THE GERMAN GIRL

THE
GERMAN
GIRL

ARMANDO LUCAS
CORREA

Translated by Nick Caistor

SIMON &
SCHUSTER

London · New York · Sydney · Toronto · New Delhi

A CBS COMPANY

Originally published in Spanish as *La niña alemana*.
First published in the USA by Atria Books, an imprint of Simon & Schuster, Inc., 2016
First published in Great Britain by Simon & Schuster UK Ltd, 2016
A CBS COMPANY

1 3 5 7 9 10 8 6 4 2

Simon & Schuster UK Ltd
1st Floor
222 Gray's Inn Road
London WC1X 8HB

www.simonandschuster.co.uk

Simon & Schuster Australia, Sydney
Simon & Schuster India, New Delhi

A CIP catalogue record for this book
is available from the British Library

Hardback ISBN: 978-1-4711-6162-9
Export Trade Paperback ISBN: 978-1-4711-6294-7
eBook ISBN: 978-1-4711-6161-2
Australian Trade Paperback ISBN: 978-1-4711-6160-5
Australian eBook ISBN: 978-1-4711-6364-7

This book is a work of fiction. Names, characters, places and
incidents are either a product of the author's imagination or are
used fictitiously. Any resemblance to actual people living or
dead, events or locales is entirely coincidental.

Printed and bound by CPI Group (UK) Ltd, Croydon, CR0 4YY

Simon & Schuster UK Ltd are committed to sourcing paper
that is made from wood grown in sustainable forests and support the Forest
Stewardship Council, the leading international forest certification organisation.
Our books displaying the FSC logo are printed on FSC certified paper.

To my children Emma, Anna, and Lucas

To Ana Maria (Karman) Gordon, Judith (Koeppel) Steel, and Herbert Karliner, who were my children's age when they boarded the St. Louis *at the port of Hamburg in 1939*

You are my witnesses.

ISAIAH 43:10–11

Memories are what you no longer want to remember.

JOAN DIDION

THE GERMAN GIRL

PART ONE

Hannah and Anna

Berlin–New York

Hannah
Berlin, 1939

I was almost twelve years old when I decided to kill my parents.

I had made up my mind. I'd go to bed and wait until they fell asleep. That was always easy to tell because Papa would lock the big, heavy double windows and close the thick greenish-bronze curtains. He'd repeat the same things he said every night after supper, which in those days had become little more than a steaming bowl of tasteless soup.

"There's nothing to be done. It's all over. We have to leave."

Then Mama would start shouting, her voice cracking as she blamed him. She'd pace the whole apartment—her fortress at the heart of a sinking city; the only space she'd known for more than four months—until she wore herself out. Then she'd embrace Papa, and her feeble moans would finally cease.

I'd wait a couple of hours. They wouldn't put up any resistance. I

3

knew Papa had already given up and was willing to go. Mama would be more difficult, but she took so many sleeping pills, she'd be fast asleep, steeped in her jasmine and geranium essences. Although she had gradually increased the dose, she still awakened during the night crying. I would rush to see what had happened, but all I could make out through the half-open door was Mama inconsolable in Papa's arms, like a little girl recovering from a terrible nightmare. Except that, for her, the nightmare was being awake.

Nobody heard my cries anymore; nobody bothered about them. Papa told me I was strong. I would survive whatever happened. But not Mama. The pain was gnawing away at her. She was the child in a house where daylight was no longer allowed. For four months, she had been sobbing each night, ever since the city was covered in broken glass and filled with the constant stench of gunpowder, metal, and smoke. That was when they started planning our escape. They decided we'd abandon the house where I was born, and forbade me to go to school, where nobody liked me anymore. Then Papa gave me my second camera.

"So that you can leave a trail out of the labyrinth like Ariadne," he whispered.

I dared to think it would be best to be rid of them.

I thought about diluting aspirin in Papa's food or stealing Mama's sleeping pills—she wouldn't last a week without them. The only problem was, first of all, my doubts. How many aspirin would he have to swallow to give him a lethal ulcer, internal bleeding? How long could Mama really survive without sleep? Anything bloody was out of the question, because I couldn't bear the sight of blood. So the best thing would be for them to die of suffocation. To smother them with a huge feather pillow. Mama made it clear that her dream had always been for death to take her by surprise while she slept. "I can't bear farewells," she would say, staring straight at me—or, if I wasn't listening, she would grab me by the arm and squeeze it with the little strength she had left.

One night I woke up during the night in tears, thinking my crime had already been committed. I could see my parents' lifeless bodies but was unable to shed a single tear. I felt free. Now there would be no one to force me to move to a filthy neighborhood, to leave behind my books, my photographs, my cameras, to live with the terror of being poisoned by your own father and mother.

I started to tremble. I called out "Papa!" But no one came to my rescue. "Mama!" There was no going back. What had I turned into? How did I end up so low? What would I do with their bodies? How long would it take for them to decompose?

Everyone would think it was suicide. No one would question it. My parents had been suffering constantly for four months by then. Others would see me as an orphan; I'd see myself as a murderer. My crime existed in the dictionary. I looked it up. What a dreadful word. Just saying it gave me the shivers. *Parricide*. I tried to repeat it and couldn't. I was a murderer.

It was so easy to identify my crime, my guilt, my agony. What about my parents, who were planning to get rid of me? What was the name for someone who killed their children? Was that such a terrible crime there wasn't even a word for it in the dictionary? That meant they could get away with it. Whereas I had to bear the weight of death and a nauseating word. You could kill your parents, your brothers and sisters. But not your children.

I prowled through the rooms, which to me seemed increasingly small and dark, in a house that would soon no longer be ours. I looked up at the unreachable ceiling, walked down hallways lined with the images of a family that was disappearing little by little. Light from the lamp with the snowy-white shade in Papa's library filtered out into the corridor where I stood disoriented, unable to move. I watched as my pale hands turned golden.

I opened my eyes and was in the same bedroom, surrounded by well-worn books and dolls I had never played with, nor ever would. I closed my eyes and sensed it wouldn't be long before we fled without a set destination on a huge ocean liner from a port in this country where we had never belonged.

In the end, I didn't kill my parents. I didn't have to. Papa and Mama were the guilty ones. They forced me to throw myself into the abyss alongside them.

∽§∾

The apartment's smell had become intolerable. I didn't understand how Mama could live between those walls lined with moss-green silk that swallowed what little daylight there was at that time of year. It was the smell of enclosure.

We had less time to live. I knew it; I felt it. We wouldn't be spending the summer there in Berlin. Mama had put mothballs in the closets to preserve her world, and the pungent odor filled the apartment. I had no idea what she was trying to protect, since we were going to lose everything regardless.

"You smell like the old ladies on Grosse Hamburger Strasse," Leo taunted me. Leo was my only friend; the one person who dared look me in the face without wanting to spit on me.

Spring in Berlin was cold and rainy, but Papa often left without taking his coat. Whenever he went out in those days, he wouldn't wait for the elevator but took the stairs, which creaked as he trod on them. I wasn't allowed to use the stairs, though. He didn't walk down because he was in a hurry but because he didn't want to bump into anyone else from the building. The five families living on the floors beneath ours were all waiting for us to leave. Those who were once our friends were no longer friendly. Those who used to thank Papa or who tried to ingratiate themselves with Mama and her friends—who praised her good taste or asked for advice on how to make a brightly colored handbag match their fashionable shoes—now looked down their noses at us and could denounce us at any moment.

Mama spent yet another day without going out. Every morning when she got up, she would fasten her ruby earrings and smooth back her beautiful, thick hair—which was the envy of her friends whenever she appeared in the tearoom of the Hotel Adlon. Papa called her the Goddess, because she was so fascinated by the cinema, which was her only contact with the outside world. She would never miss the first night of any film starring the real screen goddess, "La Divine" Greta Garbo, at the Palast.

"She's more German than anyone," she would insist whenever she mentioned the divine Garbo, who was, in fact, Swedish. But back then motion pictures were silent, and no one cared where the star had been born.

We discovered her. We always knew she would be worshipped. We appreciated her before anybody else; that's why Hollywood noticed her. And in her first talkie she said in perfect German: "Whisky—*aber nicht zu knapp!*"

Sometimes when they came back from the cinema, Mama was still in tears. "I love sad endings—in movies," she explained. "Comedies weren't meant for me."

She would swoon in Papa's arms, raise a hand to her brow, the other holding up the silk train of a cascading dress, toss back her head, and start talking in French.

"Armand, Armand . . ." she would repeat languidly and with a strong accent, like La Divine herself.

And Papa would call her "my Camille."

"*Espère, mon ami, et sois bien certain d'une chose, c'est que, quoi qu'il arrive, ta Marguerite te restera,*" she would reply, laughing hysterically. "Dumas sounds ghastly in German, doesn't he?"

But Mama no longer went anywhere.

"Too many smashed windows" had been her excuse ever since the previous November's terrible pogrom, when Papa had lost his job. He had been arrested at his university office and taken to the station on Grolmanstrasse, kept incommunicado for an offense we never understood. He shared a windowless cell with Leo's father, Herr Martin. After they were released, the two would get together daily—and that worried Mama even more, as if they were planning an escape she was not prepared for yet. Fear was what prevented her from leaving her fortress. She lived in a state of constant agitation. Before, she used to go to the elegant salon at the Hotel Kaiserhof, just a few blocks away, but eventually it was full of the people who hated us: the ones who thought they were pure, whom Leo called Ogres.

In the past, she would boast about Berlin. If she went on a shopping spree to Paris, she always stayed at the Ritz; and if she accompanied Papa to a lecture or concert in Vienna, at the Imperial:

"But we have the Adlon, our Grand Hotel on the Unter den Linden. La Divine stayed there, and immortalized it on screen."

During those days, she would peer out the window, trying to find a reason for what was happening. What had become of her happy years? What had she been sentenced to, and why? She felt she was paying for the offenses of others: her parents, grandparents—every one of her ancestors throughout the centuries.

"I'm German, Hannah. I am a Strauss. Alma Strauss. Isn't that enough, Hannah?" she said to me in German, and then in Spanish, and in English, and finally in French. As if someone were listening to her; as if to make her message entirely clear in each of the four languages she spoke fluently.

I had agreed to meet Leo that day to go take photographs. We would see each other every afternoon at Frau Falkenhorst's café near Hackescher Markt. Whenever she spotted us, the owner would smile and call us "bandits." We liked that. If either of us was later than expected, the first to arrive had to order a hot chocolate. Sometimes we'd arrange to meet at the café near the Alexanderplatz Station exit, which had shelves filled with sweets wrapped in silver paper. When he needed to see me urgently, Leo would wait for me at the newspaper kiosk near my home, allowing us to avoid running into any of our neighbors, who, despite also being our tenants, always shunned us.

In order not to disobey the adults, I bypassed the carpeted stairs, which were increasingly dusty, and took the elevator. It stopped at the third floor.

"Hello, Frau Hofmeister," I said, smiling at her daughter, Gretel, who used to be my playmate. Gretel was sad, because not long before, she had lost her beautiful white puppy. I felt so sorry for her.

We were the same age, but I was much taller. She looked down, and Frau Hofmeister had the nerve to say to her, "Let's take the stairs. When are they going to leave? They're putting us all in such a difficult situation . . ."

As if I wasn't listening, as if it was only my shadow standing inside the elevator. As if I didn't exist. That's what she wanted: for me not to exist.

The Ditmars, Hartmanns, Brauers, and Schultzes lived in our building. We rented them their apartments. The building had belonged to Mama's family since before she was born. They were the ones who should leave. They were not from here. We were. We were more German than they were.

The elevator door closed, it started to go down, and I could still see Gretel's feet.

"Dirty people," I heard.

Had I heard it right? What have we done for me to have to endure that? What crime had we committed? I was not dirty. I didn't want people to think of me as dirty. I came out of the elevator and hid under the stairs so I wouldn't meet them again. I saw them leave the building. Gretel's head was still bowed. She glanced backward, looking for me, perhaps wanting to apologize, but her mother pushed her on.

"What are you staring at?" she shouted.

I ran back up the stairs noisily, in tears. Yes, crying with rage and impotence because I could not tell Frau Hofmeister that she was dirtier than I was. If we bothered her, she could leave the building; it was our building. I wanted to hit the walls, smash the valuable camera my father had given me. I entered our apartment, and Mama could not understand why I was so furious.

"Hannah! Hannah!" she called out to me, but I chose to ignore her.

I went into the cold bathroom, slammed the door, and turned on the shower. I was still crying; or rather, I wanted to stop crying but found it impossible. Fully clothed and wearing my shoes, I climbed into the perfectly white bathtub. Mama kept on calling to me and then finally left me in peace. All I could hear was the sound of the scalding water cascading onto me. I let it flow into my eyes until they burned; into my ears, my nose, my mouth.

I started to take off my clothes and shoes, which were heavier because of the water and my dirtiness. I soaped myself, smeared on Mama's bath salts that irritated my skin, and rubbed myself with a white towel to get rid of every last trace of impurity. My skin was red, as red as if it was going to peel. I turned the water even hotter, until I couldn't take it anymore. When I came out of the shower, I collapsed on the cold black-and-white tiles.

Fortunately, I had run out of tears. I dried myself, scrubbing hard at this skin I didn't want and which, God willing, would start to slough off after all the heat I'd subjected it to. I examined every pore in front of the steamed-up mirror: face, hands, feet, ears—everything—to see if there was any trace of impurity left. I wanted to know who was the dirty one now.

I cowered in a corner, trembling, shrinking, feeling like a slab of meat and bone. This was my only hiding place. In the end, I knew that however much I washed, burned my skin, cut my hair, gouged out my eyes, turned deaf, however much I dressed or talked differently, or took on a different name, they would always see me as impure.

It might not have been a bad idea to knock at the distinguished Frau Hofmeister's door to ask her to check that I didn't have any tiny stain on my skin, that she didn't have to keep Gretel away from me, that I wasn't a bad influence on her child, who was as blond, perfect, and immaculate as me.

I went to my room and dressed all in white and pink, the purest colors I could find in my wardrobe. I went looking for Mama and hugged her, because I knew she understood me; even though she chose to stay at home and so didn't have to face anyone. She had built a fortress in her room, which in turn was protected by the apartment's thick columns, in a building made up of enormous stone blocks and double windows.

I had to be quick. Leo must have already been at the station, darting all over the place, trying to stay out of the way of people running to catch their trains.

At least I knew that he thought of me as being clean.

Anna
New York, 2014

The day Dad disappeared, Mom was pregnant with me. By just three months. She had the opportunity to get rid of the baby but didn't take it. She never lost hope that Dad would return, even after receiving the death certificate.

"Give me some proof, a trace of his DNA, then we can talk," she always told them.

Maybe because Dad was still a stranger to her in some ways—mysterious and solitary, a man of few words—she thought he might reappear at any moment.

Dad left unaware I would be born.

"If he'd known he had a daughter on the way, he would still be here with us," Mom insisted every September for as long as I could remember.

The day Dad never returned, Mom was going to prepare a dinner for the two of them in our spacious dining room, by the window from where you can see the trees in Morningside Park lit by bronze streetlamps. She was going to tell him the news. She still set the table that evening because she refused to admit the possibility that he was gone. She never got to open the bottle of red wine. The plates stayed on the white tablecloth for days. The food ended up in the garbage. That night, she went to bed without eating, without crying, without closing her eyes.

She lowered her gaze as she told me this. If it were up to her, the plates and the bottle would have still been on the table—and, who knows, probably also the rotting, dried-out food.

"He'll be back," she always insisted.

They had talked about having children. They saw it as a distant possibility, a long-term project, a dream they hadn't given up on. What both of them were sure of was that if they did have any children one day, the boy had to be called Max and the girl, Anna. That was the only thing Dad demanded of her.

"It's a debt I owe my family," he would tell her.

They had been together for five years, but she never managed to get him to talk about his years in Cuba or his family.

"They're all dead" was the only thing he'd say.

Even after so many years, that still bothered Mom.

"Your father is an enigma. But he's the enigma I loved most in my entire life."

Trying to resolve that enigma was a way to unburden herself. Finding the answer was her punishment.

I kept his small silver digital camera. At first, I spent hours going through the images he left on its memory card. There wasn't a single one of Mom. Why bother, when she was always by his side? The photographs were all taken from the same spot on the narrow living room balcony. Photographs of the sun rising. Rainy days, clear days, dark or misty ones, orange days, violet-blue days. White days, with the snow covering everything. Always the sun. Dawn with a horizon line hidden by a patchwork of buildings in a silent Harlem, chimneys spewing out white smoke, the East River between two islands. Again and again, the sun—golden, grand, sometimes seeming warm, other times cold—viewed from our double glass door.

Mom told me that life is a jigsaw puzzle. She wakes up, attempting to find the correct piece, trying all the different combinations to create those distant landscapes of hers. I live to undo them so that I can discover where I came from. I am creating my own jigsaw puzzles out of photos I printed at home from the images I found on Dad's camera.

From the day I discovered what had really happened to Dad, and Mom understood I could fend for myself, she shut herself in her bedroom and I became her caretaker. She converted her bedroom into her refuge, keeping the window overlooking the interior courtyard always closed. In dreams, I would see her falling fast asleep from the pills she took before going to bed, engulfed by her gray sheets and pillows. She said the pills helped ease the pain and knock her out. Sometimes I would say a prayer—so silent that even I could not hear or remember it—that she would stay asleep, and her pain would go away forever. I couldn't bear to see her suffer.

Every day before I leave for school, I take her a cup of black coffee, with no sugar. In the evening, she sits at supper with me like a ghost while I make up stories about my classes. She listens, raises a spoon to her mouth, and smiles at me to show how grateful she is that I am still there with her, and for making her soup that she swallows out of duty.

I know she could disappear at any moment. Where would I go then?

When my school bus drops me off outside our apartment building each afternoon, the first thing I do is pick up the mail. After that, I prepare dinner for the two of us, finish my homework, and check if there are any bills to pay, which I pass on to Mom.

Today we received a large envelope with yellow, white, and red stripes and its warning in big red capital letters: DO NOT BEND. The sender is in Canada, and it is addressed to Mom. I leave it on the dining table and lie down on my bed to begin reading the book I was given at school. A few hours later, I remember that I haven't opened the envelope.

I start knocking on Mom's bedroom door. *At this time of night?* she must be thinking. She's pretending to be asleep. Silence. I keep knocking.

Nights are sacred for her: she tries to fall asleep, reliving things she can no longer do, and thinking about what her life might have been like if she could have avoided fate or simply wiped it away.

"A package came today. I think we should open it together," I say, but there's no answer.

I stay at the door and then open it gently so as not to disturb her. The lights are off. She's dozing, her body seems almost weightless, lost in the middle of the mattress. I check that she's still breathing, still exists.

"Can't it wait until tomorrow?" she murmurs, but I don't budge.

She closes her eyes and then opens them again, turning to see me standing in the doorway, the hall light behind me—which blinds her at first, because she's used to the dark.

"Who sent it?" she asks, but I don't know.

I insist she come with me; that it'll do her good to get up.

I finally manage to convince her. She stands up unsteadily, smoothing down her straight black hair, which hasn't been cut for months. She leans on my arm for support, and we shuffle to the dining table to discover what we have been sent. Perhaps it's a birthday present for me. Someone has remembered I'm going to be twelve, that I've grown up, that I exist.

She sits down slowly, with an expression on her face that seems to say, *Why did you make me get out of bed and upset my routine?*

When she sees the sender's name, she picks up the envelope and clutches it to her chest. Her eyes open wide, and she says to me solemnly:

"It's from your father's family."

What? But Dad didn't have a family! He came into this world alone and left it the same way, with no one else around. I remember that his parents died in an airplane accident when he was nine. Predestined for tragedy, as Mom once said.

After their deaths, he had been brought up by Hannah, an elderly aunt we assumed was dead by now. We had no idea if they had kept in touch by telephone, letters, or email. His only family. I was called Anna in her honor.

The package was mailed from Canada but it's really from Havana, the capital of the Caribbean island where Dad was born. When we open it, we see it contains a second envelope. "For Anna, from Hannah" is written on the outside in big, shaky handwriting. This isn't a present, I think. It must contain documents or who knows what. It probably has nothing to do with my birthday. Or maybe it's from the last person to see Dad alive, who has finally decided to send us his things. Twelve years later.

I'm so nervous, I can't stop moving around, getting up and sitting down again. I walk to the corner of the room and back. I start playing with a lock of my hair, twisting and twisting it until it's tangled. It feels like Dad is with us again. Mom opens the second envelope. All we find inside are old photograph contact sheets, and lots of negatives, together with a magazine—in German?—from March 1939. On the cover is the image of a smiling blond girl in profile.

"The *German Girl*," says Mom, translating the title of the magazine. "She looks like you," she tells me mysteriously.

These photos make me think I can begin a fresh puzzle now. I'm going to enjoy myself with all these images that have reached us from the island where Dad was born. I'm so excited at the discovery, but I was hoping to find Dad's watch, an heirloom from his grandfather Max, which still worked, or his white gold wedding band, or his rimless spectacles. These are the details I remember about Dad from the photo I always keep with me, and which sleeps beside me every night under a pillow that used to be his.

The package has nothing to do with Dad. Not with his death, anyway.

We don't recognize any of the people. It's hard to make out such small, blurred images printed on sheets that seem to have survived a shipwreck. Dad could have been one of them. No, that's impossible.

"These photos are seventy years old or more," Mom explains. "I don't think even your grandfather was born then."

"We have to get them printed tomorrow," I say, controlling my excitement to avoid upsetting her. She goes on studying the mysterious images; those faces from the past she is trying to decipher.

"Anna, they're from before the war," she says, so seriously it startles me. Now I'm even more confused. What war is she talking about?

We go through the negatives and come across a faded old postcard. She picks it up with great care, as though she's afraid it might fall to pieces.

On one side, a ship. On the other, a dedication.

My heart starts racing. This must be a clue, but the date on the card is May 23, 1939, so I don't think it has anything to do with Dad's disappearance. Mom is handling this postcard like some kind of archae-ologist, like she needs to put on a pair of silk gloves so that it won't be harmed. For the first time in ages, she seems alive.

"It's time to find out who Dad is," I say, using the present tense just as Mom does whenever she mentions him. I stare at the face of the German girl.

I am sure my father isn't coming back, that I lost him forever one sunny day in September. But I want to know more about him. I don't have anyone else, apart from my mother, who lives shut away in a dark room overwhelmed by gloomy thoughts she won't share with anyone. I know sometimes there are no answers, and we have to accept it, but I can't understand why, when they got married, she didn't find out more about him; try to get to know him better. By now, it's way too late. But that's how Mom is.

Now we have a project. At least, I do. I think we're about to discover an important clue. Mom goes back to her room, but I'm ready now to snap her out of her passiveness. I hold on to this object sent by a distant relative who I am now desperate to get to know. I prop the small card against my bedside lamp and turn down the brightness. Then I get into bed, pull up the covers, and stare at the picture until I fall asleep.

The postcard shows an ocean liner bearing the name *St. Louis*, Hamburg-Amerika Linie. The message is written in German: *"Alles Gute zum Geburtstag Hannah."* Signed: *"Der Kapitän."*

Hannah

Berlin, 1939

*Y*anking open the huge, dark wooden door from the inside, I banged the bronze knocker without meaning to. The noise reverberated through the silent building where I no longer felt protected. I prepared myself for the blaring noise of Französische Strasse, which was full of red-white-and-black flags. People were walking along, stumbling into one another without any apologizing. Everyone seemed to be fleeing.

I reached the Hackesche Höfe. Five years ago, it belonged to Herr Michael, a friend of Papa's. The Ogres took it from him, and he had to leave the city. As with every midday, Leo was waiting for me in the doorway of Frau Falkenhorst's café, in the interior courtyard of the building. And there he was, with that mischievous expression of his, ready to complain about me being so late.

I got out my camera and started snapping pictures of him. He struck poses and laughed. The café door opened, and a man with a blotchy red face came out, bringing with him a gust of warm air and the smell of beer and tobacco. When I got closer to Leo, I was hit by the fragrance of hot chocolate on his breath.

"We have to get out of here," he said. I smiled and nodded.

"No, Hannah. We have to get out of all this," he repeated, meaning the whole city.

This time I understood him: neither of us wanted to go on living surrounded by all these flags, these soldiers, all the pushing and shoving. *I'll go with you wherever you wish,* I thought to myself as we set off at a run.

We were running against the wind, the flags, the cars. I tried to keep up with Leo as he raced along, adept at slipping through this throng of people who considered themselves pure and invincible. When I was with Leo, there were moments when I didn't hear the noise from the loudspeakers, or the cries and chants of men marching in perfect unison. It seemed impossible to be any happier, even though I knew it wasn't going to last.

We crossed onto the bridge, leaving the City Palace and the cathedral behind us, so that we could lean on the parapet and gaze down at the river Spree. Its waters were as dark as the walls of the buildings lining it. My thoughts wandered, following the rhythm of the current. I felt as if I could throw myself in and let it carry me along—become even more impure. But that day, I was clean; I'm sure of it. Nobody would dare spit at me. I was just like them. On the outside, at least.

In photographs, the waters of the Spree tended to have a silvery sheen, with the bridge looming at the far end like a shadow. I was standing in the center, above the small arch, when I heard Leo calling me in exasperation.

"Hannah!"

Why did he have to rouse me out of my daydream? Nothing at that moment could have been more important than to be able to cut myself off, ignore my surroundings, and imagine we didn't have to go anywhere.

"There's a man taking photographs of you!"

It was only then that I noticed the thin, lanky man with the beginnings of a potbelly. He was holding a Leica in his hands and was trying to focus on me. I shifted around, moving about to make it more difficult for him. He must have been an Ogre who was going to report us, or one of the traitors who worked for the police station on Iranische Strasse and spent their time denouncing us.

"He photographed you as well, Leo. It mustn't have been just me. What does he want? Can't we even be on our bridge?"

Mama insisted we shouldn't wander around the city, because it was full of rough enforcers. Nobody even felt they needed to put on a mask to offend you. We were the offense; they were reason, duty, enforcement. The Ogres attacked us, shouted insults; we were supposed to remain silent, mute, while they kicked us.

They had discovered our stain, our impurities, and denounced us. I smiled at the man with the Leica. He had an enormous mouth. A thick, transparent liquid was dripping from his nose. He wiped it away with the back of his hand, and pressed the button on his camera several more times. Take all the photos you want. Send me to jail.

"Let's grab his camera and throw it in the river," Leo whispered in my ear.

I could not stop gazing at this pathetic man, who was leering at me and almost threw himself at my feet in search of the best angle. I felt like spitting at him. I was disgusted by his big, wet nose. It was as big as those in the caricatures of the impure on the front page of *Der Stürmer*, the magazine that hated us and had become very popular. Yes, he must have been one of those who dreamed of being accepted by the Ogres. Dirty lowlifes, as Leo usually called them.

I started to tremble. Leo ran off, dragging me along like a rag doll. The man started to wave and tried to catch up to us. I heard him shout:

"Young girl! Your name! I need your name!"

How could he have thought I was going to stop and give him my name, surname, age, and address?

Attempting to blend in with the traffic, we crossed the street. A crowded tram went past, and we saw him still standing on the bridge. We laughed, and he had the nerve to shout good-bye!

We headed for Georg Hirsch's café on Schönhauser Allee. It was our favorite café in Berlin, where we usually gorged ourselves on sweets and could spend the entire afternoon without fear of being insulted. Leo was forever hungry, and my mouth was already watering at the thought of fresh *Pfeffernüsse* spice cookies, even though these weren't holidays. I preferred the ones sprinkled with sugar and aniseed extract, while Leo preferred the cinnamon-coated ones. We'd stain our fingers and noses white, and then make the Ogres' salute. Leo would change it into a traffic policeman's signal to Stop! Bending his hand up vertically, making a letter *L* with his arm. That joker Leo, as Mama would say.

As we approached the café, we suddenly froze on the street corner: the windows of Georg Hirsch's café had been smashed as well! I couldn't stop taking photos. I could see Leo was sad. A group of Ogres came around the corner marching in step and singing an anthem that was an ode to perfection, to purity, to the land that should only belong to them. Good-bye, *Pfeffernüsse!*

"Another sign that we must leave," Leo said mournfully, and we ran off again.

Leave, I knew: not this corner, or the bridge, or Alexanderplatz. Simply leave.

It was quite likely they were waiting at home to arrest us. If not the Ogres, it would be Mama. We were not getting out of this unscathed.

At Hackescher Markt Station, we got into the first car of the S-Bahn. We sat opposite two women who were complaining the whole time about how expensive everything was, about all the food shortages, about how hard it was nowadays to find proper coffee. Every time they waved their arms in the air, they gave off waves of sweat mixed with rose essence and tobacco. The one who talked the most had a smudge of red lipstick on her front tooth, which looked like a cut. I glanced at her and, without realizing it, started to perspire. It's not blood, I told myself, staring at her huge mouth. Troubled by my insistence, she flapped her hand at me to stop looking at her. I lowered my eyes, and her stale odor filled my nostrils. The conductor in his blue uniform came up and asked to see our tickets.

Between Zoo Station and Savignyplatz Station, we stared out of the window at the blackened housefronts. Dirty windows, a woman shaking a stained carpet on a balcony, men smoking at windows, and red-white-and-black flags everywhere. Leo pointed to a beautiful building that was in flames on Fasanenstrasse, near the S-Bahn level crossing. Smoke was still rising from the main roof of the shattered dome. Nobody else looked at the devastated building. They must have felt guilty. They had no wish to see what the city was becoming. The woman with the smudge on her tooth lowered her head as well. Not only did she have no wish to be a witness to the smoke, but also now she didn't dare look us in the face, either.

We alighted at the next station and walked back a few blocks to reach Fasanenstrasse. We entered the side passage of the building, its stucco façade decaying from dampness and grime. Before we even arrived under Herr Braun's window, we could hear his radio turned up to full volume as usual.

He was a disgusting, deaf old man. Leo called him the Ogre, just as he did all the so-called pure and those who wore brown shirts as well. We sat beneath the window of his messy dining room, with cigarette butts and dirty puddles all around us. It was our favorite hiding place. Sometimes the Ogre used to see us and shout insultingly "the word beginning with *J*" that Leo and I refused to pronounce. As Mama insisted, we were Germans first and foremost.

Leo couldn't understand why I took photos of the puddles, the mud, the cigarette butts, the crumbling walls, the shards of glass on the ground, the smashed shop windows. I thought that any one of these images was worth more than those of the Ogres or the buildings with their flags: a Berlin I had no wish to see.

Not even the smoke from the burning building could soften the Ogre's breath with its mixture of garlic, tobacco, schnapps, and stale pork sausage. He never stopped spitting and blowing his nose. I didn't know what made my stomach churn more: the foul smell from his house or seeing his face. Except that, thanks to his deafness, we were able to find out what was going on in Berlin.

We were no longer permitted to listen to the radio at home, to buy a newspaper, or use the telephone.

"It's dangerous," Papa told me. "Let's not go looking for problems."

The Ogre changed radio stations several times. The news—or the orders, as Leo called them—was due to start in a few minutes, and the Ogre wouldn't stop moving around and making noise. Eventually he sat near the window. Leo pulled me out of the way right when the Ogre looked out the window. We couldn't stop laughing; we were well versed in his habits.

Leo knew I'd be happy to spend the whole day here; that I felt protected when I was with him. When we were together, I didn't think of my mother fading away or of how Papa was intent on changing our lives.

Leo was a passionate person. He didn't walk, he ran, always in a hurry, with a goal to reach, something to show me that I shouldn't miss. He also visited various neighborhoods, trying to figure out what was happening in this city of ours, which was falling apart bit by bit. Occasionally he mingled with the Ogres marching and shouting in the streets with their flags, but I never dared join him. He talked to me nervously, like someone who could foresee that we didn't have a great deal of time left. Our only moment of peace was here, among the Ogre's filth and spit, thanks to an old radio playing at full volume.

Leo was older than me. Two months older. That led him to think he was more mature, and I went along with it because he was the only friend I had; the only person whom I could entirely trust.

Sometimes he used to spy on his father, who was up to something with my father ever since they'd met in the Grolmanstrasse police station, which, according to Leo, stank of urine. He used to come tell me terrifying ideas, which I preferred to ignore. We knew they were planning something big; something that might have included us or not. I didn't think they were going to abandon us, or send us to a special school outside Berlin, or to another country on our own, where they spoke another language, as some of Leo's neighbors had done with their children. But they were up to something; he was sure of it. And that scared me.

Herr Martin was an accountant who had lost all his clients. He and Leo shared a room in a boardinghouse at 40 Grosse Hamburger Strasse. Their building was next door to a shelter full of women, old people, and children—all those they don't know what to do with or where to send, in a neighborhood Mama never would have dared set foot in.

Leo's mother had managed to escape to Canada, to join her brother, sister-in-law, and nephews and nieces, whom she hadn't met before. Leo and his father had no hopes of going to live with them there anytime soon. They were looking for "other possibilities for flight," as Leo liked to say. My father was part of the plot. According to Leo, he had also been sending money to Canada since they started closing our bank accounts in Berlin.

This at least made me happy. We would have accepted whatever decision our parents made, provided it included Leo and me and both families. Leo was convinced my parents were helping his father, who had been left penniless and with no possibility of work, so that they could escape as well.

Leo was in the habit of accompanying his father to the morning meetings with Papa. He pretended he wasn't listening and that he was busy doing something else so they didn't interrupt their discussions and planning. I used to joke that he had become the spy of the Martin-Rosenthal partnership. But keeping his eyes and ears open was something Leo took very seriously.

He refused to allow me to visit him in his new home.

"It's not worth it, Hannah. What's the point?"

"It can't be worse than this horrible passageway where we spend so much time."

"Frau Dubiecki doesn't like us to have visitors. She's an old crow who takes advantage of our situation. Nobody there likes her. And Papa would only get angry. Besides, Hannah, there's no room to sit down."

He took a piece of black bread out of his pocket and put a huge chunk in his mouth. He offered me some, but I didn't accept. I had lost my appetite: I ate only because I had to. But Leo devoured the bread, and while he was doing so, I could get a good look at him.

Leo exuded energy from every pore. He was full of color: his skin was reddish, his eyes brown.

"Blood flows through my veins!" he would crow, his cheeks shining. "You're so pale you're almost transparent. I can see inside you, Hannah." I'd blush.

He didn't make many gestures and had no need to: with just one sentence, his face expressed myriad emotions. When he talked to me, I couldn't help but pay attention. He bombarded me with his words. He made me nervous; I would laugh and tremble, all at the same time. Whenever you listened to Leo, it was as if the city were about to explode at any moment.

He was tall and skinny. Although we were the same size, he appeared to be a couple of inches taller, with thick, wavy hair that looked as though it had never been combed. Whenever he was about to say something important, he bit his lips so hard they seemed about to bleed. He had frightened, wide-open eyes, and his lashes were the darkest and longest I have ever seen. "They always arrive before you do," I used to tease him. How I envied him. Mine made me sad; they were so light-colored, they hardly seemed to exist, like Mama's.

"You don't need them," he would say to comfort me, "not with those big blue eyes of yours."

The stench reminded me we were still in that disgusting passageway.

The Ogre was moving around his room. He seldom went out except to go shopping.

Leo told me that the Ogre used to work in Herr Schemuel's butcher's shop, a few blocks from there, until he himself denounced the owner. He felt in control ever since the Ogres took power; they gave him the freedom to make or unmake someone as insignificant as he was.

On that terrible November night that everyone still talked about, they smashed Herr Schemuel's windows and closed down his business. It was from that moment on that the stench took over the city: a stench of broken pipes, sewage, and smoke. Herr Schemuel was arrested, and nothing more was heard of the man who'd provided the best cuts of meat in the neighborhood.

So now this Ogre was out of work. I was curious to know what he had gotten out of denouncing Herr Schemuel.

Berlin was full of Ogres. There was a vigilante on every block. They took it upon themselves to report, persecute, and make life impossible for all of us who thought differently; who came from families that did not fit in with their idea of a family. We had to be very careful with them, as well as with the traitors who thought they could save themselves by denouncing us.

"It's better to live shut in, with doors and windows sealed," Leo would say. But we two couldn't stay still in one spot. What was the point, when our parents were going to send us wherever they felt like anyway?

It was hard for the Ogres to spot what I was. I could sit on the park benches forbidden to us and could enter tram carriages reserved for the pure race. If I'd wanted to, I also could have bought a newspaper.

Leo used to say I was able to pass for anyone. I didn't have any mark on the outside, although inside I had the stigma from all four grandparents that the Ogres detested so much. Leo was the same. They assumed that he was like them, even though he thought his nose or his gaze betrayed him. Still, Leo couldn't have cared less if they had found him out, because he was an expert at escaping and could run faster than even the great American Olympian Jesse Owens.

But my ability to pass for whomever I liked without them spitting at me or kicking me counted against me with my own people. They thought I was ashamed of them. Nobody loved me; I did not belong to either side, but that didn't really worry me. I had Leo.

We often used to hide in the Ogre's passageway to find out what was going on. If there was an afternoon when we didn't have time to get there, Leo would become anxious, afraid he might have missed a piece of news that could change our destinies.

The baker's son, who was proud of his enormous nose, interrupted us. But he was a friend of Leo's. I looked down at the ground. If Leo wanted to go play with him, let him. I'd find something else to do.

"With her again?" his friend shouted. "Come out of that filthy hole and leave *the German girl*." When he called me that, he pronounced each syllable carefully and made a face. "Leave her. She thinks she's better than the rest of us. Let's go and watch the fight out on the corner. They're beating each other to death. Come on!"

Leo told him to lower his voice and to get out of there.

"*Liebchen, Liebchen, Liebchen,*" he crooned, as if Leo and I were sweet on each other, and then vanished.

Leo tried to console me. "Don't listen to him," he said gently. "He's just a street urchin."

I wanted to go home to make my nose bigger, curl my hair, and dye it black. I was fed up with people mistaking who I was. Perhaps I wasn't my parents' daughter but an orphan—a truly "pure" orphan adopted by a wealthy impure couple who thought they were superior because they had money, jewels, and properties.

The news on the Ogre's battered radio set brought me out of my pathetic self-pity. We were going to have to comply with fresh regulations and laws. I gave a start at each new order, which echoed like a roar. It hurt.

We were going to have to list all our possessions. Many of us would have to change our names and sell our properties, our houses, and our businesses at prices they dictated.

We were monsters. We stole other people's money. We made slaves of those who had less than us. We were destroying the country's heritage. We had bled Germany dry. We stank. We believed in different gods. We were crows. We were impure. I looked at Leo and at myself. I could not see what was so different between him, Gretel, and me.

The cleansing had begun in Berlin, the dirtiest city in Europe. Powerful jets of water were about to start drenching us until we were clean.

They didn't like us. Nobody liked us.

Leo pulled me to my feet, and we left. I followed him aimlessly. I let him drag me along.

The Ogre came to the window looking smug, pleased like all of them that the cleansing was drawing nearer—about time, too!—similar to what he himself had begun in our neighborhood. The moment had arrived to crush the undesirables, burn them, choke them until not one was alive near them; nobody to spoil their perfection, their purity.

And with the satisfaction conveyed by the power to annihilate, to be who he was, to be superior to everyone else, to feel he was God in his marvelous bunker surrounded by cigarette butts and mud, he spat another thick, resounding gobbet of phlegm.

Anna

Today I woke up earlier than usual. I can't get the face of the German girl out of my mind: she has the same features as me. I want to be wide-awake so that I can forget her. On my bedside table, where I keep the photo of Dad, I've added the faded postcard of the ship.

It's my favorite picture of Dad. It's seems like he's looking straight at me. It shows his dark hair brushed back, his big, hooded eyes and thick black eyebrows hidden behind his rimless glasses, the hint of a smile on his thin lips. Dad is the most handsome man in the world.

Whenever I need to discuss something about school, talk about what went on during the day, or share my worries with someone, I take his photograph and put it under the lamp with the ivory shade decorated with gray unicorns that gallop around until the light is switched off and I fall asleep.

Sometimes we have tea together. We share a chocolate cookie, or I read him a passage from the library book for my school assignment.

If I have to rehearse a presentation for my Spanish class, I do it with Dad. He's the best listener: the most understanding and relaxed.

Mom once told me that as a boy his favorite book was *Robinson Crusoe*, and the day I started school, she gave it to me as a gift. She put her thin hands on my shoulders and looked me in the eye:

"So that you'll learn to read quickly."

I glanced at the few illustrations of those two men covered in rags on a desert island, and wondered why there weren't more pictures in this book of way over a hundred pages that Dad liked so much. I couldn't see what was so interesting about a bunch of pages full of black writing on a white background, with no color at all.

Once I had learned to read, I tried to decipher it, repeating every word, every syllable, to myself, but I still found it very hard. Those complicated sentences seemed so foreign to me, I couldn't get past the first one:

"I was born in the year 1632, in the city of York, of a good family, though not of that country, my father being a foreigner . . ."

There was no mention of dogs or cats, lost moons or enchanted forests. So it was a book of adventures. First mystery solved.

I started to read it with Dad syllable by syllable. Every night, we would conquer a page. At first, it was a struggle. Soon, though, the sentences flowed without me even realizing it.

That story of a man shipwrecked on an island where there were only two seasons, rainy and dry, stuck in the middle of nowhere with his friend Friday, whom he had saved from cannibals, filled me with hope. And later I began to create my own adventures.

Dad could be lost on a faraway island, and I would sail my majestic ship across seas and oceans, battling terrible storms and huge waves till I found him.

But today isn't a reading day. I have to tell him about the package that came from Cuba, a real family relic. Because if anyone knows anything about that boat and the dedication in German, it has to be him. I'll persuade Mom to go to a photo lab to get the pictures developed. I know he's going to help me figure out who they are. Probably his parents are there, too, or even his grandparents, because as far as we can tell, the photographs were taken before the war. The Second World War, the most terrible of all.

Every morning, when I wake up, I pick up the photo and kiss it. Then I prepare Mom's coffee. That's the only way I can make sure she gets up.

When I make her coffee today, I breathe through my mouth because the smell makes me nauseous. Mom likes it, though, and it wakes her up. I carry in her big cup very slowly, and I hold it by the handle to avoid getting burned. It's like a magic potion that will snap her out of her daze. I knock twice on her door, but as usual, she doesn't reply. I open the door slowly, and light from the hall pours in with me.

Then I see her: she's totally pale, not moving, her eyes rolled up, and her chin pointing up to the ceiling. Her body is all twisted. I drop the cup of coffee, which falls to the floor with a crash and stains the white bedroom walls.

I run out into the hall, struggle to open the front door, and then race upstairs to the fourth floor and knock on Mr. Levin's door. When he opens it, his dog Tramp leaps up at me. "I can't play with you now, Mom needs me." Mr. Levin sees how worried I am and puts his arm around me. I can't hold back my tears anymore.

"There's something wrong with Mom!" I tell him, because I can't say the word I fear most. That I've lost her, that she's gone, that she's abandoned me. From now on, I'll be an orphan not only because of my father but also because of her. Maybe I'll have to leave my apartment, my photographs, my school. Who knows where they'll send me to live. Maybe Cuba. Yes, I could ask the social workers who come looking for me if they would find my family in Cuba—to find Hannah, the only person I have left in the world.

I rush down the stairs with Tramp. Mr. Levin takes the elevator. I arrive first and wait outside Mom's bedroom, not daring to look inside. My heart is pounding. It's beating so hard my whole body aches. Mr. Levin enters very calmly, switches on the lamp, sits on Mom's bed. He takes her pulse, and then looks back at me and smiles.

He begins calling her:

"Ida! Ida! Ida!" he shouts, but the body still doesn't move.

Then I see Mom's arms slowly start to relax, and she tilts her head slightly to the left, as if trying to avoid us. Color comes back to her cheeks, and she seems annoyed by all the light in her room.

"Don't worry, Anna, I've already called an ambulance. Your mom will be fine. What time does your school bus arrive?" asks the only friend I have in the entire universe, who happens to own the noblest dog in our building.

Mom can see the tears streaming down my cheeks, and it seems like this makes her sadder than ever. It's like she's ashamed and is asking me to forgive her, but she doesn't have the strength to say a single word. I go over and hug her gently, so as not to hurt her.

I dry my tears and run down to catch the bus. From the street I see Mr. Levin out on our balcony, making sure the driver picks me up. As I climb aboard and walk down the aisle to my seat, the other kids can tell I've been crying. I sit at the back, and the girl with braids in the row in front of me turns to look at me. I'm sure she thinks I've been punished because I've done something wrong: not finishing my homework, or cleaning my room, or eating my breakfast, or brushing my teeth before leaving the apartment.

Today I find it impossible to concentrate in any of my classes. Luckily, the teachers don't bother me with questions I can't answer. I don't know if Mom will have to spend some days in the hospital or if I'll be able to live with Mr. Levin for a while.

When I get home after school, my friend is out on the balcony again. I think this must mean Mom is in the hospital and that I will have to find somewhere else to stay.

I get off the bus without saying good-bye to the driver, then wait near the entrance to our building for a few minutes because I don't want to go in. I notice the first green shoots of the Boston ivy covering the side of our building.

I pick up the mail, like I do every day, then rush up the stairs. When I enter, Tramp runs over and starts licking me. I sit on the floor and stroke him for a while, trying to postpone having to go into the living room. When I finally do, I see Mr. Levin, now with Tramp at his feet, and Mom in her leather armchair next to the open balcony door. Both of them are smiling. Mom stands up and strides over to me.

"It was nothing more than a scare," she whispers in my ear so that Mr. Levin won't hear. "I promise it won't happen again, my girl."

It has been a long time since she called me "my girl."

She starts stroking my hair. I close my eyes and snuggle against her chest the way I used to when I was little, when I really had no idea what had happened to Dad and was still hoping he might appear, walking through the door at any moment. I take a deep breath: she smells of clean clothes and soap.

I hug her, and we stay like that for several minutes. All of a sudden, the room seems enormous, and I feel dizzy. *Don't move, stay like this a little longer. Hold me until you're tired and can't hug me anymore.* Tramp comes to lick my feet and wake me from my daydream, but when I open my eyes, I see Mom is standing up, smiling, with color in her cheeks. She is beautiful again.

"Her blood pressure dropped too far. Everything will be fine," says Mr. Levin. Mom thanks him, pulls away from me, and goes into the kitchen.

"Now we'll have dinner," she announces, entering a place that's been foreign to her for the last couple of years.

The table has already been set: napkins, plates, silverware for three. The smell of salmon with capers and lemon wafts from the oven. Mom carries the dish to the table, and we start to eat.

"Tomorrow we'll go to a photo lab in Chelsea. I've called and arranged to see them."

This is what I need to hear to recover from today's scare. I feel guilty somehow; I know that sometimes I've wished she wouldn't wake up, that she'd never open her eyes again; just keep sleeping, free from pain. I don't know how I could ask her to forgive me. But for now we're going to find out who is in these photos. And I feel Mom is regaining control, or at least has more energy.

I walk Mr. Levin back to his apartment. On the way, we run into a cranky neighbor who can't stand the noblest dog in the building.

"It's a filthy dog they picked up in the street," she has told our other neighbors several times. "Who knows, he may be covered in fleas." They all think she's crazy.

But Tramp still greets her when he sees her. He doesn't care that she rejects him. He has a droopy eye. He's a bit deaf. There's a kink in his tail. That's why the old woman hates him. Mr. Levin rescued him and talks to him in French.

"*Mon clochard*," he calls him. He told me the dog used to belong to an old French woman who lived on her own like him and was found dead in La Touraine, one of the oldest apartment buildings on Morning-side Drive.

I remembered suddenly that Mom used to say, "We live in the French part of Manhattan," in the days when she would tell me bedtime stories.

When the janitor opened the old French lady's door, Tramp escaped, and they couldn't catch him. A week later, during one of his early-morning walks, Mr. Levin noticed the dog struggling up the steep steps of Morningside Park. Then Tramp sat down at his feet.

"*Mon clochard*," he called him, and the dog jumped for joy.

Tramp obediently followed Mr. Levin, a stocky old man with bushy gray eyebrows, back to his apartment. From then on, he became his faithful companion. The day he introduced Tramp to me, he said very seriously, "Next year I'll be eighty, and at that age, you count the minutes you have left. I don't want the same thing to happen to my *clochard* as it did last time. The moment they break my door down to find out why I haven't been answering, I want my dog to know the way to your home."

"*Mon clochard,*" I said to Tramp in my American accent, stroking him.

Even though Mom has never let me have a pet—apart from fish, who don't live even as long as a flower—she knows she can't refuse to have Tramp come to live with us, because we owe it to my only friend.

"Anna, Mr. Levin is going to live a long time yet, so don't get your hopes up," she told me when I insisted we'd have to look after his dog.

To me, Mr. Levin doesn't seem old or young. I know he's not strong, because he walks very carefully, but his mind is still as active as mine. He has an answer for everything, and when he stares you in the eye, you really have to pay attention.

Now Tramp doesn't want me to leave and starts whimpering.

"Come on, you bad-mannered dog," Mr. Levin comforts him. "Little Miss Anna has more important things to do."

As he says good-bye to me at his front door, Mr. Levin touches his mezuzah. I notice a single old photograph on the wall. It shows him with his parents: a good-looking young man with a smile on his face and thick black hair. Who knows whether Mr. Levin remembers those years in his village that was then part of Poland. It was such a long time ago.

"You're a girl with an old soul," he says, laying his heavy hand on my head and giving me a kiss on my brow.

I don't know what it means, but I take it as a compliment.

I go into my bedroom to tell all the day's events to Dad, who is waiting on my bedside table. Tomorrow we'll drop off the negatives at the photo lab. I tell him about Tramp and Mr. Levin and the dinner Mom made. The only thing I don't mention is the scare we had in the morning. I don't want to worry him with things like that. Everything's going to be all right, I know it.

I feel more exhausted than ever. I can't keep my eyes open. I find it impossible to go on talking or to switch the light off. I'm dozing off when I hear Mom come into the room and turn off my bedside lamp. The unicorns stop spinning and take a rest, just like me. Mom covers me with the purple bedspread and gives me a long, gentle kiss.

The next morning, a ray of sunshine wakes me; I forgot to pull down the blinds. I get up startled, and for a few seconds I wonder: Was it all a dream?

I hear noises outside my room. Somebody is in either the living room or the kitchen. I dress as fast as I can so I can find out what's going on. I don't even comb my hair.

In the kitchen, Mom is cradling her coffee cup. She drinks slowly, smiles, and her brown eyes light up. She's wearing a lilac blouse, dark-blue pants, and shoes she calls "ballerina slippers." She comes over and kisses me, and I don't know why, but when I feel her near me, I close my eyes.

I begin to eat breakfast quickly.

"Take it easy, Anna . . ."

But I want to finish as fast as possible. I want to find out who those people in the photos are, because I think we're very close to discovering Dad's family. The story of a ship that maybe sank in midocean.

As we leave the apartment, I see Mom turn back briefly. She locks the door and stands there for a moment as if she's changed her mind.

When we get outside, she walks down the six front steps that have separated her from a world she has forgotten without holding on to the iron banister. When we reach the sidewalk, she takes me by the hand and makes me speed up. She seems like she wants to gulp down as much air as possible, even if it's a bit cold, and feel the spring sunshine on her face. She smiles at the people we meet on the way. She seems free.

Downtown at the photo lab in Chelsea, I have to help her open the heavy glass double doors. The man behind the counter, who is expecting us, puts on a pair of white gloves, spreads the rolls of negatives on a light box, and starts to examine them one by one through a magnifying glass.

We have received a treasure from Havana. I am the detective in a mystery that is about to be revealed. The images we see are reversed: black becomes white; white, black. Our phantoms are about to come alive beneath powerful lamps and chemicals.

We pause at one image in particular that is marked with a white cross. In the corner, there is a blurred inscription in German, which

Mom translates for us: "Taken by Leo on 13 May 1939." There's a girl who looks a lot like me staring through the window of what the gray-haired man thinks could be a ship's cabin.

I think Mom is a bit worried when she sees me so excited by the negatives. She thinks I'm hoping they'll provide too many answers and will be disappointed. Now we'll have to figure out where they come from, which of Dad's relatives appear in the photos, and what became of them. We know at least that one of them went to Cuba. What about the others?

Dad was born at the end of 1959, but these negatives are over seventy years old, so we're talking about the time my great-grandparents arrived in Havana. It's possible my grandfather might also be among them, as a baby. Mom thinks they are photos from Europe and the sea crossing, when they were escaping the fast-approaching war.

"Your dad was a man of few words," she says again.

In the taxi back home, she takes me by the hand so that I'll give her my full attention. I know there's another piece of news she wants to pass on, something she's kept to herself all these years. She still thinks I'm too young to understand what happened to my family. *I'm strong, Mom. You can tell me anything. I don't like secrets. And it seems to me this family is full of them.*

It would have been easier if she'd just told me how I lost my father before I entered kindergarten at Fieldston. But Mom always insisted on saying the same thing: "Your father left one day and didn't come back." That was all.

"I think it's time you knew something. On your father's side, you're German as well," she says with a slight smile, as if apologizing.

I don't respond. I don't react.

When the taxi turns onto the West Side Highway, I open the window. The cold breeze from the Hudson River and the noise of the traffic prevent Mom from continuing. I can't stop thinking about this latest piece of news.

By the time we get home, my cheeks are red and freezing. We bump into Mr. Levin with Tramp; after their walk, they often rest on the stoop.

"Can I stay here for a while?" I ask Mom, who smiles in reply.

"When will the photos be ready?" Mr. Levin wants to know, but Tramp is all over me, tickling me so much I can't answer. Tramp is a very badly behaved dog, but he's very cute.

As soon as I reach the apartment, I go straight to my bedroom. In front of the mirror, I try to discover the German traits I must have inherited from a father who up till now I thought was Cuban. What do I see in the mirror? A German girl. Aren't I a Rosen?

When I ask her later, Mom tells me that the Rosen family left Germany in 1939 and settled in Havana.

"That's all I know, Anna," she says. Instead of going to bed, she sits in her armchair to read.

I don't know why I learned Spanish. German would have been better. I have it in my blood, don't I?

The German girl.

Hannah

Berlin, 1939

*D*inner was served. The dining room had become our prison, with its dark wood paneling that no one polished anymore. The ceiling, with its heavy square moldings, looked as if it could fall on our heads at any moment.

We didn't have any staff in the house now: they had all left. Including Eva, who was there when I was born. It wasn't safe for her, and she didn't want to see us suffer. Although I thought that, in fact, she'd abandoned us because she didn't want to find herself faced with the choice of having to inform on us.

Secretly, though, Eva hadn't stopped coming, and Mama went on paying her as if she were still our maid.

"She's part of the family," she explained to Papa whenever he warned her that we had to cut back on our spending or we would be left penniless in Berlin.

Sometimes Eva brought us bread, or cooked at home and came with the food in an enormous pot for us to reheat. She had a key and used to come in through the front door. Now she had to enter through the service entrance, so that Frau Hofmeister could not see her from the window.

That woman was always snooping around; she was the building's vigilante. I could feel her eyes on the back of my neck. Whenever I went out into the street, her gaze followed me and weighed me down. She was a leech who would have given anything to get her hands on one of Mama's dresses, to get into our apartment and carry off the jewels, bags, and handmade shoes that never would have fit her pudgy feet.

"Money doesn't buy good taste," Mama declared.

Frau Hofmeister spent a fortune on dresses, but on her they always looked borrowed.

I couldn't understand why Mama used to dress and make herself up as if she were going out to a party. She even used to wear false eyelashes, which gave her drooping eyes an even more languid air. She had huge eyelids, "ideal for makeup," as her friends said. But she applied only a little color to her face: pink and white, with black and a little gray around the eyes. Lipstick was only for special occasions.

Our dining room grew bigger with every passing day. I slumped in my chair and peered at my parents in the distance. I couldn't make out their faces; their features were blurred. The only light came from the lamp hanging over the table, which gave the white china plates a pale-orange tint.

We were hemmed in around a rectangular mahogany table with sturdy legs. Next to Papa's plate, I saw an edition of *Das Deutsche Mädel—The German Girl*: the propaganda magazine of the League of German Girls. All my friends—or, rather, my female classmates—had subscriptions to it, but Papa would not allow me to bring a copy of that "printed rubbish" home. I couldn't understand why he had one beside him now. Could we start eating? They both looked preoccupied, their heads lowered. They seemed not to dare talk to me. They silently lifted spoonfuls of soup to their mouths in unison and had trouble swallowing them. Neither of them even glanced at me. What had I done? Papa paused and looked up. Now he was staring at me. He turned the magazine over and pushed it toward me with suppressed rage.

I couldn't believe it. What was going to become of me? Leo would hate me. I would have to forgo our daily meetings at midday in Frau Falkenhorst's café. Nobody would drink hot chocolate with me anymore. *The baker's boy had been right, Leo. You should have left me. Don't come looking for me.*

On the cover of this magazine for pure young girls—the ones who don't bear the stains of their four grandparents, the ones with small, snub noses, skin as white as foam, blond hair, and eyes bluer than the sky itself, where there is no room for any imperfection—there I was, smiling, my eyes fixed on the future. I had become the "German girl" of the month.

The dining room seemed empty. Not even the sound of spoons dipping into the wretched bowls of soup could be heard. No one spoke to me. No one reproached me.

"It wasn't my fault, Papa! Believe me!"

The photographer we had thought was an informer had turned out to be an Ogre who worked for *Das Deutsche Mädel.* I'd thought that even though that day I had scrubbed myself so hard my skin had peeled, he had discovered my stain, and that was why he had photographed me.

"How could he have got it wrong?" I asked, but nobody answered.

"You're dirty, Hannah. I don't want to see you like that at the table," said Mama, and for the first time, to hear myself called dirty was like a caress. Yes, I was, and I wanted the world to know I didn't care about being dirty, stained, rumpled. I wanted to tell my parents that but couldn't, because, in the end, we were all dirty. Nobody was saved. Not even the smart, haughty Alma Strauss, who now was just another Rosenthal, as dirty as the undesirables who lived crammed into rooms in the Spandauer Vorstadt quarter. Not even Papa, the eminent professor Max Rosenthal, who was now pacing up and down sadly, staring at the floor.

I left the table and went to change clothes to please my mother.

I put on a short-sleeved white dress that had been perfectly ironed. *Is this what you like, Mama? I won't wear this dress the day we have to leave everything behind.* I couldn't move. If I did, it would stretch. If I sat down, it would get creased. Even a single tear could stain it. And I soaped my hands so much, they still smelled of sulfate when I returned to the dining table. As I was sipping another spoonful of soup, Mama looked me up and down, but without any bitterness.

Papa sighed. He picked up the magazine and put it in his briefcase.

"Perhaps your face on the cover of that magazine will be useful someday," he said resignedly. "The damage is done."

"Can we eat in peace now?" said Mama.

Now there was the sound of the delicate scrape of the spoons on the Meissen china that Mama had begun using only the day she realized she would soon have to relinquish it, and it would pass into the hands of a vulgar Berliner family.

"Porcelain that has been in the Strauss family for more than three generations," she sighed, and took another sip.

I didn't touch my dish. I thought that if I broke anything, they would be sure to send this "German girl" on a train to heaven knows where. And woe betide me if I made any noise sipping the clear, insipid soup, with barely a couple of potatoes floating in it and a badly cut slice of red onion—then they would send me straight to bed on an empty stomach.

"Madagascar," said Papa. I had no idea what he was talking about.

Mama lifted another spoonful of by now cold soup to her mouth and forced it down. Silence. I waited for Papa to go on. Madagascar.

"Which continent is Madagascar in? Africa? Are we going so far away?" I asked, but they ignored me.

In spite of her best efforts, the Goddess could not prevent a tear from rolling down her cheek. Hastily drying it on her white lace napkin, she smiled and brushed my hand to try to show me that the tear meant nothing to her. The sadness passed. We had to emigrate: it was our only choice.

"The farther away we go, the better," she said, confirming her approval with another spoonful of soup. Raising her snowy-white hands to her neck, she stroked it with an aristocratic air.

"Ethiopia, Alaska, Russia, Cuba"—Papa went on listing our uncertain destinations.

Mama looked at me and smiled. She began a speech that seemed to go on endlessly.

"Don't cry, Hannah. We'll go wherever we have to. We know several languages. And if need be, we'll learn others. We are different, even if they want to treat us like all the rest. We'll start again. If we can't have a house opposite a park or a river, we'll have one next to the sea. Let's enjoy our last days in Berlin."

She was so serene, she frightened me. She spoke stressing every word, extending the vowels like a litany. She paused for breath and then went on. I sensed that she might suddenly burst into tears, blame Papa, curse her terrible existence, her past, her inheritance.

She looked so fragile that I was certain she wouldn't be able to survive a journey to Madagascar. Or even a simple outing to the Hotel Adlon; or to see the Brandenburg Gate one last time; or to say farewell to the Siegessäule, the monument to the fallen in the Great War that we used to visit on autumn afternoons.

"We could go to the Adlon, Hannah. We ought to say good-bye to Monsieur Fourneau, who has always been so kind to us. And to Louis, of course."

My mouth watered at the thought of the sweets that Monsieur Fourneau served us. I remembered how when he unfolded my napkin for me his pointed nose came so close to my face I could feel his breath. Louis was the owner's son, and had now taken charge himself. He was delighted with Mama and the distinction she gave the hotel. He used to sit with us and tell us which celebrities from German high society, and even from Hollywood, were staying there at the moment.

Mama found it hard to accept the fact that she was no longer welcome in the hotel she considered her own. She used to like to boast that it was the symbol of German modernity, of elegance. It had a sober façade, but inside there were tremendous marble columns and an exotic fountain with a sculpture of black elephants.

Her parents had even been invited to the hotel opening in 1907. That day Grandpa gave Grandma the Tear—a flawed pearl—her favorite piece of jewelry, which would one day be mine, as Mama used to remind me every year. When she was twelve, the Tear passed down to her, and she wore it only on very special occasions.

Now, however, Louis was welcoming Ogres. They were the ones who gave his hotel lustre, who represented high society and power, rather than a mere heiress who thought she was more mysterious than the goddess Garbo, married to a down-at-the-heels professor. We were now the filthy ones who spoiled the reputation of a legendary institution.

Once, while the huge Persian carpets at home were being cleaned, we had stayed in two rooms with a view over the Brandenburg Gate. My room was enormous and connected to the one my parents were in. Each morning, I would pull back the red velvet drapes and open the windows to let in the noise of the city. I loved watching people running after trams, the traffic chaos on Unter den Linden. The cold air of Berlin smelled of tulips, candy floss, fresh *Pfeffernüsse*.

I would disappear among the feather pillows and the brilliant white sheets that were changed twice a day. I was brought breakfast in bed, and the maids greeted me with: "*Guten Morgen Prinzessin Hannah*." We would dress up for luncheon, change to take tea, and wear a third change of clothes at night.

"Yes, Louis's sweets, filled with cherries," I said enthusiastically, putting on the expression of a greedy child just to humor her.

I studied her closely: her slow movements, the effort she made to raise a simple spoonful to her mouth. I wanted her to look at me, to realize I existed. I went back to my room on my own. *Mama, please, go back to reading me those romantic French novels from the last century. Tell me about Madame Bovary, that bored woman so desperately in love. You nearly named me Emma after her, but Papa wouldn't permit it. Out of that story of romances and betrayals, all I could remember was Emma taking spoonfuls of vinegar so that her husband would think she was sick and haggard. One morning I got up early; I was very sad, although neither you nor Eva realized it. I went to the kitchen and drank vinegar, trying to make my face reflect what I was feeling. I also wanted to have a cotton handkerchief with drops of vinegar on it like Emma's, ready all the time, just in case somebody fainted. But in our family, I was the only one who ever passed out, as soon as I saw a single drop of blood.*

You weren't to expect me now to be the clever little girl who knew how to behave and who could discuss literature and geography in tearooms. With you, I wanted to behave badly, to run, shout, jump, cry. It was the moment for a typical young girl's tantrum. "I'm not going! I don't want to come out of my room! You two go, and leave me here with Eva!"

I took the doll in a red taffeta dress to bed with me. Mama gave it to me last year, and I hated it. I was playing at being a little girl again and blamed my parents for everything, but deep down I knew my fate wasn't in my hands or theirs; that they were simply trying to survive in the midst of a collapsing city.

There was a knock at the door. I hid beneath the sheets, but could sense somebody coming over and sitting down beside me. It was Papa, gazing at me with a look of compassion.

"My girl, my German girl," he said, and I let the man I loved most in the world cuddle me.

"We're going to live in America—in New York—but we're still on the waiting list to be let in. That's why we'll have to go to another country first. Only in transit, I promise you." My father's voice calmed me. His warmth spread to my body; his breath enveloped me. If he kept on talking to me in that same rhythm, I'd soon fall asleep:

"Our apartment in the city of skyscrapers is already waiting for us, Hannah. We'll live in a building on Morningside Drive that has the name of a mountain, Mont Cenis, and is covered in ivy. From our living room, we'll be able to see the sun rise every morning."

It's time for you to send me to sleep, Papa. I don't want to know your dreams. I want you to sing me a lullaby, like when I was little and used to fall asleep in your arms, the strongest in the world. I was a good girl again; I wasn't going to stand in the way of the grown-ups. A girl who did not want to be separated from you, and clung to you until sleep overtook her.

I would be a child again. I would wake up and think all this was a nightmare. That nothing had changed.

Papa was not suffering because we were going to lose what was ours by right, or because we had to leave Berlin for the far ends of the earth. He had a profession. He could start again without a penny in his pocket; it was in his blood. He suffered for Mama's sake, because he could see that each passing day added the weight of a year on her.

I didn't think she could adapt to living outside her home, without her jewels, her dresses, her perfumes. She was going to go mad. I was sure of it. Her life was slowly draining away between walls that had been hers for generations. The only place she enjoyed living in, surrounded by the photographs of her parents; the place where she kept the Iron Cross her grandfather had won in the Great War.

Papa was going to miss his gramophone and records more. He would have to say good-bye to Brahms, Mozart, and Chopin forever. But the good thing about music, as he always said, was that you could take it with you, in your mind. No one could rob you of that.

What I was already beginning to miss were the afternoons I had with Papa in his study. Discovering countries on his ancient maps, listening to tales of his journeys to India or up the Nile, imagining an excursion we would go on together to the Antarctic, or a safari in Africa.

"We'll do them one day," he used to comfort me.

Don't forget me, Papa. I want to be your pupil again, to learn the geography of far-off continents. And to dream, simply dream.

Anna

New York, 2014

I close my eyes, and I'm on the deck of a huge ship drifting aimlessly. I open my eyes and am blinded by the sun. I'm the girl with cropped hair on the ship, alone in midocean.

I wake up but still don't know who I am: Hannah or Anna. I feel like we're the same girl.

On the wooden dining room table, Mom lays out the black-and-white photos that reached us from an island way down on the map, in the Caribbean.

On the white wall of the hallway, next to the wooden bookcase, is the enlarged photograph of the girl at her cabin porthole. She is not looking at the shore, the water, or the horizon. She seems to be waiting for something. You can't tell if they're coming into port or are still at sea.

Her head is propped up on her hand in resignation. Her hair is parted at the side, and the cut reveals her round face and delicate neck. She seems to have blond hair, but the photograph is so contrasted it's hard for me to make out her eyes or to know if she really does look like me.

"The profile, Anna, the profile," Mom says with a smile. She, too, is fascinated by these images, especially the one of the girl.

I find the magazine with crumbling pages and faded, worn photos, and check again that it is the same girl on the front cover. I leaf through it, but find no reference to any Atlantic crossing. Nobody can solve this mystery. Mom understands some German, but she doesn't look much at the magazine because she's more interested in the photographs we had developed. She has started sorting them: family portraits, indoor scenes, the ones on board the ship. At one end of the table, she puts all those of the same boy.

I can't believe that a letter from Cuba has managed to rouse Mom from her bed. She's a different woman. I'm still not sure if it was the envelope or the previous day's fright. I feel that for the first time she's paying attention to me, taking me into account. I can see how hard she is concentrating on these images of a family fleeing another continent on the verge of war.

"It's like seeing a film from the Berlin of the twenties and thirties, a world that was about to disappear. There's not much left from those days, Anna," she says after poring over the photos.

She flicks her hair behind her ear, like she used to, and she's also started using a bit of color again. With any luck, this weekend she'll let me do her makeup and play with the cosmetics like we used to do before I started going to school and she started staying in her bed.

It's time for me to do my homework, but I prefer to stay with Mom at the table. A few more minutes and then, yes, I'll go to the kitchen and make some tea.

Smashed shop windows, the Star of David, glass shards everywhere, graffiti on walls, puddles of muddy water, a man fleeing the camera, a sad old man loaded down with books, a woman with a huge baby carriage, another wearing a hat as she jumps across a puddle that looks like a mirror, a pair of lovers in a park, men in hats dressed in black. They look as if they're wearing uniforms. All the men with their heads covered. Crowded trams. And more glass . . . The photographer was obsessed with broken panes of glass on the ground.

Mom also brought home a CD of the photos, so that I can print them as I like, crop them, make them bigger. There's a lot to discover.

Once the tea is made, I come closer to her. I take advantage of it for a moment and close my eyes, take a deep breath, and smell the perfume of her soap. I pause at the image she has in her hand of a beautiful building, its roof destroyed by fire. I look at her short, manicured nails, her ringless fingers—not even the wedding band—and stroke them. She leans her head back against me. We're together again.

"What a gruesome night that was, the ninth of November 1938. Nobody was expecting it." Mom has a lump in her throat.

As I listen to her recount the terrible drama, I cannot feel sad, because I'm happy to have her with me. I'm scared that this sorrow might send her back to bed. Better leave the photos until she has recovered completely.

But she continues.

"They smashed the windows of all the shops. Maybe one of those ruined stores belonged to your great-grandparents. Who knows. On Kristallnacht, the night of broken windows, they burned down all the synagogues. Only one was left standing, Anna.

"They took the men away, separated families. All the women were forced to call themselves Sarah, and the men, Israel," she goes on in a rush. "I told my father that if I had to change my name, I preferred to die. Some people managed to escape, others were later exterminated in the gas chambers."

A horror film. I can't imagine the two of us alone in that city then. I don't know whether Mom would have survived. Berlin was a hell for people like us. They lost everything.

"They left behind their homes, their lives. Very few survived. They lived hidden in basements. They fled the country: it was their only chance. They were attacked in the street, arrested, thrown in jail, and never seen again. Some of them chose to send their children on their own to other countries, so that they would be brought up in another culture, with a different religion, as part of families they didn't know."

I close my eyes and take a deep breath. I see Dad in Berlin, Havana, New York. I'm German. This is my family, forced to call themselves Sarah and Israel, whose businesses were destroyed. The family that fled, that survived. This is where I come from.

Mom thinks the saddest photos are the ones of interiors, but they show a well-dressed man and woman, in big rooms in what look like palaces. The woman is tall and elegant, her dress tight-fitting around her waist, and with a broad, tilted hat. She is standing in front of a window. The man wears a suit and tie and is sitting next to an ancient gramophone, with a loudspeaker curved like a gigantic flower. Another photo shows them dressed for a special occasion. He is in formal attire; she is wearing a long silk gown.

"Heaven only knows if they were separated or they managed to die together," Mom continues, her voice filled with emotion.

My favorite photos are the ones of the boy with huge black eyes. In them he is running, jumping, climbing into a window or up a streetlamp, or lying in the grass. Yes, it's the same one in all of them. And he's always smiling.

I get up and stand in front of the blown-up image. We really do look alike. The girl on the ship is the same as the one on the cover of the League of German Girls magazine. I think this weekend, I'll get my hair cut like her.

"That's Hannah, the aunt who brought your Dad up," I hear Mom say behind me. She embraces me and gives me a kiss. "You're called Anna after her."

I want to escape from this trap but can't. I have no idea where I am and try to open my eyes, but my eyelids are sealed. Air! I need air!

Is this another nightmare, or am I awake? The weight of my arms drags me toward the abyss. I can't feel my legs, they're freezing. All my strength is gone, and just when my lungs are giving out, I lose consciousness and float off to who knows where. I lift my head and my nose appears . . . on the surface? I straighten up, turn my head to the left and right, trying to figure out where I am, while the wind beats harshly against my face.

My face is soaked. My skin burns. My head is so hot it's spinning; my body is so cold it paralyzes me. I take desperate breaths, and gulp down air and salt water. I think I'm going to drown and I cough uncontrollably until my throat is scratched. I open my eyes.

I'm drifting aimlessly.

I see the reflection of my face in the surface of the water. I'm the girl on the ship.

I don't know how I got here, but now I have to see how I get back, if possible. My pupils are dilated, my eyes full of salt water. I start moving my arms to keep myself afloat; the feeling comes back to my legs. I'm awake, and alive. I think I can try to swim.

I rub my eyes and see that the palms of my hands are shriveled. Who knows how long I've been in this cold water. Am I on a beach? No: I'm floating in the middle of a dark ocean.

"Mom!" Why am I shouting, if I'm all alone? "Mom!"

No point using up what little energy I have left. *Swim as hard as you can! You're strong. Swim to the shore, take advantage of every push from the wind, a wave, the current.*

The light dazzles me. I have to keep my eyes closed. I'm thirsty, but I don't want to drink salt water. Now I have even deeper wounds, and the salty water seeps into them. My whole body is burning.

I have to swim to infinity. Away from the sun. I can see the shore. Yes, I can make out the city. There are trees, white sand. No, it's not a city. It's an island.

I swim with short strokes. The wind is against me. The waves are against me. The sun is against me. The bright light blinds me.

To the shore! That's your goal. You can do it. Of course I can. But I'm falling asleep.

No! Wake up and keep going. You can't stop! I let myself be pulled along, tumbling over and over.

Dad is waiting for me. This is the island he reached the day he disappeared; he found shelter here. Maybe he fled in a plane, had an accident, and fell into the sea. Like me, he swam and swam until he reached land.

That's why I'm stranded in the sea, because I know you're there and are watching over me. I've come to be your Friday, Dad. That's the only thing that keeps me afloat: thinking I'm going to find you. We're going to be together like two Robinsons on that desert island, and you'll protect me from cannibals, pirates, hurricanes.

After many years, after we've survived storms, earthquakes, erupting volcanoes, droughts, and attacks, we'll be rescued at last and travel together to dry land, to the continent. Mom will be there waiting for us. Because she needs you, Dad, as much as I do.

Now I'm no longer in the water. My body is lying on hot sand that sticks to my burning skin. The sun confuses me. I open my eyes and see you. Is it you?

I knew you wouldn't abandon me. That one day you'd come for me. That we would meet in a far-off land, on another continent, on an island lost in the middle of the ocean. That I would be your girl. Your only daughter, whom you would look after forever.

"Anna!" someone is shouting.

I get up quickly. It's Mom. I'm wet with sweat, in my own bed, in my room. This is my island. I look for Dad on the bedside table, and there he is, looking at me with that half smile of his, next to the postcard of the ship I got from his aunt.

Mom hugs me, and I start to cry. I'm her little girl again, and I fall into her arms so that she can soothe me, stroke me. She starts humming. I can't believe it: it's a lullaby. I close my eyes and hear her soft voice whispering in my ear: "Bye lulu-baby, bye lulu-baby, bye lulu-baby, bye lullaby."

I'm her baby once more. I hide myself in her, pull her to me, and hear her voice again. Yes, Mom used to sing me this lullaby when I was small and had nightmares. *Don't stop singing, Mom.* The two of us are still here, waiting for the day when we receive the surprising news that Dad is alive on a far-off island, that he was rescued and is coming back to us.

"What shall we do for your birthday?" She has stopped singing, and I open my eyes.

I can't remember us ever having a celebration that wasn't just the two of us, with a chocolate cupcake and a pink candle. Most of my girl-friends from Fieldston live outside the city, so usually I see them only at school during classes.

I'm not really interested in parties. I want something better: a trip. Yes, let's cross the Gulf of Mexico. Let's conquer the waves of the Carib-bean, glimpse the coast of an island filled with palm and coconut trees, with lots of sun. We'll reach a port where we'll be greeted with flowers and balloons, and there will be music. People will be dancing on the shore and will clear a way for us to enter the promised land.

"Cuba! Let's go to Cuba!"

Her face sharpens: she parts her lips, and a gleam begins to light up her eyes. I want to tell her, "Mom, we're not alone," but I don't have the guts.

"We could meet Dad's family and the aunt who raised him," I say, and at first she doesn't react.

With any luck, his aunt will look after me if anything happens to Mom. Maybe I'll even find other uncles and aunts or cousins who will take care of me until I'm old enough to decide for myself without some social worker making me go live with some family I don't know.

Now I have a goal: to discover who my father really was.

"Why don't we go to Cuba?" I insist.

Mom still says nothing. She smiles and hugs me:

"Tomorrow we'll talk to your aunt Hannah."

Hannah
Berlin, 1939

I arrived early for our rendezvous at Frau Falkenhorst's café. I couldn't see Leo, so I started wandering around the Hackescher Markt Station. It was full of soldiers. There were even more people than usual there that day. Something was going on, and Leo wasn't with me. More flags. All I could see everywhere was red and black. It was torment. The streets were crowded with banners and men and women, their arms raised to the skies.

Over the loudspeakers, an excited voice was talking about a birthday, the celebration of a man who was changing the Germans' destiny. The man we were supposed to follow, admire, worship. The purest man in a country where very soon only pure people like him would be allowed to live. The loudspeakers made it impossible to hear the announcements of the train departures and arrivals. A huge banner thanked the chief

Ogre for the Germany we lived in: "*Wir danken dir.*" Then a Bach cantata began to echo through the station: "*Wir danken dir, Gott, wir danken dir.*" "We thank you, God, we thank you." So now the Ogre was God. It was the twentieth of April.

My green dress blended with the station's tiled walls so perfectly that I felt like a chameleon. When he saw me, Leo would burst out laughing. I ran to the exit connecting to the café and bumped into him.

"What does the German girl of Französische Strasse have to say?" he laughed, with an irony that made his eyes look even more mischievous than usual. "We're going to Cuba. And you'll see how that magazine will open doors for you. The German girl is here!" he shouted and laughed.

Cuba. Yet another new destination. Leo had found out everything. He was sure it was Cuba. It began to rain, so we ran to the sprawling Hermann Tietz department store—which was no longer called that because it was too impure. Now they called it Hertie, so as not to offend anyone. Despite the rain and the time of day, all the floors seemed empty.

"Where has everybody gone?"

We found the central staircase and rushed up it. We bumped into some women who looked at us as if wondering where the adult minding us could be. We passed the floor with the Persian rugs hanging over the banister and reached the top floor under the glass roof, where we could see the rain falling.

"Cuba? Where is Cuba? In Africa, or the Indian Ocean? Is it an island? How do you spell it?" I insisted as I followed Leo breathlessly, wishing I could sit down and stop having to avoid women carrying shopping bags.

"K-h-u-b-a." Leo spelled it out in German. "They're talking about buying boat passages. Your father is going to help us with ours."

It was an island. There was nowhere else we could go. I hoped it was a long way from the Ogres.

"The rain has eased; let's go." Leo set off down the stairs without giving me time to catch my breath. Heaven knows where he wanted to go now.

We came out into the main square dotted with puddles. We went to wait for a tram, and Leo bent down and began to draw in the mud: a tiny, round island beneath an outline he said was Africa. He had made a map out of water and mud. Then he drew a city beside another puddle.

"This is where our house will be, by the seaside." He took my hand, and I could feel how dirty and wet his was. "We're going to Khuba, Hannah!"

His face fell when he realized he hadn't managed to make me as enthusiastic as he was.

"What are we going to do on this island?" was the only thing I could think to ask him, although I knew he wouldn't have an answer.

The possibility that we were leaving was becoming increasingly real; that made me nervous. Until now, we had been able to cope with the Ogres and with Mama's crises. Just knowing we would soon be leaving made my hands tremble.

Suddenly Leo began talking about marriage, having children, living together, but he hadn't even told me if we were engaged. *We're so young, Leo!* I thought he should at least have asked me, so that I could accept; that was how it was always done. But Leo didn't believe in conventions. He had his own rules and drew his own maps in water.

We were going to Khuba. Our children would be Khubans. And we'd learn the Khuban dialect.

While Leo was crouching to draw at the exit to Hermann Tietz's, a woman carrying a hatbox jumped and fell into the middle of a puddle, obliterating our map on the spot.

"Filthy kids," she hissed, glaring at Leo.

I peered up at her from the ground. She looked like a giant with fat, hairy arms, and her fingernails were scarlet-painted claws.

I couldn't bear how rude everyone was. Good manners were disappearing with each day that passed in a city where everyone was intent on smashing windows and kicking anybody who crossed their path. Good manners were no longer necessary. Nobody spoke anymore; they all shouted. Papa complained that the language had lost all its beauty.

For Mama, the German pouring from the loudspeakers all over the city had become a vomit of consonants.

I looked up and saw that the skies were about to open. A gray mass of clouds, heralding a storm. All around us, people were running toward the Brandenburg Gate to watch the parade the loudspeakers were announcing. Today was a holiday: the purest man in Germany was fifty.

How many more flags could the city bear? We tried to reach Unter den Linden but couldn't force our way through. Children and young people were thronging along windows, walls, and balconies to see the military procession. They all seemed to be screeching, "We are invincible! We will rule the world!"

Leo poked fun at them, imitating their salute with his right arm, once again bending his hand upward to signal "Stop!"

"Are you crazy, Leo? These people don't take that kind of thing as a joke," I said, tugging at his arm. We launched ourselves into the crowd again. Now the odyssey would be to get home.

A deafening noise came from on high. An airplane streaked overhead, and then another, and another. Dozens of them filled the Berlin sky. Leo suddenly turned serious. As we were saying good-bye to each other, a detachment of mounted cavalry rode past. They stared at us in amazement, as if to say, "Why are you here and not at the parade?"

The first thing I did when I arrived home was to look for the atlas. I couldn't find Khuba on the pages showing Africa, or in the Indian Ocean, around Australia, or near Japan. Khuba did not exist, it did not appear on any continent. It wasn't a country or an island. I was going to need a magnifying glass to examine the smallest names, lost in the dark-blue blotches.

Possibly it was an island within another island, or a tiny peninsula belonging to no one. It could also be uninhabited, and we would be the first settlers.

We would start from scratch and make Khuba into an ideal country, where anybody could be blond or dark-haired, tall or short, fat or thin. Where you could buy a newspaper, use the telephone, speak whatever language you wished, and call yourself whatever you wanted to without bothering about the color of your skin or which God you worshipped.

In our watery maps, at least, Khuba already existed.

❧

I always thought there was nobody more courageous and intelligent than Papa. In his prime, he had a perfect profile, Mama said: a Greek sculpture. Nowadays she no longer celebrated him. She no longer ran to his side when he came back tired from the university, where they held him in high esteem. Her face no longer lit up as it used to when they called her "the learned doctor's lady" or "the professor's wife" at society events where she looked divine in her pleated ball gowns created by Madame Grès.

"No one can touch French dressmakers," she boasted to her fans.

Papa loved to see her like that: happy, sensual, elegant. The gift of mystery so many film stars cultivated seemed to come naturally to her. Anyone seeing her for the first time could not rest until he or she had been presented to the ethereal Alma Strauss. She was the perfect hostess. She could talk expertly about the opera, literature, history, religion, and politics, and without offending anyone. She was the ideal complement to Papa, who, wrapped up in his own ideas, sometimes bewildered people with incomprehensible scientific theories.

He'd changed. His suffering, and the concern he felt about finding a country that would take us, had devastated him. This invincible man became even frailer than the leaf from the most ancient tree in the Tiergarten that Leo had given me and which I kept in my diary. Papa had a fresh complaint every day.

"I'm losing my sight," he told us one morning.

I watched him die little by little. I realized this and was prepared. I would be an orphan who had lost her father and would have to look after a depressed mother who never stopped weeping over her days of lost glory.

I had no idea how to overcome the inertia all three of us fell into when we met at home. We were not getting anywhere. I was unable to predict the path we would take, but I could sense a surprise was in store for us. And I hated surprises.

It was time for us to make a decision. It didn't matter if we made a mistake and ended up in the wrong place. We had to do something. Even if it meant going to Madagascar or to Leo's Khuba.

And I kept thinking to myself, *Where is Khuba?*

Anna

New York, 2014

Mom says my great-aunt is a survivor, like Mr. Levin. She must be full of wrinkles and spots, with sparse white hair, and be hunched and stiff. Maybe she can't walk, or uses a stick, or is in a wheelchair. But her mind is sharp enough, and she has a very special sense of humor and a gentleness mixed with a touch of bitterness that has captivated Mom. She was surprised after she talked to her. Mom says she speaks very clearly, slowly and carefully, and that her voice makes her sound younger than she really is. She switches between English and Spanish with no problem. Mom is sure we're not going to find a crushed old woman.

"She's so calm and serene," she says, as if thinking out loud. "She's not sad, Anna. She's resigned to her situation, but she wants to meet you. She said she needs to."

To me, Cuba means nothing. When from my bedroom I hear Mom chatting to Mr. Levin about our trip, they always talk of a country where everything is lacking. But I imagine a desert island surrounded by furious waves, swept by hurricanes and tropical storms. A tiny dot in the middle of the sea, with no buildings, streets, hospitals, or schools. Nothing—or, rather, emptiness. I don't know how Dad could have studied there. Perhaps that's why he ended up in Manhattan, a proper island, one step away from dry land.

Dad's family arrived in Cuba on a ship, and that was where they stayed. But he grew up and left, like almost all those born in Cuba. "You have to leave islands," he would always tell Mom. "That's what you think when the endless sea is your only frontier."

Dad was shy. He didn't know how to dance, he didn't drink, he never smoked. Mom used to joke that the only thing Cuban about him was an old passport. And the Spanish language. He spoke it without any harshness, pronouncing the *s*'s and without swallowing the consonants. English was his second language, which he spoke fluently without an accent, thanks to the aunt who brought him up after his parents' death. He obtained American citizenship because of his father, who had been born in New York. That was all the information Mom had been able to gather during the few years they were married; she verified it with the great-aunt in a phone call that was constantly cut off.

Occasionally a film reminded her of the man with whom she had decided to have a family that he never knew. It was thanks to him that Mom had discovered postwar Italian cinema. Dad was fascinated by Visconti, Antonioni, De Sica. But he also enjoyed Madonna. Those were his contradictions. When they started going out together, one of their first dates was at the Film Forum in Manhattan's Greenwich Village, to see the original version of De Sica's *Il giardino dei Finzi-Contini*, one of his favorite films. Dad always left the cinema in a state.

"I saw his eyes brimming, and he said I looked like the heroine in the movie," recalls Mom. "It was such a romantic thing from someone who said so little that I thought, *I can live with this man*. Your father never showed his emotions, but at the movies, he was always weeping."

Dad found refuge in his work, his books, and the dark theaters where stories were told through moving images. He didn't have friends. I used to imagine him as a superhero who came to rescue the oppressed and those who had nothing. Mom would laugh at my wild fantasies. But she never criticized them because she knew that, to me, he was still alive.

Mom is all alone. She was an only child, and her parents died, one after the other, when she was about to finish college. Then Dad appeared. They met at a concert of baroque music at Columbia University, where she taught classes in Latin American literature.

The day she announced she was getting married, none of her friends asked if Dad was Hispanic, Jewish, or a foreigner just passing through. His origin wasn't important: he spoke good English, and that was enough. He had a job in a center for nuclear studies, as well as a nice apartment he had inherited from his family.

Dad worked outside the city but had an office downtown where he went every Tuesday. Those were the only days he arrived home later, but she never questioned him about it. My father wasn't someone you could question, or even feel jealous about. Not because he wasn't handsome, but because he didn't like complications or anything that would disturb his space, which was already well-defined.

She never introduced him to her faculty friends, and so had no need to explain. All she knew about Dad was that his parents had died in an airplane crash when he was a young boy and that he had been brought up by an aunt. That was enough. He never spoke about his past.

"It's best to forget," he would tell her.

I go into Mom's room. She is kneeling in front of the dresser, rummaging through papers and books. She pulls out an old shoe box. I can see a pair of cuff links, a pair of men's sunglasses, several envelopes.

When Mom hears me at the door, she turns around and offers me her best smile.

"Some of your father's things," she says, closing the box and handing it to me.

I run back to my island with my new treasure, and shut myself in to examine it.

"*Look how many treasures I have. I'm sure you remember them,*" I whisper to my father so that Mom won't hear. "*There are documents, bank statements—but not a single photo. I thought I would find another photo of you. I'll keep your cuff links and glasses in my bedside drawer.*"

At the bottom of the box, I find a blue envelope. I open it carefully: inside is a small sheet of paper the same color. It's Dad's handwriting: an undated letter addressed to Mom. Suddenly I think I ought to mention it to her before I read it, but then decide not to. She gave me what she had kept packed away for twelve years, so it belongs to me now.

All at once, I feel hungry; it's always the same when I'm nervous. *I need to calm down, because I'm about to read one of your letters. I don't want to discover any secrets; there are more than enough secrets awaiting us in Cuba.*

I'll read it for you, Dad. So that you'll remember Mom, who never forgets you however many years go by.

Ida my love,

   Today is the fifth anniversary of our life together, and I remember as if it were today the moment I first saw you, in the back row of that autumn concert in Saint Paul's Chapel at the university.

   You were speaking Spanish with your students, and I couldn't stop looking at you. You became lost in the music, and I can still see how you flicked your hair behind your ears, and I could see your beautiful profile. I could have traced it with my fingers, from your forehead to your eyebrows, nose, lips, cheeks.

You still remember the concert, the music, the orchestra. I remember only you.

I never tell you I love you, that you're the best thing that has ever happened to me. That I enjoy your silences, being beside you, watching you sleep, wake up, having breakfast with you on the weekend at sunrise. Have I ever told you that those mornings together, when sometimes we don't even say a word, are my favorites because you are by my side?

You came into my life when I was resigned to the fact that nobody would accept my solitude. One day we must travel the world, lose ourselves among other people. Just you and me. Promise?

Ida my love, I'll always be here for you.

Louis

Hannah

Berlin, 1939

There were mornings when I woke up feeling as if I couldn't breathe, days when I sensed a tragedy was coming ever closer, and my heart began to beat wildly. Then very rapidly and suddenly, it seemed to stop altogether. Was I still alive? One of those days was a Tuesday. I hated Tuesdays. They should have been erased from the calendar. As soon as we got to Khuba, Leo and I would decree: "No more Tuesdays!"

When I woke up, my body was feverish, but I didn't have a cold or any pain. Papa, with his tie in its Windsor knot and already holding his gray felt hat, took my temperature. He smiled and kissed me on the brow: "You're fine. Come on, get out of bed."

He stayed with me for a while, gave me another kiss, and then left me in my room. The sound of the front door slamming startled me. Now it was just Mama and me in the apartment. Abandoned.

I knew I didn't have a temperature and that I wasn't ill, but my body refused to get up. I had even lost all desire to go out and meet Leo to take photographs. I had a premonition but could not say of what.

That day, Mama was wearing light makeup but not her false eyelashes. She had on a dark-blue long-sleeved dress that gave her a slightly formal look. I put on the brown beret she had brought me from her last trip to Vienna and shut myself in my room with the atlas, hoping to find our tiny island, which still had not appeared.

We were on the verge of going somewhere. Papa couldn't continue keeping our final destination a secret. I was ready to accept anything. Nothing more could happen to us: we were living in a state of terror in an as-yet-undeclared war; I didn't think many things could be worse than that.

Leo said Papa had even bought a house in Khuba.

"If we're not staying there long, why will we need a house?" I asked him. As ever, Leo had the answer.

"It's the easiest way to obtain an entry permit. Having a house shows you won't be a burden on the state."

I didn't know where Papa went every morning; he had been banned from the university. He must have been going to the consulates of countries with strange names to get us visas, refugee papers. Or he was with Leo's father, hatching some plot or other that could have cost them their lives.

I imagined Papa as a hero coming to save us, in a soldier's uniform and with a chest full of medals like Grandpa, who'd defeated the enemies of the German people. I saw him confronting the Ogres, who were powerless against his might and surrendered to his valor.

I was starting to get confused by all these disturbing thoughts when Mama put a record on the gramophone. That was my father's treasure, his most precious jewel. His territory.

One day, as he was placing the shellac disk in the polished wooden box, Papa had explained the workings of this marvel that kept him in ecstasy for hours. It was a real magic trick. The sound box of the

RCA Victor—which he called simply Victor, as though it were a close friend—had a moveable arm ending with a metal needle that followed at a perfect rhythm the grooves in the black disk that went around and around until I felt dizzy just looking at it. The sound waves changed into mechanical vibrations and came out of a lovely golden speaker shaped like a trumpet: an enormous bell. The first thing you heard was a whirring sound, a kind of metal sigh that lasted until the music started to flow. We would close our eyes and imagine we were at a concert at the opera house. The music poured out of the trumpet, the whole room shook, and we let ourselves be carried away. We rose into the air, an incredible experience for me.

Then I could hear the words of her favorite aria: "*Mon cœur s'ouvre à ta voix, comme s'ouvrent les fleurs aux baisers de l'aurore!*"

So there was nothing for me to worry about. Mama was carried away by the music of the French composer Camille Saint-Saëns, one of the records Papa used to look after carefully, cleaning them before and after he put them on Victor. It was a recent recording, with his favorite mezzo-soprano, Gertrud Pålson-Wettergren. He once went to Paris with Mama just to hear her sing. I could see the nostalgic look on Mama's face. By now, yesterday was a distant notion for her. I on the other hand, while listening to the desperate woman's aria, imagined myself running through meadows with Leo, climbing mountains and crossing rivers on the island where we would live.

Nothing bad was going to happen. Papa would come home for dinner. I would go out to meet Leo, and in my atlas we would find the lost island in the midst of some unknown ocean.

I knew what I had to take in my suitcase. The camera, with lots of rolls of film, of course. Only a couple of dresses; I didn't need any more. I would have loved to see Mama's luggage. She would be happy only if they let her take her jewels. The perfumes. The creams. We would need a car just to take all her baggage.

Suddenly there were two loud knocks on the apartment door. No one had paid us a visit in months. Eva had the key to the service entrance.

Mama and I stared at each other. The music went on playing. We both knew the moment had arrived, even though no one had prepared me for it. I looked at her for some answer, but she was slow to react; she didn't know what to do.

She rose from her bergère armchair and lifted the Victrola's moveable arm. The disk stopped turning, and silence filled the living room, which now seemed as vast as a castle. I felt like an insect in the doorway. Two more loud knocks followed. Mama shuddered. Her lips started to quiver, but she stood very erect, lifted her chin, stretched her neck, and walked slowly toward the door—so slowly, there was time for not just two but four loud bangs that made the room tremble.

Mama opened the door, genuflected, and gestured with her hand for them to come in, without asking who they were looking for or what they wanted. Four Ogres entered the living room one after the other, bringing with them a blast of cold air. I couldn't stop trembling. The freezing draft chilled me to the bone.

The chief Ogre reached the center of the room and came to a halt on the thick Persian rug. Mama stepped to one side so as not to obstruct the view of this man who had come to change our lives forever.

"You do live well, don't you?" he announced, without bothering to disguise his envy. He began to study the room in great detail: the coppery drapes, the silk net curtains to filter the light from the courtyard window, the imposing sofa with yellow Pompeii cushions, the oil portrait of Mama with her flawed pearl hanging around her neck and bare shoulders.

The Ogre inspected every object with the precision of a ruthless auctioneer. It was obvious from his eyes the things he liked most and he was planning to keep for himself.

Our living room was filled with the smell of gunpowder, burnt wood, smashed windows, ashes.

I placed myself as a shield between the Ogres and Mama. When she laid her hands on my shoulders, I could feel her trembling.

"You must be Hannah," said the chief Ogre in a cultured Berlin accent. "The German girl. You're almost perfect."

He pronounced *almost* with such spite that it was as if he had slapped me.

"As far as I can see, *Herr* Rosenthal isn't at home."

When he said Papa's name, I thought my heart would burst. I took deep breaths to try to calm it, to prevent them from hearing my blood pumping so loudly. I began to perspire. Mama still had the fixed smile on her face. Her cold hands were making my shoulders numb.

I had to think of something else, to escape from the room, my mother, the Ogres: I started to peer at the brocade on the silk wallpaper. Strands of fern leaves ending in bunches of flowers that were repeated endlessly. *Go on, Hannah, follow the trace of your roots and don't think about what is going to happen,* I kept telling myself over and over. One, two, three leaves on each stem.

I lost concentration when a drop of sweat started slowly to roll down my temple. I didn't dare stop it, so I let it drip onto my front.

I sensed that Mama was about to break down. *Please don't cry, Mama. Don't let them see how desperate we are. Don't lose that beautiful, cold smile of yours. Tremble all you like, but don't cry. It's Papa they've come for, and we knew this moment would arrive. It was high time we heard the banging at the door.*

The chief Ogre went over to the window to check which side of the street our living room faced and possibly also to calculate how much our apartment was worth. Then he crossed to the gramophone. He picked up Papa's fragile record, examined it, and looked straight at Mama.

"A key piece for every mezzo-soprano."

I could sense Mama was about to offer them tea or some other drink, and I stiffened to try to convey to her not to do it. *Stay as you are, proud and erect. I'll protect you. Lean on me; don't let yourself collapse and don't offer the Ogres anything.*

The man paced slowly round the room, and as he did so, the current of freezing air expanded around him. I couldn't stop trembling. I was going to have to run to the bathroom.

The Ogre waved to his two men to search the other rooms. Perhaps they wanted to steal our jewels. It wouldn't be hard to find them: they were in the box with the lonely ballerina on top, together with the Patek Philippe watch that Papa wore only on special occasions. Perhaps they were after the money Mama kept in one of her bedside table drawers. All our cash was there, apart from some she'd given to Eva in case of an emergency. The rest was in bank accounts in Switzerland and Canada.

The Ogre went back to the gramophone.

He lifted the arm with the needle and studied it intently. If he broke it, or if anything happened to the gramophone, Papa might have killed him. It was something he would never forgive.

"Herr Rosenthal is about to arrive," said Mama, and I wondered how she could be telling them that when she knew they were there to take him away.

All of a sudden it became clear to me that it was not the money they were after, or the jewels, the paintings, or even Papa's wretched gramophone: what they wanted were the six apartments in our building. First they wanted to scare us and then take them from us. No doubt the chief Ogre would move in, sleep in the main bedroom, take over Papa's study, and destroy all our photos.

Silence.

The Ogre settled into Papa's velvet armchair and began to stroke it as though testing the quality of the fabric. He took his time caressing the arm, staring intently at me all the while, telling me silently by this that he was willing to wait for Papa for as long as it took. He was comfortable and began to study the photographs of the Strauss family displayed on the walls around the room.

Until then I had never noticed how the staircase leading to our apartment creaked, but now it sounded as loud as church bells. The moment had arrived.

Silence.

The chief Ogre had also heard the footsteps and sat motionless, ears pricked. From where he was sitting, he dominated the whole room.

Another step, and I realized Papa was outside the door. My heart was about to explode. Mama's breathing quickened; I was the only one who could hear her soft moans from behind me.

I was going to shout "Don't come in, Papa! The Ogres are here! There's one sitting in your favorite armchair!" But I realized there was no point. There was nowhere for us to escape to. Berlin was a pocket handkerchief; they were bound to catch him sooner or later. And Mama was about to faint.

The Ogre and his entourage took up positions behind the door. I could hear the key scraping in the lock; it always got stuck a little.

Silence, growing longer and longer.

The delay disconcerted the chief Ogre, who exchanged glances with his men. To me, every second seemed like an hour: I even found myself wishing they would take him away once and for all—for him to disappear with them. A few more minutes like this, and I would be the one who fainted. I wanted to go to the bathroom; I couldn't hold it in anymore. I didn't want to be a witness to the humiliating spectacle that the Ogre had been carefully preparing for us, so that we would beg and weep disconsolately. Mama did not move.

The door opened.

And the strongest, most elegant man in the world came in. The one who put me to sleep and gave me a kiss whenever I was afraid. The one who hugged me, cuddled me, and swore that nothing would happen, that we would go far away, to an island that not even the Ogres' tentacles could ever reach.

The look on Papa's face showed how sorry he felt for us. He seemed to be asking himself how on earth he could have put us in such a position. We had already experienced something similar that November night when he was arrested. But this was the decisive moment. There was no going back, and he knew it. It was time for him to say good-bye to the woman he loved, to the daughter he adored.

"Herr Rosenthal, I need you to accompany us to the station."

Papa nodded without looking the Ogre in the face. He took several steps toward me, trying not to glance at Mama, because he knew that might weaken her. I was the one who could resist, who in the end would be without a father to protect her from ghosts, witches, monsters. But not from the Ogres. No one could defend us against them.

He put his arms around me and took hold of my icy hands. I could feel how warm his were. *Lend me some of your warmth, Papa. Chase this terror from my bones.* I hugged him with what little strength I had left. And I wept. That was what the Ogres wanted: to see us suffer.

"My Hannah, what have we done to you . . ." he whispered, his voice choking.

I closed my eyes tight. They were separating me from the man who until today had protected me; the one in whom we placed all our faith to save us. They were taking him away. Mama held me and drew me to her. I realized that, from then on, the weakest person in the family would be my only support. I still had my eyes shut tight, despite the tears.

"Don't worry, Hannah," I heard my father say. He was still there. Another second. Another minute, please. "Everything will be all right, my girl."

Haven't they taken him away? Haven't they changed their minds?

"Look out of the window," Papa said. "The tulips are about to bloom."

Those were the last words I heard. When I opened my eyes again, he had vanished with the Ogre. The whole building could have heard me weep. I shouted out of the window:

"Papa!"

Nobody heard me. Nobody saw me. Nobody cared.

I could sense a whisper behind me. It was Mama.

"Where are you taking him?" she asked, her voice quaking.

"It's routine," I heard one of the Ogres say from the doorway. "We're going to Grolmanstrasse police station. Don't worry, nothing will happen to your husband."

Yes, of course. They would send him back safe and sound. And he would return and tell us he had been treated like a fine gentleman. That, rather than water, they had served him wine in a big, warm, well-lit cell. But I knew what was really going to happen: he would sleep in a crowded cell and go hungry. And if we were lucky, we would occasionally hear news of his wretched existence.

From the day they took Herr Schemuel, the butcher from our neighborhood, we'd had no news of him. There was no difference between him and my father. To them, we were all the same, and I was convinced: nobody came back from that hell.

I should have clung to him until he dragged me away, to have recorded that moment I could no longer remember, because I tended to erase sad moments from my mind.

Mama rushed to her bedroom and closed the door. Terrified, I ran in after her and saw her opening drawers and pulling out documents that she scanned hastily.

"I have to go," she muttered. "I'll see you later."

I couldn't believe it. *Where are you going, Mama? There's nothing we can do. We have lost Papa!* But it was no use: with the strength of the Strauss family, which had been suppressed until that moment, Mama plunged into the street after months of shutting herself in. She slammed the front door and vanished, unconcerned about her makeup, whether her shoes and her handbag matched, if her dress was properly ironed, or if she was wearing the appropriate springtime perfume.

I closed my eyes again and told myself: you must not forget this. I started to list everything I had to engrave on my memory: the brocade wall coverings, the light in the hallway, the velvet armchair, Mama's fragrance. Even so, the most important thing escaped me: Papa's face.

I was all alone. In an instant, I knew what it was like to be without my parents. And I also knew it would not be the last time.

Anna

New York, 2014

Aunt Hannah lost her nephew, her only descendant, her last hope. I lost my father.

Until I was five, I always hoped Dad would come in one day without warning, just like that. Every time the front door buzzer rang, I used to run to the door to see who was coming.

"You're like a little dog," Mom would scold me.

He left a huge world map that I hung on the wall over my bed. I imagined Dad traveling to exotic countries in jet planes, nuclear submarines, and zeppelins. I could see him climbing Everest, bathing in the Dead Sea, emerging from an avalanche of snow on Kilimanjaro, swimming across the Suez Canal, going over Niagara Falls in a canoe. My father was an imaginary traveler who one day would come to find me and take me with him to undiscovered places. A huge adventure.

Until one cloudy September day: the fifth anniversary of the fateful day on which Dad chose to disappear. My school had organized a ceremony, and in the auditorium, packed with children, somebody read out a list of the disappeared. Dad's name was the last on it. I sat there like a statue; I had no idea how to react. The children in my class began to hug me, one by one.

"Anna lost her father," the teacher declared solemnly when we were back in our classroom.

"Those of us who lived through that day will never forget what we were doing at that time of the morning," the teacher began to say. She kept breaking off and looking at us to make sure we were paying attention.

"That morning I was in my classroom, when I was called to George's office. Classes were suddenly suspended and the children sent home. There was no public transport, the bridges to Manhattan were closed. A friend picked me up here at school, and I spent the night at her house in Riverdale. Those were such anxious days."

The teacher's eyes brimmed with tears. She searched for a handkerchief in her pocket and continued.

"Many people at our school lost family, friends, or someone they knew. It took a long time for them to recover."

I tried to react calmly, although I was completely shaken.

On the bus ride home, I sat by myself in the back row and started to cry silently. The children in front of me were shouting, throwing pencils and rubber erasers at one another. I slowly realized that, from then on, to the others, I would be the poor little girl who had lost her father one day in September.

Mom was waiting for me at the entrance to our building. I got off the bus without saying good-bye to the driver and walked to the elevator without even looking at her. When we reached our apartment, I confronted her:

"Dad died five years ago. The teacher said so in class."

When she heard the word *died*, Mom jumped, but she recovered immediately, as if to show that the news did not affect her that badly.

I went to my room; I had no idea what Mom did. She had no energy; maybe she wasn't even interested in giving me an explanation. Her mourning was over, while mine was just beginning.

Later on I went into her darkened room and saw her there, still in her clothes and with her shoes on, curled up like a baby. I let her get some rest. I realized that, from then on, we would talk about Dad in the past tense. I had become an orphan. She was a widow.

I started to dream of him in a different way. To me, it was as if somehow he was still on a faraway island. But to Mom, for the first time, he was really dead.

Every September, mechanically, I think of how Dad left the apartment one sunny morning, never to return. So am I.

That day when I was only four and a half years old and learned how Dad had disappeared, I stopped being a little girl and retreated to my bedroom with his photograph. Before then, there were parks and trees, people selling fruit and flowers on Broadway street corners. Before, we used to go out for ice cream in spring, summer, and even in winter. Mom had promised to teach me to ride a bike in Central Park. She never kept her promise.

With her head sunk in the pillow and her voice a weary monotone, Mom told me what happened that awful day in a litany that frightened me. Every September, her voice comes back to me like a prayer repeated without alteration.

When the alarm went off at six thirty in the morning, Dad's eyes were already wide-open. He turned over to make sure that Mom was still asleep, though, in reality, she was pretending. She had spent the night feeling sick, with headaches and trips to the bathroom.

For a few seconds, he sat on the edge of the bed in silence. He took his dark-blue suit into the bathroom to get dressed without making noise. He showered, shaved in a hurry, and just as he finished buttoning his shirt, he noticed a drop of blood close to his crisp white collar. He pressed his index finger against the tiny cut and then checked the mail—he'd left the letters in a pile as usual—and took two envelopes with him, Mom insists: one from his work and the other from his trust fund. He checked that Mom was still in bed and closed the door very carefully behind him.

She was planning to tell him the good news that night. She had waited three months because she wanted to be sure it wasn't a false alarm. My mother doesn't like premature celebrations. She could have told him on one of the many early mornings disturbed by the queasiness of the first three months of pregnancy. The doctor had confirmed she was twelve weeks along the day before. There were all the signs.

She bought his favorite red wine. She was going to tell him over dinner: next year everything will change. We're going to be parents. She wanted to find the ideal moment to surprise him.

Dad had no idea what she was planning. That September day was like any other. Slightly cool, but sunny, with the rush hour traffic steady. Mom watched from the window and saw him open the front door, pausing at the top of the steps to take a deep breath. There were still lingering traces of summer in the air. At the intersection of 116th Street and Morningside Drive, he glanced eastward at the early-morning sun and the still-leafy park. It was seven thirty. At that time, the superintendent always took his dog for a walk. Dad greeted him and turned onto 116th Street, heading west. He crossed the Columbia University campus and took the No. 1 train on Broadway. Mom knew his routine perfectly: just another Tuesday.

When he reached the Chambers Street station, he headed for John Allan's on Trinity Place for his monthly haircut. He had become a member of a men's club, when he began his weekly trips to the business district in Manhattan. He felt at ease there. It had an atmosphere of privacy that he enjoyed. His black coffee (no sugar) was waiting for him, and he flicked through the headlines in the *Wall Street Journal*, the *New York Times*, and *El Diario La Prensa*.

Dad never had his haircut. He never reached his office. That much is clear. I wonder now where he went when at 8:46 a.m. he heard the first explosion. He could have stayed where he was like the others did; the ones who were spared. A few minutes later, and Mom's litany would have been completely different. Only a few minutes later.

Maybe he ran to see what was happening or to see if he could save someone. The second explosion came at 9:03. Everybody must have been totally bewildered. The telephones went dead. Then the deluge of bodies began hitting the pavement. At 9:58, one of the skyscrapers collapsed. At 10:28, the other one followed.

A thick cloud of dust covered the tip of the island. It was impossible to breathe, to keep eyes open. There was a deafening wail of fire engines and police cars. I imagine that all of a sudden day turned into night. Men and women ran searching for the light in a battle against fire, terror, anguish. To the north; they had to run north.

I close my eyes and prefer to see Dad carrying a wounded person to safety. Then he goes back to ground zero and joins the firefighters and police in the rescue operation. I like to think Dad is safe—that he is still lost, not knowing where to go. Maybe he forgot his address, how to get home. With each September that passed and I grew up without him, the chances of him returning became fewer and fewer. He must have been trapped in the rubble. The buildings were reduced to shards of steel, smashed glass, and chunks of cement.

The city was paralyzed. So was Mom.

She waited two days before reporting Dad missing. I've no idea how she could sleep that night, get up and go to work the next day, and then return to bed as if nothing had happened. Always with the hope that Dad would come back. That was how she was.

She couldn't link him to that terrible tragedy; she refused to accept that he was buried among the debris. That was her defense to keep herself from falling apart. And to keep me from fading away inside her.

She became one more phantom in the extinguished city. Closed restaurants, empty markets, train lines cut off, families mutilated. A zip code obliterated. Street corners full of photographs of men and women who had left for work that day, like Dad had, and never returned. At the entrances to buildings, in gyms, offices, bookshops, thousands of lost faces. Each morning they multiplied; new descriptions appeared. Except for Dad's.

Mom didn't tour the hospitals or go to the morgue or the police stations. She was not a victim, much less the wife of a victim. She didn't accept condolences. Nor did she answer the phone when people kept calling to give her news she refused to listen to, or to feel sorry for her. Dad was not wounded or dead. She was convinced of it.

She would let time go by, and that would sort everything out. She couldn't fix something that had no solution. She wasn't going to shed a single tear. There was no need.

My mother wrapped herself in silence. That was her best refuge. She didn't hear the noise of the traffic or any of the voices around her. All the background music disappeared. Each morning, she roamed the neighborhood that reeked of smoke and melted metal, with dust and debris everywhere. Every streetlamp offered more photos. Sometimes she stopped to peer at them: the faces seemed strangely familiar to her.

She tried to continue her daily routines. Going to the market, buying coffee, picking up her medicine from the pharmacy. She lay down to sleep with the smell of smoke and charred metal sticking to her skin.

Mom left her job and has not been back since. At first, she asked for a leave, but later on that turned into an unannounced resignation. She didn't need to work. Dad's apartment had belonged to his family since before the war, and we lived on the trust fund his grandfather had set up many years earlier.

I sometimes think that withdrawing from the world was the only way she found to help her bear the pain. Not just from having lost Dad but also from not having told him I was going to be born. That he would become a father.

Hannah

Berlin, 1939

I opened the dining room windows, pulled back the curtains, let in the morning light. Then I took a deep breath. There was no odor of smoke, metal, or dust. When I closed my eyes, I could smell the fragrance of jasmine. I opened them, and tea was served on the dining room table with its delicate lace cloth, standing in the corner closest to the window so that we could catch a little sun. There were the vanilla biscuits that my friend Gretel and I liked so much. I needed a hat. Ah, and a scarf. Yes, a pink silk scarf to receive Gretel and Don, her dog. When we had finished, I would run downstairs with him.

Gretel opened the door and crossed the main living room, but Don was the first one in; he scampered around the table like a mad thing. I tried to pet him and caught him by the tail to calm him down, but nothing would stop him. He was free.

Gretel could not stop chattering: Don had said hello; he was learning to sing; he got her out of bed every morning. Don is a completely white terrier, without a single dark patch or stain, not a single blemish, and perfectly proportioned, like all the dogs of his race. He is privileged: he has even been in Villa Viola, where they train pure pedigree dogs. He was taught alongside its most famous dog, a German shepherd named Blondi.

Gretel liked to drink ice water in champagne glasses, closing her eyes coquettishly and pretending the bubbles made her feel giddy. I had such fun with her. She came to the house twice a week to have tea and champagne without bubbles.

"What are you doing sitting there in the dark?" Mama had arrived home and put an end to my daydream: my memories of afternoon tea with Gretel.

I followed her into her bedroom and was overwhelmed by the scent of 10,600 jasmine flowers and 336 Bulgarian roses. She used to explain that all this went into concocting the perfume as she subtly let a drop of it fall onto the nape of her neck and another on her wrists.

When I was little, I used to spend hours in that room, the largest and sweetest smelling in the whole apartment. Its huge chandelier, with long arms fanning out on all sides, resembled a giant spider. Frightened, I'd shut myself in the huge closet, where I used to try on pearl necklaces and parade about in voluminous hats and high-heeled shoes. That was back when Mama would laugh to see me play, smear me with bright-red lipstick, and call me "my little clown."

Times had changed, even though the rugs that no one looked after anymore, and the batiste sheets nobody ironed, and the dusty silk mesh curtains, were all still impregnated with the essence of jasmine, mixed now with the sickening smell of mothballs. Mama insisted on preserving a past that was evaporating before our eyes as we looked on helplessly.

I lay down on the white lace bedspread, peering up at the chandelier that no longer scared me, and sensed that she had come into the room. My mother headed straight for the bathroom without saying a word. She was exhausted.

It was obvious from her face and movements that this frail woman, who used to pose like the languid Greta Garbo, had somehow recovered the strength of the Strauss family from some unsuspected, remote place. She responded to Papa's disappearance with a vigor that surprised even her. I was the one now who found it hard to leave our prison. If I didn't meet up with Leo at Frau Falkenhorst's café today, he was capable of appearing at the apartment without warning, running the risk of bumping into the dreaded Frau Hofmeister and silly Gretel.

Without makeup, her hair wet, and her cheeks pink from the hot water, Mama looked even younger than she was. She walked across the bedroom to wrap a small white towel around her head and then closed the curtains so that not the slightest ray of sunshine could enter.

She had still not said a word. I had no idea if she had heard anything about Papa, what steps she was taking. Nothing.

My mother sat at her dressing table and began her beauty ritual. She could see in her mirror that I had gone to sit in her bergère à la reine armchair that was almost two hundred years old, without her even asking first if I had washed my hands. She no longer cared about getting stains on her cherished antique piece designed by someone named Avisse. She took a deep breath and, as she was examining the first signs of a wrinkle, told me gravely:

"We're leaving, Hannah."

She avoided looking at me. She spoke so softly, I found it hard to understand her, although I could sense her determination. It was an order. I didn't count, and nor did Papa or Leo. We were leaving, and that was that.

"We have the permits and the visas. All that's left is to buy our passages on the boat."

What about Papa? She knew he wouldn't be coming back, but there was no way we could abandon him.

"When are we leaving?" was the only thing I dared ask. Her answer was not much help.

"Soon."

At least it wasn't going to be that day or the one after. I had time to work out a plan with Leo; he must already be waiting for me.

"Tomorrow we'll start packing. We'll have to decide what we want to take." She spoke so slowly I became worried.

I needed to go out and meet Leo, but she went on.

"We'll never come back here. But we will survive, Hannah. I'm sure of that," she insisted, brushing her hair with controlled fury.

Mama switched off the main light and left on just the one over her dressing table. We sat in the semidarkness. She had nothing more to say to me.

I slipped out of the room and ran downstairs without even a thought for the neighbors who were so anxious to see us go. If only they knew how eager we were to finally get out of our absurd confinement.

I reached the Hackescher Markt out of breath and ran to the café. Leo was enjoying what was left of his hot chocolate.

"It's spelled C-u-b-a," he said, stressing each letter. "We're going to America!"

He stood up, and I followed him, although I still hadn't caught my breath. I was choking from having run so much. But he'd said, "We're going," and that was the only thing that mattered to me. Not our destination, but the plural *we*. I asked him again so that there would be no misunderstanding.

"We're going to America. Your mother paid a fortune for the permits."

By then, we must have completely run out of cash. We were convinced that Papa had helped pay for permits for Leo and his father. This possibility had arisen for a lot of people in Berlin, and those who could benefit would be safe and sound. Both families, theirs and ours, were among the fortunate ones.

The best news of all was that Papa was alive:

"They're going to let him leave." Leo said it with such authority that I fell silent.

Papa was lucky, not like Herr Schemuel, who never came back. We were undesirables, but the Rosenthals were also fortunate. The conditions they had imposed were that we hand over the apartment building, all our other properties, and that we leave the country in less than six months. As soon as Mama could guarantee the transfer, they would let Papa go free, and we could get his visa and the tickets for the three of us. That was why we hadn't bought them already. Now I understood.

We would have to go listen to the radio in the Ogre's stinking passageway; we needed to be aware of all the latest regulations. They were inventing new ways of making life impossible for us every day. Not only did they not want us here, they were trying all they could to get everybody else to refuse us. If we were rejected on every continent, why should they be the only ones to bear the burden? The perfect move: the triumph of the superior race.

Except that someone had already accepted us. An island in the middle of the Americas was going to take us in and allow us to live there like any other family. We would work, become Cubans, and that was where our children, grandchildren, and great-grandchildren would be born.

"We're leaving on the thirteenth of May," said Leo, striding out ahead. I followed him without asking anything. "We'll leave from Hamburg, bound for Havana."

May 13 was a Saturday. Thank heavens we were not leaving on a Tuesday, the day of the week we dreaded most.

A muddy stone. A shard of smoked glass. A dry leaf. Those were the only souvenirs of Berlin that I hid in my suitcase on the thirteenth of May. Every morning, I would wander aimlessly around our apartment, clutching the stone. Sometimes I waited hours for Mama. She always promised when she went out that she would be back before noon, but she never kept her word. If anything happened to her, I would have to go with Leo. Or perhaps Eva could say I was a distant relative and take me in. No one would discover I was impure. I would get new identity papers and would stay with the woman who had been there at my birth, and end up helping her with the chores in other people's homes.

The documents for the transfer of our possessions were all ready. The building, the apartment where I was born, the furniture, the ornaments, my books, my dolls.

Mama managed to get her most precious jewels out of Berlin thanks to a friend who worked in the embassy of some exotic country. The only thing she refused to hand over were the deeds to our family mausoleum, which didn't interest the Ogres because it was in our cemetery out in Weissensee. That was where my grandparents and great-grandparents had been laid to rest, and that was where we were supposed to end up ourselves, but I was sure they would obliterate that place just as they had obliterated so many other things.

At the time, there was a proliferation of fake documents to resettle in Palestine and England; anyone felt they could take advantage of our desperate situation to rob and swindle us. Sometimes it was the Ogres, but other times it was cruel informers who were responsible. There was nobody we could trust.

That was why Mama made sure that our permits to enter Cuba as refugees were genuine.

"As well as a hundred fifty American dollars for each permit, I paid another five hundred as a deposit. That's as a guarantee that we won't look for work on the island and won't be a burden on the country," she explained, turning her back on me.

We were going to a tiny island that boasted being the largest in the Caribbean. A spit of land between North and South America. But that tiny spit was the only place opening its doors to us.

"According to the atlas, it is part of the Western world," she declared with some satisfaction.

We were to depart from Hamburg and cross the Atlantic Ocean on a German ship. But however much we wanted to go, there was no way we could feel completely safe on a boat with a crew of Ogres.

"The first-class passages will cost us about eight hundred reichsmarks,"

Mama went on, "and the company is demanding we buy return tickets, even though they know we will never come back."

Everyone took advantage of us.

She came back early that day, because Papa was supposed to be coming home. She was wearing a black dress as a kind of anticipated mourning, and a white belt that she couldn't stop adjusting. Her face was clean, with very little makeup. She no longer used false eyelashes or penciled in her eyebrows or used eye shadow. She was a different woman.

Sitting on the edge of the seat with her hands folded on her lap, she looked as though she were an unruly pupil being punished in the school she no longer sent me to because they wouldn't have me.

"Stay calm," she told me as she saw me pacing up and down the huge, dust-filled room.

Papa was climbing the stairs. We could hear him. There he was! *We were leaving! We did it! We were going to live on a spit of land, Papa, where there were no seasons, only summer. Wet and dry. I read that in the atlas.*

When he came in, Papa seemed even taller than before. His glasses were twisted. His hair had been completely shaved off. His shirt collar was so dirty it was impossible to tell what color it was. But his gaunt appearance made him look even more noble: despite the hunger, the pain, and the stench, he was still erect. I ran over to him, hugged him, and he burst into tears. *Don't cry, Papa. You are my strength. You're safe here now with the two of us.*

I stayed there holding him tight, and breathed in his smell of sweat and sewers. I could hear his jerky breath, his heaving chest. He raised his head and looked at Mama.

He kissed me on the forehead like a baby, while Mama started to bring him up to date. I would have loved to know where this woman, who before never left the apartment and spent her days sobbing, had found this sudden strength. I could not get used to the new Alma. I was even more astonished when I heard her speak.

"We only have two exit visas signed by the Cuban state department, because they have just published a new decree restricting the entry of German refugees to the island." Mama did not even pause for breath. "But that doesn't matter: the Hamburg-Amerika Line is going to sell tourist visas for a limited period, signed by the director-general of immigration, somebody called Manuel Benítez."

She tried to pronounce his name in perfect Spanish.

"We need only one. If we can get a Benítez"—she had already christened the lifesaving visas with his name—"stamped by the Cuban consulate, you'll be able to leave with us. But we have to avoid buying it through intermediaries. It would be better to purchase three of them, so we can all travel with the same documents."

"What other option would we have if we can't get a Benítez?" I piped up. "Go anyway, and leave Papa in Berlin?"

She didn't answer me but went on with her breathless explanation:

"At least we have two first-class cabins reserved for us. That's a guarantee. The problem is we're only authorized to take ten reichsmarks per person."

That meant twenty reichsmarks for my parents and ten for me. The sum total of our fortune. We could hide some more cash, but that would be too risky: they could take away our landing permits. Or perhaps we could sneak out Papa's watch, or some other jewel. That would be a great help.

"Until we reach Havana, we won't have access to our Canadian account. It will be a two-week voyage, not much more," Mama went on calmly. "We can stay for the first few days in the Hotel Nacional, until our transit house is ready. We'll be there a month, or perhaps a year. Who knows."

She finished giving Papa all the news and then shut herself in her room. She didn't embrace him: only pecked him coldly on each cheek. We had no more family; we were alone. Over the previous few months, we had lost all our friends. Everybody was trying to survive any way he or she could.

And Leo? They must have helped Leo and his father with their tickets.

Papa's arrival prevented me from going to meet my friend. Instead, he came to look for me, and when I went down to let him in, I saw that Frau Hofmeister was harassing him.

"Get out of here, you dirty mongrel! This isn't a garbage heap!"

We ran to the Tiergarten park. We didn't have much time left, and Leo knew it. He and his father still didn't have their visas.

"They're running out of them," he told me. "And we don't have your papa's, either."

Not only that, but we had a fresh problem: our parents were planning to do away with us all if we didn't manage to leave Berlin. Leo was sure of it.

He had heard them talking about a lethal poison. He knew all about it.

"Nowadays cyanide is as precious as gold," he explained, as if he were a dealer himself.

He's spinning me a yarn, I thought, and didn't believe him. Nobody wanted to die. We all wanted to flee; that was what we most wanted in the world.

"Your father said he would prefer to disappear than to go back into a cell," Leo said in a grave voice. He had stopped running. "He asked my papa to buy three capsules for your family on the black market. Don't you believe me?"

"Of course I don't, Leo," I said, gasping for air.

"Cyanide capsules became popular during the Great War . . ." Leo adopted the tone of a traveling circus barker about to present some phenomenon of nature. His father should have realized that this boy always overheard his conversations. Leo was dangerous.

"It was better to die than to be taken prisoner. They took away your weapons, but you could hide a tiny capsule under your tongue if need be, or in a filling." Leo dramatized every phrase, waving his arms in the air. He paused to see if I was furious or scared.

"The capsules don't dissolve easily. They're coated in a thin glass film to prevent them from breaking accidentally. When the moment comes, you bite the glass and swallow the potassium cyanide." At this, he acted out a comic pantomime, throwing himself to the ground, shuddering, trembling, holding his breath, opening his eyes wide, coughing. Then he came back to life and started up again.

"The solution is so concentrated that, when it enters the digestive system, it produces brain death on the spot," he said, taking a deep breath and standing as still as a statue.

"Doesn't it hurt?" I asked, playing along.

"It's a perfect death, Hannah," he whispered. Then he began to sweep his arms through the air again. "It destroys your mind so that you feel nothing, and then your heart stops beating."

That at least was some consolation: a death without pain or blood. I would have fainted if I saw blood, and I could not bear pain, either.

If our parents abandoned us, the capsules would be perfect for the two of us. We would fall asleep and that would be that.

I leaned back against a wall plastered with posters. "Millions of men with no work. Millions of children with no future. Save the German people!" *I am German, too.* Who was going to save me?

"You have to find them," Leo ordered me. "Search your whole apartment. You can't leave without them. We have to throw them away."

"Get rid of something that's worth its weight in gold, Leo? Wouldn't it be better to keep them and sell them?"

Yet another problem: now I was going to have to check carefully everything they gave me to eat, although I didn't really think they would mix the contents of the capsule with my food, because I would notice right away. I wanted to know what cyanide smelled like. It must have a special texture, a taste that made it stand out, but Leo didn't mention that. I would have to look into it more closely. Every second counted.

They could come to my bed after I had fallen asleep, open my mouth, and sprinkle in the powder from the broken capsule. I wouldn't shout or cry. I would simply stare at them so that they could see how I was fading away; how my heart had stopped beating.

My parents were desperate, and in a crisis they'd act without thinking. Anything was possible. I didn't expect any good from them. But they could not decide for me: I was about to turn twelve.

I didn't need them. I could escape with Leo; we would grow up together. *Leo, help me get out of here.*

I went home to sleep and to try to forget about the cyanide, at least for a few hours. The next day, as soon as Papa and Mama left, I would start the search.

I woke up later than usual; Leo had exhausted me. I took advantage of being on my own to start exploring in the safe hidden behind Grandpa's portrait in Papa's study. The combination was still my birth date, but when I opened the small door, all I found inside were documents: piles of envelopes.

Next I looked in the jewelry box. Nothing. Then Papa's untouchable briefcase. I checked every drawer in the apartment, even those I had never opened before. I searched in books, behind ornaments. I went over to the gramophone and carefully felt inside the trumpet. Nothing. I searched and searched. The capsules were nowhere to be found.

They probably took them with them. That was the only possibility. Perhaps Papa kept them in his fat wallet. Or, who knew, in his mouth, convinced that the glass covering would protect him. The task Leo had given me, to find that wretched powder, was exhausting me.

I was worn-out. I had looked in every nook and cranny, and it was time for me to go out. I reached Rosenthaler Strasse at noon, but couldn't find Leo in Frau Falkenhorst's café. It was almost always him who had to wait for me: this was his revenge.

I popped in and out of the café; many of the tables were filled with smokers. Leo had not come, and I guessed he would not appear now. I went to Alexanderplatz and roamed the station. I slid my hands along the cold verdigris tiles. My fingers ended up black with a soot I had no idea how to clean off.

I took the S-Bahn and dared venture as far as the stinking passageway outside the Ogre's window. Leo might have been there, eager to catch fresh news on the radio. I had no idea what I was doing there on my own. I went closer to the window of the foulest-smelling man in Berlin, with his blaring radio set. I almost wanted to ask him: "Have you seen Leo, by any chance?" On the radio I heard there was a meeting of Ogres in the Hotel Adlon to decide what to do with the impure ones. They could have gone to the Hotel Kaiserhof, but no: they had to choose the Adlon, just to make our pain even more intense.

The Adlon was the symbol of a majestic Berlin. Everybody wanted to stay there. Now they were all fleeing. The Ogres' flags were draped from every balcony at the hotel and from the streetlamps in the sur-rounding avenues where we once used to stroll happily.

But we were leaving. That was what was most important. Luckily, there was nothing I felt attached to. Not to our apartment, or the park, or my adventures with Leo in the neighborhoods of the impure people.

I was not German. I was not pure. I was nobody.

I had to find Leo, and so I decided to take a risk: I would catch the S-Bahn again and turn up at his house at 40 Grosse Hamburger Strasse. I repeated it to myself so as not to forget it. That was in the neighbor-hood Mama had refused to move to, where all the impure of Berlin now lived. Leo could have waited for me outside our apartment block. He was not afraid of anybody, much less of Frau Hofmeister.

I got off at Oranienburger Strasse. When I reached the intersection with Grosse Hamburger Strasse, I kept my eyes on the ground, and I bumped into a woman carrying a bag full of white asparagus. I apologized, and I heard the woman grumbling behind me, "What is a pure German girl doing on her own in a neighborhood like this?"

When I reached Leo's street, I had to get my bearings. On the right was the cemetery and the so-called Free School for the impure. His house was on the left, toward Koppenplatz Park. I finally knew where I was.

The buildings were piled together in a charmless way in three- or four-story blocks that had identical façades, no balconies, all of them the same. Their mustard-colored walls were starting to fade because they had not been painted in years.

Here people walked about as if they had too much time on their hands. They were lost, disoriented. Two old men dressed in black stood in the entrance to one of the buildings. I could smell a sense of neglect and layers of sweat on jackets that were handed down without any real owner.

At least there was no smell of smoke, although there was still broken glass on the pavement. Nobody seemed to care: they trod on the shards and crushed them. The crunching sound ran down my spine.

In one shop, they had nailed up huge wooden boards to replace the windows smashed back in November. Someone had used black ink to make six-pointed stars on the wood, as well as phrases I refused to read.

I was looking for number 40; nothing else interested me. I did not want to know why the old men would not leave the doorway, or why a young boy, not yet four years old, was taking savage bites out of a raw potato and then spitting them out.

Number 40 was a three-story building painted a mustard yellow blackened by damp. The windows hung open as if they had lost their hinges. The front door, set to one side, had a smashed lock. As I climbed the narrow, dark staircase, the air inside was even colder. It was like stepping into a filthy refrigerator that stank of rotten food. The stairwell was lit only by a feeble naked bulb. Some children rushed down the stairs and pushed past me. I clung to the banister so as not to fall, and felt something sticky on the palm of my hand. I walked along the corridor with no idea how to clean it off. The doors to several rooms were wide-open. I imagined that, at some time in the past, this had been a huge apartment belonging to a single family. Now it was packed with the impure who had lost their homes.

There was no sign of Leo or his father. The last door opened and a barefoot man came out wearing a stained undershirt. I walked on warily. The man had the same nose, like a poisonous mushroom, and the six-pointed star on his chest that I had seen on the cover of *Der Giftpilz*, the book we were forced to read at school. When he saw me, he stopped for a moment and scratched his head. He didn't say a word, so I continued on my way, because I wasn't afraid of him. Or of anybody.

I peeped inside one of the rooms, where they must have been boiling potatoes, onions, and meat in a tomato sauce. An old woman was rocking in a chair. Another disheveled woman was making hot tea. A little boy was staring at me as he picked his nose.

I understood now why Leo had not wanted me to see where he spent his nights. It had nothing to do with Frau Dubiecki, the landlady, being a dreadful crow. It was because of this sadness: Leo wanted to protect me from the horror.

You could have asked for help. You could have come and lived with us. I know it would have been dangerous, but we should have opened our doors to you, yet we didn't. Forgive me, Leo.

I had reached the second floor, when someone grabbed my arm.

"You can't be here." The short woman with a huge belly thought I was not like them. That I was pure.

"I'm looking for the room where the Martin family lives," I said in a feeble whisper, trying to hide the fact that I was really very afraid.

"Who?" she asked me scornfully.

"I need to talk to Leo. It's urgent. A very serious family matter. I'm his cousin."

"You're not his cousin," spat the tiny harpy, turning her back on me. Now I was the one holding her back by the arm.

"Let go of me!" she screeched. "You won't find them. They scuttled away last night like rats with their suitcases. They didn't tell me a thing."

I didn't know whether to cry or to thank her. I stood still for a few seconds, looked her straight in the eye, and couldn't help feeling sorry for her. I ran down the stairs and out in search of the S-Bahn. I had no idea where I was heading.

On the sidewalk, the light blinded me, and I felt paralyzed by the street noise. The doorbell to a nearby bakery resounded inside my head like a struck metal bar that kept on reverberating. The conversations of the passersby intermingled in my mind. A woman shouted at her child. I could hear the breathing in the bushy nostrils of old men as though it were amplified by loudspeakers, their breath reeking of liquor, their conversations in an incomprehensible language.

I was lost. I didn't want to walk in the direction of the ancient cemetery with its headstones piled with small pebbles. Who on earth could want to live so close to the dead? There was no Leo to guide me. I had to find the station.

When I caught sight of it at last, I knew I was safe. I had to get away from there. I didn't belong anywhere. *There is a lot you needed to explain to me, Leo, because I have all these questions I can't ask my parents.*

On the way back in the tram, every time the pole jolted against the overhead wire, I jumped. The other passengers were strangely calm; they stared at the floor, and all of them seemed to be dressed in gray. Not a single splash of color in this uniform mass. My cheeks were burning, my eyes were brimming with tears I forced myself not to let out. No one wanted to sit next to me; they avoided me. I knew I looked pure, but I was as gray as the rest of them. I lived in a luxury apartment, but I had been driven out as well.

I went home alone. Nobody was ever going to accompany me again.

I still couldn't believe that Leo hadn't had the opportunity to run to my home and risk knocking on our door to tell me his father was taking him to England or wherever, that he would write to me, that we would never be distant from each other, even if we were separated by a continent or an ocean.

All I could think of was how to prepare for a journey with no future to a small island that Leo had imagined in his watery maps.

It was a Tuesday. I should have stayed in my room, staring at the ceiling. It had all been a dream, or, rather, a horrible nightmare. When I woke up the next morning, Leo would be there as ever, with his enormous eyelashes and tousled hair, waiting for me at noon in Frau Falkenhorst's café.

When I pushed open the apartment door, I saw Papa standing at the window, staring at the tulips. Now he was the one who hardly ever left. He retreated to his study with its dark wooden panels, his back to the photograph of Grandpa with his bushy moustache and the gaze of a general. He had been emptying the desk drawers, throwing hundreds of bits of papers into the waste bin: his studies, his writings.

I went over to him. He kissed me on the head and went on peering out into the garden. He was bound to know where they had taken Leo, and whether he and his father had managed to get the permits they needed to disembark in Havana.

"What about Leo and his father?" I dared to ask.

Silence. Papa did not react. *Stop staring at the flowers, Papa. This is important to me!*

"Everything is fine, Hannah," he replied without looking at me.

That meant there was no good news.

I went into Mama's bedroom. I needed someone to tell me what was going on. Whether or not we were leaving, if the journey was still happening. She was the one who now went out every morning to arrange things.

"Everything is settled," she confirmed. "There's no cause to worry."

We had our passages and had obtained the permit to disembark— the Benítez—for Papa.

"What more do we need?"

"We have to leave at dawn on Saturday. We'll travel in our car; one of your papa's ex-students will drive us. We'll pay him with the car."

"We can trust him," added Papa, who had appeared in the doorway to reassure me.

But I couldn't stop thinking about Leo.

Mama's room was in chaos: clothes everywhere, underwear, and shoes. She was flitting about nervously, and I heard her humming a song. I couldn't understand her. She seemed to have been transformed into what she had once been, or the illusion of her past. I seemed to have a different mother every day. This might have been fun, but not at that moment. Leo had vanished without saying good-bye.

Mama had four huge trunks filled with clothes. No doubt about it: she had gone mad.

"What do you think, Hannah?" She put on a gown and started to dance round the room. A waltz. She was humming a waltz.

"If we're going to America, I'll have to take a Mainbocher gown," she went on, as though we were going on vacation to some exotic island.

No one in Cuba was going to be the slightest bit interested in the brand name of the dresses she wore. She called them all by the name of their couturier: a Madame Grès, a Molyneux, a Patou, a Piquet.

"I'm going to take them all," she said with a nervous laugh.

There were so many of them that she would never have to wear the same one twice during the crossing. She knew that whenever she sought refuge in this kind of euphoria, I distanced myself from her. I knew she was suffering: we weren't going on vacation. She was aware of our tragedy but was trying to come to terms with it as best she could.

Oh, Mama! If only you had seen what I saw today. And you, Papa, you should never have abandoned Leo and his father to that nightmare.

An inventory of all our possessions had been made, the *Vermögens-Erklärung*, or declaration of property, that every family had to complete before they left. Mama could take her clothes with her and the jewelry she was wearing, but the rest of our lives had to stay in Germany. We could not lose or break anything listed in the inventory. Any silly mistake, and our departure would be postponed indefinitely. And we would be sent to prison.

Anna

New York, 2014

*M*r. Levin has put us in touch with a survivor from the *St. Louis*, the transatlantic liner that took Aunt Hannah to Cuba. We're going to visit her today. Maybe she knew Dad's family, my family. We're taking copies of the postcards and photos that we made, because, who knows, she might recognize some of her own relatives, or even herself as a young girl. That's our hope.

Mr. Levin says there are only a few survivors left. Of course, it was so many years ago.

Mrs. Berenson lives in the Bronx. We're to be met by her son, who warned Mom we would find a friendly old lady who didn't talk very much but had a vivid memory of the past. She forgets the present more each day. She has lived with sorrow for more than seventy years, says her son. She is unable to forgive. And even if she wanted to forget, she cannot.

Her son has often asked her to tell him how she managed to survive, the persecution she suffered, her odyssey on board ship, and what happened to her parents. He wanted her to set it all down in black and white, but she has refused. She accepted our visit only because of the photographs.

Mrs. Berenson has her mezuzah on the doorpost. When her son opens the door, we are hit by a blast of warm air. He is elderly, too. Their hall is filled with old photos displayed in no particular order. Recent weddings, birthdays, newborn babies. The story of the Berenson family after the war. But nothing from their life in Germany.

In the living room, Mrs. Berenson is resting in an armchair close to the window, and doesn't move. The furniture is made of heavy, dark mahogany. Everything in the apartment must have cost a fortune. There isn't much room left among the showcases, tables, sofas, armchairs, and ornaments. I'm afraid that if I sneeze, I'll break something. And every piece of furniture is protected by a lace mat. What an obsession with covering surfaces! Even the walls are draped in a sad mustard-colored wallpaper.

I'm convinced the sun has never entered here.

"You'll find she's rather nervous," her son explains, maybe so that his mother will hear him and react. But she doesn't move.

Mom takes her by the hand, and she smiles back at her.

"Smiling is the best I can do at my age," she says, breaking the ice. I can't follow what she says very well. She's lived almost her entire life in New York, and yet her German accent is still very strong.

I'm introduced, and I nod my head from the corner of the room. With difficulty, Mrs. Berenson raises a gold-ringed right hand and moves it slightly to greet me.

"My daughter's great-aunt sent us the negatives. She traveled in the boat with you. Hannah Rosenthal."

I don't think Mrs. Berenson has the slightest interest in our family. When she smiles, her eyes narrow, and she takes on the look of a mischievous child rather than a grouchy old woman who survived the war and now needs help to move.

"Those were very common names back then. Did you bring the photos?"

She's not interested in chatting. Let's get down to business: do what you came for, and then you can leave. She doesn't want to be disturbed. Smiling is more than enough.

In one corner of the room, the model of a building stands on a tall table. It has a completely symmetrical façade lined with doors and windows, and a grand entrance in the center. It looks like a museum.

"Don't get too close, child."

I can't believe she has scolded me. I quickly move to another corner of the room. Perhaps in a kind of apology, Mrs. Berenson explains:

"It's a gift from my grandson. It's the replica of the building we used to own in Berlin. It doesn't exist anymore. It was bombed by the Soviets at the end of the war. Let's look at the photos."

Mom lays out the photographs on the cloth covering the table next to the old lady, and she begins to pick them up one by one.

She settles in her chair and concentrates on the photos, forgetting about us. She chuckles, pointing at the children playing on board ship, and then mutters a few phrases in German. She seems delighted at the images: the swimming pool, the ballroom, the gym, the elegant women. Some people are sunbathing, others posing like movie stars.

She looks through them all again and reacts as though this were the first time. Her son is surprised: his mother is happy.

"I had never seen the sea before" is the first thing she says.

She picks up a second envelope of photos and adds, "I had never been to a masked ball before."

She looks increasingly anxious as she waits for a third envelope. "The food was exquisite. We were treated like royalty."

She pauses at one particular photograph. It had been taken from a port—the port of Havana? Maybe. Passengers were crowded at the rail on the side of the ship, waving good-bye. Some of them were carrying their children. Others had hopeless looks on their faces.

The old lady clutches the photograph to her, closes her eyes, and starts to sob. In only a few seconds, her gentle moans grow desperate. I'm not sure if she is crying or simply shouting out loud. Her son goes over to comfort her. He embraces her, but she doesn't stop trembling.

"We'd better go," Mom says, taking me by the arm.

We leave the photographs on the center table and don't even manage to say good-bye. Mrs. Berenson still has her eyes closed and is clutching the photo against her chest. She calms down for a moment; then the wailing starts up again.

Her son asks us to forgive her. I don't understand a thing. I'd like to know what happened to Mrs. Berenson. Perhaps she recognized her family on the boat. Did they ever disembark in Havana? Perhaps they were shipwrecked; but in the end, she had been saved, so shouldn't she have been happy?

While we wait for the elevator, her anguished cries are still audible.

We descend without a word. Upstairs, the cries continue.

I can't fail Dad the way I've failed Mom. I don't want to end up feeling the same guilt toward him. I'm only nearly twelve! At my age, you still want your parents around. Shouting at you, refusing to let you play when you want to, giving you orders and lectures when you don't behave.

Even though I had wished my mom wouldn't wake up—that she would remain forever sunk in her sheets in the darkness of her room—I reacted just in time, I ran and asked for help, and I saved her. I want Dad to wake up now, too, to emerge from the shadows, to come and get me and take me away with him, as far away as possible, on a sailboat that will defy the winds. Now I'm on my way to meet his past.

I ask him about the heat in Havana, the city where he was born and grew up. *Wake up, Dad. Tell me something.* I bring his photo closer to the light, which gives his face a reddish glow, and feel that now he really is listening to me. *I confuse you with all my questions, don't I, Dad?*

We've been told that the heat in Havana is unbearable, and that's worrying Mom. The sun is scorching, it assaults you, leaves you feeling weak at all hours of the day. We've been warned that you have to wear lots of sunscreen.

"But we're not going to the Sahara Desert, Mom. It's an island where there are breezes, and the sea is on all sides," I explain, but she looks at me as though she's wondering, *What does this girl know? She's never been to the Caribbean!* She refuses to believe that we are properly prepared.

She'd prefer us to stay in a hotel room with a sea view, but my great-aunt insisted that the house where my Dad was born also belongs to us. We can't offend her, so I've convinced Mom to forget all the hotels with names of Spanish cities, Italian islands, or French seaside resorts that she found were available in Havana.

I'm curious to see how a German woman with such a soft, melodious voice and who is so careful when she constructs her sentences in Spanish gets along on an island where, according to Mr. Levin, everybody shouts the whole time and sways their hips as they walk.

Maybe my aunt will have a big surprise for us. We'll be arriving at the Havana airport at dusk, when the sun and the heat have died down. We'll disembark from the plane, and when the glass doors separating the terminal from the city open, you'll be there waiting for us, Dad, with your rimless glasses and your half smile. Or, better still, we'll leave the airport, and when we reach the house where you were born, Aunt Hannah will open an enormous wooden door, invite us in, and you'll be sitting in the bright, spacious living room. There couldn't be a greater surprise, could there?

Oh, don't listen to me, Dad; these are just a young girl's fantasies. What I want to do is explore your room, the place where you took your first steps, where you played as a child. I'm sure my great-aunt has kept some of your toys.

I've already got my suitcase packed. Better to have everything ready ahead of time, so that I don't forget anything.

I don't tell Dad about our visit to Mrs. Berenson. Her cries are still giving me nightmares. I don't want him to worry. I know he must be pleased that we're going to Cuba. I think he would have loved to make this trip with us.

I don't believe my aunt will be like Mrs. Berenson. Maybe she never goes out and wants to forget her past, too. But she doesn't seem to be resentful or bitter.

At bedtime, I begin to go through the album where Mom has put the photos from the boat. I search for the girl who looks like me and stare at it for a long time. When I close my eyes, she is still there smiling at me. I get up and run along the deck of the huge, empty liner. I find the girl with huge eyes and blond hair. I am that girl. She hugs me, and I see myself.

I wake with a start in my room, with Dad beside me. I kiss him and tell him the news: we're leaving in a few days. We'll have a short stopover in Miami and then take a flight that lasts only forty-five minutes.

How close we are to the island. We'll reach Aunt Hannah's house by nightfall.

Hannah
Berlin, 1939

It was Saturday. The day of our departure.

I was wearing a boring navy-blue dress that Mama would have said was a little heavy for this time of year. Papa and I were waiting patiently for her in the living room. I wasn't interested in making an impression when we reached Hamburg, although I could hear one of her favorite sayings ringing inside my head: "The first impression is what counts."

Nor was I too upset at leaving behind the one place where I had ever lived and erasing twelve years of my life with a stroke. What saddened me was that Leo, my only friend, had abandoned me, and I didn't know where he had escaped to; what exotic worlds he was going to discover without me. The single consolation I had was to believe he knew he could always find me on the island where one day we had dreamed of raising a family. And he must have known I would wait for him there until my dying day.

The only good thing since Leo had disappeared was that I had forgotten about the cyanide capsules. By now, I couldn't have cared less what decision my parents made. At last we were going to escape, and we wouldn't need them. If I were Papa, though, I would never leave them where Mama could get at them: she was spending one day in bed and the next celebrating.

I asked Papa again about the Martin family. He had to know something.

"They're safe" was all he told me, but that wasn't enough, because I didn't want to be parted from Leo. "Everything is fine."

His favorite phrases now were: "Nothing is happening." "Don't worry." "Everything is fine."

He never lost his composure, even in the most difficult situations. He sat on the sofa, staring into space. I guessed that he had become indifferent to everything. The blessed leather briefcase was at his feet. When I asked if he wanted me to make some tea before we left, he was too distracted to respond. He preferred to think we were fortunate and refused to be a victim.

Seven very heavy suitcases stood in the doorway. Papa's ex-student, who was now a member of the Ogres' party, arrived and began to carry them to our car, which by the end of the day would be his. On the way out, he cast his eye over the living room: he must have thought that some of the most valuable possessions that had belonged to the Rosenthal and Strauss families for generations would fall into his hands. And who knew if, after he had dropped us at the port and returned to Berlin, he wouldn't break into our apartment and carry away Grandma's Sèvres vase, the silver service, the Meissen porcelain.

"The neighbors are down below," he told Papa. "They've formed two lines outside the building. Couldn't we go out the back way?"

"We're leaving by the front door and with our heads held high," Mama declared as she came out of her room, looking radiant. "We're not fugitives. We're leaving the building to them; they can do whatever they like with it."

As she went by, she left a faint trail of jasmine and Bulgarian roses in her wake. No one except her could have had the idea of traveling by car to Hamburg to board a liner in a full-length gown with a train. A short veil covered the top half of her perfectly made-up face: eyebrows arched to her temples, cheeks starkly white, and bright-scarlet lips. The perfect complement to her black-and-white Lucien Lelong gown, set off by a platinum-and-diamond brooch at her waist.

The dress showed off her slender figure and forced her to take short enough steps so that everyone could admire this splendid vision. That was what you called a first impression!

"Shall we go?" she said without a backward glance. Without taking leave of everything that had been hers. Without one last glance at the family portraits. Even without considering how Papa and I were dressed. She had no need to approve our outfits: her brilliance would eclipse everything around her.

She was the first to leave. The ex-student closed the door—did he lock it?—and picked up the remaining two cases.

It was Mama's perfume that reached the street outside first. The harpies waiting to shout insults at us were intoxicated—bewitched—by the Goddess's fragrance.

Perhaps they bowed their heads slightly when we clambered into the car that would soon no longer be ours. I preferred to think they felt ashamed at their evil behavior, showing at least a sliver of humanity. I had no idea if Gretel was among them. What did it matter? Frau Hofmeister would be pleased. From then on, she could use the elevator as she pleased without a filthy little girl spoiling her day.

We left our neighborhood as quickly as those shooting stars Papa and I used to discover on summer nights at our lakeside house in Wannsee. The elegant streets of the Mitte district blurred behind us. We crossed what had once been the most beautiful boulevard in Berlin, and I said farewell to the bridge over the Spree that I had rushed across with Leo so often.

Seated between Papa and me, Mama stared straight ahead, observing the traffic in a city that had once been the most vibrant in Europe. We avoided looking at one another or talking. None of us shed a tear. Not yet.

When Berlin became a dot in the distance behind us, and we were drawing ever closer to Hamburg, roughly 180 miles northwest, I began to tremble. I couldn't control my anxiety, but I didn't want anybody in the car to notice. I still had to behave like a spoiled eleven-year-old who had never wanted for anything. That could be my release. One more outburst before we reached the boat taking us out of this hell. I knew I was going to cry, and I tried to hold it back.

Then I burst into tears.

"We're going to be all right, my girl," Mama comforted me, and I could feel the fabric of her dress against my cheek. I didn't want to stain it with my stupid tears. "There's no point crying over what we're leaving behind. You'll see how beautiful Havana is."

I wanted to tell her I wasn't crying over what had been taken from me but because I had lost my best friend. That was why I was trembling, not because of some stupid old apartment or a city that already meant nothing to me.

"Take your time." At last, somebody spoke to the driver.

Mama took a mirror out of her bag and checked that her makeup hadn't been smudged.

"In fact, it would be best if we arrive at the appointed time," she said. "I want to be the last one to embark."

We stopped on a backstreet to wait for the perfect moment for her to make her triumphal entrance. The ex-student switched on the radio, and we heard one of the interminable speeches typical of recent days: "We have permitted those poisoning our people, the garbage, thieves, worms, and delinquents, to leave Germany." That meant us. "No country wants to receive them. Why should we have to bear the burden? We have cleansed our streets and will continue to do so until the farthest corner of the empire is free of these leeches."

"I think we should go to the port." That was the first thing my father had said since leaving Berlin. "That's enough." He gestured to the Ogre for us to move and for him to switch off his damned radio.

When we turned the corner, the floating island that was to be our salvation came into view. A huge, imposing iron mass of black and white, like Mama's dress, sat in the water and reached as high as the sky. A whole city on the sea. I hoped we would be safe there. It was going to be our prison for the next two weeks. And after that, freedom.

The Ogres' flag was fluttering at one end of the ship. Beneath it, in white letters, a name that would stay with us forever: *St. Louis.*

The few steps between the car and the small customs hut that divided here from there seemed almost eternal. You wanted to get there but couldn't, even if you ran. The short crossing completely drained what little energy I had left. My parents were trying their hardest to stand tall. The time for them to remove their masks and collapse would arrive soon enough.

The journey by car had been the longest, most intense, and most exhausting of my life. I was sure that the two weeks of our transatlantic journey would flash past in the twinkling of an eye; much more quickly than the trip from Berlin, the great capital, to Hamburg, the main port of great Germany.

As we drew closer to the customs hut, a small band, with all of their musicians dressed in white, began wearily to strike up "Frei weg!" I jumped with fear at the first notes. I had never liked marches: their triumphant strains made my hair stand on end. It was impossible not to feel that a march called "Here We Go!" was a huge kick in the backside. I had no idea what the shipping company was trying to do: raise our spirits or make us forget that, from the moment we set foot on the *St. Louis*, we would never return to Germany.

The ship was taller than our apartment building in Berlin. One, two, three . . . I counted as many as six decks. The small, closed portholes were the cabins. There were lots of people on each deck. Everybody must have already been on board. We were the last. Of course: as usual, Mama had gotten her way.

Two Ogres seated at a makeshift table at the foot of the gangway examined us with distaste. Papa opened his briefcase and handed over first the three documents signed by Cuban immigration officials that authorized us to travel to and to stay in Havana indefinitely. The two men checked the papers carefully—even though they could not read them, since they were in Spanish—and then asked Papa for our passports and our return passages on the *St. Louis*.

Mama was staring at the swaying ramp that was soon to separate her from the country where she was born. She knew that in a few minutes she would no longer be German. She would no longer be a Strauss or a Rosenthal. At least she would go on being Alma. She wouldn't lose her own name. She refused to answer the Ogres, low-ranking military men who dared question her, the granddaughter of a Great War veteran who had been awarded the Iron Cross.

After inspecting our documents page by page, the Ogre moistened the stamp for our departure on a pad of red ink. He thumped it down hard on our photographs, and with each blow, Mama shuddered but did not lower her gaze. We were marked with a vile red *J* on the only identity document that was to accompany us on our Cuban adventure. An indelible scar. We would belong forever to the exiles, to the people nobody wanted, the ones who had been forced from their homes since the dawn of time.

Mama was trying hard not to cry, but two teardrops were threatening to spoil the impeccable makeup with which she planned to enter this space where she hoped she could be happy for the next fortnight. Perhaps to avoid any further show of emotion, she embraced me from behind, and I could sense her lips close to my ear.

"I have a surprise for you."

I was hoping she wasn't going to do anything crazy: *Don't forget, Mama: our lives are at stake at this very moment!*

"I'll tell you in our cabin."

I thought she was only trying to calm the two of us. She made me promise I wouldn't say anything to Papa. She would tell us the news once we were safely aboard and the coast of Germany had faded in the distance.

I saw her smile. It had to be good news.

One of the Ogres could not take his eyes off Mama: without doubt, she was the most elegant passenger on the ship. Possibly, he was trying to count how many diamonds were in the brooch at her waist. We should have come dressed more simply, without showing we were different or that we believed we were better than the rest. But that was how she was. She said she had absolutely no reason to be ashamed about what she had inherited from all those generations of Strausses. Now a contemptible Ogre imagined he had the right to get his hands on that fortune that bore and would always bear her own unique stamp. And yet it was this Ogre who could decide whether she could take her jewels with her and we could leave. They could reject our documents in a flash and arrest Papa. Then we really would have had no future.

Hundreds of passengers were crowding on the decks of the ship, looking tiny up above us. Some of them were watching us; others were searching for relatives on the dockside. All of a sudden we were blinded by a camera flash. A man had begun taking photos of us. I hid behind Papa. It must have been somebody sent by *Das Deutsche Mädel*. "I'm not pure!" I wanted to shout at him.

Mama arched her body backward, at the same time setting her shoulders forward slightly and extending her neck still farther. She thrust out her chin: I couldn't believe that even when at any moment they could have searched us, taken away what we had left, canceled our departure, and arrest us, she could find the time to consider the angle at which she was being photographed.

The Ogre checked all our documents once more and came to a halt at one: Papa's. I considered running away, getting out of the port, and hiding in the dark streets of Hamburg.

"Worms," the Ogre snarled contemptuously, staring down at Papa's documents without having the courage to look him in the face.

Mama was quivering with anger. *Don't turn around, Mama. Don't pay him any attention. Don't let him hurt you.* To them we were worms, parasites, swine, cunning, unscrupulous, treacherous. That was the entire list. I thought, *Let them call us what they like.* By then, nothing could offend me.

Four seamen descended the steps toward us, observing our movements closely. Papa glanced at the Ogres, and then at the seamen, and then turned to see if our car was still there.

The seamen surrounded us. One of them picked up a suitcase; the others did the same. They shared our luggage between them and started to climb back up the still-swaying steps. At least our luggage had managed to get on board.

A wave broke against the bow of the *St. Louis*.

The Ogres were staring at Papa. They ignored us. If they arrested him, we would stay on land. We couldn't go without him! But by now, Mama had lost her fear and was thinking only of the entrance she was going to make. Rehearsing it.

"Herr Rosenthal, I hope we never have to meet again," the Ogre declared.

Perhaps he was waiting for a reply, but Papa took the documents in silence, examined them carefully, and put them back in his briefcase.

Then he leaned down to me and whispered:

"This is the most important luggage we have. We can lose our clothes, our possessions, even our money, but these papers are our salvation."

He kissed me and said out loud, looking up at the topmost point of the *St. Louis*: "Cuba is the only country that will have us. Don't ever forget that, Hannah."

The band stopped playing. Our first suitcases must have already been in our cabin. There were only two left to carry on board. And the three of us. We were still on German soil.

The steps were empty. Mama was staring at the ship's prow.

"Our cabin is on the top deck," she said, smoothing her hair and taking my hand. "It's smaller than the rooms at home, but you'll love it, Hannah. You'll see."

A seaman picked up the two remaining cases. Papa was about to follow him, when Mama took him by the arm. I realized at once that there was no way Mama would board the *St. Louis* with the luggage, even if it were hers. The moment she saw the seaman disappear through the main entrance to the ship, and had checked that there was nobody else on the gangway, she gave Papa a kiss on the cheek to signal he should start walking.

He was the first up the steps. Behind him, I held on tightly so as not to fall into the water. How the steps swayed! The ship's siren made me jump with fear. I turned round and saw Mama, who was walking slowly in that special way she had of tilting her nose in the air and ignoring everything around her. Beyond her back, I could see that the Ogres were still at their post. If we were the last people to embark, I didn't understand why they hadn't left by now. And in the distance, I could also see our car.

At the top of the gangway, a small man with a ridiculous little moustache was waiting for us. He looked like an army officer. He was stern-looking and was drawn up to his full height, as if to convey the impression that he was the one in charge of the biggest ship in the port.

"Don't be scared, Hannah. He's Gustav Schröder, the captain," Papa reassured me.

I held on tightly to the rail for support. It was a cold day, but I knew that wasn't the reason why I was trembling. *I am scared, Papa,* I wanted to tell him, and I looked at him so that he would understand how much I needed him; that I couldn't move an inch without his protection. But by now, we were nearly at the top of the ramp, and I had my ears pricked to hear if anyone called out to stop us. I didn't hear anything.

We're safe, I tried to tell myself over and over, so that I would truly believe it.

We really were the last on board. All I could hear were "I love you" and "I'll never forget you" from desperate mouths, the farewells shouted from on deck, the weeping that mingled with the sirens of ships entering and leaving the harbor.

We were not on dry land anymore. Down below, the people on the quayside looked like tiny, defenseless ants rushing about to try to get a last look at all those sailing away.

Every step I took made me feel taller and safer. We were leaving behind the port and the Ogres: they were becoming smaller and smaller. I, on the other hand, felt as big as the ship: I had turned into an all-powerful iron giant while the docks were fading from view.

I was invincible. We had climbed the mountain: Papa and I had reached the summit! As if by magic, my fear evaporated as soon as I stepped aboard this bulky vessel that was now our shield. The adventure had begun.

The noise was deafening. By now, nobody on the quayside could hear us, but lots of passengers were still shouting messages to the unfortunate ones who had been unable to obtain a lifesaving visa—a passage on the ship that would set us free.

The captain came up to us. He was so small he had to raise his head to look at Papa. With a courtesy we were no longer accustomed to, he held out his hand to my parents, who responded with distant smiles.

"Herr Rosenthal, Frau Rosenthal." He had a deep opera singer's voice.

He gently took my right hand and lifted it to his lips without touching my skin. If I hadn't been so bewildered, I would have curtsied.

We were there at last. There was no room to walk along the deck: the passengers were crowded at the rails overlooking the port, as if trying to stay close to everything they would never see again, an image that was condemned to vanish from their memories.

Mama came to a halt, terrified. She did not want to take another step and become part of this desperate throng. Then all of a sudden she realized that the three of us—Papa, me, and even her—were just as wretched as all the other exiles on board. Like it or not, we were all in the same situation.

Take a good look at them, Mama. We were a wretched mass of fleeing people who had been kicked out of our homes. In just a few seconds, we had become immigrants, something she never wanted to accept. She had to face reality now.

Suddenly a thin arm was trying to force its way through the throng and reach the captain, who was still beside us. Shoving a man still shouting good-bye out of his way, I heard a voice telling me, "Come with me! Hurry up!"

At the end of the arm appeared the black hair, more tousled than ever, the shirt buttoned to the top, the short trousers, and his huge eyes, with those lashes that always arrived before him.

"Leo! It's you! I can't believe it!"

"What? You've been struck dumb? Come on, let's run."

There was a blast on the ship's siren. We were going—together—to somewhere where no one would measure our heads or noses, or compare the texture of our hair, or classify the color of our eyes. We were going to the island you drew in the muddy water of a city to which we would never return.

To Havana, Leo. We would arrive, after two endless weeks, in Havana.

Would we plant tulips? I had no idea if tulips grew in Cuba.

PART TWO

Hannah

St. Louis, 1939

Saturday, 13 May

$\mathscr{I}$'ve heard that when you die, your life flickers before your eyes like the pages of a book until your brain gives out, but that you don't feel any pain or nostalgia. When we left Germany, I seemed to have only three memories remaining from my childhood.

The first was of being in the arms of Eva, nestling in her big, warm bosom in the bed of her tiny room by the kitchen. Papa said I was too young to have such a vivid memory, but I could clearly recall the fragrance of her lemon-bergamot-cedarwood cologne mingled with the smell of sweat and spices. This was the woman who had helped bring me into the world and took care of me while Mama recovered from a birth that kept her in the hospital for several weeks. I can still hear the tender way Mama would tell me later that it was time to go to my bedroom, and my bitter tears because I didn't want to leave Eva's room. It was the only place where I felt safe.

My second memory was from when I was five and went with Papa to the university. I hid under the desk in the gigantic hall where he was giving a lecture to a hundred or more students who listened spellbound as the most intelligent man in the world unraveled the secrets of the human body. Papa's voice sounded as if he were conducting a religious ritual or reciting the Torah from memory. He repeated the word *femur* several times, pointing to gigantic limbs displayed in a diagram on the wall, and I resolved that as soon as my parents allowed me to have a dog, I would call him Femur.

My third memory was from my fifth birthday, when my parents promised me that one day we would go on a world cruise on a luxury liner. For many nights after that, on the map beside my bed, I began to plot our route to all the faraway countries, feeling I was the luckiest girl in the world.

These were the only three things I seemed able to recall. And sadly, one of them had to do with Eva, whom I would never see again. The erasing process was already beginning. My new book of memories was blank.

Leo and I were standing at the starboard rail of the ship, watching as passengers waved to their relatives below. The people on land peered up at us not as though we were being saved but as though we were headed for some dire, inconceivable fate.

Leo and I moved away from the crowd and fixed our gaze instead on the river Elbe, which would carry us to the North Sea and from there far away from the land of the Ogres. It was high time we were leaving that port stinking of oil and fish; I didn't want my eyes to register any-thing further about it. I closed them tight, clinging to Leo so as not to feel the rolling of this enormous iron monster. I thought I was going to be seasick.

The captain was watching us from the bridge, pacing back and forth with his hands behind his back. Despite his ridiculous moustache and small stature, he was an imposing figure. He motioned for us to come up and join him. Leo was even more excited than I was; he tugged at my hand for us to run. Our adventure had begun.

From the bridge, the port looked tiny. The smell of rusty iron and the ship's rocking motion made me feel queasy again. Realizing this, the captain spoke directly to me with that gruff voice of his that seemed so much at odds with his small body:

"The ship will stabilize in a few minutes, and then you won't even see water move in a glass. Won't you introduce me to your friend, Hannah?"

Leo was bursting with pride. Previously, he had wanted to be a pilot, but now I thought that he would probably prefer to be a ship's captain. He rushed anxiously toward the controls, but the captain warned him, "You're welcome in here, but you mustn't touch anything that might endanger the two hundred thirty-one crew members and the eight hundred ninety-nine passengers we have on board. I'm responsible for the lives of each and every one of them."

Leo wanted to know exactly when we'd arrive and how fast this ship weighing more than 16,000 tons and 575 feet long could travel.

"What would happen if someone falls overboard?" Leo asked breathlessly. "Which port will we arrive at first? What other countries are we going to visit? What if somebody falls ill?"

"Our first port of call will be Cherbourg, where we'll pick up another thirty-eight passengers."

These were too many questions all at once—the captain wasn't smiling—but Leo and I had the same sensation: this man was powerful and knew a lot. And something more: he wanted to be our friend.

"Now go down to the dining room," he ordered us. "They've already begun to serve the last meal of the day."

I took the lead, and Leo followed me to the first-class dining room. When he hesitated at the door, it was my turn to take him by the arm.

"They'll throw me out of here, Hannah!"

As I opened the huge door decorated with symmetrical mirrors, leaves, and flowers, we were dazzled by the light from inside: polished wood and huge teardrop chandeliers sparkling like diamonds. Leo couldn't believe his eyes. We were in a floating palace in the middle of the sea.

A friendly steward dressed in white like a naval officer pointed out our seats, and I saw Mama waving at us from the main table as if acknowledging her admirers.

Like a perfect gentleman, Papa stood up ceremoniously and held out his hand to Leo, who took it timidly and made a slight bow to Mama.

"You need to eat properly. It's going to be a long crossing." The Goddess was back, her words silken and clear.

I didn't know how she had found the time to change and redo her makeup. The simple sleeveless pink cotton dress made her look like a schoolgirl. She had changed her pearl earrings for a pair of diamonds that glittered whenever she moved her head. Papa was still wearing his gray flannel suit and bow tie.

At one end of the room a big table was overflowing with all kinds of bread, salmon, black caviar, thinly cut slices of meat, and vegetables of various colors. This was the "light buffet" the *St. Louis* offered as we steamed out of Hamburg.

The steward served Mama her favorite champagne. Leo and I got warm milk, to help us sleep.

Papa began to thrust his chest out again, and his face looked as though he was once more at ease in his environment. Four men left the tables where their families were seated and came up to greet him, calling him Professor Rosenthal. He rose to his feet and courteously extended his hand to them. He embraced the last one, clapping him on the back, and said something no one else could hear. The men also greeted Mama, but without coming close. She smiled back from her Viennese chair, a glass full of bubbles in her right hand.

It was quite hot. Mama took out a handkerchief and dabbed at her face to prevent the perspiration from ruining her makeup. Two members of the crew drew back the red velvet curtains to open some windows. The breeze from the deck relieved the close atmosphere and dissipated the odor of smoked fish and meat, which was beginning to make me nauseous.

The steward came to ask Leo if he would like anything more, calling him "sir." I didn't know what alarmed my friend more: being called "sir" or having someone approach him in such a manner. Leo didn't answer, and so the steward continued around the table taking everyone's orders. It was obvious that Leo was not used to being treated well, especially by someone from the "pure race."

"Can you believe it?" he whispered, so close to my ear I thought he was going to kiss me. "The Ogres are serving *us*!"

He began to chuckle, raising his glass of warm milk to make a toast.

"Here's to you, Countess Hannah! This is going to be a long and wonderful trip!"

I laughed out loud in a way that made Mama smile.

"Yes, Leo, drink up your warm milk, it'll do you good," I replied with the voice of a fussy old countess.

At the next table, four young men raised their glasses high as well. Papa smiled at them and nodded slightly, taking part in their toast from a distance. Leo and I looked on, trying not to giggle.

"We're going to have such fun tomorrow!" he whispered gleefully, downing his milk in one long gulp.

13 MAY 1939

TWO OTHER SHIPS EN ROUTE HAVANA, ENGLISH
ORDUÑA AND FRENCH FLANDRE WITH SIMILAR
PASSENGERS. IMPERATIVE MAKE FULL SPEED
AHEAD. CONFIRMED, WHATEVER HAPPENS, YOUR
PASSENGERS WILL LAND. NO CAUSE FOR ALARM.

Cable from the Hamburg-Amerika Line

Monday, 15 May

I felt lost. When I woke up, I heard the notes of a violin playing the intermezzo from one of the operas Papa used to listen to in the evening at home. I was in the middle of a dream. We were back in Berlin. The Ogres were nothing more than a nightmare created by my troubled mind.

I saw myself lying at my father's feet next to the gramophone. He was stroking my head, ruffling my hair, while he told me about the opera heroine Thaïs, a courtesan and priestess in powerful Alexandria, Egypt, whom they wanted to strip of her possessions and force to renounce the gods she had always worshipped. They obliged her to cross the desert to pay for her sins.

I opened my eyes and saw I was in my cabin. The doors to Papa's room were open, and I could see the gramophone. He was reading in bed, listening to "Méditation," from *Thaïs,* just like in the good old days. The orchestra blocked out the rest of the world.

They would send us back to Berlin because we had brought the gramophone! I was sure it had been on the list of our apartment possessions we had been forced to draw up. Who on earth had thought of such a stupid idea as bringing it with us? Mama would never forgive Papa. She would start to cry and blame me as well, insisting we should all vanish. Perhaps she'd try to poison me with that terrible capsule Papa made her buy from Leo's father.

But Mama strode into my cabin looking livelier than ever. If the gramophone did not bother her, if she didn't think we'd be sent back because Papa adored music so irresponsibly, that meant we were safe.

She looked radiant and even more elegant. Having to shake off the lethargy of the past four months in order to track down our permits and comb the dusty streets of a Berlin packed with Ogres marching in sickly unison had done wonders for her. She was wearing long, loose trousers in ivory gabardine, a blue cotton blouse with matching turban, a scarf tied around her neck, and a pair of dark tortoiseshell glasses to protect her from the sun on deck. A broad golden bracelet glittered on her left forearm, and her dazzling wedding ring was back on her right hand.

The Goddess in all her splendor.

"You can go wherever you like, except to the engine room," Mama said to me. "That's dangerous. Be off and have fun, Hannah. Your father will stay here reading. It's a beautiful day."

She left the cabin as if she owned the ship, eager to breathe fresh air for the first time in many months.

We were still in Europe. I suddenly heard the noises of another port. I was longing to be out on the high seas, and was irritated by the seagulls swooping around us, the smell of fish and dried blood mixed with rust and the grease from the engines, as well as the blare of ships approaching and leaving the dock.

Out on deck, I saw Mama near the rail. She was being served tea while she stared down at the port of Cherbourg, France, carefully observing the thirty-eight passengers coming on board. Apparently she did not recognize any of them, for she moved away to one of the deck chairs on the starboard side of the ship.

I didn't think she was going to make friends with any of the other women in first class. She watched as they passed by and greeted them in a friendly enough manner but then readjusted her dark glasses and ignored all those elegant women who might wish to sit beside her. She was enjoying being alone. Spending all those months in confinement with the shutters drawn and never going out to see her friends had made her antisocial.

I knew the sea air would suit Mama. She seemed free, and could wear all her best outfits, show off her jewels, have someone always at her beck and call. But she seemed hesitant about going back into the ballroom. When she had opened the door the previous evening, she had seen a red-white-and-black flag on the back wall. She had grimaced with disgust in a way only I noticed, and left without a word. She went straight to talk to the captain. Nobody knew what she said, but the fact was that by morning the flag had disappeared. The first thing she did even before breakfast was to go to the ballroom to see whether the captain had kept his word.

"As long as we're at sea, he will look after us," she said later. "He's a true gentleman."

The ship began shuddering, and there was another blast on the horn. Now we really were under way.

Behind her dark glasses, Mama smiled peacefully in a way I had never seen before.

Leo came up behind me and covered my eyes. His hands were moist. I joined in the game and asked if he was Papa.

Laughing out loud, he tugged at my arm as hard as he could. He ruled the roost in first class. He came and went on our deck as if he were its lord and master. He was no longer afraid that someone would send him back to his father's tourist-class cabin. His place was here with me. The captain and all the stewards knew this.

I loved seeing Leo dressed smartly. His brown jacket with big buttons and breast pockets made him look older, but his short trousers and long stockings gave away his age.

He stepped back so that I could give my opinion, spreading his arms as if to ask what I thought of his transatlantic attire, and nervously awaited my verdict. I looked him up and down without a word. I was making him suffer, and he grew desperate.

"Aren't you going to tell me how I look?"

"Like a perfect count," I mocked him, and he guffawed.

"And you are the only countess on board, Hannah," he replied before dashing over to the side to start his tour of first class.

If anybody was leaning against the rail, he apologized and waited for the person to make way for him; he would not allow any modification to the route he had planned for his close study of the ship where we were going to spend the next fortnight.

I followed along like his faithful consort. This was the first time I had ever seen him happy.

15 MAY 1939

CUT SHORT STAY IN CHERBOURG. MUST
LEAVE SOONEST ALL SPEED. TENSE
SITUATION IN HAVANA.

Cable from the Hamburg-Amerika Line

Wednesday, 17 May

"*I*'ve been here hours," said Leo, leaning back against one of the iron columns on the terrace.

"Look, I've brought you a cookie. I was supposed to keep it until bedtime."

"To the engine room!"

"What? That's the only place I've been told not to go to, Leo!"

Several couples were strolling along the promenade deck, finding out where things were. There was a beauty salon, a small shop selling souvenirs from the ship, postcards, and silk scarves. I didn't think anybody would want to waste the ten reichsmarks we'd been allowed to take out of Germany on any of that.

We went down six levels and then along a lengthy corridor that ended at a heavy iron door. When Leo opened it, the noise was deafening, and the smell of burnt grease made me feel queasy. If I had leaned against the wall I could have ruined my blue-and-white-striped dress. I didn't want to upset Mama.

Leo was peering curiously at the complicated machinery that propelled the giant we were sailing on. If it had been up to him, he would have spent hours watching the pistons moving to and fro with their precise, unchanging rhythm. But all at once, he abandoned his observation post.

"Let's go back up with the others!" he shouted to me, his voice swallowed up by the noise of the engines. He set off at a run.

He had already made several friends on the *St. Louis*. It was as if he'd been on board for months. We climbed up to the fourth deck, where there was a group of boys waiting impatiently for us—or, rather, for Leo.

A tall boy with a silly-looking face stood up as Leo approached. He was wearing a tilted cap, and his cheeks were ruddy from the cold air.

"Edmund, you'll catch a cold," shouted his mother, who was wrapped in a thick brown blanket under one of the deck awnings.

Edmund paid her no attention, beyond stamping the floor like a baby about to have a tantrum.

There were two other boys as well. They were brothers, the younger one informed me, introducing himself as Walter and his older brother as Kurt, who ignored me. They both wore hats and jackets that looked enormous on them, as did their shoes and their stockings hanging loose round their ankles. I guessed their parents had bought them clothes for the journey several sizes too large so that they would last many months in Cuba, and probably wherever they were headed after that.

"So you're the famous Hannah, the 'German girl,'" said Walter slyly. I realized he was the same age as me or possibly a little bit older.

I pretended not to have heard him. Leo tried to break the ice by launching into a description of the ship: its funnel, the bridge, the mast, which was the tallest part of the ship, the difference between port and starboard. He spoke of the captain as if he were a close friend who consulted him every night about the decisions he'd have to make and then carry out first thing the next morning.

I knew someone was bound to mention "the German Girl" sooner or later. That wretched front cover of *Das Deutsche Mädel* was going to pursue me all my life. Yes, I was the German girl: So what? I felt like telling him, *I might be very German, but I'm as undesirable as you.*

"Did you know there's a swimming pool on board?" said Kurt, constantly trying to keep his hat out of his eyes. "When we're in the mid-Atlantic it'll be less cold, and they'll open it. Did you bring your bathing suits?"

The silly-looking boy suggested we go play on the promenade deck, but Leo didn't listen to him. We were merely there as followers of the most popular passenger on the *St. Louis*. He was the one in control; the one who gave the orders. All that was missing was the white peaked cap with the black visor that the captain wore. And so we all ignored Walter's suggestion.

In fact, all we did was rush about from one spot to the next, but that was enough for Leo to master the whole ship's layout. He had already memorized the labyrinths leading to the cabins, the ballrooms, the gym, and the captain's control rooms, where the crew got together to play cards and smoke. Leo came and went as he liked in the most unimaginable places. And nobody stopped him.

The children had grouped themselves according to age. The youngest remained under supervision. The girls would not have dreamed of mixing with the boys, and must have looked on me strangely, I thought, because I belonged to Leo's gang. Walter, the clumsier of the brothers—since we'd met, he had fallen, lost his hat, and gotten left behind so often that we were on the verge of abandoning him—bumped into one of the snooty girls pretending to be adolescents.

"Watch where you're going if you don't want problems," said the tallest girl, who was wearing a grotesque sailor's cap and dark glasses that kept sliding down her nose. "And you, what are you doing with this band of thugs? Why don't you stay here with us? Frau Rosenthal wouldn't be pleased if she found out you were going around with those boys."

I halted for a moment, not because I had any interest in being friendly with these girls, who had been educated for just one thing in life—to get married—but because I was tired from running around so much. Leo would come find me.

The girl in dark glasses was a Simons. Her family had owned several stores in Berlin. In order not to lose their fortune, they handed over ownership of their businesses to a "pure" German who was related to them in some way. However, they ended up exactly the same as us, fleeing to Cuba at the last minute.

Mama had known Johanna Simons, the matriarch of the family. They once went to Paris on a shopping trip together, and after that, I had to be friendly to their daughter Ines for what seemed like an endless couple of hours in the Adlon tearoom while our mothers discussed the season's drapes, designs, and colors. Ines had shot up since then, and I didn't recognize her.

"Let's go to the tearoom. They have cookies and cakes there," she said, and walked off, sure that we would all follow her.

The tearoom looked as if it had never been used. How could such a huge ship, carrying a thousand passengers on each voyage and sailing for several months each year, be kept in such perfect condition? The carpets were spotless. The gilded braid on the chairs was as good as new, the lace tablecloths without a single stain, the silver spoons polished and engraved with the emblem of the Hamburg-Amerika Line. The lighting, which was quite dim at that time of day, cast a pale-pink glow over us. Mama would have said that, in a light like that, everybody could look beautiful.

"That's how we Germans are," Ines said proudly as she surveyed the room.

Oh, Ines. Germans? I felt like shouting at her: "It's time you stop thinking you are one of them. Better remember where you find yourself!" We were about to begin a new life in some remote spot in the Caribbean Sea, where the rest of the world was no more than a hope we could not have.

"In Havana," she said, "we'll be in transit with the Rosenthal family. My mother told me we'll be going first to the Hotel Nacional for a few days, and then we'll settle in New York." Ines lived Frau Simons's fantasies. Her head was always in the clouds, Mama used to say.

At the far end of the room, a young woman was sitting on her own, a picture of sadness. She held a cup of tea in her hands, not once raising it to her lips or setting it down. Her dark dress made her look a little older than she probably was, but with her hair partially obscuring her eyes, I found it hard to tell. She must have been about twenty years old.

"It'll be hard for her to find a husband now," declared Ines, as if she were an expert with a line of suitors waiting outside her front door. "Her name is Else. Mama admits she has very pretty legs, but a girl who only gets compliments about her legs can't be very pretty, can she?"

The two other girls laughed at her joke as they sipped their tea. I wanted to get out of there; it was worse than playing with dolls. Luckily, at that moment, Leo appeared in the doorway. He was looking for me and signaled that I should come follow him. My savior! There was no time to lose: we had less than two weeks left in a place where we could do whatever we liked.

Copies of *Der Stürmer* had been left next to the deck chairs. It looked as if some of the crew didn't like us or were trying to intimidate us. I for one had no intention of reading the headlines, but Leo glanced at them and suddenly grew serious.

"They're attacking us back in Berlin," he said, adopting his typically conspiratorial tone and striding off. "They're talking about us in the papers. This is going to end badly. They accuse those of us on the *St. Louis* of stealing money and looting works of art."

Let them say what they like, Leo. We had managed to get away; they could not force us to return. We were in international waters and would soon arrive at an island where we had been given permission to stay indefinitely, although many of us would live in the tropics only for a few weeks. We would wait for the magic number to come up on the waiting list so that we could enter New York, the real island, with our immigrant visas.

A little later, Leo and I noticed the captain giving the stewards orders in a low voice. They quickly began to gather up all the newspapers.

Leo stood at attention and saluted him. The captain smiled at him and raised his hand to his brow.

GOOD RIDDANCE!

Headline in the German newspaper *Der Stürmer*
May 1939

Thursday, 18 May

The only people Mama felt comfortable with on board were the Adlers, although perhaps they were a little too old to share a late night with. Their cabin was two doors from ours, and every time we went out on deck, we had to say hello to them. Since he came on board, Mr. Adler had refused to get out of bed. His meals were taken to him, but he rarely tasted them. Mrs. Adler was very worried: she had never seen him like that before.

"It was very painful for him to have to send his son and daughter-in-law on ahead to America. He hasn't recovered from that separation," Mrs. Adler told us. "He thought things would settle down in a few months, but instead the situation grew worse. We've lost everything. Our whole lives!"

While she was talking to us, Mrs. Adler held cold compresses to the forehead of this old, white-bearded man who did not even open his eyes the whole time we were there. We watched as his wife gently looked after him. Now she was dabbing on some mentholated oil that brought tears to my eyes.

"He agreed to come only because I insisted. Ever since we left home he has been repeating that this trip makes no sense and that he doesn't have the strength to begin again."

Mrs. Adler looked as if she were straight out of some old-fashioned book. She had her hair piled high on her head and wore a petticoat under her long dress as well as a corset like a woman from the last century. Every time we visited, she gave me a gift, which Mama allowed me to keep. Sometimes it was a lace handkerchief; at others, a small gilt brooch, or some sugar-coated biscuits that were my favorites. Who knew where she got them, because they had disappeared from market shelves long ago.

We listened closely as Mrs. Adler told their story. In a way, it was the story of all of us.

"We've all lost something," Mrs. Adler said, and paused with a sorrowful smile. "Nearly everything."

The Adlers had lived to be eighty-seven, and so to me they had no reason to complain. Eight decades and seven years. We children, the ones who had our lives in front of us, were the ones who would be suffering.

The couple's physical decline became increasingly obvious with each passing hour. The old man, immobile in bed; Mrs. Adler, all alone, watching as the love of her life—her great support—slipped away slowly as this ship sailed to the island that was to be our salvation. This was the only answer they could find at an age when all you could hope for was the peace to be able to say good-bye.

"We lived on illusions and woke up far too late," said Mama, without expecting any comment from Mrs. Adler, who by now listened only to herself. "We should have seen what was going to hit us and left a long time ago."

I didn't want Mama to be sad. On board the *St. Louis*, she had become her old self again, while Papa sought refuge in music—the only true escape route that kept him sane. The old lady should have kept her sorrow to herself.

"Left for where, Alma?" Mrs. Adler replied firmly. "We can't spend our lives constantly starting over. A generation goes by, they destroy us. We start over, and they destroy us again. Is that our fate?"

Both of them looked at me, realizing suddenly that I was in the room and listening closely. They needn't have worried, though: I wasn't scared by their pessimism. They had lived their lives. I was just starting out, and I had Leo. The nightmare was behind us.

Mr. Adler began to tremble, and a racking cough made his heavy but weak body quiver. He was going to die. It was as if he couldn't breathe. We needed to call a doctor. They all looked nervous.

"He has these crises," said Mrs. Adler, who was evidently used to them. "You go along now and look at the sea."

She and Mama embraced without kissing. Their sorrow passed between them; their mutual compassion was evident.

I ran toward the corridor but heard Mama shouting my name, as if I were a little girl again. She knew very well that in a few days I would be twelve.

"Aren't you going to say good-bye?"

I smiled from a distance—that was enough—at poor Mrs. Adler, who had not been able to enjoy a single day of our journey.

Every day, the sun beat down more strongly on deck and poured fiercely through our cabin portholes. We must have been drawing closer to the tropics. What a shame the Adlers were living in darkness. They had converted their stateroom into a funeral parlor: curtains drawn, everything gloomy, the atmosphere filled with the mentholated oil and alcohol used to bring down his fever, and the labored breathing of that feeble old man who had boarded the ship only to let himself die.

A gaggle of children ran behind a man on roller skates. As he swooped round like somebody on an ice rink rather than on the slippery promenade deck, it looked as if he were about to fall at any second. He was traveling at great speed, and we were worried he might crash into the rail, but at the last moment, he always braked with the tip of his feet and came to a halt, as if waiting for applause. Then he raised his arms and made an exaggerated bow.

The children rushed to try to knock him over. Leo laughed. The man danced like a circus clown. The swarm of boys and girls followed him everywhere, and he was obviously very proud of this great feat of his in a place where nothing ever happened.

"We have to learn to roller-skate!" Leo announced. I recognized the urgency in his tone of voice: I had to take note of this new project for our life in Havana.

"Mr. Rosenthal and my father are talking to the captain. Do you think there are problems with the ship? Will it sink like the *Titanic*?" he asked, as though telling a horror story not even he believed.

"Leo, it's May. We're in the mid-Atlantic, a long way from any icebergs."

He took me to a corner of the deck far from the passengers in their deck chairs. Everything I touched on the ship was sticky with sea salt. We sat behind some lifeboats bearing the insignia HAPAG, the shipping company that owned the *St. Louis*. I was convinced there would not be enough of them for a thousand passengers if there were a shipwreck.

"I'm going to get something for you," Leo blurted.

He was always changing topics like that. I couldn't take my eyes off him when he was talking to me. I concentrated on his eyes, trying to work out what he was thinking. I felt happy he was devoting himself entirely to me, just like our days together in Berlin. But I couldn't guess what project he was dreaming up now or what it was he wanted. He must have a plan.

"Papa promised me he'll give me Mama's wedding ring. With what it's worth, we would be able to survive in Cuba, but I want the ring for you, Hannah. I have to convince him to give it to me as soon as possible. If anything happens to us, you should have it with you. We can adjust it to fit you."

He said all this without looking at me. Lowering his head shyly, he began playing with his hands, pulling on his knuckles as if he wanted to tear them off.

Did that mean we were engaged? I didn't dare ask him, but at the same time I couldn't hide my delight. He must have seen how my eyes were shining.

"*Danke,*" I said as he placed his hands on my shoulders.

"From now on, you have to forget *danke*. It's *gracias*, okay?" Sometimes Leo insisted on talking to me like a father giving advice to his little daughter.

"*Gracias. ¿Comenzarás a hablar español?*" I asked him in Spanish, knowing he would not understand a thing if I put on the accent I had polished after hours of practice.

He repeated *gracias*, stressing the *g* and the *s* in a very comical way. I burst out laughing: Leo was the only person on board who could make me forget the past, because he was so very present.

A gentle tune started to play over the loudspeakers. At first, I could make out only a few bars and didn't recognize the music.

Our brief, happy interlude ended quickly, as Leo was worried about something. His father and mine were still on the bridge with the captain, and they would not let him near. They even avoided talking in front of him. They must have realized he had his ears pricked for any little detail; he was always on alert, and then came to me with his theories and half-truths.

While Leo paused, I could study him without upsetting him. He was taller now, with a more pronounced jaw, his eyes even bigger. The music became louder: it was "Moonlight Serenade," by Glenn Miller and His Orchestra, which was all the rage in Berlin.

"It's American music, Leo!" I shouted, shaking him by the shoulders because I could see he was sad. Perhaps he was feeling nostalgic about everything we had left behind. Or possibly he was missing his mother.

"They're welcoming us, Leo! America is receiving us with open arms!"

I could hear the trombones, then the string section entering. I stood up and started humming the tune.

"Let's write some words to that music," I suggested, but he still did not react.

A serenade in the silvery moonlight, which, out there on deck, was just for the two of us. *Let's invent the words.* I started spinning around with my eyes closed, letting myself be carried away by the notes that drifted out over the ocean.

Leo took me by the hand. I opened my eyes and saw him smiling, spinning around very slowly with me. Our movements followed the rolling of the ship. I let myself go again, and the breeze ruffled my hair. So what? We were dancing. I followed the rhythm. I had no idea which of us was leading. The tune was about to come to an end. The notes lengthened. Yes, it was the end.

Now all we could hear was the ship's signal telling us it was time to go have dinner.

Entry to Cuba restricted for all foreign nationals.
To enter the country, a bond of 500 pesos is
required, together with a visa granted by a Cuban
consulate abroad and authorized by the Ministry
of State and Labor, not merely by the Immigration
Service. All previously issued documents are hereby
declared invalid.

As stipulated by Decree 937, signed by the president
of the Republic of Cuba,

Federico Laredo Brú.

Gaceta de Cuba
May 1939

Friday, 19 May

The previous night had been difficult. We almost lost Mama. I knew I had to be prepared for that. I could lose my mother at any moment and become an orphan suddenly, before I was even twelve years old. That was impossible. Mama couldn't do something like that to me, much less near my birthday, because whenever I celebrated it, I would remember her and be overcome with sadness.

Papa was shut until late with the captain in his cabin, and those mysterious meetings worried her. He always came back looking hunched, with drooping shoulders; the person who had once been the most elegant man in Berlin was now weighed down like a weary hunchback.

Mama was sick all night. I had to leave her on her own in the bathroom; I couldn't bear to see her falling to pieces like that.

"It's nothing. Go and sleep. I'll explain in the morning."

She obviously knew something she didn't dare tell me. That we had lost all our money? That the Ogres were preparing to invade America and would soon cross the Atlantic? That there was no way out for us, and they would be waiting for us in the port of Havana?

I could hear her vomiting even through the closed door. Bent over the toilet bowl, shaken by sudden spasms, she looked so frail it frightened me.

An unbearable stench began to filter out of the bathroom, through her cabin, and into mine. I pulled the pillow over my head to shut out the retching and the smell. Eventually I fell asleep.

The next morning, it was as if nothing had happened. She looked pale, with perhaps more elaborate makeup than usual. Her hair was freshly washed, and she was wearing a subtle perfume I did not recognize. This new fragrance, mixed with the smell of sea salt, confused me as much as her miraculous recovery. Mama realized this, and asked me and Papa to sit near her. Neither the perfume, nor the smell of her soap, nor whatever she had used on her hair, were enough to erase the smell of the previous night's stench from my memory.

"I have some news for you," she said, her voice dropping.

It was good news. It had to be. And at that moment, I recalled that, just before we'd boarded, she had promised me a surprise. Meeting up with Leo again had made me forget what she had promised to tell me.

She looked at Papa and then fixed her eyes on me. *Just tell us your news, Mama!*

"I waited until today because I wanted to be really sure."

She paused again. Then she looked at us with a mischievous glint in her eye, as if challenging us to guess.

"Hannah," she said, looking at me and ignoring Papa, "you won't be an only child anymore!"

It took me several seconds to take in what she was trying to tell me. *Mama is pregnant! That's why she's been so sick! She wasn't worried about Papa's meetings with the captain—that was men's business. I was going to have a baby brother—or sister!*

"Where is it going to be born?" was the only thing I could think of to ask.

How silly of me. I ought to have said something far more suited to a girl my age. I should have become all emotional, leapt toward her, hugged her. Shouted to the four winds, "I won't be an only child anymore! How wonderful!"

The spell of only children in the Strauss family had been broken. A new Rosenthal was joining the community of the impure. Papa bent over to kiss her gently but also without any show of emotion.

"We don't know yet how long we'll be in Havana. The baby will be born at the end of autumn."

She was happy that her child was not going to be born a German. She was going to get rid of that fateful weight her family had been bearing for generations, which had now disappeared as if by magic.

"Tonight we'll pass close by some islands in the Atlantic. We'll be able to see the coastline," I said, to break the silence created by this unexpected piece of news. They both looked at me is if they hadn't understood. Or as if they were thinking, *Can she be a child of ours?*

Papa went up behind Mama and pulled her toward him in a half embrace. They ignored my comment. They already knew what to expect from me: I was a silly child. But they didn't have to be too upset; now there was a new Rosenthal on the way who would live up to their expectations. Sometimes *I* thought I was a mistake.

They did not need me. This new problem Mama had brought up was something for the two of them to sort out, so it was better for me to leave them alone with their new baby. I picked my camera up and went out on deck.

"Mr. Adler is still sick," Mama reminded me, even though she didn't expect me to go and greet them on my own.

I tried to photograph the passengers in second class, but I could see it disturbed them. Some looked scared; others struck a pose when they saw me focusing on them, and that spoiled the effect I was trying to achieve. It was even worse in first class: the families there had a tendency to adjust their clothes, and some women even asked me to wait a few seconds so they could fix their makeup. The only person who didn't pose was Leo. If he saw I was interested in a shot, he would stop so that it wouldn't come out blurred.

I took a photo of him with his father. Mr. Martin looked tired, sitting in an armchair with a gray blanket across his legs. He had grown older since I last saw him. Next to him, Leo was smiling, with one hand on his waist.

"The ring will be yours, Papa promised me, in Havana he'll give it to me." Leo spoke hurriedly. He often jumbled up his sentences, and I seemed to be the only one who could understand him.

"I'm going to have a brother. My mother is three months along." That was my excuse not to have to thank him for the ring and to escape this awkward moment.

"Another mouth to feed" was his response.

This time I was the one who had been waiting to be congratulated, a "That's great, you're going to have a little brother or sister!" but as ever, Leo was practical and went straight to the point.

We were the first ones up on the promenade deck when the announcement came over the loudspeakers that we were approaching the Azores.

Leo and I joined my parents at the port rail, and we gazed at the islands appearing in the distance. Nobody shouted "Land ahoy!" as they used to in my adventure books. The decks became crammed with passengers staring at the horizon in eerie silence.

The air was freezing: night was falling. Even though Leo swore they would soon open the swimming pool, I could not imagine who would risk getting into the water with such a cold breeze. The tropics were still too far away for anyone to go out and sunbathe.

I began to feel seasick, either from staring at the horizon for too long or because of the news that a baby was on the way. For whatever reason, I found I had to hang on to the ship's rail to keep my balance. The closer we came to the islands, the more the *St. Louis* seemed to rock to and fro.

Mama leaned against Papa. She felt protected by the strongest man in the world again. Papa held her to him, but there was something like a look of panic in his eyes. I tried to guess at his feelings, what he might have been thinking, what was worrying him—whether he felt sick or exhausted or regretted having to struggle the whole time and was giving up. I had no idea why he could be afraid, if we were together. *We're safe, Papa. We managed to flee. Germany is farther and farther behind us.*

We passed by the Azores at full speed. When we saw them begin to disappear off the port bow, it felt like a missed opportunity, like someone allowing a safe conduct to freedom to slip out of their hands. What would it have been like to live there, far from the Ogres? We ought to have bought visas for the Azores.

We could have been their new inhabitants. We would have changed their name, of course. Instead of the Azores, I would have called them the "Impure Islands." Our children would speak Impure, a language we'd invented that was different from our mother tongue. The first Impure state.

This was where my brother or sister would have been born, free from the misfortune of being German, without having to speak the German language. Happy to be impure! With no need to hide from anyone, as there would not be a single pure person around. *Just think, Leo, what a paradise!*

Leo gripped my hand. My parents didn't notice, because they were so lost in their own thoughts, leaning against each other as they gazed at the horizon, where the islands were starting to fade in the midst of the sad Atlantic.

My hand was frozen, but Leo's warmed me.

"I got a pair of roller skates for tomorrow." Leo was able to get rid of any dark thoughts. I could already imagine what to expect when I woke up in the morning.

"Will you be able to learn in an hour?" I asked him. He shot me a look as if to say, "Of course I'll learn, and much more quickly than you think." His peals of laughter were contagious. Laughing was the best thing we could do.

It was then I realized that Papa was observing me rather anxiously—and there I was, daydreaming about Leo and his skates! *I think it is high time you end your silence, Papa, and make us feel like you are here with us; that you take us into account. That if anything was happening, you would tell us, because you know I am strong. We always feel safe with you.*

His voice was solemn as he announced curtly, "We're halfway there."

19 MAY 1939

SITUATION HAVANA WORSENING. PROTESTS
AGAINST EUROPEAN IMMIGRANTS. CONTINUE
ON COURSE.

Cable from the Hamburg-Amerika Line

Tuesday, 23 May

It was bound to be a Tuesday. Since we came on board, no one had even thought about what day of the week it was. What interested us was how many days were left before we disembarked. I couldn't wait for it to be Saturday, the day we were to arrive. On top of that, it was my birthday, and it fell on a Tuesday, the worst day of all. Well, anyway, what did I care? We were sailing in the mid-Atlantic and wouldn't reach our destination for almost another week. I no longer even believed in my own bad luck.

I had awakened early, because a crew member sent by the captain came to look for Papa. I decided not to mention this to Leo. He would only have started with his endless speculation and conspiracy theories.

Mama had been on edge for days. I thought that revealing her secret might have unburdened her, but that wasn't the case. Overwhelmed with foreboding, often groundless, that she kept rehashing in her mind, she remained in bed, sunk among down pillows, shrinking from the sunlight streaming in through the porthole.

Everybody knew I did not want a party, since there was nothing to celebrate. But even the captain knew it was my birthday. Leo said I would receive a very special present but that I had to be patient. I thought he was still on the trail of his mother's famous ring, although it would be crazy for his father to give away the only valuable thing they still possessed.

When Mama did finally get up, she came straight to my bed and lay down beside me. Her body felt so cold, I shivered.

"My Hannah," she said, stroking my hair.

Mama said nothing more, but I sensed she wanted to tell me something. I turned to look at her, to encourage her.

"It's time for you to have the Teardrop, Hannah."

Her freezing hands reached slowly for my neck. She began to fasten the necklace with the flawed pearl that her father had made for her mother to wear at the opening of the Hotel Adlon—the precious jewel she received at the age I was reaching that day. The delicate white-gold chain beautifully complemented the pearl, which was set in a triangle also of white gold with a tiny diamond at the tip.

The room enveloped us, and the bronze ceiling light with its three rows of snowy bulbs looked like a dazzling upside-down wedding cake competing with the sun's rays. I did not want time to pass. We were suspended in the center of this luminous space. Suddenly I was intimidated by the pearl now nestling at my neck; it brought with it a responsibility to preserve this jewel that had been in the family for generations. I ran to the mirror to examine my Teardrop, and decided to wear a soft-pink sweater to set it off properly.

When she saw how moved I was, Mama made an effort to stand up and come over to me. For her benefit, I struck a few familiar poses, to make her think I felt like a goddess, too. She laughed. For a short while, we played at being happy.

She put on a blue-and-white dress, and the pair of us headed off to celebrate my birthday.

As we approached the Adlers' staterooms, we noticed several crew members outside. We knocked on the door, but no one replied. When we insisted, we realized it had been left unlocked. Mama went in, and I followed. We found ourselves in the lounge with Papa, the captain, two seamen, and the ship's doctor, all of them looking forlorn. Papa came over and held us. I could smell the menthol odor from the Adlers' cabin on him.

"Last night Mr. Adler began to have trouble breathing. He's gone."

He's gone, he departed, he passed away, he has left us. It would have been so much easier to say "He died," but they wouldn't; they were all afraid of the word. Mrs. Adler came up, a sad smile on her face but with no sign of having cried. She took Mama by the hand.

"I wanted to bury him in Havana, but the captain has received a cable telling him that will be impossible. We'll have to hold the funeral service at night and then throw him into the sea. Can you imagine such an ending, Alma?"

The captain was talking to two of the crew, who were showing him the latest cables. At one point, he raised his head and said to me softly—so softly I could understand him only because I read his lips—"*Alles Gute zum Geburtstag Hannah.*"

So everyone knew it was my birthday. I had warned Mama I did not want a celebration like those held on previous evenings for other children on board. I was sure that, after Mr. Adler's death, nobody would be in the mood for a party.

I slipped out and went to look for Leo. He, of course, already knew everything. He also told me there had been another death during the night.

"A passenger?"

"No, one of the crew. Apparently he committed suicide by jumping into the sea. They couldn't rescue him. One tragedy after another."

Great news to start my birthday! Of course, it had to be a Tuesday.

"What happened to Mr. Adler was to be expected," I told him. "He never once got out of bed since he came on board. He let himself die. He was worn-out."

I didn't feel sorry for him, because in the end he had given up, but I did feel sympathy for Mrs. Adler: she had to bury him and continue this uncertain battle. Leo could sense my melancholy. He rested his hands on my shoulders and said, "Hannah, promise me something. We'll live together until we are eighty-seven. Beyond that, life isn't worth living. Who wants to be lying in a bed like Mr. Adler?"

I promise, Leo, of course I do. I said this to myself because he had already begun to move off without waiting for my reply.

The news about both deaths was already spreading among the passengers. Leo's friend Walter had come up with another theory. That Mr. Adler had committed suicide. That the member of the crew had been killed. That there could be more suicide attempts.

"Our visas are worthless. They say the Cuban government is now demanding a bond for each of us, a fortune that not even the wealthiest will be able to pay," he muttered. He peered around, anxious that no one else should hear his secret.

"I don't believe you," I said to him sternly. "My mother got our visas at the Cuban consulate in Berlin and bought the one for my father at the HAPAG offices in Hamburg."

I was fed up with all their speculation, their stupid theories. Everything was going to be fine: I was sure of it.

"Yes, just like ours. Those are the ones that are no longer valid." Walter sounded so sure of himself that I felt intimidated.

"If they don't let us into Cuba, do we have any other choices?" I asked, suddenly alarmed.

"Talks are still going on to see if any other Caribbean island will take us." Leo was taking control again, not wanting to appear to be behind with the news. He was the one to make announcements—not Walter, who thought he was so clever.

At least none of them said we were going back to Germany. That was not a possibility. We had already handed over our homes; there was nowhere for us to go. No one would survive. Now I understood why there were so many rumors about suicide.

"Do you think I should confront my parents so that they tell me the truth?" I asked Leo, without the others hearing me.

"No, what you have to do is find those capsules as quickly as possible. If you're refused entry to Cuba, the Rosenthals already have a plan," he said determinedly. "And we can't allow that, Hannah. Whatever happens, we have to be together."

I obeyed him, even though he was only a couple of months older than me.

We were caught up in a fresh nightmare. I didn't know if it was real or just a dream.

I reached my parents' cabin. They were sitting still, in silence, lost in their thoughts. I went to shut myself in my room and discovered on my bedside table an envelope bearing the insignia of the *St. Louis* and marked "For Hannah."

Inside was a postcard showing the biggest, most luxurious liner that had ever sailed the seas. "*Alles Gute zum Geburtstag Hannah.*" Signed "*Der Kapitän.*" It was true what Mama said: that man was a gentleman. I should have gone up to the bridge to thank him.

I could hear Mama crying outside. I clutched the postcard close to my heart and shut my eyes, wanting to hold on to the illusion that we were safe on this iron island. Choking with sobs, Mama's voice sounded so shrill I could hardly understand what she was saying:

"There's no argument. If all three of us cannot land, then none of us will. Neither Hannah, nor the child I'm bearing, nor I, are going back to Germany, Max. You can be sure of that."

23 MAY 1939

MAJORITY OF YOUR PASSENGERS IN
CONTRAVENTION OF NEW CUBAN LAW 937
AND MAY NOT BE GIVEN PERMISSION TO
DISEMBARK. SITUATION NOT COMPLETELY
CLEAR BUT CRITICAL IF NOT RESOLVED
BEFORE YOUR ARRIVAL IN HAVANA.

Cable from the Hamburg-Amerika Line

Thursday, 25 May

I wasn't afraid of death. Of the final hour arriving, of everything being switched off, of being left in darkness. Of seeing myself among the clouds, looking down at everyone still walking freely around the city. To die was like having the light switched off, and with it all your illusions.

But I didn't want my parents to decide *when* this happened. It was not yet the moment for me to return to dust. They wouldn't dare, because I would defend myself. I didn't care if our visas were worthless or that they wouldn't let us land on that nondescript island.

At night, while I slept, I could hear voices telling me to get up, leave my room, go out on deck, and throw myself into the ocean. The current would take me to the only place where I could arrive and be accepted: another tiny island that didn't figure on any map. I saw myself all alone, without my parents or Leo. From up above, I could hardly make myself out as a tiny dot, lost on the shore. That was what death must be like.

From birth, we the impure were prepared to face a premature death. For years, even in happy times, we would try to avoid it at every step, bumping into it and then continuing on. Sometimes I wondered what right we had to think we could survive when others were dropping like flies.

What I hated about the idea of death was not being able to say good-bye, leaving without a farewell. Just the thought of it made me shudder.

I would not allow others to decide my fate. I was twelve! I was not ready yet, and so I had to find those wretched capsules. If I didn't, Leo would be the one who killed me. He had explained that I had to look for a small bronze cylinder with a screw top. Inside would be three thin glass capsules with the lethal substance inside them, the ones that Mama suggested just yesterday could free her from agony if we were not allowed to land in Havana.

I had to search every corner, every suitcase, and be sure to tidy up afterward, to leave everything as it was so that nobody noticed.

That night, there was going to be a fancy dress ball, a tradition on the *St. Louis* before landing. But we still didn't know whether we would arrive, whether the ship would be allowed to dock, whether we'd be permitted to disembark. We didn't have a final destination.

A blast on the ship's horn announced it was time to go to the ballroom. Leo had already forgotten about the skates, or roaming the decks, or our game of playing at being count and countess. Playtime was over. He was a conspirator once again.

After the discussion my parents had in our cabin, I doubted whether they would want to go to such a pointless masquerade. I walked along the first-class corridor. With each passing day, it seemed narrower to me: the ceiling was closing in, and the yellow wall sconces cast shadows everywhere. I looked for the side stairs and descended reluctantly, tired of Mama's complaints, Papa's silence, Leo's demands. I reached the door to the mezzanine, and as I opened it, I heard the pop of champagne corks, the chatter of passengers as they waited for the orchestra to strike up, the laughter of those who were still confident we would be leaving the ship as soon as we reached the port of Havana.

We children were not allowed at the ball, but Leo had found a spot for us on the mezzanine balcony, which had been decorated with paper flowers, so that we could watch this crowd of imbeciles enjoy themselves before they received the slap in the face from the Cuban authorities at dawn on Saturday.

The atmosphere remained calm. The captain and the passenger committee had made sure of that, feeling responsible for these 936 wandering souls.

Walter and Kurt were unable to contain their glee, pointing out all the outlandish costumes. Leo was still in conspirator mode, analyzing every gesture of the couples on the dance floor.

The guests were like spirits as they milled around beneath the glittering candelabra bedecked with garlands intended to create a false sense of gaiety. From our observation post, the ballroom, which before had so impressed me with its majesty, now appeared little more than a shabby stage set. I could see plaster moldings based on some French palace or other, clumsy copies of bucolic scenes in elaborate gilt frames, paneling in noble woods, bronze sphinx wall lamps, frosted glass mirrors. A fantasy on the ocean. "Cheap luxury," Mama would have said.

Ines looked sad, waiting for a suitor who would never appear. She was wearing a fake diamond tiara and a tulle-and-lace gown that seemed as if it were made from cheap cotton. She had come as a princess without a throne and haughtily greeted her subjects: three girls dressed in sky blue, each with a white rose at her neckline and diamond earrings. Ines saw us watching them from above and nodded.

Walter and Kurt almost clapped when they saw a man burst into the room wearing heavy makeup. His cheeks were red, his eyebrows outlined in black, and his eyelids covered in bright-blue eye shadow. He had on a white tuxedo draped in a dramatic red velvet cape, and on his head was a golden crown ringed with laurel leaves.

A tall lady who was traveling alone was wearing a black sequined gown with wide sheer sleeves sprinkled with stars. A pearl tiara with an enormous feather completed her attire, while her bright-scarlet lips and dark lines under her eyes gave her an ominous look. She was half hidden behind an enormous ostrich-feather fan as she crossed the ballroom, where by now it was almost impossible to move.

"It's the queen of the night!" Kurt whooped.

"No, she's a vampire!" Walter corrected him, and we all laughed.

The most common costumes were pirates, a pair of young men dressed as sailors, and there were also several Greek goddesses draped in gowns with one shoulder bare.

As the noise increased, we could still hear the clink of glasses filled with intoxicating bubbles. In the space between the double staircase leading down to the dance floor, the orchestra began to play some nostalgic German tunes that darkened everyone's mood. We wouldn't be allowed to forget.

Then the orchestra paused, and there was a brief silence. Two trumpeters came to the front and started playing the tune that—for me, at least—belonged to us. Leo glanced at me: he recognized it as well. As the first notes of "Moonlight Serenade" sounded, I saw Papa enter the room in his made-to-order tuxedo. He ushered in the Goddess, who was wearing a black lace gown split halfway down, and with a train behind. Both were wearing black velvet masks, Mama's decorated with feathers and rhinestones.

They descended the staircase slowly, to the sounds of an orchestra trying hard to imitate Glenn Miller. Everyone stopped to admire the triumphant entry of the Rosenthals: if they had come to the ball, there couldn't be any problems. We would disembark without a hitch in the longed-for port of Havana. That was the message the captain wanted the Rosenthals to transmit to the disheartened passengers. But with things as they stood, not even the band's joyful music, or the brightly colored fancy dress, or my parents' air of distinction, could have lifted the gloomy atmosphere of the ball.

Concealed behind his mask, Papa looked like the hero of some cheap melodrama. Mama, frozen-faced, was trying in vain to smile. She seemed to be saying to him: "You've forced me to come, so here I am, but don't expect me to enjoy it."

The couples came together again to the strains of "Moonlight Serenade." Papa led Mama to the center of the room. She let her head droop gently onto his shoulder while he took short steps like someone dancing a waltz without following the rhythm: he didn't know this new music.

As they twirled around, Papa nodded to several of the men. Mama ignored them and avoided any eye contact.

Twelve days, that's all our happiness had lasted.

I had to leave. This was the moment for me to search the cabin.

26 MAY 1939

ANCHOR IN ROADSTEAD. DO NOT REPEAT NOT
MAKE ANY ATTEMPT COME ALONGSIDE.

Cable from the Hamburg-Amerika Line office in
Cuba

Saturday, 27 May

This was the day we were scheduled to disembark in Havana. Many on board were waiting to be reunited with family members who had already relocated to Cuba; others to go to their homes or find lodgings in a hotel. They hoped to settle on the island, learn Spanish, set up businesses. A lot of them planned to live there for only a few months, waiting to travel to Ellis Island, the entrance to New York, their final destination.

In Havana, we could create more families, and the island would slowly fill with the impure. But even though we intended to find homes and jobs there, we would always be on alert, because the Ogres had long tentacles, and who knew whether one day they would stretch as far as the Caribbean.

The destiny of the 936 souls aboard the *St. Louis* was now in the hands of one man. Who knew whether, depending on his mood when he

got out of bed, he would say yes or no. The president of Cuba might pro-
hibit us from docking and expel us from his territorial waters like stinking
rats. Then we would be returned to the land of the Ogres, where we would
be sent to prison and have to greet our premature, inescapable deaths.

I was already awake at four in the morning when the ship's horn
announced we were coming into the harbor. I had been looking for the
capsules for the past two days, and could sleep only a couple of hours a
night. I turned Mama's room upside down, and then I had to put everything back very carefully. I found nothing. Leo came to the conclusion
that Papa had concealed them in the soles of his shoes.

Walter and Kurt were convinced that we would finally be allowed
to disembark, but Leo was doubtful. As for me, I didn't know what to
expect.

All the passengers had brought their luggage out into the corridors;
it was almost impossible to navigate without tripping. There were no
suitcases outside ours, though, and that worried me. Between the blasts
of the ship's horn came the call to breakfast. This routine seemed to sug-
gest that the problems had been resolved, although in our cabin uncertainty still reigned. My parents had not packed anything. They appeared
convinced we wouldn't be getting off the ship.

Breakfast was a rapid affair. Everybody was very excited, and the
children rushed up and down. The passengers were dressed to the nines.
Not me. I was comfortable in my blouse and shorts: the heat and humidity were unbearable!

"Just you wait till the summer months. You won't be able to stand it,"
Leo said to encourage me. Just like him.

He knew I would read between the lines: if it was going to be so
dreadfully hot in the future, that meant we were going to land. He sat
down on the floor beside me, and so did Walter and Kurt. There was no
room left at the tables.

"Everything has been settled," Kurt told us. "My father says that
newspapers all over the world are reporting what is happening to us."

That meant nothing to me. Newspapers didn't win battles.

A Cuban doctor had come on board. They were going to check us all, and so we had to stay in the dining room. Who knew what they were looking for. I left my friends to their breakfasts and ran to warn Mama.

I got there as quickly as I could, stepping around all the suitcases, and opened the door to our cabin without knocking. They were both dressed, ready to go for their medical checkups. Mama was in one corner, protecting herself in the shadows. Her face was so pale it frightened me. Papa came over.

"Stay with your mother. The captain is expecting me."

His voice was not as gentle as usual. This was an order. I wasn't his little girl anymore.

I hugged Mama, but she pushed me away. Then she apologized, smiled, and began to push locks of my hair behind my ears. She didn't look at me. We sat there together, waiting for more orders from Papa.

The ship was anchored in the port but still rocked to and fro.

"I'm going to lie down for a while," said Mama, pushing me aside gently and going to her bed.

After she was back among her pillows, I returned to the dining room. Leo found me and was holding something oozing a sticky yellow liquid. A fruit.

"You have to try this."

Cuban pineapples had been loaded on board. I bit into a small piece; it was delicious, although it made my mouth sting afterward.

"First you chew to get the juice out, then you spit it out," said Walter, instructing the ignorant.

Now that we were in the tropics, our palates were discovering the shock of Cuban fruits.

"A ship left Hamburg today bound for Havana and had to change course when it was told the Cuban government wouldn't let its passengers land," said Leo, who always found out the latest news.

I could not see that this had any bearing on our situation. Perhaps they diverted the ship because, with us already here, they could not process so many passengers. Luckily, all of us on the *St. Louis* had landing permits signed and authorized by Cuba, and many even had visas for Canada and the United States, as did my family. We were on the waiting list and would stay only a short while, in transit. This would reassure the authorities. Everything would be all right.

That was my hope: there was no reason for me to think otherwise. Of course everything would be all right.

We went out on deck, where the smells of Cuba wafted to us on the breeze: a sweet mixture of salt and gasoline.

"Look at the coconut palms, Hannah!" All at once, Leo was a wide-eyed little boy, spellbound by the discovery of a new place.

As the sun came up, we could make out the majestic buildings on the Havana skyline. We saw a first group of three men, and then four more joining them on the shore. Now there were ten people running to the dock. *We're here! They can't send us back now!* My friends and I started jumping and shouting. Leo danced a comical jig.

Family members of many of the *St. Louis*'s passengers soon heard of our arrival, and within a few hours the port was teeming with people.

Small boats crammed with desperate relatives began heading toward us, although they were forced to stay at a safe distance from our quarantined ship. The coast guard had surrounded us like criminals.

We were told through the loudspeakers to have our documents ready. They were going to check the validity of our landing permits, together with other visas.

Walter arrived at a run. As soon as he got his breath back, he exploded:

"They're demanding a bond of five hundred Cuban pesos per passenger as a guarantee," he said, repeating what he had overheard from his parents.

"How much is that?" I asked.

"About five hundred American dollars. That's impossible." Leo always had a head for figures.

We had spent what little cash we had left in Germany buying valuable objects we could resell in Cuba.

"This is such a dreadful circus," said a lady in a white sun hat next to us. "Dreadful," she insisted, as though hoping somebody would hear and react.

There had to be a solution. The captain would not allow them to send us back. He was on our side; he wasn't an Ogre.

I peered at the long waterfront avenue and somehow could not imagine myself ever setting foot on it with Leo and my family.

It Is Hoped That the Problem of the Hebrews
Arriving from European Ports Will Be Resolved
Today

Diario de la Marina, Havana newspaper
28 May 1939

Tuesday, 30 May

There are moments when it is better to accept it's all over, that there's nothing more to be done. Give up and abandon hope: surrender. That's how I felt by then. I didn't believe in miracles. This had happened to us because we insisted on changing a destiny that was already written. We didn't have any rights, we couldn't reinvent history. We were condemned to be deceived from the moment we came into the world.

If Leo stays on this ship, so will I. If Papa stays, so will Mama.

Until then, they had only allowed two Cubans and four Spaniards to leave the ship. We'd never seen them on the trip across the Atlantic. They kept to themselves, never speaking to anyone.

If the process of checking our documents continued at that rate, and they let another six people disembark each time, we would have been there more than three months. By then, the swaying of the ship would have finished me off completely.

Through the porthole, Havana looked hazy, small, unreachable, like an old postcard left behind by some visiting tourist. But I kept the glass closed because I didn't want to hear the shouts from the relatives swarming around the *St. Louis* in decrepit wooden launches that a wave could capsize. Surnames and first names flew from the decks of our huge liner anchored in the harbor to the frail, hesitant craft below. Köppel, Karliner, Edelstein, Ball, Richter, Velmann, Münz, Leyser, Jordan, Wachtel, Goldbaum, Siegel. Everyone was searching for someone, but nobody found anybody. I didn't want to hear any more names, but they kept coming back. Neither Leo nor I had anyone to shout our names. Nobody was coming to save us.

On the waterfront avenue, I could see cars speeding along as though nothing were happening: to them, this was just another ship with foreigners on it, who for some reason or other were insisting on settling on an island where work was scarce and the sun destroyed all willpower.

Someone knocked at our door. As always, I shivered: perhaps they had come for Papa. The Ogres were everywhere, even on this island that my mind still could not accept as being part of our future.

Mr. and Mrs. Moser had come to see us. I said hello, and Mrs. Moser, who was bathed in sweat, hugged me. I could see they were on the verge of bursting into tears. Mr. Moser looked haggard, as if he hadn't slept in days.

"He prefers to die," Mrs. Moser explained passionately. "He wants to throw himself into the sea. But what about us? What would happen to my three children? We have no home, no money, no country."

My parents listened to them calmly. Mama stood up and steered Mr. Moser toward a chair, where he bent forward and hid his head in his hands out of shame. Mama felt great pity for this man: not so much for what he was suffering but because she could see that he and his wife believed that the powerful Rosenthals could help them somehow.

"I can't leave him on his own," Mrs. Moser continued. "He wants to cut his veins, throw himself into the sea, hang himself in our cabin . . ."

Apparently she had caught him in all his attempts at a premature good-bye. It seemed written on his forehead: it could be today or tomorrow, but it would happen.

I thought that Mr. Moser might not actually want to commit suicide, though he was gambling with his destiny. If somebody wants to kill himself, he does. It's easy, if you really mean to do it. You leap into the void or slash your wrists while the others are asleep.

"Even though our hands are tied," Papa began, trying to calm down the anguished Mosers, "we'll find a solution."

In a split second, he had become the professor again: the one who could convince, who held the truth in his hands. Mr. Moser raised his head, dried his tears, and concentrated as hard as he could on the person they all saw as the most influential passenger on the *St. Louis*. Only he could alter the fate of the more than nine hundred passengers. He and the captain.

"We ought to write to the presidents of Cuba, the United States, and Canada, on behalf of the women and children on board," Papa continued.

Mr. and Mrs. Moser smiled timidly, and their faces lit up slowly: they could glimpse their salvation and, for the first time in many days, felt there might be a reason for carrying on.

I thought they had all lost their wits. By then, no one on board seemed in his or her right mind. What difference would a letter make? The presidents wouldn't give a damn about where we ended up. No one wanted to take on our problems. No one wanted Germany as an enemy. What sense would it make to allow all these impure people into their countries, those paradises of harmony and well-being?

Our first big mistake had been to set sail from Hamburg. During all the days of the crossing, we had been living on nothing more than pathetic illusions. I didn't believe in fantasies or in an unreal world. That's why I always loathed my macabre dolls, so unresponsive and always staring at me, demanding to know why I didn't want to play with them when they were so splendid, so perfect and blond, so highly prized.

Mr. Moser's lifetime savings had vanished in the purchase of the landing permits for Cuba and in the passages for himself and his family on the *St. Louis*, and yet now he seemed to recover his faith just from listening to Papa. This encouraged him to launch into a description of his own particular drama, as though they were the only outcasts on board.

"We lost everything. My brother is waiting for us in Havana, where he's bought a house. If they send us back, we wouldn't have anywhere to go. What's going to happen to our three children? If we write to the Cuban president, I'm sure his heart will soften."

Hearing him sound so hopeful, his wife must have thought that the danger had passed. That the father of her children would no longer want to take a life that had once been so prized. They would all go back to their cabin, where she would make their beds. Tonight she could sleep soundly; she had even begun to breathe more calmly.

But that family's destiny was already written: from the moment I saw Mr. Moser leave our cabin, head down and happy, I knew what was going to happen. I lay on my bed and closed my eyes. My head began to spin endlessly, not allowing me to sleep.

First of all, Mrs. Moser would put the children to bed, sing them a lullaby, tuck them in, and give them good-night kisses. Moved by the sight of them, she would enjoy the soft breathing of these innocents, and then withdraw to rest alongside the man she had always trusted and with whom she had chosen to make a family. The man for whom she'd left her village, abandoning her parents, brothers, and sisters to take on an unknown name. She would fall asleep next to him, just as in the prosperous times.

While his family was sleeping, Mr. Moser would creep out of bed. He would go to the bathroom, look for the silver-plated razor with the leather handle bearing the insignia of the *St. Louis*, and sever his arteries with a determined stroke. First he'd feel a searing pain, but soon panic would drive out all feeling. He'd collapse to the floor, and the blood would seep slowly from his twitching body, so slowly it would allow him to see one last time, from the cold bathroom tile, how the people he had most loved in his life were sleeping soundly.

As he convulsed, his still-warm blood would start to gush out. Even though he was still conscious, his sight would grow dim, and his heartbeats would become gradually fainter. Finally he would lie still. His blood would start to dry, turning from red to black. The liquid would solidify.

At dawn, Mrs. Moser would wake up and realize her husband was not beside her. She'd touch the cold sheets that no longer bore any trace of her beloved's warmth, and then notice that the bathroom door was ajar. She'd walk slowly toward it, terrified of what she might find. Filled with foreboding, her breathing would become quicker, more urgent. She'd want to cry out, but be unable to. Coming to a halt in the doorway, she'd see the confused image of a scene she had avoided thinking about in the previous days, weeks, possibly even months. She'd close her eyes, take a deep breath, and start crying silently.

At the sight of her husband's body curled up on the bathroom floor in a fetal position, she'd kneel down to embrace him, even knowing that he no longer felt anything, that he was no longer there. A desperate cry and inconsolable weeping. The first one to join her would be her youngest daughter, aged four, clutching a white teddy bear. Then her six-year-old boy. Her eldest daughter, ten, would try to lead her brother and sister away to spare them from a sight that would haunt them for the rest of their lives.

Soon afterward, someone came to inform Papa. Neither showed any emotion: they were too preoccupied with their own anguish.

I stayed in bed. I couldn't stop thinking about Mrs. Moser when she found her husband's body. I hoped her children would never forget this day. They had to remember who was to blame.

Someone would have to pay.

Over 900 passengers, 400 women and children, ask you to use your influence and help us out of this terrible situation. The traditional humanitarianism of your country and your woman's feelings give us hope that you will not refuse our request.

St. Louis passenger committee to First Lady Leonor Montes de Laredo Brú, wife of Cuban president Federico Laredo Brú

30 May 1939

Wednesday, 31 May

"We're going to set fire to the ship today," Leo whispered in my ear almost as soon as we left my cabin and ran up on deck.

In less than ten minutes we had been up and down ladders, visited the engine room, rushed from first to third class. I had no idea what we were after.

"If they don't let us land, we'll set fire to it."

There'll be no need for that, Leo. It's so hot here that the heat is burning the ship's rails and the wooden decking. It's impossible to stay outside. The sun is another enemy.

Leo told me that, up to now, Cuba had accepted less than thirty passengers—the ones who had landing permits issued by its state department—but rejected those signed by the director-general of immigration, Manuel Benítez. He was the scoundrel who, together with his military mentor and ally Batista, had pocketed all our money. The "Benítez" had already lost its validity while we were crossing the Atlantic. Or possibly much earlier than that.

Now that military chief, the real power on the island, was in his luxury residence surrounded by his family and his escort while recuperating in bed from a cold and did not dare show his face.

His personal physician forbade him to answer the telephone, not wanting him disturbed by such trivial matters as the lives of more than nine hundred passengers!

When Mama bought the Benítez for Papa, she purchased two more for us, thinking the visas she already had might lose their validity. But we also had our US visas and were on the waiting list for entry there. I didn't know what more they could expect from us.

"It's possible everything will be sorted out *mañana*." Leo pronounced the word in his deep, ridiculous Spanish accent. *Mañana*—the only word, apart from *gracias*, that he could say in the language spoken on the island—was to be the last day of negotiations.

"*Mañana*," he said again, as if those three syllables had some other meaning and could convey hope.

Papa's passport had been stamped with a big *R*: for *return* or *rejected* or *repudiated*. They had done the same with the passports of Leo and Mr. Martin; Walter, Kurt, and their family; and Ines. Nobody would be saved. We were nothing more than a pack of undesirables, ready to be thrown into the sea or sent back to the Ogres' hell.

No one cared that we'd spent our life savings on purchasing those documents. Now a heartless president had dared to sign a decree declaring them null and void.

Leo thought that if we could set fire to the ship, they were bound to take account of us. The committee that Papa was chairman of had lost its powers of persuasion or negotiation, if it ever had any. The captain didn't know how he could face the passengers, who had put their trust in him. From the very first day, the most powerful man on board had led us to believe we would disembark—that there would be no problems when we got to the wretched port of Havana.

Two weeks wasted. We, the ridiculously gullible ones, had believed the Ogres when they authorized us to leave after handing over our businesses, our homes, our fortunes. How on earth could we have been so stupid as to trust them? It had all been planned in advance, even before Mama bought the landing permits for Cuba written in Spanish. They knew it from the moment we sailed from Hamburg; the band playing us off was another farce. It was obvious now why we were forced to have return tickets: they wanted us to cover the costs of the journey back.

In Cuba, they looked down on us; the rest of the world ignored us. They all lowered their eyes in confusion, as if trying to escape the embarrassment. They wanted to wash their hands to avoid feeling guilty.

The three young men who had toasted with us during the first banquet were now plotting with Leo—a twelve-year-old boy!—to set fire to this monstrous transatlantic liner. *Please, that's enough nonsense: keep your fantasies for when we reach dry land, if we ever do.* Some of them had no doubts about seizing the ship, changing its course, stripping the captain of his command. A kidnapping on the high seas. Or at least, in that ramshackle bay.

"What's she doing here?" the young man who looked like a matinee idol asked Leo.

"You can trust her, and she could help." *Help you do what, Leo?* If I had stopped a moment longer to think about what they were planning, I would likely have run off and left them to organize their harebrained scheme on their own.

But that young man with no future had few scruples. He was so desperate: the last thing he wanted to do was to return. He was too young and handsome to have to confront a premature death, and so he was capable of throwing into the sea anybody who got in his way, if it helped him survive. I felt like telling them that only a bunch of idiots could think that they could set fire to this sixteen-thousand-ton mammoth, but in the end I decided to leave them to their plotting and go up on deck. I had to take photos.

Let them burn it if they can. Destroy it. Sink the biggest ship in the bay. And sink us with it. That's the best thing that could happen to us.

I went to the far end of the deck, where there was no one begging to be let off the ship or people observing our despair from tiny boats. Someplace where I could not see the shoreline of a city that would pay a high price for its indifference—not today or tomorrow, but someday.

I leaned against the rail and closed my eyes, because I didn't want to see the sea, either, or El Morro Lighthouse. When I sensed there was someone behind me, I didn't need to turn around: I immediately recognized his smell of grease from the engine room, vanilla biscuits, warm milk. He stepped alongside me and took my hand. He squeezed it as hard as he could, and I smiled.

I opened my eyes because I knew I would be gazing at the long eyelashes of my only friend. *Look at me, Leo, we don't have much time left,* I wanted to tell him, but I stayed silent. If anybody knew that, it was him. Leo knew everything. Always.

On this side of the ship, we couldn't hear the shouts. The silence was ours. A boat loaded down with passengers approached. They must be "pure," I thought, because it entered the port and headed straight for its mooring, its horn sounding a warning.

And there we two were, not saying a word, hand in hand, watching them sail past and then turning around again to face the vastness of sea and sky.

Get up, Leo. Let's jump into the sea and let the current take us. Somebody is sure to rescue us far from this port. And if they ask our names, we'll invent ones that don't cause disgust, rejection, or hatred.

We would have done better to stay in Berlin. You and me, without our parents. We would be roaming streets littered with broken glass, laughing at the Ogres, listening to the radio in a dark passageway. We were free and happy then, in our own way.

My brain worked far more quickly than my tongue, and so I couldn't get the words out.

Look at me, Leo. Don't leave me alone here. Let's play. Let's go and roller-skate from deck to deck. You're squeezing my hand too hard. Into the water! I swear I'll do whatever you say. You decide. You're older than me.

Come on, it's time.

June 1939

His Excellency Federico Laredo Brú
President of the Republic of Cuba

Your Excellency,
    As a result of the meeting you were kind enough to offer
me, I have the honor of presenting the following proposal from
the National Coordinating Committee to allow the refugees
on board the SS St. Louis to enter Cuba:
    A surety from the Maryland Casualty Company,
authorized to do business in Cuba, will, with your approval,
be deposited forthwith in the name of the Republic of Cuba,
to the value of $50,000.

Lawrence Berenson, honorary advisor to the National
Coordinating Committee for Aid to Refugees and
Emigrants Coming from Germany

Thursday, 1 June

Mañana—that popular word among the passengers; the one Leo kept repeating in his strong accent—our fate was to be decided.

My parents would wait until I fell asleep to take out the bronze container with the miraculous powder from its hiding place. He would hold me down, she would pry open my mouth. I wouldn't resist; I'd chew on the glass coating to release the potassium cyanide that would bring about instant brain death. There would be no pain. Thank you, Mama and Papa, for not allowing me to suffer, for thinking of me, for putting an end to my agony. I would say good-bye happily, with a smile on my face. The time had come.

I lay down beside Papa on the bed, and we watched Mama getting ready for the last dinner on board. She went over to the dressing table and picked up her jewel case, an antique music box.

When I was little, I was hypnotized every time I opened that small black case encrusted with mother-of-pearl and saw the toy ballerina dancing to the tune of Beethoven's "Für Elise." Mama used to let me play with it and spend hours winding it up. The fragrance I associate with her jewels wafted over to the bed: the delicate aroma of lavender kept in a silk pouch inside the case. In the compartment where the ballerina's clockwork mechanism was hidden, Mama opened a tiny little drawer and took out her wedding ring, the most valuable piece of jewelry she had brought from Berlin.

At that moment, I understood in a flash. I almost jumped up but managed to stop myself: all those days trying to find the bronze container, and now it had shown up right under my nose! That must be the hiding place! If those capsules were worth their weight in gold, what better place to keep them than with the big diamond, her most precious possession.

The ship's horn sounded again. I don't think there was anything that annoyed me more than that blast. Yes, there was: strangers knocking on the door. It was time to return to the dining room, where they were going to serve our last dinner in Havana. My parents were all in white; they looked as if they were frozen in time.

"I'll be done soon, I'm not ready yet," I told them. They looked at me in surprise but decided silently to respect my routine, which was becoming more absurd by the day.

I sat at the dressing table and picked up the music box. I could have thrown it into the sea and made it disappear, jewels and all, but instead I turned the key and watched the slender ballerina spinning around and around. I was scared to open the secret compartment, because if the capsules weren't there, I'd finally give up. I couldn't stop my fingers from trembling as I opened the hidden drawer and saw the bronze container. It was so small it almost made me laugh. Then my heart began to beat so wildly I was afraid that someone, even outside the cabin, might hear it. I picked up the container with the lethal powder inside, and my hands were shaking so much I had trouble unscrewing the top.

Calm down, Hannah. Nothing is happening.

At a moment like that, Leo ought to have been beside me.

When I opened the top, I held my breath. I could see that the glass capsule really was in there, and so I quickly closed the container again. I was afraid that by opening it some tiny particles of cyanide might escape, pollute the air, and paralyze us all. A tinkling sound inside the container told me there was more than one. Of course, there ought to be three of them!

I couldn't understand how something so small could be so powerful. If you inhaled it, or a molecule got onto your skin, you would be in the next world. I thought of putting one in my mouth right then, but I couldn't do something like that to Leo. It was a decision we had to make together, and it would have been a betrayal for which he'd never forgive me. *Let's do it, Leo!*

I ran to find him.

As I hurried along, I bumped into first-class passengers who were going down for their farewell meal. As I entered the dining room, I was stunned by the noise of cutlery on plates, the sound of the diners chatting to one another, the smell of roast meat. I saw Leo in a doorway to one side, flanked by his usual cohorts, Walter and Kurt.

When he spotted me, he signaled that I shouldn't move: he would come to me. He strode across the room. Looking down at my right hand, he understood immediately that I was holding the treasure. He didn't smile. In fact, I thought that, for the first time, he was truly afraid.

When he took my hand, I opened it and let the little bronze tube with the three cyanide capsules drop into his. Leo made sure no one was looking or following him, and left the room without saying a word, like a real conspirator.

I could see my parents talking to one of the stewards. Mrs. Moser came in without her children and sat at a table on her own. Mama invited her to join them, and she accepted timidly.

The final dinner was a feast that started with black caviar on toast au gratin and celery in olive oil, followed by asparagus in hollandaise sauce and spinach in wine sauce, then sirloin steak with fried Saratoga potatoes, macaroni with Parmesan, and Lyonnaise potatoes, and lastly

California peaches and Brie cheese with raspberries. I hardly touched anything but the macaroni and the peaches: all I wanted was for that absurd farewell dinner to be over.

Then the dancing began. The orchestra launched into "Lotus Flower Waltz" and then "Come Back to Sorrento," followed by a Schreiner medley and a tune by the Hungarian composer Franz Lehár. The main ceiling lights had been switched off, making the lighting much softer: an amber glow enveloped the dancers, who seemed to be floating on a layer of fog.

All of a sudden, the orchestra fell silent.

The couples waited for the next tune without returning to their seats while the hubbub from the tables increased. The stewards were performing miracles to cross the room, which was getting more and more crowded.

A tall, slender woman wearing a strapless yellow gown and with a huge red flower behind one ear climbed reluctantly onto the stage as if forced to become the protagonist of the next act. She spoke to the musicians, who closed their scores. Apparently they didn't need them. The woman took the microphone in both hands, closed her eyes, and started to sing in a low voice.

As the first verse in German of "In einem kühlen Grunde" was heard, everybody fell silent: *In einem kühlen Grunde, / Da geht ein Mühlenrad, / Meine Liebste ist verschwunden, / Die dort gewohnet hat.* "In the coolness of a valley / A windmill is turning, / Though my beloved who once dwelled there / Is now gone."

Nobody dared move an inch. Couples embraced as the orchestra accompanied the singer. The moment the last verse was over, she stepped down without another word. By then, the atmosphere in the room was mournful. Dressed in white, Papa and Mama were the discordant note in that tide of black, gray, and brown.

Leo came up behind me, panting.

"It's done," he whispered in my ear, trying to regain his breath.

I shuddered. He had thrown them into the sea. We had lost our only chance to save ourselves together! It didn't occur to him that this could have been our escape route.

Sitting next to me, he stared in fascination at the profusion of exotic food. His eyes lit up as he piled as much as he could fit onto the china plate with the ship's emblem on it. He had already forgotten the capsules, the possibility of throwing ourselves into the sea, of fleeing.

He was hungry, and this feast that a steward described with unintelligible names was nothing more to him than salad, meat and potatoes, fruit and cheese. He devoured it as though it were his last meal. His first comment seemed to have come straight from one of the cables that the captain would receive and hand on to Papa:

"You're safe."

No need for me to be afraid: I was wearing my pearl, and my best friend was beside me.

By presidential decree, the steamship *St. Louis* is to set sail immediately. It must leave the port with the immigrants it has on board. If it does not leave under its own steam, it will be towed several miles out to sea by a Cuban cruiser.

Diario de la Marina, Havana newspaper
2 June 1939

Friday, 2 June

Mama's cries woke me. It had just dawned, and the portholes were open. The morning activity of the port began reaching us, and with it a hot breeze that I found suffocating. Mama was striding up and down in the tiny space where she had spent most of the night awake. She was in despair. The silk pillows and bedcover were in a heap in one corner of the bed.

She had come back to the cabin directly after the meal, refusing even to look at Havana, which was visible through the windows. It was the city that was never going to belong to her.

It was as though a storm had raged through the cabin. Open suitcases, the contents of the drawers spilled out, clothes strewn all over the floor, as if we had been burgled while we slept. My parents had been awake for hours. Weariness had made their movements slow. I closed my eyes, not wanting to be part of this battle with no enemies. I wanted to stay asleep, for them to think I couldn't hear them, that I didn't exist for them or for anyone, that I was invisible, and nobody could find me.

"They can't have disappeared, Max. Somebody must have stolen them. That was the only hope I had left, Max, believe me. I can't go back, Max. Neither Hannah nor I could bear it." She kept repeating Papa's name like a spell that could save her.

They couldn't find the capsules, and, in the end, they would discover it was me. That Leo had thrown them into the sea, where they dissolved in the warm waters of the Gulf. *Oh my God, what have I done? Forgive me, Mama.*

She was crying, and I felt as if with each tear she was slowly bleeding to death. Papa, his back to the hurricane Mama had unleashed in our cabin, was studying the Havana shoreline, lost in thought. The city was a shadow, a mass of lifeless air. The port was a distant horizon nobody on board could reach. I still had my eyes closed; I was squeezing together my eyelids as hard as I could, wishing I could do the same with my ears, so that I wouldn't have to listen to the sobs of this desperate woman.

The end had arrived, and it would be much worse, through my fault. Now the two of them would have to put a pillow over my head and suffocate me. I was ready: I wouldn't resist. I was there, and there would be no capsules. It would be a slow death, but I deserved it, because I was the one to blame for us losing the magic powder that would have saved us from pain. There was no turning back. I would confess my crime. I was sure they would spit on me. Beat me. Throw me into the sea.

In the end, I looked out of the corner of my eye and saw Mama sitting on the bed. She had calmed down. Ready perhaps to become a murderer. I didn't blame her.

She got dressed. Very slowly, she put on her silk stockings and her handmade white shoes. She brushed her short head of hair and applied a soft pink lipstick. Then she rubbed cream onto her arms, neck, and face. A shield against the sun.

There were three suitcases by the door. One was mine: I recognized it. I hoped they had packed my camera.

Papa seemed elsewhere, staring into space. There was no way out. Time to say good-bye.

"Hannah!" Mama's voice was no longer gentle. "*Nos vamos,*" she said in Spanish.

I pretended to wake up. I was still wearing the dress I went to sleep in. I barely had time to put on my shoes. I didn't want to cause them any more problems.

There was a knock at the door, and, as usual, it scared me. It was the Ogres: they had come for us. They were going to throw us into the bay, into the void.

A uniformed crewman told us the time had come to disembark. We would be taken in a tender to the port of this city that from the deck looked completely imaginary, unreal.

Mama emerged first. I followed her and could sense Papa walking behind me. Then he sped up, caught up with Mama, and dropped his valuable watch into her handbag.

Out on deck, all I heard were shouts and cries, families calling out their names in the hope that someone on the hazy, distant shore would hear them; someone who'd rescue them from their misery.

The captain was waiting for us. He looked tiny beside Papa. And Leo? Where was Leo? I needed to see him, to be allowed to say good-bye.

We struggled to make our way through the throng. The Cuban officials in their sweaty uniforms looked at us scornfully. We were used to that.

There was a commotion on the deck. Somebody was pushing his way through.

"Not everyone can be here. Wait your turn," shouted an old man who could hardly remain standing when his silver-handled cane was knocked to the floor.

A hand picked up the cane and gave it back to the old fellow. *Leo! I knew you wouldn't abandon me, Leo! Let's jump together, get away. The sea is ours.*

Leo took my hand and thrust something into my palm. I didn't know what it was, because all I wanted was to stare at him. I was terrified at the idea I might forget his face. I closed my hand tight, so as not to lose my gift. Then his father appeared, tugging at his arm, separating us before I could even thank him. Leo resisted and came close to me again:

"Don't open the box until we meet again, Hannah! I'll come looking for you, I swear! Today, tomorrow, or in another life, but I'll find you! Can you hear me, Hannah?"

I felt my body begin to shake, and I thought I was going to collapse. Leo was still in front of me, his lips trembling. I couldn't understand what he was trying to say. *Stay with me, Leo. Don't let them tear us apart.*

"If we never meet again, wait until you are eighty-seven to open it."

We had promised to stay together until that age.

"No, Leo. You'll come and find me. I don't want to reach eighty-seven all alone. What would be the point?" I said. I could see he was fighting back tears.

He was going to kiss me, but we wouldn't be able to embrace—the crowd was keeping us apart.

"Don't cry, Leo," I begged him, hardly able to speak.

But tears were welling in his eyes, and his long eyelashes could barely contain them. He wiped his face: he didn't want me to see him cry. I couldn't breathe; my heart was bursting.

Leo disappeared among the crowd with his father.

"Leo!" I shouted, unsure whether or not he could still hear me. In the commotion of frantic passengers, I lost sight of him.

"Promise me, Hannah!" I could hear his voice as he moved away, but couldn't see him anymore.

I didn't want anyone to see me cry. But the sun and the heat made it impossible for me to control my sobs. It was too late to respond to Leo: I didn't know what to say.

"Of course I promise. I won't leave this island until you arrive, I won't open the box until we meet again," I muttered disconsolately, knowing he couldn't hear me anymore.

I raised my hand to see what he had given me. It was a tiny indi-go-colored box. I clutched it so tightly it left an imprint on my palm.

I couldn't open it, because Leo had sealed it. I knew it was the ring. He'd finally managed to get what he had promised me. The ring would keep us united to the end, until we were eighty-seven years old.

Mama was not crying anymore. Nor was there much sign anymore of her makeup, apart from a pale pink on her cracked lips. The Cuban officials checked our documents, our Cuban and US visas. Down below a tender named the *Argus* was waiting for us. It looked tiny and ram-shackle, and was already filled with soldiers and relatives of some of the passengers. They were all crowded into the prow, and the boat was rocking dangerously in the waves, and the anxious passengers looked about to sink.

Mama fixed her eyes on Papa, and in a voice I'd never heard from the Goddess before, she swore:

"My son will not be born on this island!" She stressed the word *island* with all the disdain she could muster. "You can be sure they'll pay for it, Max. From today I am not German, or Jewish; I am nothing."

She vowed that those were the last words she would ever speak in German.

"Alma!" somebody called to her.

Above her, she saw Mrs. Moser with her three children, staring down as if begging her: "Please, take them with you! Save my children!" As if that were possible.

"Why them and not us?" moaned a woman carrying a baby, and I avoided looking her in the eye.

Mama didn't answer. She didn't say good-bye. She didn't kiss Papa.

I threw myself into the arms of the strongest man in the world and hugged him with all my might. Bending down to me, he whispered something I didn't understand into my ear. I could feel the heat of his cheeks. *Hold me tight, Papa. Don't let them take me away, don't abandon me.* Papa repeated what he had just said to me, but it was still an incom-prehensible murmur.

Even though his chest was a huge armor plate, I could hear his heart beating and how his blood was racing at breakneck speed. He whispered in my ear again. I didn't want the seconds to go by. I wanted everything to come to a halt.

A Cuban official pulled me roughly away from him. I cried out, but somebody was already hauling me down the swaying ladder. I held on to the salt-covered rail as tightly as I could. I closed my eyes to absorb Papa's smell, but all I breathed in was a wave of sweat and hair oil from the policeman guiding me down. Mama was walking firmly along in front of me. What I was most scared of then was that someone might pry the indigo box out of my hand; I clutched it to me with all my might.

"Papa! Papa!" I started to shout, but he didn't answer.

I cried uncontrollably, no longer even trying to hide it. My own sobs choked me. Papa refused to look at me, to see me go.

My tears robbed me of my voice. I was so ashamed I was leaving, I wanted to shout to my father, whom we were leaving on board. *We were being torn apart! Being abandoned on a strange island where we wouldn't be able to survive on our own! Papa!* The passengers saw me crying and panicked further. Somebody called out to me. I heard my name.

"Hannah!" I couldn't make out who it was.

Someone was saying good-bye to me. Perhaps it would be better never to know who it was. About thirty of us had been allowed to disembark. We were the chosen ones, the fortunate ones. I could see it only as a sentence, a terrible punishment.

The unfortunate ones were staying on board, the ones who had no future. Nobody knew what was going to happen to them. The captain would not be able to do anything. He would return to the high seas with 906 passengers, very slowly, in order not to have to land at Hamburg. My father would be among them, and so would Leo.

Mama stepped onto the *Argus* and slipped on the wet bottom of the boat, staining her white shoes. She clung to the rail and turned her back on the *St. Louis* without once looking at Papa, who was trying to make his hoarse voice heard above the others.

But I heard him. It was him, I knew it. I wanted them all to be quiet, for them to let me hear him. I concentrated; I shut out the noise and concentrated. I finally succeeded. He was asking me to do something. *I don't understand, Papa . . .*

"Forget your name!" he cried out.

I no longer heard the crowd's desperate shouts. Only my father existed now.

But he hadn't called me "Hannah."

"Forget your name!" he shouted again at the top of his voice.

The *Argus* moved away with a roar, covering the bay with a plume of black smoke as it left behind the biggest ship they had ever seen in the port of Havana. There would be no band waiting for us here with triumphant marches. We would hear only the shouts of the passengers who had to stay on board a ship that drifted aimlessly, without a destination.

The Ogres had snatched Papa from me. The Cuban Ogres. I couldn't kiss him. I couldn't say good-bye to him, or Leo, or the captain.

I wanted to throw myself into those dark waters that made the *Argus* pitch and roll. This was my last chance. I didn't want to hear anything more, I just wanted the engine to stop.

All of a sudden, everyone on the *Argus* fell silent: we had reached the dock, and somebody was throwing over a rope.

Silence. Now there was complete silence. In the calm, I heard Papa's voice floating out over the water one last time, echoing through a space where we had dreamed we could be happy.

"Hannah, forget your name!"

PART THREE

Hannah and Anna

Havana, 1939–2014

Anna
2014

*T*oday I'm going to find out who I am. *I'm here, Dad, in the land where you were born.*

When we leave the plane the sunlight outside is blinding, but then we pass through immigration and customs almost in darkness.

They search Mom's luggage, and the female official congratulates her on her dresses.

"I've never had anything like that. How many days are you going to be here? You've got enough to change lots of times," she says, lengthening the vowels while the muscles of her face are in constant motion. Just looking at her exhausts me.

Today I'm going to meet Aunt Hannah. I tell myself to stay calm.

The man helping us close our suitcases asks Mom if she has a bottle of aspirin to spare.

"They're hard to get here."

We're not sure whether it's a test or if this badly shaved man in a military uniform wants the bottle because he has constant headaches. She gives it to him, and we're pointed toward the exit.

"This is the first time I've been nervous going through customs," Mom whispers. "I feel like I've done something wrong."

We push our way through the crowd waiting for passengers outside the exit and board the taxi sent by Aunt Hannah.

The smell of gasoline makes me feel sick: first when we got off the plane, then in the car, and now as we enter the city. I try to put on my seat belt, but it doesn't work. Mom glances at me out of the corner of her eye. She's trying to be nice to the driver, who seems intimidated.

"Would you like to listen to music?" he asks.

"No!" we both reply at once, and then laugh.

We wind down the windows to lessen the smell of tobacco coming from the torn seat upholstery.

The potholes and the car's awful suspension make me feel like we'll be catapulted through the windshield at any moment. Mom never stops smiling at the driver, who now launches into a long speech about the difficulties in the country and the lack of resources to keep Havana's streets in good repair.

"Some are better than this," he says, as if apologizing.

The farther we get from the airport, the heavier the atmosphere becomes. I wonder if all Havana is like this.

A young boy without a shirt who is riding a rusty bike comes to a stop alongside us under a traffic light.

"Hello! Tourists? Where are you from?" he asks.

Our driver only has to give him a look, and he lowers his head and pedals off without waiting for a reply.

"A vagrant!" he says, heading for Vedado, the neighborhood Aunt Hannah has lived in since she came here from Berlin. The place where Dad was born.

"It's one of the best neighborhoods in the city," the driver tells us. "It's right in the center. You can walk everywhere from there."

Leaving behind the airport avenue, we cross a big square, with a gray obelisk beneath a sculpture of one of the island's historic heroes. It's surrounded by huge propaganda billboards and modern buildings that, our guide informs us, are government headquarters.

The square opens onto a wide avenue with a tree-lined walkway in the center and run-down mansions on either side. On several street corners, groups of people are lining up outside big buildings with faded paint that appear to be markets.

"Are we in Vedado already?" I ask, breaking the silence, and the driver nods with a smile.

Several young people in uniform wave to us from a school. It seems like the word *tourist* is stamped on our foreheads. We'll soon get used to it!

Somehow I can tell we are arriving. The driver soon slows down, pulls over, and parks behind a car from the last century. Mom takes my hand as she stares at a faded house with withered plants in the garden. The porch is empty; there are cracks in the roof. A battered iron gate separates the building from the sidewalk, which is raised here and there by the roots of a leafy tree that seems to have been planted there to protect it from the harsh tropical sun.

A boy sitting under the tree greets me, and I smile back. Mom walks toward the house with our suitcases. The boy comes over.

"So, are you relatives of the German woman?" he asks in Spanish. "Are you German? Are you coming to live here, or are you just on a visit?"

He asks so many questions at once that I can't even think of a reply.

"I live on the corner," he says. "If you like, I can show you Havana. I'm a good guide, and you won't have to pay me."

I burst out laughing, and so does he.

I try to get into the garden without having to touch the iron gate, but the boy gets there before me.

"My name is Diego. So, have you rented a room in the German's house? Everybody here says she's a Nazi, that she fled to Cuba at the end of the war."

"She's my father's aunt," I reply. "When he was my age, he became an orphan and she brought him up. Yes, she's German, but she fled with her parents before the war broke out. And she's not a Nazi, that's for sure. What else do you want to know?" I ask him harshly.

"Okay, okay, take it easy! And I'll still show you Havana if you want. All you have to do is come outside and shout my name, and I'll be here in the blink of an eye. I don't mind if you're a Nazi, too."

His boldness makes me laugh out loud again. Then I turn my back on him and am just stepping onto the porch when someone opens the front door. I hide behind Mom and clutch her hand. She squeezes mine tightly.

As the rotting door opens, we can smell the perfume of violet water.

"Welcome to Havana," says a weak voice in English.

It's the little girl from the ship.

I can't see her face yet. From her voice, it's hard to tell whether she is a young girl or an old woman. Aunt Hannah is standing inside the doorway as if she doesn't want to be seen. She doesn't come out to greet us but spreads her arms to invite us in.

"Thank you for coming, Ida," she says in a low voice, and then looks down at me and says with a smile, "How pretty you are, Anna!"

I go in and hug her quickly, feeling shy. To me, she is still a shadow. Her hair looks the same way it does in the photos of her as a girl, parted on the side, with the ends curling inward and tucked behind her ears. Except that now she isn't blonde and doesn't have bangs. I begin to study her curiously. Mom lays a hand on my shoulder, as if to say "That's enough!"

In the semidarkness of the living room, my aunt looks as young as Mom. She is tall and slender, with a strong jaw and a long neck. As she emerges more into the light, wrinkles appear on a face that seems incredibly calm. I have the feeling I have known this woman for a long time.

She is wearing a beige cotton blouse with pearl buttons, a long, narrow gray skirt, stockings, and low-heeled black shoes.

Aunt Hannah speaks softly. She stresses the vowels and pronounces the consonants at the ends of words with great care.

"Come on, Anna. This is your father's house, and yours, too."

I hear her clear voice waver almost imperceptibly. Close up, I can see deep lines on her face, liver spots on veiny hands. Her blue eyes are striking, and her skin is so white it seems as if she has never been exposed to the fierce tropical sun.

"Your father would have been so happy to see you now," she sighs.

She takes us down a hallway with checked tiles to the back of the house. The windows are covered by thick gray curtains.

In the dining room, there's a strong aroma of freshly made coffee. We sit at the table; its top is a cracked mirror covered in stains.

Aunt Hannah excuses herself, goes into the kitchen, and returns with an old black woman who has difficulty walking. They serve themselves and my mother coffee, and offer me lemonade. The medium-built black woman comes over and gently holds my head against her stomach, which smells of cinnamon and vanilla.

She says her name is Catalina. It's hard to tell who helps whom, because they both appear to be about the same age. Hannah stands straight, but Catalina leans forward, due to her height. When she walks, she drags her feet, although I don't know if this is just a habit or because she's tired.

"My girl, you're just like your aunt!" she exclaims, rumpling my hair with a familiarity that surprises me.

While Mom and Aunt Hannah talk about our journey, I look up at the ceiling. There are patches of damp everywhere. The paint on the walls is peeling, and the room is filled with the battered furniture of a family that must have lived well a long time ago.

While Mom is busy telling her about our life in New York, Aunt Hannah doesn't take her eyes off me. She asks if I'm bored, if it wouldn't be a good idea to let me go out into the street so that the boy who talks so fast can take me to explore the city.

"You can go out and play for a while if you like," she insists.

I'm not sure there's anything around here for me to play with.

"Better if you stay and get some rest," says Mom. She pulls the envelope with the photographs out of her bag.

This doesn't seem like the right moment. We just got here. Perhaps it's asking too much of Aunt Hannah to make her go back to such a distant past, but apparently Mom can't think of anything more to say.

I'd like to explore upstairs, where the bedrooms must be. I wish they'd leave me alone so I can see where Dad used to sleep, where he kept his toys and books.

Mom lays out the photographs from Berlin on the cracked mirror tabletop. Hannah smiles, although I get the impression she would prefer to go on studying me than to have to return to the past.

"Those were the happiest days of my life," she says.

As she remembers, her blue eyes grow more intense. She seems to be coming to life, although it's obvious she is not particularly interested in that dramatic Atlantic crossing. I'm surprised to hear her say those were happy days.

"I was your age, and was free to run all over the ship's decks, sometimes until really late at night," she explains. I don't know what to say.

She pauses for a long while between sentences.

"My mother was so beautiful! And Papa was the most distinguished and respected man on board the *St. Louis*."

She picks up the photograph of a man in uniform and shows it to us.

"Oh, and the captain . . . we adored him!"

Mom points to a snapshot of a boy who appears both in the images from Berlin and those from the boat:

"Who is this boy?"

"Oh, that's Leo!" Aunt Hannah falls silent for a moment. "We were very young." Another silence, before she finally looks at us again. "He betrayed me, so I erased him from my life. But I think the time has come to forgive." Another pause. "Will we be able to forgive someday?"

We don't know what to say. We were hoping she would tell us the story of the only person who posed naturally—the one who was obviously the main protagonist of the photo collection. I was intrigued. I wanted to know more about this Leo: if he had reached Cuba at a later date; how, exactly, he had betrayed her. But if I ask her, Mom will kill me. The silence deepens. Then Aunt Hannah picks up a postcard showing the boat in midocean.

"Back then the *St. Louis* was the most luxurious transatlantic liner ever to reach Havana," she recalls with a sigh. "It was our only hope, our salvation—or so we thought, Anna my dear, until we realized we were being tricked yet again. One man died during the crossing, and his body was thrown into the sea. Only twenty-eight of us were allowed to disembark. All the others were sent back to Europe, and less than three months later, war broke out. Nobody wanted us. We were the undesirables. But I was your age, Anna, and I couldn't understand why."

Mom stands up and goes over to hug her. What I want is for the conversation to finish, to end the torture we've made this poor old woman suffer. We've only just arrived! And it's obvious she thinks that the only cure for her illness is to forget. She seems more interested in learning about our lives in the present, because we are all that's left of the boy who grew up to be a man in her house, only to disappear beneath the rubble of two tall towers in a far-off city she never knew.

"Every day I wonder why I'm still alive!" she whispers, suddenly bursting into tears.

Hannah
1939

The car hugged the coast, leaving the port behind. We could hear the *St. Louis*'s horn in the distance, but my mother did not even react. I turned to look through the back window of the car, and saw how we were moving apart. The boat was leaving the bay, while we were heading for the center of the city. I stopped crying. My father was nothing more than a dot in infinite space, lost again on the enormous liner where we had been a family for the last time.

The lady sitting alongside the driver chose to talk to us just as I was drying my tears.

"I'm Mrs. Samuels," she explained. "We're going to the Hotel Nacional. I hope it will only be for a couple of weeks, until the house in Vedado is furnished and ready. Mr. Rosenthal left everything well organized."

When I heard Papa's name, a shiver ran down my spine. All I wanted to do was to erase the past, to forget, not to suffer anymore. We were safe on land, but my father and Leo were gone.

"So this is the Cuban equivalent of the Hotel Adlon?" asked the Goddess, raising an eyebrow ironically as we entered the Hotel Nacional.

Fortunately, our room did not look out to sea but faced the city, so that we did not have to watch boats entering and leaving the harbor. In any case, the view hardly mattered, for during our entire two weeks' stay in the hotel, Mama kept the curtains closed.

"We have to protect ourselves from the sun and the dust," she insisted.

Whenever they came to straighten up the room, she would shout a stern "No!" if the maid tried to draw back the curtains. Each day it was someone different, and we never left before she arrived, just so that my mother could instruct her that she didn't want a single ray of sunlight in there.

Not once in those weeks did she mention Papa's name. She met Mrs. Samuels every day on one of the terraces of the inside courtyard— the only place we were sheltered from an orchestra that, in her opinion, knew how to play only those fast-paced Cuban *guarachas*.

"Island music," she declared disdainfully.

Sometimes she would ask the waiter if the musicians could please play less loudly or even if they could stop playing altogether.

"Of course, Señora Alma." The reply irritated her still further because the waiter used her first name, possibly because he couldn't pronounce her German surname, whereas she, a foreigner, could speak perfect Spanish.

Meanwhile, the *guaracha* music continued unabated.

My mother decided to wear the same indigo-blue suit whenever she met Mrs. Samuels. When we returned to our room, she would send it to be cleaned and pressed. This was our routine in the Havana hotel to which she swore she would never return.

In the morning, she would meet with our lawyer, Señor Dannón, who was handling the permits for our stay in Cuba. In the afternoon, she saw the representative of the Canadian bank where Papa had transferred most of our money, and who was in charge of our trust fund. After that, she would go to see the hotel manager, always with some complaint or other, usually about the orchestra and the noise that invaded the room even with the windows shut.

I could tell she was happy the day our Cuban identity cards arrived. Not because we finally had the legal right to stay, and the right to reside in the house that until then she had refused to visit, but because she could, once and for all, be free of her ancestral name—thanks to Cuban bureaucracy or the ignorance of incompetent officials unable to spell *Rosenthal*. Now that our names had become more Spanish-sounding, she would be known as "Señora Rosen." My first name was changed from *Hannah* to *Ana*, although I decided to tell everyone it should be pronounced with a *J*, like *Jana*.

Mama never asked for her name to be corrected, although she insisted to her lawyer—a cigar smoker whose hair was thick with grease—that he should immediately try to get her a temporary American visa, because she had to be in New York within four months. He bewildered us with his talk of the decrees and legal resolutions passed by his government where the division of power between civil and military was precarious. When we were back in our room, Mama insisted to me—as if I hadn't heard it already on board ship—that my sibling would be born in New York.

At first, I continued to speak to her in German, just to see if she would keep the promise she had made to Papa, but she always replied in Spanish. I soon decided this ought to be the language we communicated in during our short stay on the island.

She protested from morning to night, whether it was about the heat, the wrinkles we would get from the sun, or the Cubans' lack of manners. They didn't speak, they shouted. They were always late, used far too much cumin in their cooking and sugar in their desserts. The meat was always overcooked, and the drinking water tasted of rusty pipes. I realized that the more she detested everything around her, the busier she was, and so she forgot more quickly what had happened to the 906 passengers stranded on the *St. Louis* and did not have to speak of Papa. At that time, we had no idea what would happen to them: if they would find another island to take them in or be sent back to Germany.

The day we finally descended to the lobby to meet the driver who was to take us to our house in Vedado, Señor Dannón told us that the *St. Louis* had docked at Antwerp, Belgium, and it had been agreed that the passengers would be taken in by Great Britain, France, Holland, and Belgium.

"Señor Rosenthal has already taken a train to Paris."

Mother did not react. She refused to show any emotion in front of a stranger who no doubt was charging her more than he should have for his services. She glanced at a group of men entering the hotel wearing flimsy palm hats and shirts with pleats down the front and mother-of-pearl buttons. "The Cuban uniform," she called it, considering it vulgar.

Mrs. Samuels presented us to a driver in a black suit with gold buttonholes and a cap that made him look like a policeman. He had bulging eyes, and I found it impossible to tell how old he was: sometimes he looked very young; at others, he seemed older than Papa.

"Good morning, señora. My name is Eulogio."

He removed his cap with his left hand, revealing a dark, shaven head. He extended his enormous, callused right hand first to Mama and then to me. I had never felt such a hot hand. He was the same man who a few days earlier had picked us up at the port, but we had not paid him much attention then. I found it hard to identify his accent: I didn't know whether it was typically Cuban—swallowing parts of words and aspirating the *s*'s—or a foreigner who had come from another island or possibly Africa. Now our driver had a name, although we didn't know yet what his family name was, and he was to accompany us throughout our stay in Cuba.

We left the Hotel Nacional along Avenida O and then took Calle 23. The avenues all had letters, in ascending order as we progressed. I opened the car window to feel the hot breeze and hear the noise of the city. Then I closed my eyes and tried to imagine Papa on the train with Leo and Herr Martin arriving at the Gare du Nord Station in Paris. They would take a taxi to the Marais district and share a temporary apartment until our American visas were ready.

I began to see not the streets of Havana but Parisian boulevards. I pictured Papa as in the books he had shown me: sitting at an outdoor café, reading his newspaper, and me running with Leo to one of the oldest squares in the French capital, the Place des Vosges, where Papa told me you could look up at the window of the room where Victor Hugo used to write.

Then the car braked sharply, bringing me back to an island where I had no wish to stay. I passed the time counting the white stone markers identifying each street.

We turned onto an avenue called Paseo, and then again into Calle 21. After we passed Avenida A, the car pulled to a stop a few yards before the next corner.

Mother recognized the house as soon as she saw it. She pushed open the heavy iron gate, and we entered a garden full of yellow, red, and green croton bushes. At the far end was a small roofed-in porch. It was a solid two-story house that was quite modest in comparison with the mansion next door, which occupied a plot twice the size of ours. Señor Eulogio began to unload our suitcases, while I remained on the sidewalk, eager to explore the neighborhood we were going to live in for the next few months.

Mother came to a halt on the threshold, waiting for the man with the darkest skin she had ever seen in her life to open the door for her. A stocky woman with graying hair appeared on the step. She was wearing a white blouse, black skirt, and blue apron.

"Welcome," she said in a gentle but firm voice. "I am Hortensia."

The entrance led straight into a square room with moldings on the walls and ceiling. A tiny palace in the middle of the Caribbean! The furniture was an imitation of classical French styles: armchairs with medallion backs, cabriole legs, and gilt edgings. When she saw them, the new Señora Rosen burst out laughing:

"Where on earth have we come to? Hannah, welcome to the Petit Trianon!"

A long passageway linked this room to the back of the house. At the far end was the dining room, filled with heavy pieces of furniture and a table with a mirror top. A staircase led up to four spacious bedrooms on the second floor. There were gilt-framed mirrors everywhere and endless elaborate marquetry.

My bedroom was above the porch, looking out onto the street. The furniture there was light green, with a small half-moon dressing table surrounded by mirrors, and a wardrobe with hand-painted flowers on it. I opened a door thinking it was a closet and found it was my bathroom. I had another surprise when I saw the floor tiles, which immediately took me back to Alexanderplatz Station: they were the same verdigris color as in the café where I used to meet Leo at midday.

My mother's bedroom was at the back of the house: the dark wood furniture there had clean, straight lines. Hortensia and I peered out of the window—which was to be kept shut from now on—looking across at the guesthouse above a garage that took up most of the yard.

"That's where I live," said Hortensia. "Eulogio's room is next door."

Mother was far from pleased at having people living on the property, but she said nothing. Eventually, she realized that it was probably better than having them in the house. Mrs. Samuels had insisted, "They are absolutely trustworthy."

On the ground floor was a study for my father; I was pleased we were still taking him into account. Next to the study, a small library woke Mother from the lethargy she had been plunged into by her first conversation with that small, plump woman who was to be our only companion for who knew how long. She went through titles and authors, rejecting most of them with her typical expressions: raising an eyebrow, chewing her lip, shaking her head, or rolling her eyes.

"Cuban literature? I don't want a single author from this island in here," she said dismissively.

I wasn't sure Hortensia knew who these authors were, but she nodded anyway. Each time Mother passed by a window, she closed it, but she did allow the sun into the kitchen and dining room, calculating that this would be where Hortensia spent most of her time. And anyway, they did not open onto the street but onto the backyard.

"Eulogio is a very hardworking young man," Hortensia said protectively. This settled my question: Eulogio was not old; he wasn't even my parents' age. I thought he must be ten or twenty years older than me, even though his face had the weary look of an old man. I was itching with curiosity. I wanted to know where he was from, who his parents were, if they were alive or dead.

I went up to my room and heard Mrs. Samuels arrive. From upstairs, you could hear everything that was said in the house, as well as the sounds from outside. I was beginning to learn what it was like to live in an open house in a city full of noise.

I flung myself down on the bed, closed my eyes, and thought of Papa and Leo. We should have stayed with them: *We would all be in Paris now!* I tried to fall asleep, to slow down my mind, but I heard my name being mentioned and listened again: we were going to stay here three months, and we had to be absolutely discreet as long as we stayed in the Petit Trianon.

"In this country, they don't look kindly on foreigners," Mrs. Samuels was explaining. "They think we're here to steal their jobs, their properties, their businesses. Avoid wearing jewelry or too-striking outfits. Don't take anything valuable with you. If you go out into the street, avoid crowds. Things will gradually return to normal, and the *St. Louis* will be forgotten."

This list of the restrictions we would have to live with didn't bother us at all.

"Classes start in two months," Mrs. Samuels added. "Baldor is the best school for Hannah. It's quite near. I'll arrange the details."

Two months! An eternity! It suddenly flashed across my mind that our "Havana transition" was not going to be for just a few months. It would be a year at least.

When it rains, the smells of Cuba explode. Wet grass, whitewash on walls, the breeze, and the tangy sea air all mingle together. My brain was alert, trying to identify each odor separately. I could not get used to the downpours: it was as if the world were coming to an end.

"Be prepared for the hurricanes! From your window, you'll see tiles flying through the air, trees toppling. Only in Cuba, Ana!" exclaimed Hortensia.

"My name is Hannah, and in Spanish you have to pronounce it as if it has a *J* at the beginning," I corrected her at once, as sternly as I could.

"Oh, my girl, *Ana* is so much easier, but as you wish, *Jana* it is! We'll see, though: in school you won't be able to correct everyone all the time."

At that moment, I thought of Eva. It was the first time she had crossed my mind since we had left Berlin. Eva had been with me since I was born and yet she always treated us deferentially. Hortensia, who had only just met us, treated us with a familiarity we were not used to.

When the summer was almost over—if it is ever not summer on this island—we received the first news from Papa. His letter, postmarked Paris, took more than a month to reach Havana. When Eulogio handed my mother the mail, she ran to shut herself in her room. She refused to come down to eat and wouldn't answer when we called up to her.

"I'm fine, don't worry" was all she said.

We thought that perhaps her withdrawal had to do with her medical checkups, because she went to see the doctor on her own, and would never allow Hortensia or me to accompany her. Hortensia thought that perhaps there were problems with the baby, or she had low blood pressure, or was bleeding.

"We should let her rest," she advised me.

Mother waited for the lights to go out in the house and for Hortensia and Eulogio to return to their quarters before she came to my room.

"We've had a letter from Papa," she said simply. Then she lay down beside me, just like in the days when we had the world at our feet.

It wasn't easy for Papa to get in touch with us. The plan was for us to meet up in Havana or New York. He was living austerely, in a fairly quiet neighborhood in Paris. The situation was tense there, too, but nowhere near as bad as it had been in Berlin.

I wanted her to tell me more; to give me details.

"He says we're to look after ourselves, to eat well, and to think about the baby that's on its way. We have to be patient, Hannah."

I would try to be. What choice did I have? But I needed to see Papa. To hear Papa.

"Why didn't he write a few lines for me?" I ventured to ask.

"Papa adores you. He knows you're very strong—much stronger than I am—and he's told you so."

I fell asleep in her arms. I didn't have nightmares but fell into a deep sleep. Tomorrow would be another day, although in Cuba, the worst thing was how heavily and slowly time passed, with too many intervals. A day could be an eternity, but we would get used to it.

In fact, it was Leo I wanted to know about. To hear if he and his father were sharing the same room. If they were safe. Papa should have mentioned it in his letter. I wanted to ask Mama, but decided against it: better to go into her room and find the letter so that I could read it in secret—or even keep it. Only fear of what had happened on board the *St. Louis* held me back: I didn't want the episode with the capsules to be repeated. If Mama's mind faltered in Havana, I could lose her: she could be taken to a clinic, be shut away or even deported, and I would never see her again. Oh, but I so much wanted to see and touch Papa's handwriting!

Mother never agreed to show me the letter. I even came to think that she had invented it to keep my hopes up, when she knew perfectly well that neither of us had a future, that Papa had died during the journey back across the Atlantic, or that he never found a country to take him in and had to return to Germany.

I never really understood her. I tried, but the problem was that we were not alike. She knew that.

With Papa, it was different. He was not ashamed to express what he felt, even if it was pain, frustration, loss, or a sense of failure. I was his little girl, his refuge, the only one who understood him. The only one not to make demands on him or blame him for anything.

Before breakfast on the day that Mama finally left to give birth in New York with her temporary American visa, wearing a loose-fitting jacket to hide her pregnancy, she called Hortensia and me into the living room. She took Hortensia's hands firmly in hers and looked her straight in the eye.

"I don't want Hannah to leave the house. Stay here whenever you can. Every Monday morning, Mr. Dannón will come by to see what you need. Look after Hannah for me, Hortensia," she said, sealing her plea with a fleeting smile.

While Mama was far away, I kept hoping Papa would write and that his letter would reach me rather than her—but there was nothing. By then, war had broken out. England and France had declared war on Germany two days after its September 1 attack on Poland. I imagined Papa unable to leave his dark garret amidst the unending gray of a Paris autumn and winter.

Life was easier after Mother had left. We opened the windows, and I helped Hortensia with the chores. She taught me how to cook custard, rice pudding, bread pudding, pumpkin flan—recipes she had learned from her maternal grandmother, who was from Galicia, Spain, and had always made marvelous desserts.

One day I told Hortensia I wanted to learn how to make a cake with frosting for when we celebrated somebody's birthday. She went on with her task without replying.

"When is your birthday?" I insisted.

She shrugged.

I thought perhaps they didn't register newborn babies in Cuba, or that Hortensia might have come from another country—from Spain, like her grandmother—and so she didn't have her birth certificate.

"I'm a Jehovah's Witness," she said cautiously. "We don't celebrate birthdays or Christmas."

With that, she turned her back on me and went off to wash the dishes. I was ashamed at being so indiscreet and for putting her on the spot. I tried to imagine her feelings. I remembered our last months in Berlin, how bitter we had felt at the contempt we were shown. An impure religion. So Hortensia herself was also impure in a way. I closed my eyes and saw her pursued along the streets of Berlin, beaten, arrested, driven out of her home.

From her reaction, I thought these "witnesses" must also be seen as undesirables in Havana. Hortensia hadn't shown pride in her beliefs, although she didn't seem ashamed of them, either: it was more that her tone of voice implied they were something to be kept private.

"Don't worry," I wanted to tell her, "we don't celebrate Christmas, either." *That is, unless in her new life here Mama decides to do so in order to pass for a "normal" person and hide the fact she is a refugee that no country will accept.*

I loved spending time with Hortensia, who was a widow, as she told me on one of those airless Havana nights. At that time, so that I wouldn't feel all alone in the house, Hortensia slept in the room next to mine. I insisted I wasn't afraid and that I could be left on my own—that I was already twelve years old—but she had promised Mama, and making a promise meant it was a debt she had to honor.

Her husband had died of a terrible illness I preferred not to ask about, and she had a younger sister, Esperanza, who lived on the outskirts of Havana and had recently gotten married.

"It was such a lovely wedding," she told me, eyes shining, perhaps because her own had been nothing special or because it had ended so sadly.

Hortensia had never had children. Now it was up to her sister to add to a family that had seemed at risk of dying out.

"She is a Witness, and so is her husband," she said in a low voice.

Another secret between us, one that we resolved not to share with anyone.

By now, I had started to attend the Baldor School, and every afternoon I came back more convinced than ever that there was nothing new for me to learn. I was bored at school, where the intention was to make a young lady out of me. We had lessons in dressmaking, cooking, typing, handicrafts, and handwriting. I was known as "the Polack," and accepted it. I didn't try to make any friends, because I knew that in the end we would be leaving this island where we had nothing of value to lose. At school there was constant talk of the war, and that was what truly frightened me.

Whenever we got mail, I hoped to receive a letter from Papa, but all that came were postcards from Mama in New York. Flights could be suspended, because anything could happen during a war: it occurred to me that, for the good of the baby, she might decide to stay and live in our Manhattan apartment. Who then would handle all the expenses? My visa and documents? I didn't have access to anything. I felt abandoned and took refuge in Hortensia, who spoke more about the life of her parents in Spain than her own life in Cuba. Perhaps this was also a transit island for her, a childless widow condemned to bury her loved ones here—a country where she would probably be buried, too, because Spain was an illusion that belonged to the past.

"It's a boy. He weighs seven pounds. They've named him Gustav. Señora Alma sent word while you were at school."

Hortensia was even more contented than me. She told me the details while she was stirring a dessert on a slow heat. I think I would have liked the idea of having a sister more, so that I could have played with her and could have gone with her to live in Paris with Papa.

"Having a boy is the best thing that could have happened," Hortensia assured me. "A man can make a life for himself and look after the pair of you—two women all alone in this country."

When I heard I was no longer an only child, I went to our small home library, intending to give my mother a surprise on her return. I made a great effort to remove from the shelves all the books written by Cuban authors, as she had wanted when we first arrived. That would be my gift to her.

Eulogio drove us to a bookshop in the center of Havana where we looked for whatever they had of French literature. The only problem was that the books were in Spanish; there were no editions in the original. Hortensia pointed out the man who worked in the bookshop, or who was possibly its owner.

"He's a Polack, like you."

"I'm not Polish!" I burst out. "What is this obsession with Poles?"

When he saw me, the man smiled; it seemed he had realized immediately that I was a phantom like him. That I had the same mark on my face. That we were both undesirables, lost in a city mercilessly punished by the sun's rays. Hortensia and I went over to ask about books in their original language.

At first, he spoke to me in Hebrew, which made me jump. He went on in German, but I replied instantly in Spanish. When he realized I wasn't going to change, he reminded me, again in Hebrew, that no one would understand what we were saying, and that there was no need to be afraid. My eyes started to tear, and he must have seen how fearful I was.

Don't cry, Hannah, nobody's done anything to you, stay calm, I told myself, although my legs felt suddenly weak. I never should have left home; I should have followed Mrs. Samuels's advice! To have stayed hidden, not attracting any attention, avoiding all Cubans, living with the windows closed, in total darkness.

I recovered, determined not to give in.

"Where can I find books by Proust in French?" I asked in Spanish.

The man, who had a huge nose, curly hair, and dandruff all over the shoulders of his jacket, answered in German-accented Spanish that, because of the war, he couldn't guarantee the arrival of books from Europe.

"Before, any order from France would get here in under a month."

Smiling in a friendly way, and following a lengthy explanation in French that was much more fluent than his Spanish, he asked if I was French.

All I managed to do was thank him. Hortensia was taken aback by my timidity, but she didn't ask me anything. We left the bookshop loaded down with works my mother was bound to love: Flaubert, Proust, Hugo, Balzac, Dumas—all in Spanish. The perfect addition to her Petit Trianon. It remained to be seen whether Gustav would allow her time to read, which had always been one of her greatest pleasures.

Eulogio could not understand why we needed more books when we had not read all the ones in the library. He thought they were good only for making the shelves look less empty. The things rich people did!

Since "Señora Alma" was absent, we broke the rules. For example, Hortensia sat with me in the back of the car and insisted I should find friends:

"The next few years will fly by, and if you don't get married, you'll end up an old maid. And a stuck-up young woman, which is never a good thing."

Her comments made me laugh as we rode along, the wind streaming in through the open windows and ruffling our hair. In my mind's eye, I saw Leo's face. I was convinced he would come for me and that we would be together all our lives. But that was my most precious secret, and I had no reason to tell it to Hortensia.

The best thing about my days with Hortensia was that, to some extent, they helped me forget our real problems. I learned that, to survive, it was best to live in the present. On this island, there was no past or future. Your destiny was today.

Shortly before we reached our house, traveling along streets full of drivers who ignored all directions and signs, I plucked up the courage to ask Eulogio about his parents. He told me his family was very poor. His father had left his mother with nine children: six boys and three girls. Eulogio was the middle child. He had managed to escape this poverty thanks to an uncle on his mother's side who was a driver and taught him the skills. His uncle used to say that of all his brothers and sisters, he was the only one who was honest and had "character." He helped his mother and whenever he could went to visit her. The rest of the family had grown up and was scattered all over the island. His grandparents had been African slaves, but his family was from Guanabacoa, a very pretty little village surrounded by hills, where everyone knew one another.

"Where is Guanabacoa?" I asked, intrigued.

"It's in the southeast part of the city, not far from here. I'll take you there one day. I bet you'll like it. I grew up there and know it like the back of my hand."

He braked sharply to allow a woman pushing a carriage to cross in front of us.

"That's where your people's cemetery is, too," he added.

I couldn't understand what he meant. There was a moment's silence. It was an embarrassing situation, particularly for Hortensia, who felt guilty for having let me be so familiar with an employee. If my mother heard about it, both she and Eulogio could be dismissed.

But rather than remaining silent, I kept asking questions:

"What people's cemetery?"

Hortensia looked at him, waiting to see what he would say. As we turned the corner on Paseo to enter Calle 21, Eulogio explained:

"The Polack cemetery."

Anna

2014

The first place we visit in Havana is a cemetery. I had never been in a city dedicated to the dead before. Aunt Hannah has insisted on visiting Alma—her mother, Dad's grandmother, my great-grandmother—who was laid to rest in Cuban ground in 1970. Mom wasn't too happy about the idea, but when she sees I am enthusiastic, she gives in.

We climb into another wreck of a car; Catalina up front, the three of us in the back. Aunt Hannah has bathed in violet water, and Mom is wearing a thick layer of sunscreen that makes her look like a corpse. As we go up Avenida 12 and cross Calle 23 to enter the cemetery, I'm assaulted by the smells of all kinds of flowers that have been cut to comfort the living.

The heavy scent of roses and jasmine mixes with traces of orange blossoms and basil. Wreaths of an intense green, as well as red, yellow, and white roses, are piled on a cart pulled by a gaunt old woman with messy hair and leathery skin.

I want to start taking photos, but the car is still moving. Then we stop for Catalina to buy her roses. The combined smell of cigarettes and sweat coming from the old woman with the cart, the flowers, and the stench in the road make me hold my breath as I point my camera at her. She pulls back in fear. My lungs are crying out for oxygen, I cling to my aunt to protect me with her fragrance of violets. Too many smells!

Aunt Hannah takes this as a demonstration of affection and strokes my cheeks, which are burning from the heat. Mom is proud of me—me, the one who is always so solitary and removed, being friendly toward the only other person who is a link to the father I never knew. I close my eyes and let myself be. For the first time, I feel close to my aunt.

The cemetery is a real walled city. The entrance arch is crowned by a religious sculpture.

"It represents faith, hope, and charity," Catalina explains when she notices me looking at it. We park inside the cemetery and get out to walk the rest of the way. Catalina is carrying red and white roses, and has sprigs of basil tucked behind her ear.

"They're refreshing," she explains.

Seeing that I am trying to take in everything around me, she becomes my guide.

"Señora Alma has not yet found peace. She suffered a lot. She left with a heavy suitcase, and you should go to your grave as lightly as possible. Remember what I'm saying, child. And that goes for you, too," she says, raising her voice so that Aunt Hannah can hear.

We're surprised at the familiarity with which Catalina treats Aunt Hannah. She doesn't use the polite form of address in Spanish, although she is always respectful. She talks to Aunt Hannah as if she had more experience.

"We have to leave the past behind," says Catalina, sniffing the roses. She goes on: "These are for Señora Alma. She still needs a lot of help!"

We walk along slowly, not because of my aunt but because of Catalina, whose legs are heavy. She is constantly fanning herself. Aunt Hannah leans on Mom's arm as she gazes at the avenues lined with mausoleums. Leaving the main avenue, we are surprised by a sea of marble sculptures: there are crosses as far as the eye can see, laurel wreaths, and upside-down torches adorning the monuments. It's a real ode to death.

Some of the mausoleums look like plundered palaces. According to Aunt Hannah, a lot of them have been vandalized. "A great society in decay," Mom whispers.

I stop to read some headstones. One is dedicated to the heroes of the republic, another to firemen, another to martyrs, and, of course, to military and literary heroes. On one tomb I read this inscription: "Kind passerby: Absent your mind from the cruel world for a few moments, and dedicate a loving, peaceful thought to these two beings whose earthly happiness was cut short by fate, and whose mortal remains lie at rest in this sepulcher in fulfillment of a sacred promise. We thank you from eternity." This helps take my mind off the unbearable May heat.

At Catalina's request, we head for the central chapel. She says she wants to pray for her dead, and for ours as well, I suppose. While we wait for her, we stand in silence. When she comes out, we turn onto Avenida Fray Jacinto to look for the Rosen family plot, and finally arrive at a mausoleum with six columns and an open porch. A temple that provides shade for its dead and for those who come to visit them. The family name is engraved near the top.

There are five tombstones, one for each of the Rosens, whether or not they were born, lived, or died in this supposed place of transit. The first reads "Max Rosen, 1895–1942"; the second, "Alma Rosen, 1900–1970"; the third, "Gustav Rosen, 1939–1968." The fourth is the one for my father: "Louis Rosen, 1959–2001." A fifth stone is still blank: I guess it is reserved for my aunt, the last Rosen on the island.

Catalina kneels down with great difficulty in front of my great-grandmother Alma's tomb, because in the end, she explains, that was the only one that really had a body in it. The others are symbolic burials. The mausoleum will keep for all eternity only the two women who one day disembarked from a liner that had no destination. The men of the family died far away, and their bodies were never recovered.

Catalina joins her hands together, lowers her head, and then stands for a few minutes saying her prayers for a woman who "came into this world to suffer and left it full of sorrow." She lays the roses on my great-grandmother's tomb, then straightens up very slowly. Mom takes four stones from her bag—where did she find them?—and places them on each of the four named tombs. Catalina looks almost offended—her eyes open wide in astonishment, as if she is waiting for an explanation for such rudeness, but nobody bothers to offer one.

"There isn't a dead person in the world who would prefer a stone to a flower," she says to me in a whisper, so as not to upset Mom or my aunt, who seems pleased at this gesture by a woman who also loved her beloved Louis.

"Flowers wither," I explain to Catalina. "Stones last. They will be there forever, unless somebody dares to move them. Stones protect."

However much I explain, Catalina will never understand. To her, the roses cost money: they were cultivated and cared for. The dusty stones had appeared from heaven knows where. It's not right for them to be placed near the dead.

Still grumbling about this, Catalina pauses, takes my hand, and asks me to follow her. Aunt Hannah and Mom are still standing in silence at this mausoleum my great-grandmother had built when she received the news of Great-grandfather's death. On our way here, my aunt told us that on that day, Alma had made a vow: all the Rosens who ended their days on the island, as well as those born here, were to be buried in the family plot. For Great-grandmother, forgiveness did not exist. She blamed this island for the misery, and swore that "for at least the next one hundred years" Cuba would pay for the tragedy of her family.

"The curse of the Rosens!" Aunt Hannah concludes with a resigned smile, recognizing the hatred her mother had tried unsuccessfully to instill in her.

Catalina leads me to a much-visited tomb strewn with flowers. I can see several people standing reverently before a white marble sculpture of a woman with a baby in her arms, leaning against a cross. The worshippers move away without turning their backs on the figure.

When I raise my camera, Catalina shoots me a stern look.

"Not here," she says, covering my lens with her hand.

She closes her eyes for several minutes before speaking again.

Finally, she says without explanation, "This is the tomb of Amelia la Milagrosa."

Waiting for her to continue, I watch the silent ritual of the pilgrims visiting the tomb.

"La Milagrosa was a woman who died in childbirth. They buried her with the baby at her feet, but when the tomb was opened years later, they found the child in her arms."

Catalina forces me to go up close and stroke the child's marble head. "For good luck," she whispers to me.

When we return to the family plot, we see Aunt Hannah with one hand on her mother's tombstone. As she straightens up, it occurs to me that it will be up to us, her descendants, to engrave her name on the headstone left blank for her. Someday we will come here and leave a stone on it. If Catalina outlives her, she'll bring her flowers.

"I think the time has come to reclaim our real name," Aunt Hannah says gravely, staring at the name engraved over this tiny Greek temple in the midst of the Caribbean. "For us to become Rosenthals again."

As she is talking to her mother, she places another stone on the tomb.

At dusk, we return home, and Mom and I go to bed without supper. I think this worries my aunt and Catalina, but the fact is, we are exhausted. In bed, Mom talks endlessly about Aunt Hannah until I fall asleep.

She says that Aunt Hannah is thin and frail but is protected by her dignity. I, too, am amazed at the way she holds her body erect like a ballerina. Mom says her gestures are feminine; there is an unusual gentleness about them. And despite everything she has suffered, she refuses to let any hint of bitterness show in her face.

"I can see you in her, Anna. You've inherited her beauty and her determination," she whispers in my ear. I barely hear her, as sleep is creeping up on me. "We were so lucky to find her!"

Hannah
1940–1942

My mother missed cold mornings. She detested the endless summer and the constant tropical downpours on the island.

"It's an archipelago of frogs and savages. Aren't you nostalgic for the seasons? Do you think we'll ever enjoy autumn, winter, or spring again? Summer should be a season of transition, Hannah," she would repeat.

We lived on an island with only two seasons, dry and wet: where the vegetation grew ferociously; where everybody complained and talked of nothing but the past. As if they knew what the past really was! The past didn't exist; it was an illusion. There was never any going back.

She returned to Havana with Gustav on a warm, humid thirty-first of December. He was the smallest baby I had ever seen. Not a hair on his head, and very grumpy.

"He's like a grouchy old man," laughed Hortensia.

The baby's arrival had changed the demanding Señora Alma, at least momentarily. She didn't complain about the open windows letting in sunlight, or the noise of voices and clattering dishes from the neighbor's when she was feeding her children rice and black beans. Nor did she seem to mind that we listened in the kitchen to absurd radio soap operas full of betrayals, tears, and illegitimate pregnancies, or that Hortensia taught me to cook delicious doughnuts, or that we flooded the house with the smells of vanilla essence and cinnamon.

That first night, we were left alone with the baby. Eulogio had gone to celebrate the New Year with his family in Guanabacoa, and Hortensia had asked for a few days' leave. Neither would be back until January 6. As soon as they had left, Mother gave me a big surprise:

"Papa is fine!"

I didn't ask how she knew. If she had got another letter, she wouldn't tell me. I tried not to let any emotion show on my face and went on trying to entertain that blob of a baby, who did not react to any of my songs or funny noises.

No news of Leo, was my only thought. I found it hard to understand why I hadn't received any sign of life from him.

I realized we were on our own for the first time in a strange, hostile city. Alone, with a newborn baby, and without a family doctor or anybody we could turn to in an emergency. Hortensia had left us some cooked meat; I would see to the rest. When she saw me taking charge of the kitchen, my mother couldn't believe her eyes. She seemed to be thinking, *I've lost her! If I'd been away another month, I wouldn't recognize her.*

She went back to her room, with the baby in the wicker basket that Hortensia had brought home before Mother returned from New York. She had lined it prettily with blankets embroidered with blue silk and called it a "Moses." She would say, "Move the Moses over here." "Don't put the Moses so high!" "Rock the baby in the Moses, and you'll see how he falls asleep." At first we didn't understand what she was referring to.

That Moses turned out to be a great help during Gustav's first months, because we could carry it easily around the house and even take it out onto the patio so that at sunset or early in the morning he could get some sun when it was at its most gentle—if it could ever be called that. My mother said that, like plants, babies needed warmth and light to grow, and so I took over giving my brother his daily sunbath.

That last day of December, the three of us fell asleep around nine o'clock in my mother's room. It had been a long, exhausting day. Gustav demanded to be fed every three hours; otherwise his cries would have reached the North Pole. Every time she breast-fed him, he fell asleep, but as soon as he woke up, he started protesting again. It was an endless cycle.

We were not in the mood to celebrate. In reality, there *was* nothing to celebrate: the two of us were stranded in the Caribbean; Papa was in hiding with other "impure" people in Paris, with the Ogres snapping at his heels. And now we had a baby boy who made me wonder with each passing moment why we had brought him into this hostile world. So we went to bed almost without realizing that one year was ending and another beginning, just as terrible as the previous one.

At midnight we heard explosions and an unusual commotion in what was normally such a quiet neighborhood. Mother woke with a start, and then closed the window and curtains. We went to my room to peep out through the shutters and saw our neighbors throwing buckets of water into the street. Some of them were even throwing buckets filled with ice. We couldn't understand what was going on, if we were being threatened, or if this was just some exuberant local custom.

Our next-door neighbor opened a bottle of champagne with an extravagant gesture: the cork flew off and almost hit our window. She drank straight from the bottle and passed it to her husband, a bald, shirtless man with a very hairy chest. Then the music began: *guarachas* mixed with shouts of "Happy New Year!" from all sides.

We were leaving another decade behind as well. The sinister 1939 already belonged to the past. My mother was observing the extraordinary spectacle from her Petit Trianon, protected by the walls of a house she would gradually transform into a fortress.

When she saw us at the window, our neighbor raised her frothing bottle and wished us a "Happy Nineteen Forty!"

We went back to sleep. When we woke, we were in another decade. Our life had changed. We had a new member of the family: a little boy who would spend more time in the arms of a stranger than in his mother's. Little by little, even if we found it hard to admit, Hortensia, in her own way, became another Rosenthal.

I couldn't understand why that woman was so determined to cover Gustav all over with talcum powder and to wet his head with cologne every time she changed him. He would start to cry the moment she sprinkled him with that lilac-colored alcohol.

"It cools him," she insisted.

On this island, "cooling oneself" was a mania. Or rather, an obsession. The idea of "cooling yourself" explained the presence of palms, coconut trees, parasols, electric fans, and handheld ones, as well as lemonade, which they drank at all hours of the day and night. "Sit here by the window, so you can catch the breeze . . ." "Let's walk on the other side of the street, where there's some shade . . ." "Let's wait for the sun to go down . . ." "Go and have a dip . . ." "Cover your head . . ." "Open the window so there's some air . . ." Few things were seen as more important than cooling oneself.

Hortensia had my brother's room painted blue and hung lace curtains on the windows that matched the white furniture. Gustav was little more than a pink blob in the midst of his blue sheets, and his freckles and reddish hair were just beginning to show. His only toys would be a wooden rocking horse standing unused by the window and a sad-looking gray teddy bear.

We talked to him in English, to prepare him for our journey to New York to live with Papa. Hortensia stared at us in bewilderment, trying to decipher a language that to her sounded harsh.

"Why do you want to complicate the life of a poor child who hasn't said his first word yet?" she muttered to herself.

She spoke to Gustav in Spanish, with a maternal softness and rhythm to which we were unaccustomed. One morning, while she was changing him, we heard her conversing with him.

"What does my lovely little Polack have to say?"

Our eyes opened wide, but we said nothing. We simply laughed and let her carry on. That was the day I realized my mother had not had Gustav circumcised, violating an ancient tradition. I didn't judge her: I had no right to. I understood she was doing everything she could to erase all possible traces of guilt—the guilt that led us to flee a country I once thought I belonged to. She wanted to save her son; to give him the chance to start again from zero. He had been born in New York, was for the time being in Cuba, and would never know where his parents had come from. It was a perfect plan.

But, circumcised or not, here Gustav would be just another "Polack."

Without asking, Hortensia had given the boy a little jewel. This made my mother uncomfortable, because she did not know whether to thank her, give it back to her, or pay her for it. She also thought that wearing a pin on his nightgowns was dangerous, even if it was made of gold. The small bead dangling from a safety pin was always attached to his white linen gown, on the same side as his heart.

"It's made of black amber, to ward off evil," Hortensia explained to my mother very seriously. She wasn't seeking Mother's approval or disapproval, because she was sure we also wanted only what was good for the boy.

That black stone on his chest was to become his inseparable talisman. We accepted it because, if at least part of Gustav's childhood was to be spent in Cuba, then he would have to learn to live with the customs and traditions of the country that had taken him in.

In a matter of months, my body began to change: curves and shapes began to appear where I least expected them. I started wearing loose-fitting blouses, mostly because of the heat, but one morning, when she saw me lifting Gustav out of the Moses, Mother seemed suddenly to realize what was going on and immediately went off to the kitchen to have a secret chat with Hortensia.

I was not ready to become a woman. In my dreams, I still saw Leo as a child, and it terrified me to think that while I was growing up, he was still as small as I saw him in memory.

A few days later, Eulogio appeared with the delivery that was to change our lives in the Petit Trianon. It was a Singer sewing machine, together with a supply of material that was almost too big for the entrance to the dining room. I was delighted, because at least now we had something definite to do, and I set about organizing the different-colored rolls of cloth in a wardrobe, together with boxes of buttons, balls of yarn, silk ribbons, bundles of lace, elastics, and zippers. That wasn't all: there were also long reams of tissue paper, measuring tapes, needles, and thimbles.

The small iron table contained what Hortensia called "the arm": a mechanism containing a needle, a bobbin, and a pulley. At the bottom was a treadle I loved to operate whenever I was asked to rethread the bobbin, because I was the one "with the best eyes." We called the machine simply "la Singer."

Designer and seamstress spent their time measuring me and coming up with patterns for my new wardrobe, which we decorated with bows and lace. They forgot their worries and concentrated on tucks, flounces, and pleats. Soon afterward, Eulogio brought a mannequin that made my mother almost euphoric. I think that in those days she was happy, even if her new "Cuban uniform" gave the opposite impression: a black skirt with a white long-sleeved blouse, buttoned up right to the top.

The Goddess's Berlin glamour had given way to the most discreet simplicity. The truth was she didn't have the time or energy for nostalgia. Her beauty rituals had also been reduced to having her hair cut at home. Scissors in hand, Hortensia made sure her locks remained at shoulder length.

"Cut away, Hortensia, don't be afraid!" she would encourage her novice hairdresser, who gingerly snipped off another inch.

Hortensia knitted cardigans for Gustav that he refused to wear, and put so much starch into his collars that he began to howl the instant he saw them. To calm him, she would clutch him to her breast and sing him boleros about deaths and burials that made my hair stand on end, but which for some unknown reason seemed to soothe him.

By the time he was two and a half, Gustav was a curious child, restless and rebellious. He had none of the Rosenthal reserve: he was more than ready to show his emotions openly. He saw me more as an aunt than a sister; and, far from disturbing us, Mother and I were touched by his closeness to Hortensia.

To him, Spanish was the language of affection, games, tastes, and smells. English meant order and discipline. Mother and I obviously were part of the latter.

Without our realizing it, Gustav, the ship captain's name, slowly became Gustavo, and we accepted it. The Spanish version was better suited to that impatient young boy who almost always went around half naked and covered in sweat.

He had a voracious appetite. Hortensia fed him Cuban food: rice with black beans, chicken fricassee, fried plantain and sweet potato, thick soups full of vegetables and sausage, as well as the desserts I had learned to make like an expert. In the afternoons, I would help Hortensia prepare the sweets she used to spoil him with. In fact, she would have liked to have him all to herself; she spoke to him all the time in diminutives.

Gustavo had not inherited anything from Mother or me. We had not succeeded in transmitting to him a single habit or tradition of our own. We had no idea if one day he would discover that his first language was German, and that his family name was not Rosen but Rosenthal.

Gustavo was Hortensia's. Still under the shadow of Papa's absence, Mother gradually had less and less to do with his upbringing. Insecurity, misinformation, and the impossibility of being able to think of the future prevented her from focusing on a child she had not asked to bring into the world. Sometimes Gustavo even slept in Hortensia's room, or went with her to spend weekends at her sister Esperanza's house, where they also didn't celebrate birthdays, Christmas, or the New Year.

For Gustavo, life outside the Petit Trianon existed thanks to a simple woman whom we paid to look after us. At nighttime, Hortensia was the one who put him to bed, told him scary stories about witches and sleeping princesses, and sang him lullabies: "*Duérmete mi niño, duérmete mi amor, duérmete pedazo de mi corazón.*" That was her formula to make Gustavo capitulate until the next morning.

He was playful, even mischievous. He liked sitting on Eulogio's lap behind the wheel of the car, pretending he was driving at top speed.

"You'll go far in this country, my boy," Eulogio would encourage him. "This boy knows a lot!"

This prediction terrified us. Who wanted to go far in "this country," when all we wished was to get out as quickly as possible and settle as far away as we could from this interminable heat?

Three years later, I was as tall as an adult woman; too tall for the tropics. I was even taller than the boys in my class, who for that reason avoided me. They saw me as an ally of our teacher. Occasionally the poor woman did call on me for help in controlling that bunch of ignoramuses, who, because they came from rich families, thought they were better than her. They taunted me all the time: Polacks only married among themselves, they didn't wash every day, they were mean and greedy. I pretended not to hear them: in the end, I thought, those idiots were never going to realize I wasn't a Polack and that there was no way I would ever want to be accepted by them.

Mother continued to design and make her one black-and-white tropical outfit. Communication with Papa had been cut completely, and we had heard nothing about Leo and his father. What else could we have done? The Second World War was at its height: every night before I closed my eyes, I prayed for it to end. But in my innocent prayer, I never spoke of who might lose. What interested me was for order to be reestablished— and by "order," I meant above all international mail service: I wanted to be able to receive and send letters to Paris, to hear news of our loved ones.

One Tuesday afternoon—it had to be a Tuesday!—in midsummer,

the worst time of year in this godforsaken city, the lawyer looking after our finances appeared without warning at our home.

That day, which was to be added to my list of tragic Tuesdays, I understood that Señor Dannón was one of us. Even though the tropics had softened his "impurities," he was as undesirable as the Rosenthals, whom he helped for a monthly fee. He was never called a Polack, though, because his ancestors had come from Spain or possibly even from Turkey. Like us, his parents had fled and found shelter on an island that admitted his entire family. Without splitting them up, as they had done with ours.

In a gruff voice, Señor Dannón asked us both to take a seat in the living room. Hortensia took Gustavo out onto the patio to leave us alone. Even though she did not entirely trust him, she knew that the lawyer always brought important news.

I can't reproduce what he said, because I didn't properly understand it. Only the words *camp* and *concentration* made an impression on me. I found it impossible to understand why we still hadn't finished paying for our guilt. I wanted to run out into the street and shout "Papa!" But who would hear me? What had we done? How long would we have to go on carrying this burden of grief? I buried my face in my hands and began to sob uncontrollably. *Papa! Papa!* I could at least shout his name silently inside and weep in front of Señor Dannón, even if Mother did not like it. *Papa!*

In a sudden show of solidarity, the lawyer—who, after all, was nothing more than a stranger to us—told us that he had lost his only daughter. A typhus epidemic that had claimed the lives of thousands of children in Havana had kept her in bed until her tiny, frail body finally succumbed. That was why he and his wife had decided to stay in Cuba, close to their child's remains.

I felt like saying to him, "We don't have the strength to weep over an unknown girl. How stupid of me. We have so few tears left, señor. Don't expect compassion from us. We still have a lot to weep over."

"*Papa!*" It was more than I could bear, and I shouted his name out loud. Alarmed, Hortensia came bustling in. Behind her, Gustavo began to yell.

I ran up to my room and shut myself in. I tried to comfort myself by thinking of Leo but avoided imagining him in Paris. I had no idea what his fate had been! Only the Leo I had known, the one I had run with along the streets of Berlin and the decks of the *St. Louis*, could be of any help to me at that moment.

I shed all the tears I had left. I waited for the pain to subside in my chest, for my eyes not to show the anguish and hatred eating me up. I longed for a typhus epidemic or any other calamity that could get me out of there. I saw myself in bed, yellow and weak from typhoid fever, my hair falling out in clumps on the pillow, surrounded by doctors, and Mother pale and nervous in a corner of the room. What about Papa? And Leo? Neither of them appeared in this daydream of mine, even though I was the one who decided how it began and ended.

Mother, also shut in her room, spent the night in despair. She stifled her crying in her pillow, but I could still hear her.

I stayed in my room until the next morning, until I felt I had run dry of tears. Hortensia did not ask what it was all about. She must have thought the worst, but we had breakfast as though nothing had happened. After all, we did not really know Papa's fate.

I didn't dare ask if it wouldn't be better to go to our apartment in New York, where Mother had once told me we could see the sun coming up from our living room overlooking the park. To a city where there were four seasons and where tulips grew. I understood that perhaps Mother was afraid she would not be able to escape the Ogres' tentacles, now that they had reached the farthest corners of Europe. Paris was filled with the loudspeakers of terror and draped with the most awful combination of colors: red, white, and black.

Soon we would feel their presence in Cuba, a country that seemed to be favoring them already. In fact, I was sure the Cubans had reached an agreement with the Ogres to prevent the arrival of the ship that could have been our salvation.

From that day on, Mother never went near "la Singer" again. I sensed that our stay on the island would no longer be a temporary one but would last forever.

Anna

2014

*D*iego appears freshly bathed, with wet hair, and in his smartest clothes: an ironed shirt tucked inside wrinkled shorts, white socks, and the black sneakers he wears on special occasions.

I have to define his scent, but it's not easy: a mixture of sun, the sea, and talcum powder. In Havana, all the people dust themselves in talcum powder. You can see it on women's chests, babies' arms, the napes of men's necks. The white powder contrasts vividly with Diego's skin. I realize why he leaves his hair wet: it looks combed. As they dry, his curls start to become one big, messy tangle.

Things I'm not allowed to do in New York seem to be fine here. It's not so much that Mom has great faith in Diego, who must be the same age as me; it's more that she doesn't want to go against Aunt Hannah, who insists she shouldn't worry, that Diego is a good boy liked by everyone in the neighborhood.

"Let her enjoy herself. Nothing's going to happen to her," she reassures Mom.

I think I could live in Havana. I feel free; Diego senses this and laughs. He takes me by the hand, and we run together down a side street. "To the sea," he says. On the corner, we come across a skinny dog, and Diego comes to a halt.

"Better go this way," he says, and heads off in the opposite direction toward the tree-lined avenue I recognize at once: Paseo, the one we drove down when we first arrived.

Diego is afraid of dogs. I don't ask him why but follow him without a word. I don't want to embarrass my only friend here. We walk down the middle of Paseo, heading for the shore.

"Beyond that, there's nothing but the North, where you live," he explains. "My father went there one day and never came back."

We reach the seawall called the Malecón. I can't tell from here how far this crumbling cement structure stretches. I ask Diego if the whole of Havana is surrounded by a wall like this.

"Are you crazy, girl? This is just one part. Come on, let's go!" he says, setting off at a run.

Even though I can hardly breathe, I run for a while, too, because I don't want to lose sight of him: I'm not sure I'd know how to get home. *Up Paseo to Calle 21*, I repeat to myself, so I won't forget. Paseo and Calle 21, and from there, yes, I think I could find my aunt's house. Besides, she's the only German in that neighborhood, so everyone must know her and would give me directions. I'm not lost. I'm not going to get lost.

At last, Diego stops and sits on the rough wall that's dripping with salt spray and blackened from car exhaust.

"How is it going with your aunt?"

He makes me laugh. He doesn't hold back, simply asks whatever he feels like. I think I should answer like that, play his game, but he speaks before I have the chance to.

"My grandma says a long time ago your aunt smothered her mother with a pillow. That the old woman wouldn't die, so your aunt grew tired of her and killed her."

I can't stop laughing, and when he sees I'm not offended, he goes on with his cheap soap opera:

"There was no funeral. People say she still keeps the dried-out body in a bag hidden in a wardrobe."

"Diego, yesterday we went to the cemetery. We visited my great-grandmother's tomb. I saw the headstone with her name on it. Believe me, there's no mummified body in the house. But if you want, you can come and ask my aunt to her face. I dare you!"

"The Rosens have been cursed ever since they came to Cuba," he babbles, pouring out words he only half pronounces. "One died in a plane crash. Another, when the Twin Towers went down."

"That was my father," I interrupt him, and it's the end of the game. Diego turns serious, eyes downcast, ashamed of himself. I wait a few moments, to prolong the torment. I don't tell him that I never knew my father; that he died before I was born. That it doesn't upset me if he talks about his death, because this is how it's always been for me: I have no memories of him.

He's the one who breaks the silence and again sets off running along the Malecón, until we come to a plaza filled with black flags and banners with weird messages on them. Some kind of speech is coming from loudspeakers that I can't really understand: "We owe everything to the Revolution." "Socialism or death." "No one here will surrender." And "We will keep fighting."

"What is this?" I ask. Diego can see I'm frightened.

"It's nothing," he says, laughing. "We're used to it."

But even though he tries to calm me, I'm sure I have stumbled into a danger zone. The men in uniform could come and arrest us.

"Don't worry. You're a foreigner, and that's more valuable than being a Cuban. No one is going to arrest you. If they arrested anybody, it would be me, for being with you."

"Let's get out of here, Diego. I don't want them to worry at home. We've gone too far."

Between the screeching loudspeakers and Diego's explanations, I begin to feel even more nervous and start shaking.

❦

The next day at the breakfast table, Aunt Hannah is waiting with a yellowing photo in her hand. Her lips are curled in a smile, and there is a special gleam in her eyes.

"It's all we could recover that belonged to Papa," she says, showing us the small image of a little girl sitting on a woman's lap. "There was also his yellow star, which was placed in his tomb in the Rosen mausoleum. Another of Great-grandmother Alma's ideas."

The photo is of Alma and Hannah. It was the last snapshot they took before leaving Berlin; my great-grandfather Max kept it through his entire long ordeal.

"After the *St. Louis* was turned back from Havana and was also refused entry into the United States and Canada, Papa was one of the two hundred twenty-four passengers placed in France. Perhaps because he was fluent in French, or because he knew the city, Papa ended up there rather than Holland or Belgium, two other countries that took in passengers. If he had been among the two hundred eighty-seven they sent on to England—the only ones who were spared in the Second World War and did not end up in concentration camps—today we would have a body we could honor in the mausoleum alongside my mother's."

Aunt Hannah tells the story rapidly in a low voice, as if she herself did not want to hear it. She mentions figures and dates so coldly it surprises Mom. Aunt Hannah's smile starts to fade, and her eyes are now a misty blue.

"On the night of July 16, 1942, my father was one of the victims of the infamous Vélodrome d'Hiver roundup when all the impure were arrested by the French police. He was transported to Auschwitz, the death camp . . ." She sighs. "He didn't survive. He was very weak, and I'm sure he let himself die. In our family, we don't kill ourselves; we let ourselves die."

She stares us in the eyes and clasps our hands. Hers are cold, possibly because she has blood circulation problems or because she is telling us something she wanted to forget but couldn't.

Mom, who until now has kept her composure, begins to weep silently. She doesn't want to upset Aunt Hannah, who is struggling to finish her story.

"A friend of your great-grandfather's named Mr. Albert, who was with him during the first months in Auschwitz, managed to save the photo and star."

"Papa asked him to send them to me, because he thought my mother must have succumbed on the way and would be resting in peace. They all underestimated Alma." She smiled again. "She was stronger than we thought. Until the day came when she could no longer go on."

Mom looks like her heart is about to break. Aunt Hannah continues:

"We should have stayed together on the *St. Louis*." Now my aunt is speaking resignedly, and her blue eyes have turned to gray.

"Mr. Albert, who closed Papa's eyes, visited us in Havana after the war." She smiles again, as though remembering how grateful they were for this. "He felt he owed a debt to the man who had helped him survive. When Papa reached the death camp, Mr. Albert was finding it impossible to get over the loss of his wife and two daughters, and he had fallen ill. Papa looked after him, doing all the work he had been ordered to do in his place until Albert had recovered a little."

At this, Aunt Hannah closes her eyes and is quiet for a long time.

"'Work will set you free,' is what they claimed," she said with a sigh. "'*Arbeit Macht Frei.*' That was the inscription in German over the entrance to that hell. One day it was Papa who could take no more and let himself die."

Another long silence.

"'You keep Max's yellow star. He was a good man,' Mr. Albert told us years later in Havana. He said that he had been sent to Auschwitz because he and his family were Jehovah's Witnesses. Then he said sadly, 'But I don't have anybody to leave my purple triangle to.'"

"To me, Mr. Albert was lucky," my aunt goes on. "But to him, Max was the lucky one. What sense did it make to survive after witnessing the annihilation of his wife, his parents, his two daughters—all his family? As he saw it, Papa had fallen by the wayside, but the two of us were safe. Mr. Albert would have preferred that fate. He was all alone, with all that loss in his heart and the purple triangle of the Jehovah's Witnesses in his pocket."

"What happened to Mr. Albert?" I ask.

"We never heard from him again," replies Aunt Hannah.

Catalina bustles in and out of the dining room without paying much attention to Mom's tears, my aunt's sad smile, or even the story, which she must know by heart—all those dead people she never met. She has her own problems, and yet she always seems ready to help. Now she comes in with a pot of coffee.

"This house needs lots of red and white roses," she says, filling the tiny cups.

In my memory, the scent of roses mingles with the aroma of the hot coffee Catalina prepares in a strict ritual. In Havana, people drink coffee all the time, to keep their eyes wide-open. My aunt takes a sip before continuing.

"My mother had shed all the tears she had left by the time she heard they had arrested Papa. Perhaps that's why she didn't cry in front of anyone when his death was confirmed. After all the tears in Berlin, on the *St. Louis*, and in this dark house in Havana, she could only feel indignant at confirming that what had happened in Berlin was being repeated in Paris, and that Papa had been defeated by the horror of Auschwitz. Her pain was replaced by a cold serenity."

Aunt Hannah said that from that day on, the windows were never opened again in the house, or the curtains drawn back, or music played. Great-grandmother decided to live in darkness. She rarely spoke and ate only because she had to. She spent all the time shut in her bedroom, reading French literature in Spanish, translations that made those stories from earlier centuries seem even more remote. I find it hard to imagine what she must have been like.

My aunt received a surprise when Great-grandmother had a family mausoleum built—not in the cemetery at Guanabacoa, which was the so-called Polack cemetery, but in the Colón Cemetery, the biggest in Cuba.

"'There'll be room for us all here,' she used to say whenever she went to supervise the building of the mausoleum," recalls Aunt Hannah, imitating her mother's firm tone of voice. "She did it less to honor the memory of her loved ones than for her body and mine to end up in Cuba, which she always blamed for not accepting us all when our boat arrived in the port of Havana."

Another silence. Catalina opens her eyes wide and shakes her head.

"She made me promise her I would never leave Cuba," Aunt Hannah says. "My bones were meant to rest alongside hers on this island she wanted to curse until her dying breath.

"'They're going to pay for the next hundred years,' she would insist." She imitated Great-grandmother Alma once more, waving her hands dramatically in the air. Then she falls silent again.

We stare at her in astonishment. Staying sane all those years must have been really difficult. She must have fled as far away as she could from the curse on her here.

Catalina is busy with her chores, but when she hears what Alma intended to do, she shivers and runs her hand over her head as if to cleanse it of the evil that might still be in the house. She brings Aunt Hannah a glass of water to help clear her throat and allow all the sorrow choking her to come out. She runs her hand over her head, too, and mutters, "Let go of her! Get away! Godspeed, Alma!"

Aunt Hannah trembles. There is an awkward silence as Catalina paces around the dining room. I decide to say something:

"What happened to Leo?" I ask, although Mom looks at me as if to try to shut me up.

"That's another story," replies Aunt Hannah, smiling again. Then she swallows hard.

"After the war, I managed to get in touch with a brother of Leo's mother in Canada. She had passed away shortly before Germany surrendered. That was a time of searching, of desperate attempts to find survivors, to reunite fragmented families. Nobody knew anything. Until one day I got a letter sent from Canada."

Lowering her head, she tucks her hair behind her ears and dries the perspiration on her brow with a napkin.

"Leo and his father never left the *St. Louis.*"

Hannah
1950

$\mathcal{M}$other had become a ghost, and Gustavo was increasingly elusive. Eulogio drove him to and from the Colegio de Belén Catholic School, but we never met any of his friends. From the time he was a toddler, Hortensia used to take him every weekend to her sister Esperanza's house, because she had a son named Rafael. Despite their age difference, Gustavo had at least one friend to play with, although he wasn't particularly happy about visiting a wooden shack that could be flattened by any hurricane, and where they talked constantly of the apocalypse and a god he couldn't have cared less about.

He gradually began to grow apart from us, and especially from Hortensia. He displayed all the vitality, lack of inhibition, and spontaneity that Cubans have. I suppose he was ashamed of Mother and me: two women who found it impossible to reveal their feelings in public and who were riddled with secrets. A couple of crazy women shut up in a house where there were never any newspapers, where they didn't listen to the radio or television, or celebrate birthdays, Christmas, or the New Year. A house where the sun never shone.

Gustavo was angry even at the way we spoke Spanish, which he found complicated and pretentious. We watched him come and go like a stranger, and often avoided speaking in front of him. Over family dinners, when Gustavo tried to talk politics, we would switch to topics he considered feminine and frivolous. His place at the table stayed vacant increasingly often.

Hortensia insisted this was just typical adolescent rebelliousness, and she continued to try to spoil him as if he were her eternal baby. As far as he was concerned, though, Hortensia was now merely a household employee.

It was thanks to Gustavo that *guarachas*, the sentimental music of Havana that drove my mother mad, soon infiltrated the house. He took the radio—which had not been switched on for years—up to his green-painted room and listened all day to Cuban music. Once, as I was passing his door, I saw him dancing on his own. He was swinging his hips, and then made a sudden dip, his feet crossing rapidly to the rhythm of that mindless music with its unfinished phrases and verses that were often no more than raucous shouts. Yet he was happy in his own way.

I started studying at Havana University and decided I wanted to be a pharmacist. I didn't want to have to depend anymore on the money Papa had deposited in an account in Canada, since we didn't know how much longer we would have access to it. As I focused on my studies, Mother and Gustavo faded into the background. In addition, Leo's betrayal, which I had learned of rather late, allowed me to think of him less frequently, and so my world was reduced to organic, inorganic, quantitative, and qualitative chemistry. Each day, I would climb the university steps, passing the bronze statue of the *Alma Mater* before entering the stately halls of the Faculty of Pharmacy. Only then did I feel secure.

The mansion in Vedado receded for a few hours. My stain vanished, and no one called me a Polack anymore, at least not to my face. Once, one of my favorite professors, Señor Núñez, a small, bald man with two tufts of red hair behind his ears, came up to me and rested his hand on my shoulder as he checked my equations. The weight of his hand made me feel an inexplicable link. He was someone else like me! Maybe Núñez wasn't his real name—maybe he had managed to come here with his family or as a child.

Without understanding why, I started to tremble. I was so weary of stumbling over my ghosts! Professor Núñez realized this: perhaps he himself had been in a similar situation. He didn't say a word, simply patted me on the back and went on reviewing the students' work. But from then on, even when I didn't really deserve it, he began to give me top marks.

Each time I left classes and took a different way home, or got lost in the backstreets of the city, I would think of Leo. I could feel my small hand in his as he guided me along the streets of Berlin. Who knew why he had made the decision he had? In an unhappy time that made us all unhappy, we all saved ourselves as we thought best.

It would have been better for me to have discovered his betrayal as soon as I arrived in Havana. As it was, I had to wait for many years to discover that Leo never got rid of those valuable capsules of ours—of the Rosenthals, not the Martins. He never threw them into the ocean, as he swore he had during our last dinner on board the *St. Louis*.

So it was that for a long time I lived in the hope of meeting him again, of us creating the family we had dreamed of in those days when he drew maps on water in Berlin.

Leo was not one of those who surrender. But the Leo who was left behind on the *St. Louis* was another person. The pain of loss transforms us.

I would never know what really happened the day the *St. Louis* sailed off back toward Germany. I decided to think that Leo, proud at recovering the capsules, told his father he had them. Should he throw them in the sea? Impossible! He had succeeded in snatching them from the despairing Rosenthals. To have saved my life was much more important to him.

Close to the Azores, more than halfway back to hell, when they saw they had been abandoned in midocean and without any hope that a country would take them in, perhaps Leo and his father took refuge in the only space where they felt safe: their small cabin that smelled of varnish. Then they lay down to sleep.

Leo dreamed of me. He knew I was waiting for him, that I would wait for him with my little indigo box until he returned and placed on my finger the diamond ring that had been his mother's and that his father had given him for me. We would go live by the sea, far from the Martins and the Rosenthals, from a past that had nothing to do with us. We would have lots of children, with no stains or bitterness. The best dream of all.

At midnight, Herr Martin, watching over his only child's deep, happy sleep, got up. He gazed down at the boy with those long eyelashes. *How much he looks like his mother!* he thought. This was the being he loved most in the world: his hope, his offspring, his future.

He stroked Leo and lifted him in his arms as gently and slowly as possible, so as not to wake him. He felt his body, warm with life, beating against his chest. He didn't think, he didn't want to analyze what he was about to do. But he knew there was no other way. There are moments when we know the sentence passed is final. For Herr Martin, that moment had arrived.

He took the treasure from his pocket: the little bronze container that, paradoxically, he himself had bought on the black market for Herr Rosenthal. He unscrewed it. Taking out a tiny glass capsule, he carefully placed it in the mouth of his son, still only twelve years old. With his first finger he pushed it toward the back, behind the molars, making sure the boy did not wake up.

Leo gave a sigh, wriggled, and pressed himself closer against his father, searching for what only he could give him: protection. His father embraced him again. *The last embrace,* he thought. He put his lips up close to the cheek of the child who had such blind faith in him and who admired him so much.

Herr Martin closed his eyes. He thought he could somehow absent himself from this moment, which it was already too late to avoid. He pressed his son's delicate jaws together. He heard the small glass capsule crack, and the sound echoed deep inside his mind. The boy's eyes opened, but his father did not have the courage to watch his son's life ebb away. Leo's breathing began to falter, he was choking, he couldn't understand what was going on, or why the bitter, burning taste in his mouth was taking him from his father, from the man with whom he had set out to conquer the world.

There were no tears, no complaints. No time for that. His open eyes, framed by their enormous lashes, stared at nothingness.

Herr Martin raised the remaining capsules to his own mouth. This was the best way to make sure he did not survive this terrible tragedy. He did not dare weep or cry out: all he felt was a deep loathing for everything around him. He had taken his son's life from him. Only a diabolical force could have driven him to commit such a dreadful atrocity. He had no wish to prolong the agony any longer. As the potassium cyanide mixed with his saliva, he could not even detect the taste or texture of the lethal powder. Instant brain death. A few seconds later, his heart stopped beating.

They found the bodies of father and son the next day, when all the passengers had received permission to land outside Germany. A cable informed the captain that, for health reasons, it would not be possible to wait until they docked at Antwerp for their funeral. The boy with the longest eyelashes in the world was thrown overboard with his father, close to the Azores.

This is how I preferred to imagine the end of my only friend, the boy who believed in me. My beloved Leo.

Anna

2014

Aunt Hannah's room is very plain. She has made an effort to erase every last trace of the past. That is why she sent us the negatives, the postcards from the boat, the copy of the *German Girl* with her photograph on the front cover. She doesn't want to keep anything.

"It's enough having it up here," she says, touching her temple. "I wish I could get rid of it there, too."

She can close her eyes and find her way around the big room overlooking the street without bumping into the dresser, the bed, the night table, the rocking chair, the stand for her hats and shawls. In her mind's eye, she can see every inch of this space she once thought would be only temporary. The young girl's bedroom is now that of an old woman.

There aren't any photos on the walls, furniture, or shelves. She doesn't have any books, either. I thought I would find her room covered with photographs from her childhood in Berlin, her ancestors. We're very different. I spend my life plastering my bedroom walls with pictures, and she gets rid of them.

Sometimes I think she never had a childhood, that the Hannah in the photos from Berlin and on the magazine cover is another girl who died during the crossing.

On the chest of drawers, there is a white china pot decorated in blue.

"It's from my pharmacy, but I lost that. Back then they took everything from you in this unpredictable country," she says without explaining.

She doesn't keep the pot out of nostalgia for the Farmacia Rosen, which used to be on a street corner in Vedado, but as somewhere to put anything she doesn't want covered by the constant tropical dust.

In the wardrobe with a door that sticks constantly, I see the collection of soft white cotton blouses and dark skirts made of some heavy material that became the uniform she used in her later years in Havana.

She opens her night table drawer and shows me a little blue box.

"This is the only thing I've kept from my three weeks on board the *St. Louis*. It will soon be time for me to fulfill my promise. It won't be long now before I open it."

I wonder how she could keep the box for so long without wanting to know what was inside it. She already knew Leo wasn't coming back and that she had lost him forever.

She also shows me the Leica her father gave her before they boarded the *St. Louis*.

"Take it, Anna," she tells me. "It's yours. It's been put away ever since we arrived in Havana, so perhaps it still works."

Before she shuts the drawer, I catch sight of the back of a photograph that has something written on it. I manage to read: "New York, August 10, 1963."

Seeing my interest, she picks up the photo and stares at it for a long time. It shows a man in an overcoat at an entrance to Central Park.

"That's Julian, with a *J*," she says, smiling.

I had never heard that name before, so I wait for her to explain.

From the way she is gazing at it, and also because it wasn't in the envelope that reached us in New York, I guess he can't be from our family.

"We met when we were both studying at university in Havana. It was a very chaotic time."

She continues to stare at the black-and-white photograph, which is blurred and creased slightly.

"We didn't see each other for some years, because he had gone to study in New York. Then he came back, and we met again at my pharmacy. We were inseparable, but then he left again. Everybody leaves here, except for us!"

When I ask if he was her boyfriend, she laughs out loud. Then she returns the photograph to the drawer, struggles to her feet, and goes out onto the landing.

Between her room and ours, there are two locked rooms. Aunt Hannah realizes that even though I can't bring myself to ask her, I am studying the doors with great curiosity.

"That was Gustavo's room! It was our fault we created such a monster! I didn't have the nerve to put your father in there when he came here to live with us as a child. In those years, your father was our only hope. Now you are."

I hold on to the banister behind Aunt Hannah, who carefully places her foot on each step as we go downstairs. Not because she is afraid of falling, but to maintain her upright posture. I touch the walls with my hand, trying to imagine Dad on these stairs at my age, following the aunt who saved him from growing up alongside a "monster." His parents had been killed in an airplane accident and his grandmother was prostrate in bed, and it was his aunt who devoted herself to looking after him. He grew up protected by this small fortress in Vedado. He was to be the only one who left the island where the Rosenthals had made a vow to die.

Aunt Hannah seems to have come to the end of her explanations. But ever since she said that word *monster* to describe Gustavo, she knows I'm curious. There's a big gap between the years when Gustavo was a student and the airplane accident. But I'll get another chance; there's a time for everything.

We stand together in the front doorway. We stare for a few moments at the garden, where, she tells me, there were once poinsettias, bougainvilleas, and multicolored croton bushes.

"Everything here dries out. And I so much wanted to grow tulips. My father and I loved them."

For the first time, I sense a deep nostalgia in her voice. My aunt's eyes seem to be brimming with tears that never fall but well up and make them seem an even brighter blue.

I leave her with Mom, because Diego is waiting to take me to discover another secret part of the city. When I meet him, he says something awkward, as usual:

"I think your aunt must be at least a hundred!"

Hannah
1953–1958

$\mathcal{T}$hings in Cuba change without warning. You go out into the street under a scorching sun, then the breeze pushes along a cloud, and everything gets transformed. You can be soaked in a second, even before you have time to open your umbrella. The rain comes lashing down, the wind buffets you, branches are snapped off, gardens flood. When the rain stops, a stifling vapor rises from the asphalt, all the smells mingle, paint has been washed from the housefronts, and terrified people run everywhere. In the end, you get used to it. They're tropical downpours: you can't fight them.

I felt the first raindrop on the corner of Calle 23. I turned right into Avenida L, but by then, I was soaked to the skin. By the time I climbed the stairs to reach the Faculty of Pharmacy, the sun was shining again, and my blouse was starting to dry, but water still dripped from my hair.

In the blink of an eye, dozens of students began rushing down the steps, pushing and shoving one another as if they were running away from something. I saw others perched on top of the *Alma Mater* sculpture, waving a flag in the air. They were shouting slogans I couldn't make out because they became confused with the police sirens from patrol cars that had pulled up at the foot of the staircase.

One girl next to me was so frightened that she clung to my arm, squeezing it without a word. She was crying, panic-stricken. We didn't know whether to climb the stairs or to run off down Avenida San Lázaro and get away from the university.

The shouts became deafening. Then there was the sound of something striking a piece of metal; it might have been a gunshot. We were petrified. A boy came down the stairs telling us to fling ourselves to the ground. We did, and I found myself facedown against the wet steps. I buried my face in my hands. All of a sudden, the girl next to me stood up and ran off down the staircase. I edged over as close as I could to the wall to avoid being trampled on, and then stayed as still as possible.

"You can get up now," said the boy, but I didn't respond at once.

I lay there a few seconds longer, but when I saw everything was calm again, I looked up and saw he was still there, with my books under his arm. He held out his hand to help me.

"Up you go; I have to get to my classes."

Without looking at him, I leaned on him as I straightened my skirt and tried without success to clean my blouse.

"Aren't you going to introduce yourself?" he asked. "I won't give you your books until you tell me your name."

"Hannah," I replied, but so quietly he didn't hear me. He frowned, raised an eyebrow: he hadn't understood, and insisted in a raised voice, "Ana? Your name is Ana? Are you in the Pharmacy Department?"

Yet another one! I had to be forever explaining what I was called.

"Yes, Ana, but pronounced like it begins with a *J*," I said irritated. "And yes, I'm a pharmacy major."

"A pleasure, 'Ana pronounced with a *J*.' Now I have to run to my classes."

I saw him bound up the steps two at a time. When he reached the top, he paused between the columns of the building, turned, and shouted:

"See you later, Ana-with-a-*J*!"

Several professors did not come in that day. In one of the rooms, some scared students were whispering about tyrants and dictatorships, coups and revolution. I wasn't frightened by anything happening around me. The university was in turmoil, but I wasn't interested in finding out what the protests were about, and still less in taking part in something that had nothing to do with me.

When it was time to leave class, I stayed behind for a while trying to do something about my blouse in the lavatory. But no use: it was completely ruined. When I finally left the building in a bad mood, I saw him again, leaning against the doorway.

"You're the boy from the staircase, aren't you?" I asked without stopping, pretending I wasn't really interested.

"I didn't tell you my name, Ana-with-a-*J*. That's why I'm here. I've been standing in this doorway for an hour."

I smiled, thanked him again, and continued on my way down the stairs. He kept pace with me, observing me in silence. His presence didn't bother me; I was more intrigued to know just how far he was going to follow me.

The sky had cleared a little. Dark clouds were visible in the distance, at the far end of Avenida San Lázaro. I thought of saying that possibly it was raining a few blocks away, but I preferred not to talk nonsense just to make conversation. A few moments later, he decided to speak to me again.

"My name is Julian. You see, it's the *J* that unites us."

I didn't think that was particularly funny. We reached the bottom of the stairs, and I still hadn't said a word.

"I study law."

I had no idea how he expected me to respond to that, so I stayed silent until we reached Calle 23, where I would turn left each day to head home. He had to go down Avenida L, so we said good-bye on the corner. Or, rather, *he* said good-bye, because all I managed to do was to shake his hand.

"See you tomorrow, Ana-with-a-*J*," I heard him say as he disappeared down the avenue.

He was the first Cuban boy who had ever taken notice of me. And apparently even Julian refused to say my name properly. His hair was a bit long for my taste, with unruly curls that cascaded down his brow. He had a long, straight nose and thick lips. When he smiled, his eyes narrowed beneath a pair of thick black eyebrows. At last I had met a boy who was taller than me.

But what struck me most about Julian were his hands. His fingers were very long and thick. Powerful hands. He was wearing a shirt with the sleeves rolled up, no necktie, and his jacket slung nonchalantly over his shoulder. His shoes were scuffed and dirty, possibly because of the chaos we had been through a few hours earlier.

Ever since we had arrived in Havana, I had never had the slightest interest in making friends in a place we still thought of as being temporary. But when I got home that day, I found myself still thinking of him. What most puzzled me was that whenever I remembered his face or his voice when he called me Ana-with-a-*J*, I caught myself smiling.

Going to classes had been my escape. Now there was another reason to escape: to see "the boy with a *J*" again. The following day I arrived early at the department, but didn't see him. I even waited at the entrance for a few minutes, until I was afraid I would be late for my class. Better to forget somebody who hadn't even bothered to try to pronounce my name properly, I told myself. Just as I was about to enter, a few minutes before they would close the door to my class, I got a shock when I felt his hand on my arm. Before I knew what I was doing, I turned to Julian and found myself smiling.

"I came because you didn't tell me your family name, Ana-with-a-*J*."

I could feel myself blushing uncontrollably. Not because of what he had said to me, but out of fear that he would see how delighted I was.

"Rosen," I told him. "My family name is Rosen. But now I have to go, or they won't let me into class."

I should have asked him his last name as well, but I was too nervous.

When I left that afternoon, I was disappointed to find he wasn't there. Nor the next day. A week went by, and the boy from the staircase did not appear again. Yet I continued thinking of him. Whenever I tried to study or sleep, I recalled his laugh or saw his curls and wanted to straighten them.

But I didn't see him again.

When I finished my university studies, I talked with my mother about opening a pharmacy I could run myself. She wasn't very enthusiastic about my project, because it implied a sense of permanence she was still refusing to accept, even though, after seventeen years, everything seemed to indicate we had no other choice. She discussed the matter with Señor Dannón, and he was the first to support me enthusiastically, especially as it would mean a new and stable source of income.

We opened the Farmacia Rosen one cloudy Saturday in December. It was very close to our house, opposite the park with the flame trees. Mother wasn't keen on the idea of opening a business on the weekend. She would have preferred a Monday, but for me, Mondays were too close to Tuesdays. When I didn't back down, she decided not to come to the ribbon-cutting ceremony.

That was a time when I spent all day, and very often part of the night, preparing prescriptions in a world measured in grams and milliliters. I employed Hortensia's sister Esperanza, who became the "face" of the pharmacy. Or of the "apothecary," as she liked to call it. She was the one who attended customers behind the narrow counter. She was "good with people," as they say, which was something supposedly not common among Cubans. She was extremely patient and listened indulgently to the locals' complaints. Sometimes they came in not for medicine but simply to be listened to, and to relieve their woes by talking to that placid woman with candid eyes. Although she was much younger than Hortensia, they looked the same age. Esperanza didn't pluck her eyebrows or wear lipstick: there was never a trace of makeup on a face that looked harsh and yet radiated goodness.

Esperanza brought her son, Rafael, from middle school, and he started helping us with home deliveries. Rafael was tall and thin, with straight, dark hair, an aquiline nose, almond eyes, and an enormous mouth. He was as polite and respectful as his mother. Both of them lived in a state of constant agitation. On an island where most people belonged to the same religion, they had a different faith: they shared the sin of being different.

That was the reason I could never understand why, although they lived in fear, both of them sometimes took the opportunity to slip "the word of God" into their consoling messages. "Our mission is to spread the word," they would tell me. Fortunately, they never attempted to convert me. I was sure that Hortensia had told them I was a Polack, and that it was best to leave all Polacks in peace.

I felt safe with Esperanza and Rafael, at a healthy distance from my mother's increasing bitterness and pain. She had lost Papa, was trapped in a country she loathed, and had lost control of her son, Gustavo. She regarded the pharmacy as my attempt to be happy, and that was too much for her: she was certain that, for the Rosenthals, happiness would always prove unattainable. Premature death was an essential part of us. There was no point pretending anything else.

Leaving home also implied risks. Ghosts could take me by surprise on any corner. That was why I put Esperanza at the counter: I knew that if I waited on the customers myself, at some moment or other, somebody like me would have appeared, recognized me, and tried to enter into a dialogue that until then I had managed to avoid.

Rafael went with me to the warehouses to pick up any bulky packages. On the way, I tried not to establish visual contact with any passerby. If anyone came too close, or if there was a group of youngsters on a corner, I would lower my eyes. If I saw an old woman, I would cross to the opposite sidewalk. I was convinced I was bound to meet one of *them* somewhere. That was my greatest fear.

One Tuesday we were walking down Calle I to Línea, when we came across a garden. I began to admire the roses growing on both sides of the main entrance. Looking up, I saw a modern-looking building that had ancient inscriptions over the door, inscriptions I had not seen for years but recognized immediately. Three girls dressed in white came out of the building. I was paralyzed: there was no doubt they had recognized me. Yet again, the ghosts had found a way to catch up with me. I began to perspire like mad.

Rafael, who had no idea what was going on, held me up. I looked away, trying to ignore them, but when I glanced back, I saw ironic smiles on their faces—a look of perverse satisfaction. They had found me; there was no way I could hide. We were the same breed: refugees on an island. We had fled from the same thing, but there was no way out for us.

Rafael looked at me, uncomprehending.

"It's the Polack church," he told me, as if I didn't know, and without realizing that, in fact, I would have preferred not to know.

On our way back from the warehouse, we took another route. From that day on, for me, that street no longer existed.

Most evenings, before we closed the pharmacy doors, Esperanza, Rafael, and I would sit down to chat for a while. We turned down the light to avoid anybody coming in and interrupting our conversations about the old grouch who lived above the store and counted out every pill he got in his prescription, or the woman who received her ampules and asked Rafael to inject them for her, or the man who each time he picked up medicine for his wife warned my employee he had absolutely no interest in hearing anything about God. Sometimes I stayed on my own for hours, watching the blades of the noisy fan go around and around. It hung so low that if I raised my arm, I almost brushed against it.

Often in the evening, the three of us listened to music: Esperanza would search the radio dial for a station that played boleros. We delighted in songs about impossible loves, ships without destinations, abandonments, obsessions, sorrows, forgiveness, moons like dangling earrings, rustling palms, stolen embraces, and sleepless nights. These sung melodramas mingled with the sweet smell of the potions, camphor, menthol, ether, Vichy salts, and alcohol to reduce fever, which in those days was what sold the most.

We would laugh together. Esperanza sang to the rhythm of the boleros as we rested after a long day. Then they would go home, while I had to go back to the dark Petit Trianon.

Hortensia could not thank me enough for giving her sister and nephew work. She never could have understood that I was the one who was grateful. It would have been very hard for me to find employees I could trust for my pharmacy, which according to Mother was condemned to fail because it had been opened on a Saturday.

A few years later, Gustavo began to study at law school and came back to sleep less often. We never dared ask him with whom or where he stayed, but we were afraid for him. According to Hortensia, a wave of violence had been unleashed on the streets of Havana, but after all we had been through in Berlin, nothing kept Mother and me awake at night. To me, the city was the same as ever: the invasive noise, heat, humidity, drizzle, and dust never changed.

One night, after we had all gone to bed, Gustavo arrived home unexpectedly with his shirt torn. He was dirty and had been beaten up. Hortensia took him to her room so that we wouldn't be scared, but we managed to see him from the half-open window of my bedroom. Mother did not flinch.

After washing and changing, Gustavo went up to his own room and did not leave the house for a week. We had no idea if he was running away, if the police were searching for him to arrest him, or if he had been expelled from the university, where we continued to pay the fees punctually. Mother's answer was always the same:

"He's an adult. He knows what he's doing."

At the end of the week, he told us the news over dinner: a student leader had been murdered; the University of Havana was closed. I couldn't help thinking of Julian at the foot of the staircase. "Ana-with-a-*J*," I could hear quite clearly, and imagined him coming out of the Law School. *Where did you go, Julian? Why didn't you look for me again?*

The smell of the chicken fricassee Gustavo was wolfing down brought me back to the present. His voice full of passion, my brother was waving his arms about as he spoke of deaths, dictatorships, oppression, and inequality. Hortensia had placed a gauze bandage over his temple; I couldn't stop looking at it as his face reddened with fury and impotence. Though he raised his voice, I responded in a whisper. He was growing desperate, trying futilely to stir me with his words. Hortensia came and went nervously, clearing away our plates, pouring water, and, finally, bringing in the dessert with a great sense of relief. She thought that meant dinner was coming to an end, that the argument would be over, and the two of us would go up to our rooms.

At a certain moment, I saw a red blotch appear on Gustavo's bandage. It started as a small dot that the others did not see; then it spread until a thin trickle of blood began to run down to his ear.

I came to on the floor between Hortensia and Gustavo. He had a fresh bandage around his head, with no trace of blood. I felt warmth flowing back into my body. Hortensia was smiling.

"Up you go, my girl. Eat your pudding. Are you going to faint over a little drop of blood?"

Mother had not moved from the table. I saw her slowly raising a spoonful of rice pudding with cinnamon to her mouth. As I stood up, she excused herself and went up to her room.

My fainting had not alarmed her: what disturbed her was that Gustavo had involved Hortensia in a family conflict, and also that he might in some way be linked to that murder, whether on the side of the criminals or the victim. She found either option unacceptable, because she had made the decision to survive on the island without drawing attention to herself. After making so many sacrifices to erase the stain she had brought him into the world with, she now saw him mixed up in conflicts that could prove fatal for the Rosens.

Gustavo could not understand how we could be so cold, not reacting to injustices in a country that he saw as his; how we could live so isolated from everything going on around us. He asked me why, but by then I did not have the energy to continue a dialogue that would not get us anywhere. I had a mother who could lose her mind overnight and a pharmacy to run, I kept telling myself endlessly.

In his usual passionate way, Gustavo harangued me about social rights, tyrants, corrupt governments. I felt like saying to him, "What do you know about tyrannies?" but my brother was born with the need to confront power and to change the established order. The passion he put into his speech, his aggressive gestures, and the intensity of his voice left Hortensia and me in a state of panic. We felt that one day he might wake up, go out into the street in a fury, and organize a national revolt. He no longer believed in the laws or the order of a country that, in his opinion, was falling to pieces.

"You were born in New York and are an American citizen. You can leave here without a problem," I reminded him, trying to offer my brother an alternative. To him, this was like a slap in the face.

"Not one of you understands me! Don't you have any blood in your veins?" he shouted at me in exasperation, clutching his head in his hands.

Getting up furiously from the table, Gustavo flung his plate of dessert to the corner of the dining room. Hortensia ran to clean the stain it had left on the wall. She gave me a pleading look to say no more.

"Leave him, he'll soon get over it," she begged me in a whisper, like a mother protecting her son from his own mistakes.

She was the one who suffered most from the chasm opening between Gustavo and us. She was worried that her adored child would get into trouble.

"Who would defend him if anything happened to him? Three women shut up in a mansion like this?" she muttered.

That night, Gustavo went up to his room, slamming the door. He threw things onto the floor and paced back and forth, talking to himself. Then he switched on his radio, forcing us to listen to a *guaracha* at full blast. A half hour later, he came down again, carrying a suitcase. He slammed the front door behind him and disappeared.

We heard nothing more from him until after a turbulent year's end, when everything changed radically. That morning, Mother predicted that before long we would be living in a state of terror once again.

Anna
2014

*M*om and Aunt Hannah now have a project. They're busy empty-ing the rooms of a family that no longer exists. I catch them whispering together like they've known each other all their lives.

Aunt Hannah has a hard time opening an old drawer and then takes out a bunch of woolen scarves of different colors. Mom is surprised to see them: Scarves in this tropical heat?

"Bring them with you to New York," says my aunt, wrapping them around my neck one by one.

She also takes out her knitting needles and a ball of yarn. This time I'm the one who's surprised, trying to understand what sense there is knitting things no one will ever wear.

"It helps my arthritis," Aunt Hannah explains, starting down the stairs while leaning on Mom's arm.

I leave this new collection of scarves on my bed—the last gift I expected to find in Cuba—and tell them I am going out with Diego. His mother has asked us to lunch, and he has come to get me.

Diego's house, which used to be white, has a solid wooden door that seems like it's been through a lot over the years. On the right-hand side of the doorframe is a small object you can hardly see because it's covered with coats of paint. Diego can't understand why I've stopped there. When I get close, I see it's a mezuzah. A mezuzah! I can't believe my eyes.

Inside the house, there are boxes everywhere, like they're about to move. Diego explains they use them to store things in.

"Like what?" I ask him.

"Things," he says, slightly surprised at my curiosity.

In the dining room, the table is set. It's covered by a vinyl tablecloth. Diego's mother comes in, smiles without introducing herself, and gives me a kiss. She is as thin as he is, with black, curly hair, a long neck, and droopy breasts. Her stomach also looks huge in a very tight dress. Before we sit down, Diego quickly explains to her that my mother is a Spanish teacher and that is why I speak Spanish, that I'm not German, that I live in New York, and that we're close in age. I smile at her without saying a word.

His mother brings in a steaming bowl of white rice, a dark-looking soup, and a colorful plate of scrambled eggs. I glance at this quickly to see if it has sausage, vegetables, or tomatoes in it, but it is impossible to tell what the yellow and green strips are.

I serve myself as little as possible so I won't upset them if I don't like it. While we're eating, I look at the family photos on the walls, trying to see if any of the people look like my Cuban friend or his mother. Maybe they're his grandparents or great-grandparents.

I discover something else: on the sideboard, there is a menorah, its seven branches covered in candle wax. Surprised and intrigued, I stop eating. Diego's mother notices:

"Don't worry, we probably won't have a power outage today. We don't have any candles left. Last month they cut the electricity several times—they do it to save power. Eat, my girl, eat."

First the mezuzah, now the menorah. And the portraits of their ancestors. I decide it's best to ask. I choose one of the portraits showing a couple.

"Are they your parents?"

Diego's mother can't help laughing out loud, her mouth full of rice and beans. Raising her hand to her mouth, she chews rapidly so that she can reply before I go on.

"They're photos of the family that used to live here. We were given their house a few days after they left the country. I was your age at the time."

I can't understand how that family's possessions came to belong to this other one. Apparently they moved into an abandoned house.

"Over thirty years ago, there was a crisis, and the government allowed lots of people to leave. They crossed the sea in boats their relatives sent from the United States," Diego's mother starts to explain. "Those were terrible months. The newspapers said that those who were leaving were enemies of the people. They called them scum or traitors. 'Good riddance!' read the headlines. I remember that the day the family who were living here were leaving, the neighbors waited outside to insult them in what used to be called 'an act of repudiation.'"

She doesn't stop eating while she is talking. I guess so many years have passed since then that it doesn't upset her as much.

"They spat at them and shouted, 'Get out of here, you worms!'" she continues. "The girl from this family used to go to school with me. I couldn't understand what crime they had committed to be treated like that, or why on earth they would call a twelve-year-old girl a 'worm.' I still remember the way she looked at me from the car as they drove away."

I try to see if the girl is in any of the photographs on the wall but can't find her.

"There was so much hatred and pain in her eyes," says Diego's mother. She seems serious now and doesn't have food in her mouth anymore. "Nowadays those 'worms' have suddenly turned into butterflies, and we receive them with open arms," she says, and then laughs again. "Everything changes with the years. Or with our needs."

She goes on with her story, and I try to understand, but it's hard to follow.

"The government handed over the property to my parents. They had been on the waiting list for a house ever since a hurricane blew the roof off ours."

I imagine Diego's mother in the room that once belonged to the girl who looked at her with such contempt. Her clothes, her toys, became hers. She had become an impostor.

"At first, I couldn't sleep in that huge room full of drapes, but little by little I got used to it."

She breaks off, goes into the kitchen, and then returns with a vanilla pudding in a syrup that tastes a little like licorice.

"My parents kept the house exactly as it was," she says after serving the dessert. She eats it quickly, as if afraid it might suddenly vanish. "They left the portraits, the furniture—everything—where it had been before."

The dessert and the house's history are done. With a smile, Diego's mother starts to clear the table. I go over to a dusty bookcase and stop in front of an antique book with a leather binding. It has an English title—the longest I've ever seen: *The Life, and Strange Surprizing Adventures of Robinson Crusoe, of York, Mariner: Who lived Eight and Twenty Years, all alone in an un-inhabited Island on the Coast of America, near the Mouth of the Great River of Oroonoque; Having been cast on Shore by Shipwreck, wherein all the Men perished but himself. With An Account how he was at last as strangely deliver'd by Pyrates. Written by himself.*

I turn to Diego.

"I can almost recite this book by heart," I tell him. "To me, my father was Robinson, and I was jealous of Friday."

Diego looks at me, clueless. He doesn't understand a thing.

I turn back and start looking through the book. Just like Robinson, some nights I used to write down all the good and bad things that happened to me. I still remember many of my notes: "*Bad*: I never knew my father. *Good*: I have his photo and talk with him every day. I know he's with me and is protecting me." Or the first page of my diary, imitating Robinson, on my seventh birthday: "May 12, 2009. I, the poor and wretched Anna Rosen, having been orphaned of my father in the middle of an island during a terrible attack, have reached this shore all alone." I say this out loud in English, forgetting that Diego can't understand me.

My friend looks at me as though I'm crazy and starts laughing.

"Can I take the book from the shelf?" I ask.

"Of course, and you can take it with you if you want. Nobody reads in this house."

The edition is from 1939, and on the first page is a dedication in Hebrew: "To the girl who is the apple of my eye."

It is signed: "Papa."

Hannah
1959–1963

On this turbulent island, new years always bring great upheavals. Everything can change drastically overnight. You go to bed, fall asleep, and wake up in a different, completely uncertain world. Typical of the tropics, Mother used to say.

On New Year's Eve, Hortensia had filled the house with the scent of rosemary. We had planted it on the patio, and were amazed how well it grew. We picked it at the end of summer and dried the leaves, which Hortensia kept in a cardboard box; in the autumn, she had prepared infusions for us, and as we sipped, she'd regale us with the herb's magic properties. On the last night of 1958, my hands, my hair, and even my sheets smelled of rosemary.

The next morning, Hortensia seemed anxious to bring us up to date in her usual doomsday fashion. She had become our only contact with the outside world. We learned about everything that happened there through the filter of a woman who felt that the island was falling to pieces, and tinged every event with her alarmist vision. To her, we were drawing ever closer to the apocalypse, to Armageddon; we were living the last days; the end of the world was nigh. We always discreetly ignored her harangues about the coming of the longed-for Kingdom of God.

"It's war! There's no government!" she shrieked when she saw us come into the dining room, even more worked up than usual.

Even though she was in the habit of addressing us without pausing in her domestic chores—sometimes, if she was busy, with her back to us, we found it hard to understand her—this time she sat down at the table and lowered her voice. We quickly joined her; I could see that Mother was becoming agitated.

"They left in an airplane, after midnight."

"Who left?" I interrupted her.

Oh, the way Hortensia spoke! She always assumed we already knew what was going on.

"The one who always used to wish us good health at the end of his speeches. Now we can wish him the same," she explained.

I imagined that the joy, perhaps clouded by the fear of what might come next, would be felt throughout the island, especially in Havana. But we lived on another island within this island, shut up in the Petit Trianon, and so we had no reason to celebrate.

That New Year's Day 1959, very few people in our neighborhood were celebrating. Most of the excitement was around the hotels and the city's main thoroughfares. Our noisy neighbor had been very cautious: she didn't open her bottle of champagne at midnight. Only a few people threw buckets full of icy water into the street. Uncertainty reigned.

Gustavo flung open the front door without knocking. He had on a uniform that we didn't recognize. When we saw him come in wearing his olive-green fatigues with a red-black–and-white armband—that fateful combination of colors—Mother closed her eyes. History was repeating itself. She regarded it as her punishment.

Gustavo went up to her and kissed her, a broad smile on his face. He grabbed me by the waist and called out to Hortensia, who came running from the kitchen as soon as she heard his voice, without even stopping to dry her hands. Behind him, a young woman, also in uniform, appeared in the doorway.

"This is Viera, my wife," he said. When she heard this, Mother was thunderstruck. She quickly surveyed the newcomer from head to toe, studying her build, her features, her profile, her teeth, the texture of her chestnut hair, the yellowy-green of her eyes.

"We've just got married. Viera is pregnant, so there's another Rosen on the way!"

When I looked at my mother's face, I could tell what she was thinking: *We mustn't lose this child. Look what we've done to Gustavo after fleeing here, by constantly thinking of those who remained on the far side of the Atlantic, by never really settling on this island where we had to remain.* This baby would now be the family's salvation, the only one who would not have to bear our burden of guilt. She got up from her armchair, ignoring Gustavo, and went over to embrace Viera.

Delighted, she placed her hand on the still-flat stomach of this stranger who was going to bring into the world a longed-for baby, her first grandchild. Although Viera seemed startled, she let herself be patted by this old woman whom her husband had told her lived in the past, turning her back on the country where she now lived.

Alma did not know whether to celebrate or lament that her son—whom she had not had circumcised and whom she had sent to a school where they would do all they could to erase any trace that might incriminate him—had ended up marrying an impure woman, someone as impure as we were. She was sure of it. Who knew where Viera's family had come from, or how she had integrated into life on the island. Alma did not dare ask her family name. What was the point? The damage was already done.

That new year, we also lost Eulogio. He decided it was time to start his life beyond the control of a family that was not his. Overnight, he went from being a driver to becoming a worker, and felt for the first time he was a free man in the midst of a revolution that was just beginning. At last, he told Hortensia, we were all equal in this country, without regard to the amount of money we had or what family we were born into. He soon packed his bags and left without saying good-bye.

Hortensia never forgave him, but for Mother, his departure had a positive aspect: it was one less salary to pay.

In the coming days, the streets began to fill with bearded, long-haired soldiers, all of whom wore the armband that was impossible to ignore. The neighbors went out to cheer them; women threw themselves in their arms; some even kissed them. Paseo became a military thorough-fare. Crowds marched alongside them, heading for the main square, where they listened to revolutionary speeches that could last an entire night from a young leader who evidently loved the sound of his own voice. Hortensia told us proudly that Gustavo was up on the podium near the man who had seized power by force of arms. Mother listened to her, horrified, but did not shed a single tear. She had none left.

One afternoon in October, Viera got out of a car with a baby in her arms. Gustavo stayed alongside the driver. When Viera saw us, she didn't say hello but announced straight out:

"This is Louis." She said it in a whisper, so as not to wake him.

We looked at one another in consternation: *Louis?* Gustavo never ceased surprising us. Mother held the baby in her arms, and then Hortensia. I kissed him on the forehead, thinking he looked more like Papa's side of the family. He was born with a mop of dark hair.

Viera did not want anything to drink; she wouldn't even sit down.

"Gustavo is waiting for me in the car, and he gets impatient. I don't want to upset him," she said. The two drove off in a hurry.

Hortensia had busied herself finding out "where Viera had come from," even though, in the end, it was completely unimportant, because from the very first day, Mother had been convinced that Viera was one of us. One evening Hortensia confirmed the news:

"Viera is a Polack. She was born in Germany like you, and at the age of five was sent on a ship to Cuba to live with an uncle who had arrived earlier. Apparently she lost all her family in the war."

Mother's eyes opened wide, and it seemed as if she was trying to catch her breath.

"Her uncle, an older man with liberal ideas, is linked to the new people in power on the island," explained Hortensia. "His real name is Abraham, but he changed it to Fabius when he reached Cuba."

I left for the pharmacy delighted with the arrival of this new Rosen and refused to let Hortensia's news worry me. When I got there, I saw Esperanza in the doorway talking animatedly with a tall man. I couldn't tell whether they were arguing or chatting. When she saw me, Esperanza smiled. The man turned toward me as Esperanza went back inside.

From where I stood, the man was in shadow, and the bright sunlight prevented me from making out who it was. All I could see was that he was wearing a beige suit and that he had broad shoulders. Then I saw his hands. And recognized them.

It was Julian. Without his curls, with a broader, squarer jaw, a strong neck, and thick eyebrows that divided his face in two. We smiled: his eyes narrowed just as they used to. His mouth was the same, and so was his mischievous look.

"My dear Ana-with-a-*J*. Did you think I'd forgotten you? I like your Farmacia Rosen!"

Without thinking, I embraced him. He looked surprised, but responded with a laugh and said my name again.

"Ana-with-a-*J*," he whispered this time. "You must have so much to tell me."

I took him by the arm, and we crossed the street to sit under the flame trees in the park.

He told me that, during the crisis at the university, his family had decided to send him to study in the United States.

"I finished my law studies, and now I've just come back to help my father in his practice . . . only to find the city full of soldiers."

While he was speaking, I couldn't take my eyes off him. Julian was no longer a young university student.

"I thought of you the whole time," he said, looking down in embarrassment.

I had always been a stranger in this city. Now he was one, too, and that united us. For the first time, I felt hopeful. Perhaps a circle would close for me.

From that day on, Julian came to the pharmacy every night, just before we closed. We would stay in the park chatting for a while, and then he would see me home. Sometimes he came at midday, and we would walk along Calle 23 to have lunch at the charming El Carmelo café.

Julian wanted to know more about me, but there was little to tell: Papa had died in the war while we were waiting for him in Havana to go to New York, and what was supposed to be a stay of a few months in Havana seemed to be permanent.

We held each other's hands, and he sometimes put his arm around my shoulder, and even occasionally took me by the waist to hurry me across the street. We spent hours together like that. The most daring thing I did was rest my head on his shoulder one evening while we were waiting for a traffic light to change.

Esperanza called Julian my boyfriend, and I didn't correct her. I was weary of trying to explain: that my name wasn't Ana, that I wasn't a Polack, and now, that Julian was nothing more than a good friend whose company I enjoyed.

He never asked to go into our dark mansion. Nor did I ever invite him. As the days passed, we enjoyed silence more than conversation. We could spend hours with each other without speaking, sometimes simply enjoying the cheerful hubbub of the students coming out of the college that looked onto the park.

I realized that sometimes Julian seemed distant, that his mind was elsewhere, that he was very worried about something but didn't have the heart to tell me what it was.

One evening he called me at the pharmacy. Esperanza told me he was on the line, and in that instant I had a strange premonition. His parents had gotten an exit permit to go to the United States. He had just bid them farewell at the airport. He had no idea when he would see them again.

This man full of energy and optimism who made me feel secure, who resolved every problem with a smile, who was as big and tall as a tree in the Tiergarten, had been knocked flat. He asked me to go to his apartment.

I picked up my bag and left the pharmacy without a word to Esperanza. I walked to the corner of Línea and L, where Julian lived, by coincidence above a pharmacy.

It was a white building with wide balconies. I took the elevator up to the eighth floor, and when I knocked on the door, I realized it was open.

"Julian?" I called out softly, but there was no reply. I went down a short hallway that led to a room without furniture, and with light patches on the walls where there had once been framed pictures. Julian was out on the balcony, staring northward toward the sea.

Approaching him slowly, I suddenly found I was looking at the sea from on high, as I had done so many years earlier. I took a deep breath, and my lungs filled with the breeze from the Malecón.

"Julian?"

Silence. I took another step forward and could feel the warmth of his body. I was so close I could touch him. My heart began to beat wildly; I closed my eyes and put my arms around his back. He turned, hugged me tight, and started to cry.

"What's wrong, Julian?"

He was disconsolate. His parents had been forced to flee: there was no room for their businesses under the new government. Before they left, they had managed to sell the furniture and some valuables. They smuggled their family heirlooms out through an embassy. With the currency changes the new government had brought in, the money they had in the bank had lost its value.

"I've stayed to wrap things up here," he said, his voice quavering.

"Are you leaving as well?"

I knew he would not answer. I stared at him for a few seconds, and then closed my eyes and kissed him. I didn't want to think. I didn't want to regret it. When I opened my eyes, I could see the waves beating against the Malecón. I could taste my mouth filling with salt spray and tears. I found it hard to grasp what was going on. I was feeling emotions previously alien to me.

Julian took me by the hand. I followed him as if I had lost all willpower. He led me to his room. In the center stood a bed with white sheets. I closed my eyes, and his face became blurred with mine.

"Ana, my Ana-with-a-*J*," he kept whispering in my ear. His fingers traced my features with a delicacy I would not have expected from his big, heavy hands. My eyebrows, my eyes, nose, lips . . .

I have no idea when I left the apartment that evening, how I found my way back to the pharmacy, or how I slept that night.

From that day on, at lunchtime I went to smell the sea from the eighth floor and to lose myself in his arms.

Havana began to take on a different aspect. Together with Julian, I looked more closely at the foliage of the enormous trees in Vedado, for example. We used to walk down Paseo and sit on any bench we came to. Alongside him, the days, weeks, and even months seemed like only a few hours.

Sometimes we would walk from Paseo to Calle Línea, and from there to his apartment building. We didn't care if the weather was hot, or if it was raining, or if there was a demonstration in favor of or against causes that meant nothing to us.

Then one Monday he called me at the pharmacy to say we wouldn't be able to meet that week: he needed time to do a few things. This didn't worry me. But when the following week he didn't even call, I began to grow alarmed, even though deep down I had always known Julian was bound to disappear.

On the day the soldiers came to seize the pharmacy in the name of the revolutionary government, I arrived at work early. When I opened the door, I found a letter pushed underneath. It was from Julian.

Dearest Ana-with-a-J,

> *I didn't know how to say good-bye: I'm no good at farewells. I'm going back to New York with my family. We've lost everything. There's no place for me here.*
>
> *I know you can't abandon your mother, that you owe a debt to your family. It's the same for me with mine. I'm all they have left.*
>
> *I want to have you beside me, for just you and me to exist. And I know that someday we'll meet again. We've already been apart once, and yet I found you again.*
>
> *I'm going to miss our evenings in the park, your voice, that white skin you have, your hair. But above all I will remember the bluest eyes I have ever seen.*
>
> *You will always be my Ana-with-a-J.*

Julian

Another one who was leaving me.

I didn't cry, but I couldn't work, either. I read the letter so often I knew it by heart. I read it silently and then out loud, went back over every sentence. My encounters with him in his eighth-floor apartment with a view to the sea were engraved in my heart, in my head, on my skin.

And the rain as well. From that moment on, whenever it rains, I see Julian lending me his arm, lifting me, embracing me. I had a lot to thank him for.

I promised myself that, from then on, I would let nobody else into my life. That kind of hope was not made for me. With each passing minute, Julian's face began fading from my memory. What I could still hear clearly was his voice: "Ana-with-a-*J*."

And then the soldiers arrived.

I saw them clamber out of their vehicle and come toward the front door of the pharmacy. I kept repeating the words of Julian's farewell letter to myself, as if it were a spell that could protect me. Fortunately, Esperanza remained very calm and managed to transmit her serenity to me. I waited for them behind the counter, without a word. They had come to rob me of what was mine—everything I had built with my hard work. There was nothing more for me to lose.

Staring them straight in the eye, I tore the letter into a thousand pieces. My great secret ended up at my feet, in a small wastebasket.

I didn't allow them to speak. Taken aback, the soldiers simply stared at me. Still without saying anything, I gave Esperanza and Rafael a hug and left the pharmacy without a backward glance. Let them have it all. I no longer felt any fear.

On my way home, I quickened my pace and kept telling myself: this is a city of transit; we didn't come here to put down roots like these ancient trees.

When I reached the house, Gustavo and Viera were in the living room with the baby, who had just turned three. Gustavo had been determined to keep Louis as far away as possible from us: I didn't know if this was to punish us or to prevent us from instilling in his son our bitterness toward a country he himself was willing to die for. I thought he had probably shown up after such a long time simply to find out how we had reacted to the seizure of the pharmacy.

What had been ours was now in the hands of a new order that my brother was part of.

⁘

Nights became increasingly difficult for me. If I managed to sleep, my memories were a senseless jumble. I confused Julian with Leo. Sometimes I woke up with a start because I had seen Julian on the deck of the *St. Louis* holding my hand, climbing up and down the ship's ladders, and Leo as a grown man sitting beside me under the flame trees in the park.

I returned to our domestic routine and began to give English lessons to children who couldn't give a damn about learning it. I became the German teacher who taught English in a neighborhood where I was known as the Polack. The children and adolescents who came to our front porch for me to teach them that "Tom is a boy, and Mary is a girl" were on a waiting list to leave the country with their parents. One of them, a youth who was due to perform his military service when he finished school, was desperate to leave the island but was told that his being of "military age" made that impossible. I had become a teacher, and my porch a confessional.

Esperanza and Rafael hadn't lost their jobs following the takeover of the pharmacy. They came to visit occasionally and told me how things were under the new owner: the State. Another new development was that Esperanza's husband had ended up in jail for practicing a religion that was not recognized by the makeshift government. They regarded it as a sect that undermined the patriotism they were trying to instill into a fervent mass of people anxious for change. Esperanza and her fellow Jehovah's Witnesses refused to salute the flag or sing the national anthem and were opposed to war. That made them unacceptable in a society that had to be constantly on the alert for a battle that was never declared.

One evening as they were saying good-bye, I could see that Esperanza was worried. Without my really understanding what she meant, she whispered that the new government "had turned into a melon: green on the outside, red on the inside."

Viera began to work day and night alongside Gustavo, with the result that they started leaving the boy with us. We spoke to Louis in English, and within a few months he could understand us. After a year, his English was better than his Spanish. When they found out, neither Viera nor Gustavo protested. They were caught up in a chaotic social process to which they devoted all their time. In those tumultuous days, family was not the most important thing.

Louis ended up sleeping in the house almost every weeknight. Mother decided he needed a room of his own, and so we prepared the one next to hers. We had a hope. Of what, exactly, I had no idea, but those were joyful days. I was happy above all at seeing a child grow up who was free of the guilt of the Rosenthals.

We were slightly surprised that Hortensia kept her distance from Louis, in a way she hadn't when Gustavo arrived from New York as an infant. I think that back then she thought we needed help, but with this child, it was different: we devoted our time to him and showed him affection. Or perhaps she did not want to get emotionally involved, only to find herself back in the role Gustavo had relegated her to in the end: that of a mere employee, not someone who had cared for him, fed him, given him her love in the years when he most needed it. One summer—the warmest of all those we had suffered until then—I got an envelope from Julian in New York. Inside was a photo of him in a park similar to the one where we used to meet.

There was no letter, only the photograph, the date, and a dedication. Julian never said much. I took the few words he had written on the back as his farewell message: "For my Ana with her *J*. I shall never forget you."

Anna

2014

Day dawns here in a rush. One minute it's night, the next it's day. There's no in-between. I'm woken by sunlight piercing my eyelids and can feel Mom behind me. She is studying me with a smile and untangles my hair. Today she, too, has woken up with a scent of violets.

I turn to the photo of Dad I brought with me. I prop it up beside the lamp. We look at each other, and I can see he is happy. This trip has changed us all.

"I haven't been paying much attention to you," I tell him, "but now you're in your home!"

Mom smiles when she sees me talking to the photograph. Ever since we arrived, Mom and Aunt Hannah have become inseparable. They spend hours talking together, and I wonder what Dad makes of that.

The pair of them have scoured every nook and cranny, every ward-robe. Mom knows that each folded blouse, or brooch, or old coin holds a story she wants to rescue.

"You shouldn't get rid of this," she tells Aunt Hannah, pointing to some yellowing sheets of paper tied with a red ribbon. "Keep them; you never know."

They are the title deeds to the apartment building in Berlin, which for her now are sacred.

"Even if they're no longer valid, they are family heirlooms," she insists, stroking my aunt's hand.

Dad is closer to her each day. He is no longer simply the man she met at a concert in St. Paul's Chapel. Now he has a past, his family has a face, he had a childhood. Aunt Hannah has opened Dad's book, told us his story. Mom's reasons for complaining are gradually disappearing. It's true she lost her husband, and I lost my father, but Aunt Hannah has lost her entire life.

I think that seeing the headstone in the cemetery with Dad's name on it and having contact with the Rosenthals' past has helped put Mom's grief into perspective. I hug her, and just in case she's worried, I tell her everything will be fine—that I feel like I've known Dad; that now we have someone we have to look after.

As the days go by, Aunt Hannah seems increasingly frail. Some-times she even seems lost, not knowing what to do or where to go. The first time I saw her standing in the doorway, she was almost as tall as the doorframe. Now she seems more bent and walks with the slow, heavy step of an old woman.

Maybe it's just that I've gotten taller here. That's what Mom told me.

She also says that she would like to get back to New York.

I don't understand why. Maybe she wants to return to her Spanish literature classes at the university, to renew the life she abandoned years ago. If it were up to me, we'd stay here, live in Aunt Hannah's house, and look for a school I could go to.

Aunt Hannah's silences when she tells her stories are growing longer and more frequent. They are from a faraway past, but she often tells them in a present tense that confuses us.

I sit with her for hours, listening closely to this kind of monologue that leaves no room for anyone to interrupt. Sometimes while she's telling her endless stories, I take photos of her, but this doesn't seem to upset her. When she falls silent, Mom and I can see how vulnerable she is. When she is talking, though, a little color returns to her pallid cheeks.

By the end of our trip, there won't be anything more for Mom to learn about Dad. But we'll probably leave here without finding out what really happened to my grandfather Gustavo. Aunt Hannah always concentrates on Louis.

Diego is impatient. I can see him from the front door. He doesn't know what to do and starts throwing stones at the tree. He digs up a piece of the sidewalk that makes us trip, and then wipes his hands on his trousers. He tries to call me without attracting attention. He's afraid that the old German woman, who to him is still a Nazi, will complain to his mother about him.

When I do at last manage to get away, he gives me a warm hug. I look back to see if anyone has spotted us. I still can't believe a boy is hugging me in broad daylight, in a city I don't know. It's my secret, and I'll keep it that way.

Diego and I walk beneath a sun that scorches the asphalt. We reach a park, where he shows me a pharmacy on the corner.

"Look, my granny says that used to be your aunt's pharmacy."

There are still traces of yellow paint on the damp-covered walls. Above the cement doorway is faded lettering that shows my name: Farmacia Rosen.

We run down Avenida Calzada until we come to a narrow passageway between two big houses. I don't want to ask Diego where we're going or if he has permission to enter. It's too late anyway, because we're already on someone else's property. We reach the patio and climb a spiral metal staircase that sways as if it is about to come loose. As we climb, we hear someone playing the piano and a woman's voice giving instructions in French as she counts out a strange beat.

Jumping over a low wall, we're on a flat roof. Through a window, I see a ballet class taking place below. The girls are lined up perfectly; their arms stretch up toward the ceiling as if they are reaching for the infinite. They probably want to seem light as air, but from above, they look heavy—weighed down by gravity. Diego sits with his back to the window. He's concentrating on the music.

"Sometimes they have an orchestra, or two violins accompanying the piano," he says dreamily.

Diego is always surprising me with things I am least expecting. Normally he can never stay still in one place, but here he's sitting hidden on a private terrace and listening to monotonous musical exercises.

I want to leave. I feel uncomfortable in a place where we haven't been invited. But Diego wants to continue with his music therapy.

"Be careful, you might be stepping on my ants."

Up here on the roof, Diego has an ants' nest. He brings them sugar or bread crumbs, and studies them. They're his pets. He takes a carefully folded piece of paper containing his magic powder out of his pocket. When he pours the sugar crystals into a corner, they appear at once. Some are red, others black. They form a long line from one end of the wall to the other. Diego pauses to watch them carrying the tiny white grains back to their nest. Then he picks up one and looks at it closely.

"These don't bite," he tells me, carefully putting the ant back down. "In a few years, I'll learn to swim well. Then I'll climb onto a raft and come over there to be with you."

"You, too, Diego? So it's true that everybody here is obsessed with the idea of sailing off to sea?"

"There's no future here, Anna," he replies very seriously.

He speaks with the pessimism I've already noticed in adults here.

"Do you want to be my girl?" Diego asks out of the blue. He obviously finds it hard to say; he doesn't look at me. Just as well, because I can't bear anybody seeing me blush, even when it's something I have no control over: anybody can tell what I'm feeling. And my feelings are my own business, not to be shared.

I instantly see myself back at Fieldston, telling the girls in my class that I'm in love with a boy who has black, curly hair, big eyes, and suntanned skin. Someone who speaks only Spanish, who swallows his *s*'s until they completely disappear, who hardly ever reads, who runs through the streets of Havana, and who wants to leave his own country on a makeshift raft as soon as he has learned to swim.

"Diego, I live in New York. How can I be your girlfriend? Are you crazy?"

He makes no reply, and still has his back to me. He must regret what he's just said but not know how to get out of it. And I don't know how to help him.

I take his hand, which makes him jump—did he think that meant I was accepting? He grips my hand so tightly I am unable to free it. It's too hot to be so close to each other. I don't want to be rude.

Finally, he lets me go, stands up, and walks over to the rickety staircase.

"Tomorrow we'll go for a swim at the Malecón."

Hannah
1964–1968

Señor Dannón came to visit us for the last time. He entered with his usual swagger, smelling as ever of tobacco, but his hair was disheveled. There was not much brilliantine on it, and his unruly locks would have needed a lot more to make sure they lay flat on his enormous head.

This time Mother did not receive him in the living room but showed him into the dining room. I think she realized that the lawyer was there to draw a line under a relationship that had always been based on money and mutual convenience, but she was grateful for it, even if she never told him so.

In fact, I didn't know what would have become of us without Señor Dannón through all those years. He charged us a fortune but never abandoned us. Nor did he swindle us, I was sure of that.

Hortensia served him freshly made coffee and a glass of ice water, and then came over to me and whispered that she felt sorry for him.

"The poor man, he doesn't know what to do."

Although Señor Dannón had never mentioned any of his problems, she could tell what they were from the way he was sweating, anxiously mopping his brow, and trying to arrange his rebellious curls. Ever since he had told us about losing his only daughter, Hortensia regarded him differently. I think Mother did, too.

The rank smell of tobacco he gave off was what prevented me from getting near him: it was all I could do to stay in the same room. Now he sat close to Mother and spoke almost right up against her ear while she listened calmly. Neither Hortensia nor I could gather if he had brought good or bad news. All at once, Mother got to her feet and went upstairs. Señor Dannón gulped down the ice water, dried his lips on a napkin that he left stained brown, picked up his heavy briefcase, and followed her up to her room.

"Something bad is going on," declared Hortensia, but I decided not to pay her much attention. In fact, I was rather nervous, but I didn't want to start asking myself questions that led nowhere. I was tired of going through all the worst that might happen so that I would be relieved when things turned out less dreadfully. Besides, I could never foresee what was going to happen. That was a trick I had given up on by then.

I went to sit with Hortensia on the patio steps, waiting for Señor Dannón to leave so that I could learn the news about our legal and financial situation in Cuba. Maybe we would even have to leave for another country.

In an hour's time, I had to go pick up Louis from his school with the name of a martyr, where he had begun kindergarten and was happy. On his first days, he cried when I left him in his class. When I picked him up, he cried disconsolately again, as though to make me feel guilty. A week later, he had already adjusted, and although he did not have a gift for making friends, he was learning quickly how to survive socially. His only complaint about the school was that the other children spoke very loudly. I said to myself, *You're living in the Caribbean; you'll get used to it.*

Señor Dannón came downstairs looking very nervous and said he wanted to say good-bye. I don't think he was expecting me to embrace him, but he did look surprised when I held out my hand. Rather than shaking it, he took hold of it gently, so that my fingers were engulfed by his soft, moist palm. That was the first time in all those years that we had come into physical contact.

"Take good care of yourself. And the best of luck," Hortensia said, patting his broad, sweaty back.

He left the house with a much lighter briefcase. He paused at the iron gate and turned to say good-bye. He stared at the house, the trees, the bumpy sidewalk, for a few seconds, and then sighed and climbed into his car. We came out onto the porch to watch him go.

I was anxious. Not for whatever news he might have brought but because I was convinced he would never be back. I understood we were now left all on our own in a country heading into the unknown and prepared constantly for war. A country ruled by angry military men who had set themselves the task of reinventing history, of telling their own version of it, of changing its course as they saw fit.

Our American visas had long since expired, but I was sure we could find a way to leave if we wanted to. But that possibility had never even occurred to Mother. She had already decided her bones would rest in the Colón Cemetery. She was even more determined to stay now that her bitterness and rancor had been softened by Louis's arrival. I think she felt that in some way her presence in Cuba was necessary, and would be until the day she chose to be her last. In fact, not even then would they be free of her, because this tropical land "would have to keep my bones for at least another century."

Nor was she going to abandon Louis to parents who were convinced they were inventing a new society, which she saw as nothing more than an absurd game of "Move over, it's my turn," as a popular saying had it. Power was taken from the rich and given to the poor, who then became rich, took over houses and businesses, and thought they were invincible. So the vicious cycle started up again: there was always somebody crushed at the bottom.

Mother called me up to her room; Hortensia gestured to me not to keep her waiting. She knew that Mother would never share the news with her, whether it was good or bad. Besides, she had no need: when she saw us at dinner, she would know at once.

As was to be expected, Señor Dannón's legal practice had been taken over. The United States had broken off diplomatic relations with Cuba three years earlier, but he and his wife had obtained exit permits and were going to leave from a port near Havana where boats came from Miami to pick up entire families. It wouldn't be good for us if he visited anymore, because now he was seen as a "worm."

When Mother heard that word, she shuddered. That was what they had started to call those who wanted to leave the country or did not agree with the government. To her, it was as if she was reliving a nightmare. People were being dismissed as worms once again. History was repeating itself. What a lack of imagination, I thought.

Señor Dannón had left her a considerable sum of money. From then on, it would be more difficult to gain access to our trust account in Canada. It might even be seen as illegal by the new government, and we would probably have to give it up.

We decided it was not worth worrying. We could survive on the money we had. I received a ridiculously small sum each month as indemnity for the pharmacy that the government had expropriated; I also had my English classes. We didn't need much more.

That night, after dinner, Hortensia received an urgent call from her sister, who did not want to go into details over the telephone. They were both afraid that their conversations were listened into by government agents. She asked for two days' leave and hurried off in a panic. I had never seen Hortensia like that before.

The two days turned into five. Then she called to say that a woman named Catalina would come to help us. From that day on, that stocky woman took control of the house and never left us.

Catalina was a hurricane. She was obsessed with order and perfumes. She insisted we never leave the house without a splash of fragrance. It was then that I, too, began to use the violet water that Hortensia used to sprinkle on Louis's head every day before he went to school.

"It's to ward off the evil eye," she explained.

She was the descendant of African slaves mixed with Spaniards during the colonial period. Her mother was the only family she had known. Catalina came from the far eastern end of the island and had arrived all alone in Havana two years earlier after a cyclone destroyed her house and floods buried her village in mud. Following the devastating cyclone, she also lost her mother. She said she had worked very hard all her life and never "had time for husbands" or for a family.

Thanks to Catalina, life returned to its old routine, and the house was filled with sunflowers.

"Wherever you put them, they seek out the light," she would say.

She soon became my mother's shadow and communicated perfectly with her despite Catalina's abrupt way of speaking, full of colloquial expressions that we often found hard to understand. Catalina used familiar forms of Spanish with me and was so open with us that we soon found it amusing.

"We're in the Caribbean. What more can we expect?" Mother said.

We gradually got used to life without Hortensia. Her sister, Esperanza, with her husband in prison, had more need of her than we did; or perhaps someone in their family was ill. In reality, we had no idea what had happened to her.

Catalina began to plant mint along the patio, which she used for her infusions. She also planted basil to keep off insects she called guasasas, or fruit flies; and star jasmine so that when we went to bed, a fragrant breeze would blow in through the windows and help us rest.

A week later, Hortensia and her sister appeared without warning late one night. Louis was asleep already, and we had retired to our rooms. Catalina asked us to come down, as there were people waiting for us in the dining room.

They did not say hello or acknowledge my smile; in fact, they ignored me. They were both looking expectantly at Mother, who went to sit at the head of the table. Apparently she was the only one who could do something in the desperate situation they found themselves in, and they quickly placed themselves on either side of her. Catalina and I remained standing at the back of the room, because I thought they might want some privacy, but they were so anxious to talk to Mother they didn't even notice us.

Hortensia was trying to stay calm, even though it was obvious she found it hard to control her rage. She couldn't even speak, because apparently if she said anything, she would end up shouting, and she knew she ought to show us respect. I realized that not only was she never coming back to work for us but also this would be the last time we saw her. She didn't dare look me in the eye, but her expression was one of complete repulsion, even disgust, at having to be under the same roof as us.

Esperanza was the one who eventually spoke:

"One evening, just as we were about to close the pharmacy, they came looking for Rafael. In a vehicle full of soldiers. I plucked up the courage to challenge them and ask why they were arresting him, what he had done wrong, where they were taking him, but none of them answered me. They ignored me and took away my son."

In her despair, Esperanza visited all the local police stations, but with no success. The next day, she learned that they were rounding up all the young males, sixteen years old and up, of their faith and taking them to a stadium in the Marianao district. When she understood what was going on, she threw herself onto the floor at home and burst into tears. She cursed herself, blaming herself for the religious fervor with which she had brought up her son. Rafael was a boy who knew only good and was incapable of doing anybody harm. They had been trying to leave Cuba for a long while, but it had become impossible for them to obtain an exit visa ever since the "great leader" had accused their religious group of being a "terrible blight on society." They had no money or relatives abroad who could help them. They depended on the compassion of their congregation, which was already officially considered illegal.

Mother remained motionless as she listened to Esperanza, arms tight against her sides and hands folded on her lap. This time she wasn't facing racial cleansing that aimed to create physical perfection, size, and color to achieve purity. Now it was a cleansing of ideas. It was people's minds they were afraid of, not their physical traits. The doubts expressed by a crazy philosopher from her own country whom she used to read flitted through her mind: "Is man God's mistake, or God man's mistake?"

As Rafael was considered a minor—he was a few months short of his eighteenth birthday—they obtained permission to visit him in a work camp in the center of the island. This was where those hostile to the new government as well as people with religious beliefs were imprisoned. God had become the new rulers' main enemy. The government devoted itself to political, moral, and religious purges. The forced labor camp where Rafael had been interned was surrounded by barbed wire fences, and at the entrance was a huge sign that read "Work will make men of you."

They were allowed to see him for a half hour. Rafael did not have the chance to tell them—it was impossible, because there were guards present the whole time—how bad things were for him. He had lost more than twenty pounds. His head had been shaved.

"His hands were blistered," Esperanza went on. "He was forced to salute the flag, to sing the national anthem, to deny his religion. He refused, and so they increased his punishment day by day. He's only a boy, Alma, a boy . . ."

Rafael did have time, though, to tell them that a delegation had been there to inspect the camps, which were known as "therapeutic rehabilitation work camps." In the group were several members of the government who were concerned about the prisoners' conditions and asked how the reeducation process was going. He had recognized one of them, who returned his gaze. Rafael smiled and suddenly felt a glimmer of hope.

"Gustavo was part of the delegation," said Esperanza, looking straight at Mother.

On hearing her son's name—the boy she had not had circumcised, whom she brought up to be free—Mother began to tremble. She did not shed any tears, but her body shuddered with silent sobs. It was obvious it was not only her soul that was in torment: she was suffering physically.

Catalina put her arm round me. I was struck dumb; I couldn't believe it. Hortensia got down on her knees in front of Mother and clasped her hands.

"Alma, you are the only one who can help us. Rafael is our life, Alma," she pleaded.

Mother shut her eyes as tight as she could. She did not want to listen. She could not understand why she still had to pay for her guilt.

"Talk to Gustavo. Beg him to get Rafael back to us. We won't ask anything more of him. If Rafael dies . . ." Hortensia left the sentence unfinished.

Mother was still far-off, staring at the wall. Her whole body was shaking.

After a lengthy silence, Hortensia rose to her feet. Esperanza took her by the arm, and the two of them strode to the door. They did not say good-bye, and we never heard from them again.

Still trembling, Mother tried to get up out of her chair. Catalina and I rushed to help her. She had difficulty walking, and we had to struggle—almost carrying her—to put her to bed. She hid under the white sheets, buried her head in the pillow, and appeared to have fallen asleep.

At dawn the next morning, I went into her room with Louis so that he could say good-bye before going to school. When he gave her a kiss on her brow, she opened her eyes, caught hold of his arm, and stared at him. Summoning what little strength she had left, she whispered in his ear in a language he could not understand:

"Du bist ein Rosenthal."

Since we had reached the port of Havana and disembarked from the ill-fated *St. Louis*, this was the first time Mother spoke German. It was also the last.

Anna
2014

This trip has been more difficult for Mom than she imagined. When Aunt Hannah tells her about what happened to Rafael, Mom can't understand how Cuba, the country she idolized as a bastion of social progress, could have created concentration camps to purge its "undesirables" while the world simply looked on. Perhaps Grandfather Gustavo thought he was behaving correctly: that he really was rehabilitating those who had gone astray, that "blight on society" that needed reforming. Grandfather Gustavo's crime was a gesture of salvation. What I can't understand is why Aunt Hannah never asked her brother to do something to help Rafael. She left it all up to my great-grandmother.

It was a year before they released Rafael and let his whole family leave the country in exile. Catalina tells us that when she found out, she ran to tell the news to Great-grandmother, who had taken to her bed in an act of perpetual self-punishment. Great-grandmother wasn't satisfied that Rafael had been set free by now. The guilt went much deeper than that, and Gustavo would have to pay as well.

Eventually, when Gustavo and Viera appeared one day to tell Alma they were going to a distant country as ambassadors of the nation she detested so much, Catalina says my great-grandmother turned her face from them. That was her only response. Catalina says it showed that she cursed her son, that she wished to see them both dead. Her gesture wounded Gustavo to the depths of his soul. Dad remained with Aunt Hannah from the day his parents went off to the far side of the world.

Catalina devoted herself to looking after Alma. She fed and washed her, changed her sheets every day, and treated the terrible bedsores that slowly ate away at her body. Strangely, as she withered, her hair began to regain its former brilliance.

I go up on my own to Great-grandmother's room, which smells of disinfectant. The gray bedcover, drawn up over the mattress with its broken springs, still seems to hold some of her presence. I sit on a corner of it and can sense her, the pain of her last years while she was lying here in endless silence.

Aunt Hannah keeps a lock of Alma's hair in a black wooden chest together with their most precious jewels. It's a Rosenthal family relic. I also see there a faded leather notebook, and the small blue box my aunt has never opened, keeping the promise she made on the ship a long time ago.

Catalina comes in and puts an arm around my shoulders.

"That's all we have of Viera's. It's her family photo album and some letters her mother wrote when she left her in Havana with her uncle. She must have had a feeling they would never meet again," Catalina says, and then falls silent.

"Alma was a good woman," she goes on after a while, as if to reassure me. "I was the one who told her that her son and Viera had died in a plane crash. However much you hate your son, death is always a blow, my child. Another tomb in the cemetery without a body."

According to Catalina, Great-grandmother had not really been alive for a long time but did not know how to let herself go, although she knew it was time to join her husband and son.

"If you don't have faith and are not willing to forgive, if you don't believe in anything, there's no way that your body and soul will leave together. I haven't got long left. The day I'm struck down, I'll let myself go, and that will be it! What's the point of all that suffering?"

Catalina is a wise old woman.

Great-grandmother's final days were terrible: she couldn't breathe well or swallow. Catalina sat at her bedside in an armchair, and spent both day and night whispering in her ear:

"You can go now, Alma. Everything is all right. Don't suffer anymore."

Catalina tells me that one morning when she woke up, she saw that Great-grandmother Alma had stopped breathing and that her heart was no longer beating. Catalina closed her eyes, and ventured to make the sign of the cross over her cold, gray face before giving her a farewell kiss.

I understand now why my aunt says that nobody in our family dies: it's more that we let ourselves go; we decide when it's time to leave. That makes me think of Dad. Maybe he, too, once trapped, let himself die under the rubble.

I ope
New York
the huge
the cars, t
one arour
corner. I
what is ab

All ol
after, anot
I ran
baby. He
his fragra
I started
wieder ger

"Let's
Spanish. I
That
daughter.
A law
I was inte
my father
a claim I
was a Ro:
the burde
We cc
day was tl
also a dau
you often
I laug
world bea
cially whe
In ou
the instar

Hannah

1985–2014

*E*very day now when I open my bedroom window and see the leafy
trees that protect me from the aggressive morning sun, I discover I am
still alive and still on this island where my parents brought me against
my will. My mind starts to travel at a speed my memory cannot keep up
with. My thoughts fly more quickly than my ability to capture them. I
don't remember what I dream. I don't remember what I think.

My nights are disturbed. I can't find peace. I wake up with a start
without knowing why. I'm no longer in our apartment in the center of
Berlin; I can't see the tulips from the living room. The *St. Louis* has been
relegated so far from my mind, it's impossible for me to summon up the
smells from on board.

The years in Havana have become confused. Sometimes I think
Hortensia is about to come into my room or that I'm going with Eulo-

gio to a
with Juli
together.
see Loui

He's
Afte
Center f
the offic
book he
hands: s
relativity
great co

He
She kne
give me
returned

He
one ther
Afte
us he ha
infreque
terrible
a while.
of our tr
call: Lou

The
long tim
"Do
had alre
I kn
On
bath wit
me. I fel

using a few of its purple drops on my gray hair each day. Then it always remained with me.

I was about to turn eighty-seven, the age when one should begin to say good-bye. I thought I should get in touch with Anna, the only trace our family would leave in this world. It would have been unjust toward my parents if I had concealed her legacy. You need to know where you come from. You need to know how to make peace with the past.

By now, all I had left was a single debt, a single desire yet to be fulfilled: to open the little indigo-blue box with Leo.

The last time I had blown out a birthday candle had been on board the *St. Louis*. So long ago. The moment to celebrate had arrived.

Anna
2014

Dad grew up very close to Aunt Hannah and Catalina. They both dedicated themselves to making him an independent man and also, maybe without wanting to, a loner.

"The deaths of Gustavo and Viera did not affect your father too badly, because he was only nine at the time," my aunt tells me. "What did distress him was to see them lower the almost weightless body of his grandmother into her grave at the cemetery. To Louis, his parents had simply left one day and never come back. That was enough for him. But this time it was a corpse, the first he had seen, in a box, which they were going to bury."

My father lived between two languages. English became the one he spoke at home, and Spanish the one he used for school, which he didn't like. Aunt Hannah decided he wouldn't need German. He studied nuclear physics, and shortly before he graduated, Aunt Hannah went with him to the US Interests Office in Havana, near the Malecón. She took with her Gustavo's birth certificate to apply for American citizenship for his son, Louis.

"It was your father who finally had the chance to free himself from the stigma of the Rosenthals," she said.

Aunt Hannah herself felt she had to stay in Cuba with her mother's remains, to have her own bones lie alongside hers, so that the country would pay for not allowing her husband to enter. But however much she explains the reasons why she didn't go live in New York, I can't understand.

When he reached his new country, Dad took over what is now our New York apartment and reactivated the trust accounts Great-grandfather Max had set up.

There is no sign of his presence in his room or anywhere else in this house. Those of Aunt Hannah and Great-grandmother Alma are too strong for any trace of him to survive.

There are no family photographs here, either. The only snapshot my aunt has is the blurred, yellowing image where she appears seated on her mother's lap: the photo her father kept until the day he let himself die in lands overrun by the Ogres. We are the ones who now have all the other images, from her years in Berlin or on the *St. Louis*.

I feel exhausted, so I go to find Diego. He promised we would go swim at the Malecón. At least, *he* was going to have a swim: I don't dare plunge into those dark waters where violent waves come crashing against the seawall. At this time of day, the shore, with its reefs and sea urchins, is where all the neighborhood kids hang out. At first, I think the smell of rotting fish, seaweed, and urine will make me nauseous, but I'm surprised a few minutes later to realize I've forgotten it. Diego dives into the rough waters. It seems as though he's drowning: his head goes under, and he struggles to return to the surface, but then he laughs and plays with the other boys in the water.

When I point my camera at him, he leaps and smiles in the midst of the crazy waves.

When he comes back to the wall, I see he's limping. I take another shot of him, and he poses with his injured leg raised. The sole of his right foot is full of sea urchin spikes. He sits beside me, and I patiently start pulling out the black needles one by one. He bears the pain without a murmur, although tears well up in his eyes. He smiles again, puffing out his chest and baring his teeth, as if to say, "This is nothing, I've seen worse!"

After I remove all the spikes, he dives back into the sea. The sun is setting on the horizon, and my thoughts fly elsewhere. I want to take as many pictures of him as I can back to New York. A cloud hides the sun, and for a few minutes we are in shadow.

I put down my camera and suddenly feel overwhelmed. I can't stop thinking of Diego and this family—my family—which I am only now discovering. I am a Rosenthal! It's too late to go back now.

As we walk home, Diego is upset. He knows Mom and I are leaving in a few days. Soon classes will start, and maybe we'll write to each other. I have to convince Mom to come back to Cuba. Now that we've met Aunt Hannah, I don't think we'll be able to just abandon her. We are the only family she has.

Diego talks endlessly about his plans to leave the country. He doesn't want to be like his uncles and aunts, forever worried their house will fall down, living bitter, hopeless lives. One catastrophe per family is enough. Maybe he'll find his father in the United States, or I could help him find him. Maybe he's in Miami, where there are lots of Cubans; maybe he will feel sorry for his son and take him in. Diego says that in the blink of an eye he could be in the North. He talks all the time about leaving, not about us being separated.

It's time to get some rest; tomorrow's another day.

Before we return to New York, Mom wants us to visit the cemetery again to say good-bye. Just the two of us go, and the taxi leaves us near the chapel. Mom doesn't enter, but stands outside for a few moments, closes her eyes, and takes deep breaths.

I don't want to read headstones, either, or to admire angels frozen in marble, or to see weeping people. Here are all the pungent smells again!

We can see the family mausoleum in the distance. Mom realizes that Aunt Hannah has had the inscription on the pediment changed. It now reads in Spanish "Rosenthal Family," and under that, what the name means in German, "Rose Valley." She has returned to her essence. She is no longer a Rosen but has become what she always was: her father's daughter.

The headstones are there, with their inscriptions. My great-grandparents Alma and Max, my grandfather Gustavo, Dad's, and—my aunt's! Hannah Rosenthal, 1927–2014. When we see this, our only reaction is to clasp each other's hands. Aunt Hannah must have decided this will be her last year. And, as we know by now, in our family we don't die but let ourselves go.

Mom doesn't want me to worry, so she tries to pretend this discovery of ours is not important. But I can't help noticing a look of terror on her face that I have never seen before. She tries to lessen the tension:

"I'm sure she'll change the date. At her age, you think you already have one foot in the grave. Don't worry, Aunt Hannah will be around for some time yet."

Catalina's withered flowers are still there, as well as the stones Mom put on each of the headstones apart from Aunt Hannah's. She offers another stone to each of our dead relatives. She pauses in front of Aunt Hannah's headstone, probably thinking she'll leave one there, too, but then decides not to. She knows what I know: Aunt Hannah has already made up her mind, and nobody can make her change it. She slips the stone back in her bag.

As we walk back to our taxi, the sun beats down on this white sea of marble, blinding us. I think my aunt has reached an age she never dreamed she would, in a country where she never thought she would stay. She prefers to go back to her rose valley.

We return home and start preparing the birthday celebration. Catalina and I are going to bake a cake for my aunt. I beat the eggs until they become frothy and rise so much they almost overflow the china bowl. The flour gradually makes the froth thicker. A spoonful of oil, a pinch of salt, grease the tin, and into the oven with it! Before that, though, I sprinkle it with vanilla, and the air becomes sweet and warm. My first cake!

Next, I make the icing. The white froth rises; I sweeten it until it thickens. A few drops of lemon juice, salt, and cinnamon powder. The icing covers the cake, turning it into a lopsided snowball: my gift to Aunt Hannah.

Mom is astonished and says we must bake a cake together every year.

The birthday girl has been watching us the whole time with that lovely smile of hers. She radiates a gentle sense of peace that I have never seen before. To know that we are leaving the island, that the possibility denied to her and her mother from the day they disembarked from the *St. Louis* is open to us, is enough to make her happy.

Catalina sits in an armchair for a rest, and falls asleep. Whenever she gets the chance, she settles down anywhere she can, closes her eyes—and we have to shake her to wake her up. She hears less and less. There must be such a symphony of sounds inside her head that she cannot make out clearly what is going on outside.

"It's old age, there's nothing to be done," she says with a brief smile, and then gets up to do something—anything—to keep busy.

Mom thinks Aunt Hannah and Catalina need someone to help them. She talks about them both as though they were family. They are.

Aunt Hannah asks us to celebrate her birthday at dusk: the hour when the captain of the *St. Louis* appeared in her cabin with a postcard for her that we now have. Her twelfth birthday. What followed was a long life in this place where she never felt at home. For her, the years in Cuba are the least important. Her real life took place in Berlin and on board the *St. Louis*. Most of the rest has been a nightmare.

Catalina found a half-burned candle in a kitchen drawer and has stuck it in the center of the white sponge cake. I go out in search of Diego and invite him in to taste my first cake.

We switch off the dining room lights, and Mom lights the candle. First we sing in English, because of me, although my birthday has already come and gone. My aunt insists, and we do it to please her. I close my eyes and make a wish. What I most want at this moment is to be able to come back to Havana.

We light the candle again, this time for Aunt Hannah. Catalina sings a Spanish version of the song I have never heard before: "Congratulations on your birthday, Hannah, may you be happy and joyful, many years of peace and harmony to you, happy, happy birthday . . ."

Moved, Aunt Hannah leans over the cake, closes her eyes, and makes a secret wish. There's a lengthy pause, and then she blows at the candle, but her weak breath does not put out the flame. In the end she snuffs it out with her fingers, smiles at all of us, and gives me a big hug.

When I go to bed that night, I find on my pillow a small bottle of violet water and a note written in big, shaky writing: "For my girl."

PART FOUR

Hannah and Anna

Havana, Tuesday, May 24, 2014

Anna

*I*t's time for us to leave, and I don't know how to say good-bye. Mom is coming and going in and out of the house with our cases. She smoothes her hair nervously and wipes away the sweat while I stay out on the sidewalk, halfway between Aunt Hannah, who is on the front porch, and Diego. He is standing at the street corner with his back to me.

"Anna, it's time to go! We can't put it off any longer. Come on, we're not going to the ends of the earth!" Mom's voice snaps me out of my daydream.

I run back to my aunt, and as I hug her, I can feel her leaning against me so she won't fall.

"Be careful!" Mom warns. "Remember, your aunt is eighty-seven."

Eighty-seven. I don't know why she thinks she has to remind me.

"Give me another hug, Anna. That's it, my child; now get off this island as quickly as you can," my aunt says, her voice shaky.

I can feel her cold hands on my shoulders, but I keep my arms around her. I don't know whether Diego is still there or has gone.

"Look, Anna, this teardrop is for you. Can I put it around your neck?" Her voice seems really weak now. "It's a flawed pearl, and you are somewhat like it: unique. It's been in our family since long before I was born, and it's time you had it. Take good care of it. Pearls last a lifetime. Your great-grandmother always said every woman ought to have at least one."

I touch the tiny pearl. I mustn't lose it. When I get home, I'll have to keep it safe, in my bedside table, together with Dad's souvenirs.

It seems as though the minutes are flying by and that we will never come back.

"My mother gave it to me in our cabin on board the *St. Louis* on my twelfth birthday. It's yours now."

I clasp the pearl and try to move away from her, but she is still holding me tight.

"Don't forget, when you reach New York, you must plant tulips, Anna," she whispers. "Papa and I used to love to see them flower from the window looking out onto the courtyard of our apartment in Berlin. Tulips don't grow on this island."

I run to Diego and hug him from behind. He doesn't dare look at me because I know his eyes must be full of tears.

He turns and gives me a kiss I can't avoid. Diego kissed me! I wonder if anyone saw. My first kiss! I want to shout but haven't got the nerve.

"This is for you," he says, staring at me.

Opening his right hand, he holds out a small shell that is yellow, green, and red. I take it from him very carefully and then give him another hug.

"We'll meet again soon, you'll see." I want him to be sure I'll be back.

I walk away from him, counting each of my steps to the car, where Mom is waiting. Aunt Hannah is still standing on the porch, but I don't want to look at her; I don't want to cry. All at once, the breeze drops. All of them are frozen in time, and I take the last step in slow motion.

"Anna!" my aunt shouts, and I walk back to her. "Here's another story for you to explore."

She hands me my grandmother Viera's brown leather album that she had kept with the blue box. We embrace again.

"It's yours now."

Slowly she lets go of me. I get into the car and lean on Mom, who opens the window just as we are pulling out, without looking back.

In one hand, I have the shell. In the other, the photo album.

"My first kiss, Mom. I just had my first kiss . . ."

"You will never forget your first one," she says, smiling.

We remain silent as we pass by the old redbrick school where Dad studied. I imagine him in the blue-and-white uniform my aunt described to me. There he is, marching in some procession they have to take part in. Or sitting on the school wall with his classmates, waving a paper Cuban flag.

Good-bye, Dad. I take his photo out of my blouse pocket.

"We're here, fulfilling your dream," I tell the photo, giving it a kiss. "We made the journey together."

I put the photo into my grandmother Viera's album and close my eyes.

We reach the airport, which is crowded with families carrying huge suitcases. I study their faces, which seem familiar to me: a frail old lady off on a visit to Miami, a soldier carefully checking the travel documents of a couple with a daughter, a little girl who takes a look at me and then runs to hide behind her mother. In their eyes, I discover a fear of being shunned by the ones who stay.

Through the plane window, I say good-bye to the country where the father I never knew was born. We leave Havana behind and fly over the Straits of Florida. I can't help wondering if this will be the last time I see Diego and Aunt Hannah. I don't know if someday we will return to the land where my great-grandmother is buried. I lean my head against the window and fall asleep until they announce we're arriving in New York.

I look up at Mom, who is stroking my hair, and see she has tears in her eyes.

We're about to land. I open the photo album, and the first thing I see is a postcard of an Atlantic liner with the insignia *St. Louis*, Hamburg-Amerika Linie.

"Remember the tulips, Mom. We're going to plant tulips."

Hannah

I still have a destiny; at least today, a Tuesday. And I'm going to choose it. I can decide where I go, where to aim for. I can be whoever I like, abandon everything and start over, or end things once and for all. That is my sentence. I feel set free.

I can wander one last time among the colorful croton bushes, the poinsettias, the rosemary, basil, and mint herbs in the neglected garden of what has been my fortress in a city I never came to know. I let the aroma of recently filtered coffee envelop me, mixed with the smell of cinnamon coming from the oven. I am able to see and experience whatever I like. How fortunate I am!

On the threshold of our Petit Trianon, where I first caught sight of Anna and recognized myself in her, I clasp her warm hand and around me see the world I will never know through her eyes, which are mine.

Mother hated farewells. She did not have the courage to say good-bye to me. She hid herself away in bed with her eyes shut tight and let her body shrivel.

But the truth is, I *need* farewells. So much time has passed, and yet still I cannot forget that they did not allow me to say good-bye to Leo, my father, the captain, or Gustav, Louis, or Julian. Today nobody is going to stop me from doing so. With every minute, I see myself in Anna; in what I might have been but wasn't.

I'm confused. Anna stands in the shadow of the ship sailing out of the bay. I can't make out the faces of those still shouting good-bye to us, but all of a sudden I hear Papa's voice:

"Forget your name!"

I can't say good-bye to Anna calmly. I hold her in my arms while in my ears I hear the desperate cry of the noblest man in the world.

If I close my eyes, I am with Diego and Anna, who are embracing. Yes, Diego, it's so sad to say good-bye. Go on, kiss her, take advantage of every second. Thank you, my children, for giving me this moment.

The sky has turned a deeper blue, the clouds are scudding along, leaving the sun to shine as it sets, its dying rays less painful on my skin, which cannot take much more. The smell of the sea invades my nostrils. The breeze starts to ruffle our hair. The three of us, alone on this corner in Vedado. What about Leo? Leo isn't here.

Next to Anna I am happy. We're so close . . . Diego kisses her. It's her first kiss. I can't believe it, either. She has kissed a boy at the start of her thirteenth year, and I have to endure saying good-bye to her.

I open my eyes and let her go. Everything comes to a halt. She is leaving. I lose her. The distance between Anna and Diego, between Anna and me, starts to widen painfully.

Diego and I are left at a loss. He can't stop crying, but when he realizes I'm watching him, he runs off.

These last two weeks have been an eternity. I have relived every instant of a life that was always deprived of meaning. Seventy-five years trapped in an unreal city, seeing so many people leave, flee, and abandon us here, condemned to be laid to rest in a land that never wanted us.

I should have liked to be Anna for a few minutes more. I leave the past in this run-down mansion: I have had enough of paying for other people's sins, for their curses. I don't care if everything we have suffered is forgotten. I'm not interested in remembering.

They have all gone. Only Catalina is here behind me. I turn and embrace her. I don't know how to say good-bye to her, either. She looks at me and knows; she understands but prefers not to say anything. She turns her back on me and walks slowly and heavily back into my Petit Trianon, which is hers now. The door slams shut.

I hear the ship's siren. That's the signal. Time to return to the sea.

I descend Paseo, counting every step I still have to take to reach the Malecón. I discover new buildings, overgrown gardens, the roots of leafy trees that refuse to stay beneath the asphalt.

Anna is no longer with me, and that hurts. I try my best to look at the faded houses and the children hurtling down Paseo on their bikes, but I find it impossible. All I can see is her, even if I know she wasn't born to live on this island where I am condemned to die, as Mother used to say. In the end, I'm comforted by that idea.

A day like today, after I have celebrated my birthday, I find it hard to understand how I have survived everyone in my family. Leo, who drew our fate in maps made of water and mud in the alleyways of Berlin. Julian, a vain hope that from the start was destined to vanish into nothingness.

I have no wish to return to the past. Time to end it all: even pain has its expiration date. I live in the present, yes, the here and now, whatever can give me another breath, even if it is the last. The goal is in sight, and I feel I have a voice. I exist, even if now I am no more than the ghost of what I once was.

It seems as if everything I am wearing is smothering me. The pearls pull me down toward the ground like a deadweight. My dress is a suit of armor that prevents me from breathing. My shoes cling to the sidewalk as if unwilling to take another step. The faint rouge I've dabbed on to show myself I am still alive is no more than a childish weapon in this battle to live in the present.

My memory is dense—so dense that the good-byes are lost in forgetfulness.

I can reconstruct every last detail of the dress Mother was wearing when she boarded the *St. Louis* seventy-five years ago, but I cannot recall what I did before I said good-bye to Anna. Did I close my bedroom door? I've no idea if I left the lights on, if I said good-bye to Catalina, if Anna accepted our pearl. I at least know I'm wearing rouge. Yes, my face has some life in it. Or at least the semblance of it.

The only thing I'm interested in is today. Yesterday and tomorrow are for other people, not for an old woman who has reached the age of eighty-seven. Anna, you are in charge of the remaining traces of a family that should never have survived. That's why I passed on those photos and the pearl.

Yes, the moment has arrived, and I'm here for you.

Can you hear me, Leo? I'm carrying my little brown bag. In it are the keys, my compact, the lipstick, the threadbare lace handkerchief Papa brought me from Bruges on one of his trips. And your gift, Leo, the last one, the one I have waited until today to open: the small indigo box you put in my hand before I was torn from you. We didn't have the chance to say good-bye, not like Anna and Diego did. I was never able to give you the promised kiss.

I still have a voice, I tell myself again, to convince myself, but the rouge on my cheeks separates me from you, from my childhood. Yet I know that every step I take brings me closer to you.

At last, I see the horizon. I lean against the wall that protects the city from the sea, eaten away by the years and the salt spray.

"I'm eighty-seven," I say out loud, surprising a loving couple sitting on the Malecón wall. They respond, but I can't hear what they say. I've grown accustomed to living in a constant murmur. As time goes by, I understand less and less what other people are saying. I no longer even try to make out phrases or learn new words. At my age, what would be the point?

I continue walking until I come to the tunnel linking Vedado with Miramar. I find it hard to breathe; I feel cold and start to tremble, but that doesn't mean I'm afraid. My heartbeats are fading, and my breathing is failing.

Here among the rocks by the ruins of an abandoned restaurant, I collapse onto an iron chair that was once silver. I sit and watch the waves break on the reefs, far beyond the port. I've reached the age we promised we would share together. *Remember, Leo?*

"I am the only survivor of my family, but I am not prostrate in bed like the Adlers," I say, to convince myself that this wait was worth it. "No need for more thought. I'm ready."

I have kept all my promises, and it comforts me to know that Anna is the best thing that could have happened to us, the Rosenthals. So many lost generations . . .

I search carefully in my bag for the indigo box you gave me when we were separated on that chaotic deck of the *St. Louis*. I kept my promise, Leo. I can't help but smile, even as I realize that during all those years of solitude in the city my parents condemned me to, you were always with me.

The moment has come to stain my hands with indigo. With all the strength I have left, I grip the small box you gave me seventy-five years ago while my father was pleading with me to forget my cursed name.

It's time for me to say good-bye to the island. The small, faded box has been my amulet right up to today. Eighty-seven years old. *We've made it, Leo.*

I muster what little energy I have left to devote to you. This is our moment, the one for which we have waited so long. *Thank you, Leo, for this gift, but I can't open it on my own. I need you here with me.*

I close my eyes and feel you drawing close. You, too, are eighty-seven, Leo, and you walk slowly. Don't rush. I've waited for you so long that one minute more will not change our destiny. I breathe in deeply, and you come to me with all the intensity you used to convey in those childhood years of ours in Berlin, when we were playing at being adults.

You are close. I can feel you. You are here.

You take me by the hand, and I stand up to embrace you, something we never dared to do back then. You are trembling, and I lean against you so that you can gradually pass me your warmth. This is no moment for tears: this is our dream.

You are taller and stronger than me. Your skin looks even darker now that your curls are white, as white as my poor tresses. And your eyelashes? They still arrive before you do . . .

You waited seventy-five years to reappear, because you knew for certain I would be here, on the seashore, as the sun goes down, so that together we can unearth the treasure I guarded for you.

I'm dreaming, I know that. But it's my dream, and I can do as I like with it.

Together we open the box very slowly. Here it is, intact: your mother's diamond ring. Look how it glitters in the sunlight, Leo. And beside it, I can't believe my eyes: a small piece of yellowing glass.

My heart looks for strength where there isn't any and beats a little more rapidly. I must hang on.

I close my eyes and finally understand: it's the last cyanide capsule my father bought before we embarked on the *St. Louis*. The third capsule, the only one left. *You kept it for me, Leo!*

I regret—and it is one of the few occasions in my life that I have done so—I regret accusing you of betraying me, thinking that you and Herr Martin had stolen the capsules meant for me and my parents. I understand now: you had no way of knowing how many other islands would be closed to you. All the islands in the world hidden behind silence. And as we know, in wars, silence is a time bomb.

It was inevitable that you should keep them. It was written in all our destinies.

The old, priceless capsule you kept for me is out-of-date now. It cannot cause me instant brain death or paralyze my heart. But I no longer need it. I waited this long because I gave you my word: I kept the promise I made to the boy with the long eyelashes. It's time to be on my way, to let myself depart.

I see you closer to me than ever, Leo, and I'm so happy, I tremble. Yet I can't help feeling guilty, because my parents are absent from my final thoughts. Because in all truth, it is you and Anna who are my hope and light, whereas Max and Alma are an intrinsic part of my tragedy.

I don't want to feel guilty. Lightness is essential from the moment you have made up your mind to leave.

Sunset is all the more intense when it's the last one. The breeze takes on a different dimension. My body is still too heavy, so I concentrate on the waves, the awful smell of sea spray that always made Mother feel nauseous, the noisy youngsters going through the tunnel, and the music blaring from passing cars. And, of course, all the time I can feel the humid, irritating heat of the tropics that I've had to put up with until today.

I lose all sense of time. I let my mind drift away, and just as I feel my heart is about to give out, you slip the diamond ring onto my finger. I raise the capsule to my lips—the last thing you touched with your still-warm hands—as if at last I were kissing you. In that instant, we are together in my parents' luminous cabin on the *St. Louis*.

The tulips, Leo, soon the tulips will be in bloom, I whisper in your ear as I gaze at you—can you hear me? With your eyes tight shut and those long, long eyelashes that always arrive before you.

You are twenty now, and a handsome young man. I am also twenty, an age neither of us was able to enjoy. I bring my face up to your still-warm one and at last give you the kiss I promised for the day we met again on our imaginary island. We are still holding hands, closer than ever, and I see you next to me, at the top of the mast, the closest point to the sky on the magnificent *St. Louis*. The weight I have been carrying since we were torn apart drops away, and I acquire the lightness I need to let myself leave.

We start to fly over the long Malecón seawall, look down on the avenue from up on high. For the first time, Havana belongs to us. Crossing the bay, we settle by the silent Castillo del Morro and gaze back at the city, which looks like an old postcard left by a passing tourist.

We are twelve again, and nobody can separate us. The day is not ending, Leo, it is about to dawn. Havana is still in darkness, dimly lit by the amber glow of the streetlamps. All we can make out are a few buildings in the midst of all the palms.

Then we hear the deafening blast from the ship's siren.

We are in the same spot on the deck from where we first caught sight of the city. At an age when we could not understand why nobody wanted us. But now everything is silent. No one is pleading; there are no desperate voices shouting names into the empty air. Once again, my parents insist on separating me from you, dragging me against my will to a tiny stretch of land between two continents.

And I don't cry out, I don't shed tears, nor do I beg them to let me stay beside you, Leo, on the *St. Louis*, the only place where we were free and happy. I take mother's delicate, smooth hand and, without a backward glance, allow them to launch me into the abyss.

And this time, I can say to you *Shalom*.

Author's Note

At eight in the evening of Saturday, May 13, 1939, the transatlantic liner *St. Louis* of the Hamburg-Amerika Linie (HAPAG) set sail from the port of Hamburg bound for Havana, Cuba. The ship was carrying 900 passengers, the vast majority of them German-Jewish refugees, and 231 crew. Two days later, another 37 passengers boarded at the port of Cherbourg.

The refugees had landing permits issued by Manuel Benítez, the director of the Cuban Department of Immigration and provided by the HAPAG company, which had offices in Havana. Cuba was to be a transit point, as the travelers already had visas to enter the United States. They were meant to stay in Cuba while they waited their turn: a stay that could last between one month and several years.

A week before the ship set sail from Hamburg, Cuba's president, Federico Laredo Brú, published Decree 937 (so called because of the total number of passengers aboard the *St. Louis*) invalidating the landing permits Benítez had signed. Only the documents issued by the secretary of state and labor of Cuba would be accepted. The refugees had paid 150 US dollars for each permit, and passages on the *St. Louis* cost between 600 and 800 reichsmarks. When they left, Germany had demanded that every refugee buy return tickets, and permitted them to take with them only 10 reichsmarks per person.

The ship arrived in the port of Havana at four in the morning on May 27, 1939. The Cuban authorities would not allow it to dock in the area corresponding to the HAPAG company, and so it was forced to anchor in Havana Bay.

Some of the passengers had relatives waiting for them in Havana, many of whom rented boats to go out to the ship, but they were not allowed on deck.

Only four Cubans and two non-Jewish Spaniards were authorized to disembark, together with twenty-two refugees who had obtained landing permits from the Cuban state department prior to the ones issued by Benítez, who was supported by the army chief, Fulgencio Batista.

On June 1, lawyer Lawrence Berenson, a representative of the American Jewish Joint Distribution Committee, met with President Laredo Brú in Havana but was unable to reach an agreement to enable the passengers to land.

The negotiations continued, and the next development was that the Cuban president demanded from Berenson a surety of 500 US dollars per passenger before they could disembark. Representatives of various Jewish organizations, as well as members of the US embassy in Cuba, held unsuccessful talks with Laredo Brú. They also tried to contact Batista, only to be told by his personal physician that the general had caught a cold on the same day that the *St. Louis* arrived in Cuba, that he had to rest, and could not even come to the telephone.

When Berenson made a counterproposal reducing the amount of money demanded as surety by $23.16 per passenger, the Cuban president decided to break off negotiations and demanded that the ship leave

Cuban territorial waters by eleven in the morning on June 2. If this order was not obeyed, the *St. Louis* would be towed out into the open sea by the Cuban authorities.

The ship's captain, Gustav Schröder, had protected his passengers ever since their departure from Hamburg, and began to do all he could to find a non-German port where they could disembark.

The *St. Louis* steamed for Miami, but when it came very close to the Florida coast, Franklin D. Roosevelt's government denied it entry into the United States. This refusal was repeated in Canada by the government of Mackenzie King.

The ship was therefore forced to head back across the Atlantic toward Hamburg. A few days before it arrived, Morris Troper, director of the European Committee for Joint Distribution, came to an agreement for several countries to take in the refugees.

Great Britain accepted 287; France, 224; Belgium, 214; and Holland, 181. In September 1939, Germany declared war, and the countries of continental Europe that had accepted the passengers were soon occupied by the armies of Adolf Hitler.

Only the 287 taken in by Great Britain were safe. Most of the remainder of the former *St. Louis* passengers suffered the horrors of war or were exterminated in Nazi concentration camps.

Captain Gustav Schröder commanded the *St. Louis* one further time, and his return to Germany coincided with the outbreak of the Second World War. He did not set to sea again but was given desk jobs in the shipping company. The *St. Louis* was destroyed during Allied air raids on Germany. After the war, during the denazification process, Captain Schröder was put on trial, but thanks to testimonies and letters in his favor from the *St. Louis* survivors, the charges against him were dropped. In 1949 he wrote the book *Heimatlos auf hoher See*, about the journey the *St. Louis* had made. In 1957 the federal government of Germany awarded him the Order of Merit for his services in the rescue of the refugees.

Captain Schröder died in 1959 at the age of seventy-three. On

March 11 of that year, Yad Vashem, the official Israeli institution dedicated to the conservation of the memory of the victims of the Holocaust, recognized him posthumously as Righteous Among the Nations.

In 2009 the United States Senate passed a resolution "acknowledging the suffering of those refugees as a result of the refusal by the governments of Cuba, the United States, and Canada to offer them political asylum." In 2012 the US State Department apologized publicly for what had happened to the *St. Louis*, and invited the survivors to its headquarters so that they could tell their stories.

The year 2011 saw the unveiling in Halifax, Canada, of a monument financed by the Canadian government and known as *The Wheel of Conscience*. It recalls and deplores the refusal by that country to take in the refugees from the *St. Louis*.

Until now, in Cuba, the tragedy of the *St. Louis* has been a topic absent from classrooms and history books. All the documents related to the arrival of the ship in Havana and the negotiations with Federico Laredo Brú's government and Fulgencio Batista have disappeared from the Cuban National Archive.

Acknowledgments

To Johanna V. Castillo, my editor, who encouraged me to revisit the tragedy of the *St. Louis*. She was my first reader and the driving force behind this story.

To Judith Curr and the entire, fantastic team at Simon & Schuster's Atria Books for believing in me, for your support, and for your thorough work on *The German Girl*.

To my grandmother Tomasita, the first person who told me, when I was a child, about the tragedy of the *St. Louis*, and sent me to have English lessons in Havana with a neighbor who had emigrated from Germany in 1939 and who was unjustly known in the neighborhood as "the Nazi."

To Aaron, my Jewish friend in Havana.

To Guido, my Jehovah's Witness friend at primary school.

To my aunt Monina, for her stories about being a pharmacy student at the University of Havana and for helping me get to know the life of Jehovah's Witnesses in Cuba though her family.

To Lydia, "la madrina," who relived for me her days as a student at Baldor during 1940s Havana.

To Scott Miller, head curator at the United States Holocaust Memorial Museum in Washington, DC, an expert on the *St. Louis* tragedy, who provided access to more than 1,200 documents and put me in touch with survivors.

To Carmen Pinilla, for acting as my guide in Berlin, and for the care with which she read the first part of the book, and for her valuable advice.

To Nick Caistor, my translator, for capturing the essence and voice of Hannah and Anna in the English language version. Thank you for an excellent translation.

To Elaine, for your meticulous revisions to the English language edition.

To Néstor and Esther María, for their meticulous work as copy editors.

To Ray, for his support and trust.

To Mirta, who believed in this project from the outset.

To Mirta's mother, who didn't allow Hannah to leave without Leo.

To Carole, who fell in love with my novel even before reading it, and encouraged me to write it.

To María, who was moved as soon as she met the German girl, and who made sure Hannah was not entirely unhappy in Havana.

To Annie Philbrick, with whom I traveled to Cuba after writing the book. Thank you for being the first to read it in English, for your kind words, and for being the godmother of *The German Girl*.

To Leonor, Osvaldo, Romy, Hilarito, Ana María, Ovidio, Yisel, Diana, Betzaida, Rafo, Rafote, Herman, Sonia, Sonia María, Radamés, Gerardo, Laura, Boris: my family and friends, who patiently endured my obsession with the *St. Louis*.

To my mother and sister, who were more than the protagonists of these pages.

To Gonzalo, for his unconditional support, and for taking care of the family when I needed time to write.

To Emma, Anna, and Lucas, the true source of inspiration for this story.

To the 907 passengers on the *St. Louis* who were denied entry into Cuba, the United States, and Canada, to whom we shall forever be in debt.

Bibliography

Afoumado, Diane. *Exil impossible. L'errance des Juifs du paquebot "St-Louis."* Editions L'Harmattan, 2005.

Almendros, Néstor y Jiménez Leal, Orlando. *Conducta impropia*. (Documental) 1984.

Arditi, Michael. *A Sea Change.* London: Maia Press, 2006.

Bahari, Maziar. *The Voyage of the* St. Louis. National Center for Jewish Film, 2006.

Bejar, Ruth. *An Island Called Home: Returning to Jewish Cuba*. New Brunswick, NJ: Rutgers University Press, 2007.

Bejarano, Margalit. *La comunidad hebrea de Cuba*. Instituto Abraham Harman de Judaísmo Contemporáneo, Universidad Hebrea de Jerusalem, 1996.

———. *La historia del buque San Luís: La perspectiva cubana.* Instituto Avraham Harman de Judaísmo Contemporáneo, Universidad Hebrea de Jerusalem, 1999.

Breitman, Richard, and Allan J. Lichtman. *FDR and the Jews*. Cambridge, MA: Harvard University Press, 2013.

Buff, Fred. *Riding the Storm Waves: The* St. Louis *Diary of Fred Buff. May 13, 1939 to June 17, 1939*. Margate, NJ: ComteQ, 2009.

Castro Ruz, Fidel. Speech given (against Jehovah's Witnesses) at the end of the ceremony commemorating the sixth anniversary of the assault on the presidential palace, celebrated on the staircase of the University of Havana, March 13, 1963. Departamento de versiones taquigráficas del gobierno cubano.

De la Torre, Rogelio A. "Historia de la enseñanza en Cuba". Proyecto educativo de la escuela de hoy. Ministries to the Rescue, 2010.

Goeschel, Christian. *Suicide in Nazi Germany*. New York: Oxford University Press, 2009.

Goldsmith, Martin. *Alex's Wake: A Voyage of Betrayal and a Journey of Remembrance*. Boston: Da Capo Press, 2014.

———. *The Inextinguishable Symphony: A True Story of Music and Love in Nazi Germany*. New York: John Wiley & Sons, 2000.

Hassan, Yael. *J'ai fui l'Allemagne nazie. Journal d'Ilse (1938–1939)*. Gallimard Jeunesse, 2007.

Herlin, Hans. *Die Tragödie der* St. Louis. *13. Mai–17. Juni 1939*. Herbig, 1979.

Hitler, Adolf. *Mein Kampf*. Montecristo: 2011. Kindle edition.

Kacer, Kathy. *To Hope and Back: The Journey of the* Saint Louis. Toronto: Second Story Press, 2011.

Kidd, Paul. "The Price of Achievement Under Castro." *Saturday Review*. May 3, 1969.

Korman, Gerd. *Nightmare's Fairy Tale: A Young Refugee's Home Fronts, 1938–1948*. Madison: University of Wisconsin Press, 2005.

Lanzmann, Claude. *Shoa*. (Documentary) France, 1985.

Levine, Robert N. *Tropical Diaspora: The Jewish Experience in Cuba*. Gainesville: University Press of Florida, 1993.

Lozano, Álvaro. *La Alemania Nazi. 1933–1945*. Álvaro Lozano. Marcial Pons, 2008.

Luckert, Steven, and Susan Bachrach. *State of Deception: The Power of Nazi Propaganda*. Washington, DC: United States Holocaust Memorial Museum, 2011.

Mautner Markhof, Georg J. E. *Das St. Louis-Drama*. Leopold Stocker Verlag, 2001.

Mendelsohn, John, and Donald S. Detwiler, eds. *Holocaust Series*. Vol. 7. *Jewish Emigration: The S.S.* St. Louis *Affair and Other Cases*. New York: Garland, 2010.

Meyer, Beate, Hermann Simon, and Chana Schütz, eds. *Jews in Nazi Berlin: From Kristallnacht to Liberation*. Chicago: University of Chicago Press, 2009.

Montaner, Carlos Alberto. *Otra vez adiós. Tres mujeres, tres vidas, una huida infinita*. SUMA de letras, 2012.

Ogilvie, Sarah A., and Scott Miller. *Refugee Denied: The* St. Louis *Passengers and the Holocaust*. Madison: The University of Wisconsin Press, 2006.

Ortega, Antonio. "A La Habana ha llegado un barco". Bohemia. Número 24, 11 de junio de 1939.

Padura, Leonardo. *Herejes*. Tusquets, 2013.

Porcheron, Michel. *"Le drame du paquebot* Saint Louis *à La Havane (mai 1939) : Une page de honte de l'histoire des USA, et donc de Cuba aussi"*. Tlaxcala, 2010.

Reinfelder, Georg. *MS "St. Louis": Frühjahr 1939 - Die Irrfahrt nach Kuba. Kapitän Gustav Schröder rettet 906 deutsche Juden vor dem Zugriff der Nazis*. Hentrich & Hentrich, 2002.

Ros, Enrique. *La UMAP: EL gulag castrista*. Ediciones Universal, 2004.

Rosenberg, Stuart. *Voyage of the Damned*. Sir Lew Grade for Associated General Films, 1976.

Schleunes, Karl A. *The Twisted Road to Auschwitz: Nazi Policy Toward German Jews, 1933–1939*. Champaign, IL: Illini Books, 1990.

Schröder, Gustav. *Heimatlos auf hoher See*. Beckerdruck, 1949.

Seiden, Othniel. *The Condemned Journey of the S.S.* St. Louis: The Jewish Series History Novel Series Book 6. A Books to Believe In Publication, 2013.

Shilling, Wynne A. *Over the Big Water: Escaping the Holocaust Twice*. CreateSpace Independent Publishing Platform, 2012.

Shirer, William L. *Berlin Diary: The Journal of a Foreign Correspondent, 1934-1941*. Rosetta Books, 2011 (ebook).

———. *The Rise and Fall of the Third Reich: A History of Nazi Germany*. Rosetta Books, 2011 (ebook).

Sosa Díaz, Adriana. "Aproximaciones lingüísticas al estudio del antisemitismo en la prensa cubana: Diario de la Marina". *Perfiles de la cultura cubana*. Número 14, mayo-agosto, 2014.

Sotheby's. *The Greta Garbo Collection*. (Catalogue) 1990.

The Jewish Virtual Library. "U.S. Policy During the Holocaust: The Tragedy of S.S. *St. Louis* (May 13–June 20, 1939)."

Thomas, Gordon, and Max Morgan-Witts. *Voyage of the Damned: A Shocking True Story of Hope, Betrayal, and Nazi Terror*. Skyhorse Publishing, 2010.

United States Holocaust Memorial Museum. *Voyage of the Saint Louis*. (Catalog.)

Whitney, Kim Ablon. *The Other Half of Life: A Novel Based on the True Story of the MS St. Louis*. Alfred A. Knopf, 2009.

Wyman, David S., ed. *The World Reacts to the Holocaust*. Baltimore: Johns Hopkins University Press, 1996.

Yahil, Leni. *The Holocaust: The Fate of European Jewry, 1932–1945*. New York: Oxford University Press, 1990.

THE PASSENGERS OF THE *ST. LOUIS*

What follows is a reproduction of the original list of the 937 passengers who boarded the ill-fated *St. Louis* and photographs that capture their quest for freedom. *The German Girl* is dedicated to them.

The materials included in this section were generously provided by the United States Holocaust Memorial Museum in Washington, DC.

United States Holocaust Memorial Museum, courtesy of Julie Klein, photo by Max Reid.

Erna Levy

Gertrud Scheuer   Erwin Herz   Walter Heyse

Ludwig Berggruen   Walhol Herz   Regi Blumenstein

Nina Herz   Toni Berggruen

Heinrich Strauss   Selmar Wiener   Armin Oppé

Elsa Biener   S. Fritz Kassel   Johanna Heilbrun

Bella Weis   Elsa Blumenstein   Julie Fuld

Ludwig Fuld   Charlotte Atlas   Emma Strauss

Leontine Schaschewitz   Walbaum   Elise Loewe

Ruth Loewe   Felix Neuhaus

Manfred Fink   Herta u. Michael Fink

Leopold Salm   Ida Salm   Bruno Berwin

Levi Nussbaum   Ruth Gerber   Rosa Gerber

Regina Krohn   Fanni Moskiewicz   Kurt Bolm

Fritz Gabriel   Kurt Rosenfeld   Heinz Bolm

Heinz Grünstein   Max Pauch   Berta Pauch

Hilde Pauch   Werner Feig   Fritz Sommer   Regina Gottschalk

Jacob Gottschalk   Blumenthal Fink   Wolfgang Uhlin

Lea Blumenstock   Alex Hamburger   Max Lebrecht

Hermann Moser   Edith Friedheim   Siegfried Hoffmann

Erich Jacobsohn   Margarete Jacobsohn   Rudolf Cohen

Thomas Jacobsohn   Else Goldschmidt   ... Goldschmidt

Max Maier   Freya Maier   Sonja Maier

Carl Maier   Irma Maier   Helene Maier

Herman Hirsch   Hermann Grunewalker

Liesel Joseph   Rose Guttmann

Dr Lewith Julius u. Valerie   Siegfried Weinstein

J. Sofier   Siegfried Frank

Heymann   Walter Weinberg

Lea Sietz   Arno Heyne

Max F. Epstein u. Frau   Fritz Strauß

Susanne Jacoby   Alfred Braun

Wilhelm Goldberg   Dr. Ruth Lewin

Emil Maas   Hans Wolfgang Philippi

A. Wolf Israel   Ruth Hirschmann

Walter Hirschberg   Heinz Gembitz

Oskar Flechner   Günter Groß

Kurt Schwarz u. Frau u. Kind   Manfred Frank

Egon Lustig u. Frau   Alfred Stern

Otto Jacoby und Familie   und Samuel Schillinger

Bruno Dzialowski   Marie Schillinger

Lici Dzialowski.   Lotte Meyer

Adolf Grünthal   Oskar Wutschmann u. Frau

Berta Grünthal   Johanna Fischer u. Kinder

Walter Grünthal   Moritz Salomon

Grete Grünthal   Sibilla Salomon

    Siegfried Pfann u. Frau

Eduard Weil   Johann Pfann u. Familie

Emma Weil   Rosa Stahl

    Lilli Bornstein

Alfred Friedheim   Joseph Wachtel u. Frau

Herta Friedheim   Hermann Goldstein u. Familie

Elly Reutlinger   Julius Herrmann

    Ernst Roth u. Frau

    Lehmann

Cäcilie Michaelis   Walter Michaelis

Richard Schlesinger   Ruth Fellner

Meta Schlesinger   Margot Bernstein

Julius Schulhof   Dr. Adler

Stella Schulhof   Günther Skotzka

Moses Singer

Amalie Singer   Julius Marx

Josef Singer   Val. Fröhlich

Aron Secemski   Rudy Leisalette

Luise Secemski

Otto Löwenstein   Gerda Heim

Arthur Britzmann   Kurt Schloff

Ludwig Meyerstein   Hugo Israel

W. Lehmann   Dr. Willy Zimmer

Dr. Oscar Schwartz   Alice Meyers Feil

Siegfried Marcus   Dr. Arthur Thassel

Richard Dresel   Felix Weil

Ruth Dresel   Val. Spitz

Rudy Levy   Else Spitz

Lena Wagner   Erich Spitz

Flora Karliner   Arthur Ernst

Herta Arndt   Georg Moses

Paula Kahnemann   Lucie Cohn

Salomea Carr   Friedrich Weiss

Hilde Falkenstein   Grete Löwy

3

Martin Rothmann

Karl Alexander u Braut

Fritz Gotthelf u Frau

Max Herbert Lichtenstein

Dr Georg ......

Herbert ......

Herbert Maurice u Frau

Walter Grove

Arthur Blau

Alfred Heldenmuth + Frau

Gustav Kahn u Frau

Max Haus

Regina ...... u Tochter

Frau Ida Feldstein

Günter ......

......

Familie Ernst Silberstein

Frau Johanna Jordan

Familie Adolf ......schmidt

Familie Isaac ......

Adolf ......

Frau Milly Joseph

Rudolf Ball + Frau

Dr Heinemann

Heinz Rosenbaum

Ernst Weil

Wilhelm ...... Neuberg

...... u Else ......

Dr. Ernst Löwenstein u Frau Alice

A. ......

Albert ......

Resi Schwarzer

Siegf. Rosenzweig

......

Dr. ......

......

Gustav Weil

Siegbert Seligmann

Adolf Hahn

Max u. Fritzi Schlesinger
Lilli Huber
Walther Fuchs-Marx
Anna Fuchs-Marx
Lea Sietz.
Laur ham
Kurt Levin
Mannheimer.
Hermann Gronowetter
Benjamin Gelband
Chana Gelband
Adel Grossmann
Helene Grossmann
Friedrich Grossmann
Nathan Halbe
Maja Knepel
Gisela Knepel
Sonja Knepel
Minna Leinkram
Klara Marx
Julius Weil
Klara Weil
Willy Barz
Susanne Weil

Bertha Ackermann
Lieselotte Arndt.
Frank Haurwitz
Hermine Obstfeld.
Donath
Paula Oberndorfer
Adolf Weil
Anneliese Weil
Ingeborg Suse Weil
Max Goldschmidt
Helmut Goldschmidt
Sally Guttmann
und Frau Ruth Guttmann
Herbert Glass
Leinkram Rosa
Eva Rothschild.
Berthold Adler
Robert Hesse
Fritz Hirndler
Josef u. Grete Guttmann
Helga Guttmann
Harry Guttmann

9

Hermann Riesenburger

Georg Cohn - Frau

Jenespany

Kurt Rosenthal u. Frau

Sara Cohn

Dr. H. Borchardt u. Frau

Dr. Möllemann   Gertrud Schönemann

Berthold Weil

Westheimer Frau

Alfred Behrens

Emma Behrens

Hermann Strauss.

Moritz Frank u. Familie

Selig Rosenberg

Louis Rosenberg

Erwin Richter Rosenberg

Moritz Sehy u. Frau

Olga Loeb u. Hans Otto Loeb.

Aron Einhorn u. Frau

Dr. Ina Finkelstein

Dr. Fritz Herrmann

Frau Gusti Callen

Betty Unger

Max Czeminski u. Frau

Ernst Philippi u. Familie

Thea Thermed u. Kracker

Emma Hoffmann

Dr. Heinrichsdorf u. Familie

Max Hirsch u. Familie

Herta Liepmann

Herbert Liepmann

Philipp Banemann u. Frau

Erwin Rothschild

Sophie Gronik

Moritz Gronik

Adolf Gronik

Anna Aberbach

Marie Gronik

Hermann Gruber

Gisella Gruber

Max Gruber

Alex Gruber

Kurt Stein u. Familie

Frau Betty Sklar

Frau Grete Oppé

Max Herz

Dr. Brodnitz

Harry Fischler

Lina u. Fischler

Etty Hamberg

Paul Silzer

Leontine Silzer.

Jula Lauchheimer.

Hilde Levin 3 Kinder.

Ernst Ostrodaski.

Gisela Alexander

Herrn Moritin

Fritz Neufeld

Dr Walter Cohn

Sofi Aron

Ernst Heim

Leopold Marx

Blanka Brenner

Justin Levi

Cilly Hofmann

J. Köppel

Josef Köppel u. Familie

Alfred Aron. —

Walter Greve u. Familie

Herbert Manasse u. Fam.

Joseph Katzin

Berthold Rottholz

Stella Bianca Bak

Hans Fraenkel

Georg Haengler

Rosa Klara u. Familie

Grete Waldbaum u. Tochter

Berthold ...

Levi Birnbaum

Blanka Tridel —

Leopold ...

Ruth u. Margot Heyse

Henri ...

Ritta Goldstein

Maria Kurendler
Siegf Rosenzweig

Kurt Löwenstein
Addi Löwenstein

Julius Bernstein
Paul Kahane

Gottfried Burgheim

Joseph Neufeld
Andor Adler
Abraham Srog + Frau
Erich Guilbaum

Leo Wartelski

Anton Haas
Rieder Elisabeth
Hirsch Herman

Grete Stein

Erich Stein
Henriette Schapira
Julius Schapira
Henriette Altschüller
Selma u Karl Hoffmann

Max Spanier jr.
Hilde Ito
Inge Ito

Charlotte Mühlenthal
Jacob Wolfenann Stern
Rosa Rosentann
Kurt Silberstein
Thea Silberstein
Renate Silberstein
Gert Silberstein
Herbert Cyper
Karl Cyper
Elise Guttmann.
Max Falkenstein
Julius Weinberg
Regina Weinberg

PHOTOGRAPHY CAPTIONS AND CREDITS

Top row:

Elly Reutlinger and her nine-year-old daughter, Renate, pose near a dining area on the ship.
(*United States Holocaust Memorial Museum, courtesy of Renate Reutlinger Breslow*)

Herbert Karliner poses with his father, Joseph, on the deck of the MS *St. Louis*. Herbert and his brother, Walter (not pictured), were the only members of their family to survive the war, immigrating to the United States in 1946.
(*United States Holocaust Memorial Museum, courtesy of Herbert and Vera Karliner*)

Group portrait of Jewish refugee children. Among those pictured are Evelyn Klein (*back row, center*), Herbert Karliner (*front row, left*), Walter Karliner (*front row, second from the left*), and Harry Fuld (*first row, far right*). The Kleins were allowed to disembark in Cuba.
(*United States Holocaust Memorial Museum, courtesy of Don Altman*)

Portrait of Gustav Schröder, captain of the MS *St. Louis*.
(*United States Holocaust Memorial Museum, courtesy of Herbert and Vera Karliner*)

Middle row:

Ana Maria (Karman) Gordon and her mother, Sidonie, on deck, May 1939.
(*Courtesy of Ana Maria Gordon*)

Passengers aboard the MS *St. Louis*.
(*United States Holocaust Memorial Museum, courtesy of Dr. Liane Reif-Lehrer*)

Fritz (now Fred) Buff and Vera Hess dance in the ballroom. After disembarking the *St. Louis* in Belgium, Fritz was later able to secure passage for New York in 1940.
(*United States Holocaust Memorial Museum, courtesy of Fred Buff*)

Bottom row:

Pictured in the foreground from left to right: Ilse Karliner, Rose Guttman, Henry Goldstein (Gallant), Harry Guttman. *Behind, at the right*: Alfred and Sophie Aron.
(*United States Holocaust Memorial Museum, courtesy of Herbert and Vera Karliner*)

From left to right: Irmgard, Josef, Jakob, and Judith Koeppel, a German-Jewish refugee family. Irmgard and Josef later died in Auschwitz, and Judith was sent to live in the United States with her aunt and uncle.
(*United States Holocaust Memorial Museum, courtesy of Judith Koeppel Steel*)

Passengers attempt to communicate with friends and relatives in Cuba, who were permitted to approach the docked vessel in small boats.
(*United States Holocaust Memorial Museum, courtesy of National Archives and Records Administration, College Park*)